Mismatched in Manhattan

Mismatched in Manhattan

TASH SKILTON

piatkus

PIATKUS

First published in the US in 2020 by Kensington Books
First published in Great Britain in 2020 by Piatkus

1 3 5 7 9 10 8 6 4 2

Copyright © 2020 by Sarah Skilton and Sarvenaz Tash

The moral right of the author has been asserted.

A CIP catalogue record for this book
is available from the British Library.

ISBN 978-0-349-42566-5

Printed and bound in Great Britain by Clays Ltd, Elcograf S.p.A.

Papers used by Piatkus are from well-managed forests
and other responsible sources.

Piatkus
An imprint of
Little, Brown Book Group
Carmelite House
50 Victoria Embankment
London EC4Y 0DZ

An Hachette UK Company
www.hachette.co.uk

www.littlebrown.co.uk

To the four sisters—Haideh, Homa, Haleh, and Hengameh—
who gave me my favorite love story. —*S.T.*

For my parents, Earl & Ros Hoover, who are overdue for a
dedication; who taught me to love books; and whose Meet
Cute will never be matched. —*S.S.*

When you're attracted to someone, it just means that your subconscious is attracted to their subconscious, subconsciously. So what we think of as fate is just two neuroses knowing that they are a perfect match.

—Nora Ephron, *Sleepless in Seattle*

CHAPTER 1

To: All Tell It to My Heart Employees
From: Leanne Tseng
Re: New "Office Space"

Team,

Although the last couple of months have been
challenging, I want to take a moment to com-
mend you for being so open and adaptable to
our new direction. I also hope you are all
enjoying the freedom and independence of
working remotely. (I came across this article in *Wired* about the future of offices.
We're trendsetters!)

Also, whoever programmed my phone to play
"Tell It to My Heart" for all incoming messages . . . I appreciate the joke. It played
very well at our "Farewell Office" office party.
But no one—not even the so-called geniuses
at the Genius Bar—can seem to disable it.

```
Would you please come clean and get over
here to change it back? For obvious reasons,
if I ever have to listen to that song again,
I will 100% murder someone. And no one gets
paid if your CEO is in jail.


Yours,
Leanne
```

MILES

It's fine. It's absolutely fine.

So what if my ex-fiancée just posted a photo of her ringless fingers cradling what is very obviously a baby bump. So what if we only broke up six weeks ago and, look, I cannot claim to be an expert in women's reproductive health or anything, but I'm pretty sure that is not what six weeks pregnant looks like. So what if I, in a split second of confusion and elation, texted her "Are we having a baby?" with an actual goddamn baby emoji next to it just in case she needed a visual representation of the word "baby" and got absolutely no response even though the read receipt confirms she saw it.

So either the baby is mine and Jordan has decided she's not going to let me be a part of his or her life. Or . . . Jordan was cheating on me before she dumped me, shattered my heart, and stole the apartment.

I'm not sure which is worse.

I get a ping on my laptop, a message next to a tiny picture of a smiling brunette girl.

Jules478: Hi, how are you?

Fucking great. And now I have to work. Now I have to work trying to get other people's love lives in order. What a cosmic joke. Not only that, but I no longer even have an office to go to, or colleagues to make small talk with, or a coffee machine that will dispense caffeine to me at will. Just a totally unfathomable espresso maker that could double as a 747 cockpit and a corner of this borrowed couch that I swear is made from burlap, because my friend Dylan lives in a Pottery Barn catalog. (You may say that couch surfers can't be couch choosers, but I—in the throes of my melancholy and with half my hair in a permanent state of static cling—say we can all be critics.)

I close my eyes and try the breathing exercise that, of course, Jordan once taught me—inhale for four, hold for seven, exhale for eight—before I respond.

PerseMan: Hey there. I'm great. How are you doing?

It's okay. I can do this sort of idle chitchat in my sleep. I haven't spent the past two years becoming the top ghostwriter at Tell It to My Heart for no reason. I've honed these skills enough that I can practically be on autopilot. Right?

Jules478: Good.

Right. Except I just broke the cardinal rule of online dating: Much like improv, never ask a question that can be responded to with a one-word answer.

I try to rectify.

PerseMan: Have you seen the summer concert schedule for Forest Hills Stadium, by the way? It's pretty amazing this year.

My guy . . . I scan my open files for his name . . . Farhad. That's it. He's a music buff, so I know this is important.

Jules478: Yes! Belle and Sebastian and Greta Van Fleet? Amazing!

PerseMan: I know, right?

I type the response automatically and then scroll over to the schedule myself, trying to figure out which one of these god-damn stupid bands Farhad might be into. Oh, right. He had mentioned LCD Soundsystem in his questionnaire.

PerseMan: Super excited for LCD myself.

Jules478: Yeah? They're cool too.

Okay, so she's less excited about that one. But, hey, they can each bring different musical tastes to the relationship. That's the beauty of romance, right? Everyone brings their own interests into it, and then they mix and mingle, and sometime later, there is a little embryo that has genetically combined those passions into something that can be cradled in an artsy, black-and-white Instagram post.

PerseMan: Do you like kids?

Whoa. WHOA! What the hell are you doing, Miles? As the *Tell It to My Heart Style Guide and Freelancer's Handbook* suggests on page twenty-two, there are certain things you never, ever bring up on a first chat: politics, religion, marriage, meeting the parents, and—of course—children. Not in any way, shape, or form. I know this because I *literally* wrote the handbook. As Leanne's first employee, I got to sculpt a lot of what my job—and the company culture—is.

There is a noticeable pause before Farhad's match writes again.

Jules478: Yeah. I like them.

PerseMan: Do you have any idea what a six-week pregnant belly looks like?

I have no idea what's happening. My fingers are 100 percent working independently from my brain.

Jules478: Uh . . .

PerseMan: It's not obviously pregnant, right? Like, usually, you wouldn't be able to see a bump?

At this point, what the hell does it matter? Jules might have more insight into this than me considering she, at least, has the requisite parts and has, I don't know, probably attended a baby shower or something.

Jules478: I don't think so?

PerseMan: That's what I thought.

The thing is, I know the baby isn't mine. I probably always

knew it, but the blank screen on my messages, gut-punched by that *Read 8:37 AM* confirms it. Jordan wouldn't raise a baby alone, not if its father wanted to be an active part of his or her life. How many times had I held her while she told me another example of why her absentee dad was such a shithead and how it had directly impacted some aspect of her life or personality?

Jules478: So . . . listen. I think I've got to go.

Shit. I've been spiraling into a deep, dark thought hole instead of doing my job and convincing this girl that Farhad is a great match for her and worthy of at least a meetup.

Time for some damage control.

PerseMan: Ha! Sorry, I didn't mean to freak you out.

I'm now racking my brain for some sort of valid excuse to ask this girl about pregnancy symptoms.

PerseMan: I'm writing a song. And this is research.

Look, if there can be songs about lady humps, why not about baby bumps, am I right?

Jules478: Oh . . . are you a musician?

PerseMan: It's a hobby.

I scan Farhad's questionnaire again.

PerseMan: I work in finance by day.

Good, good. Worked in the stable job bit smoothly. I might be back on track here.

Jules478: What kind of band are you in?

I scan the questionnaire one more time. Oh, fuck.

PerseMan: A string quartet.

There is another long pause.

Jules478: Right . . . I'm sorry, but my lunch break is over and I really do have to go.

It's 8:52 in the morning.

Jules478: Maybe talk later?

But then she logs off before I can respond.

Honestly?

I probably did both Farhad and this girl a favor.

There is no such thing as love anyway. Not to get all hair metal power ballad about it, but love is an illusion. It's just a smokescreen for future heartbreak. Why do it to yourself? Why? Either they'll leave you, or you'll leave them or—best-case scenario—you live together happily until one of you dies and leaves the other one completely destroyed and a shell of their former self.

Why the fuck bother?

A message pops up from Leanne.

Leanne T: Miles? I think you need to come into the office for a meeting.

Fuckity fuck fuck.

Miles I: I'll be there in twenty minutes. Is that okay?

Leanne T: Yes.

And then, before I can think better of it.

Miles I: Hey, Leanne. Question for you. Do you know what a six-week pregnant belly looks like?

Leanne's office is in a building that was clearly a warehouse until maybe three minutes ago, when some enterprising real estate mogul realized he could create about 450 closet-sized offices in there and charge people an exorbitant amount of rent for the privilege of working right next to the West Side Highway, which is at least a fifteen-minute, windswept walk from any subway line.

I wait for her to buzz me up, and then take one of the many freight elevators up to the ninth floor, until I end up in front of Leanne's cupboard.

Up until two and a half months ago, Tell It to My Heart was located in a small, but airy office space in the Meatpacking District. Full-length glass windows looked out over the cobblestone streets where high-end shoppers in designer sunglasses and Jimmy Choos and/or hungover clubbers in designer sunglasses and taller Jimmy Choos hobbled to and fro. I used to look out and think it was very possible one of those clubbers was a client of ours, coming back from a successful date night that ended at seven a.m., rushing to get home and change and look presentable for work, but unable to hide that secret smile only a hot date with someone new was able to conjure up. It wasn't a walk of shame, it was a walk of *pride*. Who wouldn't feel proud and exhilarated to have come off of a night of passion and connection? And, maybe, just maybe, I'd had a hand in that. It used to make *me* feel proud and exhilarated, by association.

Now I know better.

Now I know one hot night will probably turn into agony somewhere down the road—whether it's because of unreturned text messages, or fights over the other one's overbearing parents, or splitting up and trying to figure out who gets the houseplants. I'm facilitating nothing but ruin and damnation.

And as for the office? Well. We can chalk that one up to another brilliantly catastrophic idea from Leanne's ex-husband, Clifford.

To paraphrase Taylor Swift, once upon a time, many mistakes ago, Leanne and Clifford were two of those idiots who thought they were in a loving, long-lasting relationship. So not only did they exchange vows, and buy an apartment (a co-op no less, another nightmare), and adopt a cat together—they decided to take it to the next knuckleheaded step: co-owning a business.

Yup, they started Tell It to My Heart together, although it was Leanne's idea originally. As both a writer and a person enthralled by love, she'd been watching her single friends struggle through the tortures of online dating, of constructing the perfect profile, and of saying the right things over e-mails, IMs, and texts. And one day she realized: She was a copywriter. She could help them craft their message better.

It snowballed from there, the idea to create a ghostwriting agency that would help people get their foot in the door on their paths to true love. "We're not ghostwriting, we're cupid-writing," Clifford said.

That was Clifford's task: taking care of the marketing and operations.

Meaning it was Clifford's idea to name the company Tell It to My Heart (which was probably the last time Leanne and Clifford agreed on anything). And then his next logical step was to get the rights to that Taylor Dayne song to use in all the commercials.

It sounded fine in theory, of course. Except Taylor Dayne and the songwriters did not want to be associated with some weird, unknown, online dating ghostwriting agency thing, and had asked for an exorbitant fee to secure the rights.

Any normal person would have tried to either negotiate or realize the song wasn't worth it.

If Clifford is one thing, it's abnormal.

He agreed to their terms right away, without consulting Leanne or the lawyers or anybody.

Leanne got the company in the divorce, but she was also stuck with the consequences of Clifford's poor business decisions.

So, yes, do have the pleasure of getting "Tell It to My Heart" stuck in your head if you come across any of our radio or occasional TV ads. While I and the other three full-time TITMH (pronounced *tit-mee*) employees have the pleasure of no longer having an office.

And poor Leanne, CEO, is relegated to this musty, windowless closet that can barely fit her desk and two chairs let alone all of the cool, eclectic artwork and sculptures she used to have as her backdrop at our old digs.

Still, despite her surroundings, she looks as impeccable as always. Leanne is Chinese-American, with long, straight black hair, the posture of a prima ballerina, and a wardrobe that almost entirely consists of structural pieces that look like they ought to come with blueprints. She somehow makes them work, whereas I'm pretty sure anyone else wearing them would look like they were dressed as the Empire State Building in a questionable Miss New York pageant.

"Care to explain what happened today, Miles?" she asks in her calm, deep voice, the kind you know has the potential to unleash a tsunami of devastating barbs if necessary.

I clear my throat. "What do you mean?"

"Let's start with not knowing our client was in a string quartet. And move on to the whole pregnant belly debacle."

"You know about all that?" I ask weakly.

"Miles. After the fiasco of the last three clients, I told you I'd be logged on to your computer to see your chats. And then you accepted my remote access request this morning."

"Oh, right," I say. Shit. I definitely had. And I definitely planned on being on my game today, but that was before Jordan announced to the world (and, oh yeah, me) that she was with child.

Leanne sighs. "Look. I know you're going through a hard time right now." I haven't told her too much about what's been going on, just that Jordan and I broke up. And that I moved out of our apartment into Dylan's living room. And that Dylan's boyfriend, Charles, has been passive-aggressively leaving me notes about how disruptive I am to their lives. And that he made me return the single-ply toilet paper I bought as a thank-you gift because, as he claimed, nobody's ass deserves the degradation of single-ply, not even mine.

Okay, so maybe I have told Leanne a lot. The problem is that in the eighteen months we were together, I ended up co-opting most of Jordan's friends, and now I'm stuck trying to scrape together some semblance of a social circle.

"Here's the thing," Leanne says, "I can't afford this meltdown, Miles. I *literally* can't afford it. Clearly, we are in some serious trouble here." She waves her arms vaguely at the horror show of peeling paint and Formica office furniture she's some-how ended up captaining. "And losing *four* clients in the span of a month? That's just not acceptable."

I nod, suddenly realizing it's very possible that—on top of everything else—I am about to get fired. I'm like the pilot epi-sode of a sitcom about a man whose life goes to shit before he changes careers and decides to become a cattle rancher in that quirky town his grandmother lives in. Except all of my grandparents are dead and, in the real world, losing your job doesn't actually lead to a hilarious but poignant epiphany about what you're supposed to be doing. Just a sudden need to add LinkedIn to the daily ritual of social media that makes you feel like crap about yourself.

Leanne must see the panic in my face, because she tries to soften the blow. "It's no secret that you've always been my best employee, Miles. You were great at what you did. Nobody has as many success stories as you. How many weddings have you been invited to? Three?"

"Four," I mumble. Always as an old friend of the groom be-cause, of course, none of them could bear to tell their future wives that their relationship was built on what is—let's be hon-est here—something of a lie.

"That's incredible," Leanne says gently, before her voice takes on the firm but fair tone that made her a superstar cre-ative director back in her agency days, when I was working as a copywriter under her. "But I can't rely on what you *did*; I have to rely on what you *do.* I have to know I'm sending someone out there who's going to listen to our clients' wants and needs and work his hardest to get them to meet up with their perfect match."

"Right," I say, not adding that what Leanne needs is someone who actually believes in such a thing as a perfect match. Once upon a time, that was me. But not anymore.

"So this is what's going to happen," she says, and I'm expecting her to produce—if I'm lucky—a severance package from within her desk to hand to me. Instead, she takes out her iPad. "You have one more chance to make good here. One more client who's going to need the old Miles to reappear and give him the real Tell It to My Heart Experience™." Obviously, she doesn't say the trademarked bit, but I can practically hear it in her voice. Another one of Clifford's brilliantly expensive ideas. "So, pick one. Go ahead. There are three to choose from."

I reluctantly take the tablet from her, and flip through the familiar file format of our clients: a smiling photo and the answers from the initial questionnaire. This one ideally wants to be married within two years. That one is new to the city and wants someone to "eat his way through New York with." (His words, not mine. And obviously we are going to have to do something about them if I take him on.)

And then there's Jude Campbell. There's nothing very special about Jude's profile. He's good-looking enough. His answers are normal enough. Or, I should say, there's *almost* nothing very special about Jude's profile.

Jude apparently moved here from Scotland a couple of years ago. Which means Jude has an accent. And if I am going to stake my whole career on one guy's love match?

I'm picking the dude with the Scottish accent.

CHAPTER 2

To: My rock stars
From: Clifford Jenkins
Re: Ch-ch-ch-changes! (New Company Name)

What up, my dudes? That's what Justin Bieber
said when he met President Obama, according to eyewitnesses at the time. But I don't
want to discount our hard-working dudettes,
of course! So. Here's the deal. We are dunzo
with Best Foot Forward. Erase it from your
hard drive, remove it from your e-mail signa-
tures, bleach it from your brains. It's gone.
Let's all agree it never happened, right? New
URL, new e-mail domain, new start, new name.

We are now officially called Sweet Nothings,
LLC, and we're going to kick all manner of
butt with this.

IF YOU CONTINUE TO GET CORRESPONDENCE FROM
FOOT FETISHISTS, DO NOT RESPOND. Forward
it immediately to customer service (heyyyy

Crystal) and delete it. Simple as that. Crystal will take care of the particulars.

I'll be happy to answer any questions at the monthly meetup, but in the meantime, scrub any and all references to BFF (and YOB for you seniors among us) and replace them with Sweet Nothings. Our portal will reflect all changes within the week.

Smell you later,
Clifford
CEO, Best Foot Forward fka You, Only Better

ZOEY

Get across the street. That's all you have to do: Get across the street.

Except of course it's not that simple, because it's not a normal street and it's not a normal city, and before I can cross the street I have to leave my apartment. "Apartment" being the oh-so-hilarious code name for rathole. Although I guess for actual rats, it would be a palace. Actual rats are out there, by the way, waiting to run across my shoes and up my legs, little rat teeth chittering, dropping diseases on me, plumes of germs surrounding them like a deadly cloud around Pig Pen.

Okay. It's okay. Just because the "apartment" is half-a-room total, and the couch doubles as a bed, and the shower is in a corner of the kitchen, and you have to climb over the furniture to go anywhere, is no reason to get upset. You're having a new experience! Still, if I don't escape I'll go mad, so here we are.

Laptop, check. Purse, check. Keys, check. Unlock the chain and the deadbolt. Slowly open the door the tiniest crack.

"Coming out," I yell, the warning I was taught to use on the day I moved in, by a neighbor I haven't seen since. I used to hear her, the way I assume she hears me, announcing her movement into the hallway. There's only room for one person to use it at a time, and if you don't announce yourself and there's someone already there, you risk bodily harm, and one of you will have to retreat to give the other person room to finish using the hallway. When no one responds, I open my door all the way, briskly exit, and relock it behind me.

"In the hall," I yell, updating someone who might not even be there. For some reason my voice is a baritone when I do this. I want to make sure she hears me. My combat boots guarantee the people on the floor below hear me, at any rate.

New obstacle: the stairwell. I'd use the elevator, except the last time I did, someone was asleep inside. (Mary, my former boss and current landlord, was unsympathetic: "In my day, they'd have been passed out in their own vomit.") I have this fear there will *always* be someone asleep inside, and that the next time I go in, the person's eyes will pop open and they'll grab my ankle.

In LA, I worried someone might be hiding under my car to slice my tendons, so this is not an unfamiliar fear of mine. Once I'm outside in the "fresh" air though, all similarities, real or imagined, to the City of Angels evaporate.

Honk! Screech! Beep! Sizzle! "Hey!"

I'm assaulted by noise. Smells. Garbage, floating in the air and piled outside front stoops. Cacophony. I fight the urge to cover my ears, close my eyes, and pray for a teleportation device. Does it have to be so loud? Does there have to be unidentifiable steam shooting out of a nasty-ass grate in the middle of the sidewalk? Does everybody have to hustle past me, elbows knocking me, at such a frenzied pace? At least my boots will protect me. They don't help with speed, though, that's for sure.

Get to the corner. Just get to the corner, so you can cross the street.

I understand the appeal of newsstands; really, I do. And food carts. Sure. It's just that now I have to move around them without accidentally bumping someone or getting grease on me or smelling something I'd rather not smell this early in the morning.

Jesus, I've only gone half a block and I've been glared at, eye-fucked, stepped on, jostled, and surrounded. What I wouldn't give for the peace and tranquillity of my car in California. I know, I know, we have the worst traffic in the world, but you know what else we have? Space to ourselves. Temperature control. Room to breathe, the option to listen to whatever music or podcast or radio station we want, and the ability to HEAR IT in the quiet of our cars, while we sip an iced latte or brainstorm a line of dialogue.

I'm at the intersection at last, and the WALK sign comes on, but I know better than to step toe off the curb. The first three cars don't stop. Two of them slide on through, and the third honks, like the car is swearing at me, ordering me to not even think about it.

Know what else we have in California?

Mountains. Trees. The beach. *Grass.* (Both kinds.)

Before I know it, the red flashing hand of doom is back and I've lost my chance. I hang back, frustrated and embarrassed. Why can't I get my feet to move? A few more people gather close and I tense up, preparing for full body blows as they fence me in. Then, as one unit, all of them cross the street! Even though it clearly says DON'T WALK! Apparently, they all have death wishes. I should have grabbed a shirt corner, let them drag me along with them. It's probably the only way I'll make it to Café Crudité.

Two more green lights and the WALK sign comes back on. I force myself to dart, quick as I can, head down, barreling forward. Take that, mofos! Past the cheese shop and a Duane Reade and I've made it inside the café. I got off to a late start, but no one's claimed the big table by the window, so the day is looking up. I promise myself I'll be productive. I'll spend the next six to eight hours toggling between my spec script and the Sweet Nothings portal to see if new clients have entered the system so I can nab one. The last four days I haven't been quick enough on the draw, and my freelance checks are going to reflect it. I wonder if the other freelancers have installed some type of alert system and that's how they're able to beat me to the punch?

My stomach rumbles. All I have in my fridge right now are ketchup packets and half a bottle of Riesling, and I can't spend my taxi money on an expensive quiche for breakfast, so it looks like another biscotti morning. (Café Crudité offers free "day-old baked goods" on a plate at the counter.) The place is mostly empty; just one person in front of me on line and no one behind. I watch in slow motion as the guy in front of me reaches his greedy hand straight for the free biscotti, aka My Breakfast. There are two left, enough for a sad, quasi-meal. I'm so hungry I feel saliva gathering in my cheeks.

I *need* the biscotti.

"Wait!" I bellow. It's my "I'm in the hall" voice, weirdly resonant. I start over. "It's just—those are mine, so . . ." I trail off in a normal voice.

The guy's hand pauses in midair and he turns to look at me. He's tall and tan, like the California dreams of my past, but there's nothing easy, breezy, or ocean-sprayed about him. His dark hair sticks straight up, intense and angry, he wears hipster glasses he probably doesn't need, and the not-quite-a-beard on his face can't decide what it wants to be when it grows up. He looks like if Zayn Malik were a stressed-out dental student.

"How are they 'yours'?" Zayn Malik, DDS, asks, complete with air quotes.

"You can have the day-old muffins," I say, pointing. (Heh. They've got vegetables in them, but Hipster Glasses may not know that. He may not know "crudité" is vegetables.) "They're bigger, more filling, and I'm doing you a favor by letting you have those instead," I add, my teeth gritted.

"How magnanimous of you. They're *stale*."

"That's why they're free!"

"And they're probably stuffed with zucchini or kale."

Oops. He does know.

"The biscotti are already hard, they won't taste any worse," he snaps, reaching for them again. "The muffins will be CRAP. Besides, I was here first."

His raging case of bedhead is infuriating. Someone's fingers obviously clutched his hair in a moment of passion last night and he hasn't bothered to make himself presentable. He thinks he's Bringing Disheveled Back, the morning after Sexy had its triumphant return; he probably slept in late with his loverrrrr, leisurely feeding her eggs and toast in bed, and now he thinks he can have *my* breakfast, too? Still, he hasn't picked up the biscotti yet, so maybe he's open to reason.

"I *always* get the biscotti," I mutter. I can practically taste them. "They're saving them for me."

The barista appears and hands the guy his grande coffee. Her name tag reads "Evelynn."

"Are you saving the day-old biscotti for this insane person, Evelynn?" he asks.

"I've never seen her before, and no. It's first come, first served."

"I come here every day," I protest. "Monday through Sunday, seven days a week."

Evelynn shrugs. "I don't remember you."

"I bring you more business than he does," I say desperately. "I'm a regular, every day since I moved to New York."

"When was that?" Hipster Glasses says.

"A month ago."

"Oh, wow, gosh, yeah, you're like a LEGEND," he says

loudly. " 'The coffee lady!' An entire month, you say? Yeah, that's impressive . . . except I'VE BEEN COMING HERE FOR ALMOST FIFTEEN YEARS."

He's *yelling* at me. A complete stranger. In public! In LA, only celebrities could get away with that shit. The reptilian part of my brain shrieks, *Retreat!* but the hunger part of my brain replies, *Don't you fucking dare,* so I stand tall. "How come I've never seen you, then?" I demand.

"Probably because *I spread out my visits* like people are supposed to do."

"Maybe you could spread them out farther next time," I reply. I know I sound crazy but he doesn't need the biscotti the way I do. He's a local, free to move about the city, whereas I'm stuck on this one block for the foreseeable future.

"Wait." Evelynn snaps her fingers at me. "I do remember you. Bottomless cup of coffee, no food."

"That's not bringing them business," Hipster Glasses points out. "It's taking business *from* them."

"Evelynn, I'll give you ten cents for the biscotti," I blurt out.

"Twenty-five," the guy interrupts.

Evelynn looks between us.

"Seventy-five," I counter.

"The point is they're free," Evelynn says slowly. "Because they don't taste very good."

"This'll just be for you, Evelynn," I remark. "Under the table. No need to declare it."

"Two dollars," Mr. Moneybags says, pulling the cash out already. "Final offer."

"The point is they're free," I protest. I can't compete anymore. I need the two dollars for my bottomless cup of coffee.

Evelynn pulls the plate toward her.

"Great," the guy fumes. "Now no one can have them and no one's happy ever again!"

"Wow, okay. 'Ever again'?"

With gloved hands, Evelynn breaks both bars of biscotti in half. She swipes two broken pieces into my open hands, and two broken pieces into his. Why did she break them in half first? Was it the only way she had of showing her anger? Was it so we'd both still get two pieces, shut our mouths, and go away? Or was she reminding us who has the power in this scenario? (Irrelevant, I know. But those are the details that make up a character. I take note of them whenever I can.)

Biscotti pieces and crumbs secure in my fist, I order a large Americano and place seventy-five cents in the tip jar since that's what I'd bid during the auction. My cheeks feel warm and I avoid Evelynn's gaze when she hands me my order. Dramatic Sex Hair McGee got to scurry off with his ill-gotten bounty after yelling at me, while *I* had to stay there and accept the annoyance pouring off Evelynn like a heat wave. I mumble a "thank you" and pivot away. I can feel her eyes on me as I walk to my large, lovely window table, and I don't blame her. I set my coffee down and—

Are you freaking kidding me? There's a bag on the opposite seat, the nice long bench against the window. *My* window.

It's a messenger bag with a front Velcro flap, one of those bright, one-of-a-kind upcycled jobs from Switzerland or something, made up of rubber tarps and an old seat belt that goes across the shoulder and clasps at the collarbone. It's morally superior to every other bag, which is the only reason to buy it, and now it gets my table, too. Whoever owns it is elsewhere, so I could technically . . . *push* the bag off the bench and pretend it fell and I never saw it. Possession is nine-tenths of the law. I look left and right and lean over with my combat boot to tip it when . . .

"That seat's taken," says a male voice.

I freeze, caught.

And of course, *of course*, it's the asshole again. To prove his point, he moves around the other side of the table and makes a show of lifting the messenger bag off the bench and plopping it in the middle of the table.

I pick up my coffee. "All right, geez. I'm going."

Evelynn squints at us and I refuse to make another scene, so, with as much dignity as I can muster, I slink off to another table. He'd better not stay there long. He probably doesn't even need it—he's just one of those people who has to have the "best" of whatever's available. It's clearly the king table of Crudité, the rest of them surrounding it like peasant-subjects. The others are so tiny they don't have room for my laptop *and* purse. .

I wouldn't be this angry if I hadn't been in the middle of another shit morning in this shit city, or if my script were going well, or if I weren't so hungry for both food and clients, and, okay, if he were average-looking. With his scruff cranked up to eleven, his deep brown eyes, his slim frame, and his thick hair, he's ridiculously attractive, which means he's never had to work on his personality, so he probably goes through life showing up anywhere he wants and people just give him stuff. Well, not this girl. I come from the land of models-slash-actors, so his exterior means nothing to me.

It's the first time someone's snatched the big table from me, but I'll just have to wait him out. There's no way I can work from my rathole; and there are no other cafés within my self-defined comfort radius.

It's been forty minutes and he's still there, lollygagging, his long legs stretched out within tripping distance of anyone who comes near. My coffee's gone and I need to pee.

Leave, I order him telepathically. *Leave!* I get up to use the restroom, willing him and his stupid hair to be gone by the time I get back.

He's not, though. When I return, he's typing madly on his laptop. He's got the look of somebody who's settled in for, like, the duration. I open my laptop (perched on my actual lap for the first time in its existence, probably giving me thigh cancer) and log in to Best Foot Forward's—I mean, Sweet Nothings'—portal and get the dreaded message: *There are currently no ghostwriting jobs. We are working to attract more clients. Your patience is appreciated. While you're waiting, why not add a line to the Drop-Down Database? Smell you later!*

Beneath the message is the familiar logo of a sexy woman's foot in a high heel. Guess they haven't finished "scrubbing" the portal of all references to the prior name yet.

While I was hate-waiting for the Table Thief to leave, all the new clients must have been snatched up. This happens a lot; Clifford has so many independent contractors working for him that the ratio of ghostwriters to clients is lopsided. He says we're expanding every day, and I believe him (I think), but it's tough to earn regular paychecks this way. There are bonuses—so he claims—for getting clients across the finish line, but that hasn't happened for me yet. I sigh and click over to the Drop-Down Database. One of Clifford's ideas is a DIY package, wherein clients pay the company to access a list of timely, provocative subject lines and messages—categories include Flirty, Sassy, Sexy, Casual—and create their own buffet of communications to use on unsuspecting would-be matches. Every time I add to it, I get five dollars per line and the sinking suspicion I'm hastening my own demise by making my job obsolete.

I've sent out at least thirty résumés since I arrived in the worm-infested Big Apple, but for now, Sweet Nothings provides my sole income. I've got to make this work, even if it means logging in to the portal fifty thousand times a day.

Ping.

A new message pops up on my phone.

Why'd you ghost me?!!!

Oh no—did I mess up? Leave a job hanging when it was my turn to chime in? That's a serious taboo in this business. We respond right away unless we're under orders for strategic delays. My client Tess never signed up for that, so I gotta fix this immediately.

Oh gosh, I type, I'm so sorry, things have been crazy busy but I really—

Then I see who sent the message. Nick, not a client. Nick, the guy I was sort of seeing in LA. (Emphasis on "sort of." He was Mary's weed delivery guy, so our hours were . . . irregular.)

I didn't ghost you, I correct him. I told you I was moving.

You didn't respond to any of my messages! THAT'S GHOSTING.

No, that's saying goodbye. Ghosting is a mystery that's never solved.

Have a nice life, I GUESS. Your boss owes me 2k in back weed.

I'm sure that's true, but what am I supposed to do about it?

You'll have to take that up with Mary.

Block, move on.

For the next two hours I alternate between working on my spec script and logging in to the Sweet Nothings portal. On my sixteenth try, three clients have become available, so I frantically move my cursor to click on one of the boxes but I'm not fast enough because the screen refreshes into the usual wah-wah: *There are currently no ghostwriting jobs.* The graphic has changed, at least, from the sexy foot to a person whispering something into another person's ear. (Sweet nothings, one must presume.) At least the tech guys are keeping busy. It's a much nicer look for the site. Now if only I could get a piece of the action.

I shoot another glare in Table Thief's direction. I would've been quicker on the uptake if he hadn't stolen my breakfast and workstation.

Two p.m. rolls around and he's still there.

I mosey over to the counter—mercifully, Evelynn's shift has ended, so I have an opportunity to seem normal to the current barista—and get a refill on my coffee. I stare longingly at a black bean and quinoa bowl. It's the cheapest thing on the menu, but it's still too rich for my one-client blood.

Back at my child-size table, an e-mail has arrived from Clifford. Probably another NDA to sign, or an updated protocol handbook (rumor has it he stole it from his prior company). I click the Dropbox link in the body of the text and music suddenly bursts out of my laptop speakers: The Weeknd, crooning loudly that, due to the way I work it, I've er-er-er-er-er-earned it.

What is happening! I stab my finger on the lower-volume key until the song is muted. The people in line raise their eyebrows. One of them shakes her head at me. And I just know Table Thief heard it, too.

Blushing, I put my headphones on, attach them to the laptop, and tentatively bring the volume back up, double-checking to make sure no one else can hear. It's a video. Heart pounding, but convinced it will be a private viewing this time, I reload the file. Over a black screen, The Weeknd assures me again that I earned it. Then Clifford appears. He actually walks toward the camera like he's approaching me across a room in real life.

"Greetings, Rockstar! Don't worry, that song cost us nothing because it's for parody purposes. But girl, you earned it."

Does he have one auto-message for female ghostwriters and one for men? I wonder idly. *And if so, is that offensive to either group?*

"If you're seeing this message, it means you totally powered up! Your latest client . . ."—a weird pause, followed by an overdub in postproduction of—". . . Tess Riley . . ."—before returning to his regular voice, "has deleted his or her dating profile. Which means you have a success story! Yes!" (Pause for overdub again . . .) "Tess Riley . . . has found true love! What does this mean? It means YOU get a $500 bonus" (KA-CHING sound effect, with animated coins falling around Clifford) "and a DIY party in your honor. Check your mail, alligator, for a bubbly surprise. Most important for YOU, it means you automatically get the next client that comes down the pike. No need to scramble, it's all yours. Congratulations, and have a great day or night."

I'm still reeling from the unexpected communiqué from Clifford and The Weeknd, but there's no denying it's wonderful news. Five hundred bucks will pay for countless taxi rides. If I ever went anywhere, I'd be psyched.

It finally hits me, the reason it's so difficult to nab clients in the portal: Most of them are filtered into the accounts of freelancers who've proven themselves. Clifford's either a dick or a mastermind when it comes to motivation. Those with no aptitude for the job won't even need to be fired; they'll simply never get clients, without knowing why. Like being ghosted. I'm not sure how I feel about that, but regardless, I *did* earn it, dammit. Tess Riley wanted an architect, twenty-eight to thirty-seven, with a soccer-player body. She crossed her fingers for a man of South American or Dutch descent. Did I deliver? You bet your sweet ass I did!

Mateo Van de Berg was *both*.

I close my laptop and pack up, floating on a wave of satisfaction. Time to call it a day, leave on a high note (if only; some weed would be a great way to calm down for the trek home). A siren rages in the distance, drawing ever closer, and I cringe, reminded of what I'm about to walk out into. The city, alive and unrelenting, ready to toss me around like an old hacky sack.

I pass Table Thief on my way out. He glances at me and I look away just as quickly, but not before we make eye contact. I take a deep breath and push the exit door. And then, despite the noise and crowds threatening me, I smile, briefly, to myself. Because he doesn't know it, but today is the last day he will ever sit there.

CHAPTER 3

To: All Tell It to My Heart Employees
From: Leanne Tseng
Re: Word of the Day

Team,

At the risk of sounding like a certain someone we all know and hate, the word of the day
is "upsell." This week, I want you to keep
in mind that we are a full-service boutique
with a variety of services to offer. Let's
help our clients take advantage of our tal-
ented pool of consultants. Take a deep dive
into your clients' files and see how we can
help them to put their best foot forward.

Speaking of which, although we have not
taken legal action yet, please be aware that
we are looking into whether any intellectual
property or other proprietary information
has been breached by any companies offering

similar—though obviously subpar—services. For our freelance contractors who may be doing business with said companies, we're hoping to have this matter resolved as soon as possible without letting it affect your duties or loyalties to either.

Having said that, the ultimate goal is to get the company to a place where I can hire all of you as full-time staff who won't have to spend half your week scrubbing off the newest inappropriate comment from your other boss.

Word of the day, folks. Word of the day.

Yours,
Leanne

MILES

Evelynn wasn't kidding about the bottomless cup of coffee. I Am Legend is over there in her corner table, hunched over her laptop for almost the whole day, every now and again shooting a dirty look my way. But like I said, I've lived in New York City for fifteen years. If I can't handle death ray eyes from some doe-eyed brunette, I deserve to have my MetroCard revoked.

By the way, even if she hadn't told me, I'd have figured out she wasn't from New York by virtue of her outfit. It's the end of April and she's in a tank top and shorts. We had a blizzard less than two weeks ago, which might—though really doesn't—explain the combat boots. Although maybe it's just her way of letting the world know she has a smoking hot bod but will also kick your ass if you stare too long. Which I can respect. Less obvious to decipher is the bizarre fingerless knit glove things that come up to her elbows and were clearly homemade by someone who was either drunk or gleefully looking to use the #nailedit hashtag. Wherever she's from, it's probably devoid of seasons and, let's face it, culture. Maybe someplace utterly predictable, like Florida.

Whatever her story, I need to ignore her. Just like I need to ignore why I haven't been to Café Crudité in six weeks. It's not that this was exactly "our place," mine and Jordan's. But we used to go here sometimes, together, back when she lived around the corner with three roommates, back before we made the leap to cross a bridge and moved to a borough that didn't start with "Man" and end with "holy hell, that's how much you're charging for this closet, but Jesus that is a nice terrace, I can fit a chair out there and have, like, outdoor space, where do I sign?"

I mean, we also made the leap to move in together, of course, but at the time, the Brooklyn thing seemed like the bigger deal. Sidenote: Last year Miles was such a douchebag.

And a moron. A goddamn romantic in this day and age—*and* at his age? Like it took him thirty-one years to realize that happily ever after literally belongs in a fairy tale. For children. As Gemma, the British girl I briefly dated before Jordan, used to say: what a nob.

But, anyway, this nob has stayed away from this café lately because there were too many memories of grabbing a cup of coffee on mornings after spending the night, or sometimes loitering here after dinner because they were lax about that and we didn't particularly have a hell of a lot of money. Which was why when the TITMH offices vanished in a poof of whatever Clifford was smoking, it was my go-to place to park my ass and get some work done. Even if it was a bit of a trek from Brooklyn, coming here kept up my daily routine of heading out to "the office."

Which is why I'm here, now. This is the last place I remember actually giving a shit about my job. And if I'm now forced, by threat of professional disgrace and unemployment, to try and show up as some semblance of former Employee of the Century Miles Ibrahim . . . this seems like the logical place to go.

I open up Jude Campbell's questionnaire and read it. Then I reread it, again and again, until I memorize it. No more string quartet surprises for me. I click over to the three dating website profiles he's linked out to and peruse them. I start to make notes on what we can change. He doesn't have a lot of info out there, which is a rookie mistake. You don't want to write a dissertation, but you do want to have enough content to show that you took time to fill the profile out. That demonstrates follow-through and dedication to the cause. Of course, there is a fine line between being thorough and TL;DR, which is a lot of where I come in. The words should be carefully chosen to reflect our clients' (enhanced and copyedited) personalities; they should sparkle . . . but leave you wanting more.

I e-mail Jude, introducing myself as his Tell It to My Heart writer and asking him when he might be free to meet, letting him know I could do it as early as today. I've just hit send when music comes blasting from a corner table, warranting a glance in that direction.

It's I Am Legend, whose face has turned bright pink, Bambi lashes fluttering as she frantically hits keys on her laptop. I'm pretty sure that's a song from *Fifty Shades of Grey*. Is that what she's doing here? Does hoarding free food while she watches soft-core porn in public get her off or something? I watch her for a second, curious whether I can discern if she's turned on. Then I catch myself. Under no circumstances am I to be checking out women again, even if it's purely anthropological.

A *whoosh* alerts me that I have an incoming message. An e-mail from Jude, who says he can meet at four p.m. today. Excellent. Eager and communicative is a good sign in a client. I e-mail him back with directions to Café Crudité.

Then I take out my phone to test myself on how well I've absorbed my client's profile.

I open up 24/7, one of the scores of dating apps I have downloaded (as a work thing, of course, because I, myself, am obviously never dating again. The profiles aren't even set up as me, but as a hodgepodge of background info I made up and pictures stolen from a Google Images search that I'm pretty sure are from a random Czech college brochure). I look over the twenty-four thumbnail images and short profile snippets that have popped up as the daily matches for "me." And then I pick the five that I think Jude might be most likely to select. I hesitate, choosing between a financial analyst who plays softball on the weekends and a marketing coordinator who is a Pilates instructor. I end up going with Miss Pilates: probably has more free time along with being more limber. I'll check my answers with Jude at the end of our meeting.

Now I just have forty-five minutes to kill before he gets here. I'm feeling a little hungry, but the biscotti are gone (obviously) and some desperate person even took the kale muffins. I glance over to the corner table and see that I Am Legend is on her way out too, throwing one last glare my way before she reaches the door. Fare thee well, Tampa Bay. You better toughen up fast or New York will break you within a week, sending you back to the sun-soaked swamps whence you came.

Despite my rumbling stomach, I decide against buying anything to eat. Even with my due diligence today, who knows if I'm still going to be employed next week, and I'll be kicking myself if I have to skip out on dinner because I got tempted by a four-dollar cake pop. And now that Legend is gone, there's no one interesting here to even look at/stare down as an unofficial tour guide on the Real New York Experience.

I take out my phone again. And before I know exactly what I'm doing, I've opened up Instagram and have navigated over to Jordan's pregnancy post. This time, I only spend a minute or so looking at the picture itself before I get whirlpooled into the rabbit hole of comments.

In between the congrats and the OMGs are some real gems.

"Way to go, Miles and Jordan!" from Greta, the German foreign exchange student my parents hosted one summer. Aha! At least I'm not the only one who thought the baby might be mine. Though I should probably write her . . . not that I'm exactly sure how that e-mail is going to go:

```
Hey Greta,
Long time no talk. Hope you're well. By the
way, could you please defriend my cheating
ex-fiancée from your social media?
Danke,
Miles
```

Then a simple "Congratulations" from . . . is this for real?! My aunt Fatma?

And then, as if she can sense both my impending breakdown and the incredulous thoughts I'm having about her own mother, I get a text.

How's it going?

It's Aisha, my cousin.

Is your Spidey sense on high alert? I write. Aisha has a knack—or I like to think we both do—for sensing the exact moment when the other person is in need of a check-in. It probably has something to do with both of us being only children. She's the closest thing I have to a sibling, and vice versa.

I hope you are not looking at Jordan's post. Or writing her. Or thinking about her, she writes.

Of course not, I type back. Why would I ever write her? I mean, aside from this morning, but obviously it was pure adrenaline steering that boat. But speaking of writing things, you might want to have a talk with your mother.

Oh God. What did she do now?

Oh, nothing, I type. Just congratulated my ex-fiancée on the baby she's having with another man. On Instagram. NBD.

There's a considerable pause before Aisha writes again. You know how they have parental lock features on phones? They should really have one that goes the other way too. FOR parents. I'll talk to her. Again. I'm sorry.

I laugh despite myself. Honestly? It's probably the first time I've laughed since Jordan's "We need to talk." So maybe you should thank her.

Do you need me to tell you Jordan doesn't deserve you and you're better off and you'll be over her before you know it?

I type out No and then, thinking better of it, delete it and replace it with, It couldn't hurt . . .

Well, then, she doesn't deserve you. You are absolutely better off without her. And you'll be over her much, much sooner than you think. It wasn't meant to be.

I laugh, bitterly this time. I don't believe in meant-to-be.

Yeah, right, she types back. This is Dumped Miles talking. Write me again in two months when you're back to Secret Rom-Com-Loving Miles.

Hey, I write. It was never a secret.

True, she types back. Heart on Your Sleeve Miles. I'll be waiting for you.

Yeah, yeah.

In the meantime . . . just delete Instagram from your phone.

I look down at my phone and hesitate. Can I really do that? I mean, can *anyone* really do that?

Yes, you can do it. Aisha responds to my brain signals again. And, trust me, I'll be making sure my mom does too.

I sigh, and then click the buttons to remove the app. Fine. Anything else?

Yes. ♥ you.

♥ you too.

And if I ever see Jordan again, I will 100% kick her ass.

I laugh. Aisha is about four foot eleven but does an intense kickboxing boot camp class three times a week. I wouldn't take any bets against her. Thank you, I write back. Though maybe not in her condition.

You're right, she writes. I'll give her an IOU for . . . let's say . . . 8 months postpartum?

Sounds fair.

The front door jangles and I look up to see a familiar face walking through it. Gotta run. My client's here.

Ooh. Scope him out for me? I could definitely use a little extra work this month.

Will do.

I stand up as I put my phone away, calling out Jude's name to get his attention since I have the advantage of knowing what he looks like. He's got artfully styled reddish-brown hair and an equally well-groomed beard. His eyes are green and he's almost definitely picked out his form-fitting T-shirt to highlight both them and his biceps, obviously a perk of his job as a personal trainer. If this was twenty years ago, and this guy was just trying to pick up girls in a bar . . . he definitely wouldn't need my help.

As it is, it won't even be a stretch to recommend Aisha's photography services to him. Considering what he's got to work with, and Aisha's magic mix of the right lighting, the right poses, and her secret-sauce filter . . . I'm pretty sure she could make him look like Jude *Law* if she wanted to.

"Hello. Miles, is it?" he says, as he walks over toward my outstretched hand.

Yeah, the accent was the right choice. Sure, it might be a little hard to figure out exactly what he's saying, but it's probably just hard to hear over the sound of all the dropping panties.

"Yes. Hi, Jude. A pleasure to meet you. Please have a seat." We shake hands, and he gets settled down at the table across from me. "Can I get you anything? A cup of coffee?"

"Oh, no, thank you," he says. "I'm actually off of caffeine these days." Noted. He thinks for a second. "But do you think they'd be able to get me a cup of hot water with some lemon in it?"

"I'm sure that can be arranged. I'll be right back." I wait in line and give my drink order to Evelynn's replacement barista, who doesn't comment on the fact that I've been sitting here for hours and have now ordered something she has to give me for free. I leave a dollar in her tip jar for good karma.

"Ta," Jude says when I place the mug in front of him, and then laughs. "Sorry, this is a little awkward, isn't it? Meeting someone who's supposed to be impersonating me."

I put up my hands. "Don't think of it like that. Just think of it like a coach. Or a copy editor. I'm helping you come across as the best version of yourself on paper. Or, you know, the screen."

Jude nods. "Yeah, I've gathered I need some help in that department. The problem is, I absolutely never know what to write back, and then I forget, and before I know it I've accidentally 'ghosted.' Or something. That's what a couple of the girls called it."

I nod. "Writing is a skill set. You're basically just hiring a consultant to help you with getting your foot in the door. No different than if you hired, say, someone to help you with your résumé."

"Right, right." Jude nods as he takes a sip from his mug. "So, how does this work exactly? Do I get to pick my matches?"

"Well," I begin, settling into my spiel. "We essentially offer packages. So with your basic package, you can pick your matches and our goal is to get you to an initial in-person date. Now, you can always add à la carte services like, for example, getting one of our matchmaking consultants . . ." (Georgie, also known as Leanne's assistant/graphic designer/social media manager) ". . . to help you select your possible matches. Another add-on we do is a photography package. Our photo consultant—who is absolutely fantastic by the way—can help with picking and enhancing your profile pictures," I say, planting the seeds for throwing some work Aisha's way. "We even have conversational coaches who can help with in-person dates." That would be Giles, Leanne's lawyer who—for reasons unbeknownst to us— owes Leanne some sort of epic favor.

"I see," Jude says.

"Now, we do offer other packages. Our silver package will get you up to a third date and includes three photo enhancements built in, along with a phone consultation with our conversational coach. Or our gold package, which is the whole shebang: We will work with you up to and including a tenth date. We'll set up a photo shoot and provide you with up to ten retouched and varying photo options for your profile. Our conversational consultant will be available to you on demand and can even surreptitiously attend a date to help you with your speaking skills via a headset." Which we can only offer because no one ever picks the gold package. We certainly don't own the equipment and I'm pretty sure Giles has no idea that's even an option.

"Wow," Jude says, nervously squeezing out the lemon in his drink. "Sounds very James Bond."

I can sense he's overwhelmed; time for me to rein it in with the perfect combination of self-confidence and ego boost. "We've had a lot of success with all of our packages. But in your case, I'd recommend the basic package. I don't think you're going to be needing too much help from us."

"Really?" he says, looking up at me hopefully.

"Absolutely," I say, not even really lying. From the corner of my eye, I can see the barista looking at him wistfully. I'm either gonna have this guy married off by the end of the year or surrounded by a harem—all depending on where he currently stands on the spectrum of relationship-seeking adult male. Though, usually, if they're coming to us, they tend to be after something a little more serious. "And, if you happen to need any add-ons, we can take it from there." I'll bring up Aisha's wunderskills at our next meeting.

Jude nods. "Okay."

"For today, I'm going to show you a couple of places in your profiles that you can spruce up. Just so you can see how we operate and know that we're not changing anything about who you are."

"Sounds good," Jude says.

"Great." I navigate over to his Chemistrie profile. "Okay, like here. Under 'Likes,' it says: 'A pint.' Which is good, honest. But what do you like about drinking?"

Jude stares at me as if I might have three heads. "Er, mostly getting drunk, mate."

I smile. "Of course. But aside from that . . . is there a particular drink that you like? A particular bar?"

"Oh," he says. "Well, actually, I'm on this weird little quest. It's stupid, really." He takes another sip of his water, holding on to his mug like a security blanket, as if revealing his nerdy, though I'm sure absolutely charming, quest is just oh-so-slightly embarrassing. This guy. He is 100 percent the lead in a rom-com.

"No, no. Please tell me. Quests are good. Quests show character," I egg him on.

"Well . . . I'm trying to find a gluten-free, low-calorie craft beer that tastes like the regular kind. I've been going all over the city, trying everything they have on tap." Yup, what did I say? "Not a ton of luck so far. But Brooklyn seems promising." It would.

"This is good," I say. "We can work with this."

"Really?" he asks.

"Definitely. And, I mean, wouldn't you want a companion to go on this self-designated pub crawl with?"

"That'd be bloody fantastic," he says with a chuckle.

"Well, that's why I'm here. So, let's do this. Do you mind logging in to your account?" I turn the laptop to face Jude and let him put in his password. Then I bring it over so he can see as I type.

Likes: On the hunt for the perfect craft
beer and the perfect girl to find it with. Do
you like quests? Exploring this amazing city
with both a purpose and no real reason at
all except to enjoy the company you're in?
If so, drop me a line.

I finish with a flourish.

"Oh, that's good," Jude says. "That's really good."

"Thanks," I say. "So, if you're ready to sign up, I can e-mail you the contract and it'll have instructions for changing the log-in passwords to your dating profiles so that you can give us access. FYI, nothing will be changed without your approval."

"Right," Jude says, nodding and taking a final swig from his cup. "What the hell? Let's do it, right?" He smiles at me and offers his hand again.

"Great," I say, shaking it. "And, listen, before you go, there's a little game I like to play." I take out my phone and click into the 24/7 app again. "Since I'm going to be helping you craft your voice, I like to try and see how well I get to know my clients just through the questionnaire. So, tell me, which five of these women would you pick as your matches?"

"Hmmm . . . okay," Jude says, as he takes my phone and looks closer.

"Just jot down your answers," I say, handing him my notepad and pen.

He has my phone for a long time. I actually start a game of KenKen on my laptop before I hear him clear his throat.

"All right. I think I'm ready."

I look over his notepad. And then I grin, flipping it over to reveal the ones I had picked for him earlier. Of course, I maybe wouldn't have shown him my answers if my results hadn't been so good.

But they usually are.

Four out of five. Miles Ibrahim: Love Wordsmith is back.

CHAPTER 4

To: All the Baes
From: Clifford Jenkins
Re: GIFT CARDS ARE WORKING

Turns out the Beatles were wrong. Say whaaaat?
You CAN buy love! Super psyched to report
the gift card glitch sitch is under control. I also set it up so the default base-
line starts at $299. Treat our gift carders
like the royalty they are, 'cause they'll be
expecting a premium love match FAST. We're
talking crunch time, Cinnamon Toast-style.

(That said, if their first choices sizzle out,
remind them the gift card has unlimited re-
fills. With wedding season upon us, we're going to be marketing DIRECTLY to brides and
grooms. It's the perfect thank-you gift from
the hitched to the ditched when tension and
emotions are through da roof.)

Wish I'd bought *myself* a gift card on the
eve of a certain Save the Date event, but of

course, they didn't exist back then. Guess
my loss is the world's gain. #perspective

Reminder: Our next meeting will be Tuesday,
May 12, and I'm renting out the back room at
Porchlight, so prepare to get your drank on!
Till then, enjoy these April showers.

Clifford
CEO, Sweet Nothings (NOW GIFT CARD CAPABLE)
P.S. If you understand blockchains, DM me.

ZOEY

My alarm splits the air at four a.m. and my hand flails around
to shut off my clock and knock it to the floor, like I'm in the
opening of a movie. I've lived here a month, but I still calculate
what time it is on the West Coast (i.e., The Real Time). One
a.m. sounds a lot better to me than four. One a.m. is fun and
frivolous. It's midnight showings of *The Room* at the Sunset
Five. Ravenous trips to Pink's Hot Dogs, or skinny-dipping in
an infinity pool overlooking the Hollywood Hills. (I only did
that once, but still. It could have conceivably happened every
night.) One a.m. means trying to keep up with Mary's extraor-
dinary brain, Frank and me nipping at her heels while she paced
in her kitchen. Frank is her emotional support ferret. I'm pretty
sure he worked his magic on me, too. He'd ride on my shoulder
while I transcribed her quips into dialogue for screenplays that
needed a tune-up. Watching the sun rise outside her floor-to-
ceiling windows overlooking Studio City was the last time I
remember feeling content with my place in the world.

Working for Mary wasn't exactly calm, of course. It was the
elevator drop at the Haunted Mansion; twists, turns, and sud-

den mood shifts, followed by gale forces of screaming laughter. Mary swept into rooms as though they were towns. She held no illusions about her "quirks," and greeted me each morning with some variation of "Let's spin the wheel on my personality!" Twice my age but with the soul of a college student, she dillydallied for weeks and then pulled all-nighters twelve hours before her doctored pages were due. I practically lived at her house, often staying overnight in the guest room with its own balcony and mini-fridge. Some days all she asked was for me to read her the latest celebrity blind items while she lay on the couch with cucumbers on her eyes and Frank sleeping on her feet. The next week we'd spend ten-hour days at the Museum of Television and Radio aka the Paley Center on Beverly Drive, bingeing old award shows from decades past for inspiration (she was occasionally hired to write introductions for one actor to say about another actor during the Golden Globes, Emmys, or Academy Awards).

The name of her script doctoring company was Mary, Fuck, Kill. I blushed every time I answered the phone, smooshing the words together so they'd be indistinguishable. "Mary Fuckle, how may I assist you?"

She'd chastise me, "They're going to think I married some schmo named Fuckle. Enunciate."

"Let them think that, then."

"If you don't say it properly, I'm going to change the company name to George Carlin's Seven Words You Can Never Say on Television," she warned me. "Look, I'm filling out the paperwork now. 'Shit, Piss—'"

I threw an *Undersea* PEZ dispenser at her. "Okay, okay."

The *Undersea* PEZ dispenser represented her former life as an actress. In the mid-eighties, before I was born, she had portrayed Duchess Quinnley in a sci-fi/fantasy film about intergalactic mermaids. An on-set injury the final week of filming stripped her of all enthusiasm for performing and she'd successfully sued her way out, bankrupting future productions before they could start. She'd been trying to live it down ever since; fans still blamed her for the abrupt end of what was intended to be a trilogy, while in other circles, her departure added to the cult appeal of the one film that *had* been made. At least this way, they argued, it couldn't be "ruined" like other long-running franchises because it would never have an ending. Fan conventions and cosplay tournaments kept the cult alive, and invites to appear on panels still filled Mary's inbox on a daily basis. One of my jobs was to delete them, unread, each morning.

Of the seemingly infinite collector's items on eBay (toys, games, and action figures instilled with her likeness), the only one she owned was the PEZ dispenser, because it symbolized her current work as a script fixer: "People pay me to lift up my neck hinge and shoot out something tart and sweet on command, with ten more of equal quality lined up behind it."

Seven weeks ago, she told me I was the best assistant she'd ever had, and that's why she had to fire me. Instead of living my own life, I was living hers. I needed to throw myself into new situations if I was ever going to grow as a writer, as my *own* writer. I begged for another six months of time while I figured out where I wanted to go and what I wanted to do, and she said she'd sleep on it. The next morning, when I knocked on her door, she handed me a one-way ticket to New York, paperclipped to the address of an apartment she'd leased in my name. (I found out later she'd purchased the building in the mid-1980s with her Duchess Quinnley money. It was worth a fortune now, but she preferred to rent to starving artists and offer them merit-based discounts.)

She blew me a kiss, closed the door, and locked it. I saw Frank in the window for a split second before the blinds snapped shut, too.

Now here I am at four a.m. in the Big, Rotten Apple, forcing myself to wake up on a weekday so I can be the first customer at the only place I'll go all day, which happens to be across the freaking street.

Somehow, I don't think this was what Mary meant by "living." But until and unless New York stops being frightening and grotesque, I don't see anything changing.

When I arrived home yesterday, there was a basket outside my apartment door. Inside was a barely legible, handwritten card: "Champers for my Champ! You're money, baby!— Clifford." The rest of the basket was empty. Someone *stole* my champagne.

That about sums up my view of Manhattan. Everything's there for the taking, and it's been taken by someone else.

I roll across my lumpy couch bed and land in "the kitchen," aka the area where the hot plate and mini-fridge are. Another piece of advice from the neighbor I've only seen once: "Use your oven to store your winter coats." (Without a closet or cooking skills, that made pretty good sense to me. Unfortunately, I'm sans oven. Instead, I hang my sweaters in the empty pantry.)

Out the window, the city is dark and unfriendly. The noise of a truck backing up—*beep, beep, beep*—fills the air. Is there a single quiet hour here? Ever? I make a deeply ironic cup of coffee so I can wake up enough to sit outside Café Crudité and insure I'm the first customer to arrive and purchase more coffee. Then I plop down cross-legged in front of the lopsided mirror hanging on the door and scrutinize my face. I looked like a human Xanax withdrawal yesterday, blinking into the light, but today that won't do. It's not enough to beat the Table Thief; I want to look good doing it (but not as though I'm *trying* to look good). I dab on tinted moisturizer, a swipe of eyeliner, and a muted lip. I'll still wear my stomping boots and the arm warmers Mary knitted because I refuse to be miserable in an overly air-conditioned building, but other than that, I'm less Manic Pixie Nightmare and more "Oh, did I put on makeup?" I smile at my reflection, pleased with the results.

Outside on the darkened sidewalk, I'm flooded with adrenaline. There aren't many people out, which is nice, but on the other hand, there aren't many people out, so if something happens to me, or I need help in any way, there will be no one to hear my cries.

Boots, start walking. Fast.

I make it across the crosswalk on my second try. Progress. Then, at precisely 5:01, Evelynn strides toward the café entrance to unlock the door and jumps when she sees me.

"Hi! Sorry. Hi. I guess I'm the first one here today, ha ha ha. *Am* I the first one here?" I sputter.

"Yes," she says. "Can you stand back while I . . ."

"I'm curious, is the biscotti already sitting there waiting for me? Or do you have to bring it out and display it?"

"We discontinued that policy after the events of yesterday."

My mouth falls open. "Are you serious?"

"No." She motions with her hand. "Can you give me a little space?"

Five minutes later, I've set up my mobile office at the glorious, big table, devoured all the free biscotti, thank you very much, and swallowed half my second cup of coffee. Ten minutes after *that*, the place is jumping with commuters, yet there's no sign of the Table Thief. In between hostilities, he'd mentioned he "spreads out his visits," so maybe he's off to the next coffee shop on his rotation. I'll be pissed if I got up early and went to all this trouble for nothing; is it so wrong that I want him to show up, witness his own defeat, and *feel* the loss of the good table before exiting my café and my life?

I'm downing my last dregs of coffee when who should walk in but Mr. Personality. He scans the room and his gaze rests on me.

"Not today, Satan," I mutter triumphantly.

His brown eyes whip toward mine. "What'd you say?"

"Uh, I said, 'Seat's taken.' "

"I can see that. Given that you're sitting in it."

"Just wanted to make sure we're clear. I'll be here all day, by the way, so don't get any ideas that you can, like, wait me out."

"Well, *Fifty Shades* can't watch itself," he says disdainfully.

"Excuse me?"

"Six straight hours of mommy porn is admirably rigorous."

"I have *no* idea what you're—oh. The Weeknd." Dammit, Clifford! "Uh, it was a parody video," I stammer.

"Parody porn *is* underrated," he says condescendingly.

"I didn't come here to watch porn," I hiss.

"Just do me a favor and keep the volume down, okay? Some of us are here to *work.*"

Asshole!

"Miles, your order's up," Evelynn chimes in.

Miles, eh? So, he's got a name. But he doesn't have a place to sit. Every table's occupied, and more customers are piling in. He busies himself adding cream and sugar to his coffee while scanning the café for the next available place to sit. Unfortunately, the cream and sugar station is right next to me. I sense his gaze roving around and glance over in time to see him pour roughly half the café's sugar supply into his mug. (And I thought he was tense *before*? He is going to Hulk Out when his blood sugar spikes.)

Out of nowhere, "Last Dance with Mary Jane" by Tom Petty pours out of my speakers. Not again!

A video chat box hijacks my screen.

I try to press Do Not Accept as fast as humanly possible, but in my haste I click Accept by accident.

"Should Frank get his own Instagram page, and if so, what should the sub-theme be?" Mary shouts.

I manage to hang up while dozens of eyes swing toward me in irritation.

"There's a class for people who are new to computers coming up at the Y," Miles says, lifting his mug (aka "sugar with a splash of coffee") to his lips.

I don't have time to counter this bit of snideness before he adds, "Wait. Was that—was that the real Mary Clarkson trying to FaceTime you?"

The image attached to her screen name is a faux-retro photograph from an old issue of *Interview* magazine. She's got curlers in her hair, a bright red mouth, and a joint dangling from her lips. The song starts up again, with an added notification: **Contrary, Quite** would like to FaceTime. This time I mute the call and hang up simultaneously.

"Hmm?" I feign ignorance.

"Mary Clarkson. *Undersea.* Mary *Clarkson*!"

"Maybe." Don't you wish you'd been nicer to me before, so you could ask me about her?

"And you just . . . you just . . . you hung up on Mary Clarkson."

"I'm texting her instead. Volume control, remember?"

I always forget that for dudes of a "certain age" (such as Clifford), Mary as the brave, feminist Duchess Quinnley of Undersea and her brief, forced mermaiding is everything golden and good from their childhoods. She was those guys' first crush, and for some of them, their first, well . . . "self-love." I wonder if that's true of Miles. He looks younger than Clifford, though. He's in way better shape, that's for sure. Cutting remarks burn a lot of calories.

Confession time: I've never seen *Undersea.* It's actually the reason I got the job as Mary's assistant.

The temp agency I signed with after graduating from Santa Monica City College sent me on a mystery assignment to an anonymous female writer who lived above Studio City on Mulholland. I had no idea who she'd be or what she was looking for. I recognized her when she (and Frank) opened the door, but not the way a fan would. Just a vague thought of, "Oh. It's her. Huh."

A standard résumé scan and work history interview commenced. At the end, she said, "Now for the most important question. What is the name of the home planet of the Sworkas?"

"Uh . . ." This wasn't something I could fudge my way out of. I was pretty certain the Sworkas were a loathed component of the fandom, cutesy and high-pitched. I seemed to remember they resembled dolphins, but as to the name of their planet, I hadn't a clue. If I'd known Mary Clarkson was the person I'd be meeting, I'd have downloaded *Undersea* and prepared myself. Ah well, guess it wasn't meant to be.

I looked up with a shrug. "Planet Merchandising?"

She grinned at me and it happened that quick: My life changed.

"There are only two rules," she said, eyes twinkling. "The first is, if I ever become someone who cares whether or not you know the answer to that question, shoot me. The second is, never see the movie. You made it this far; stick to your guns. You in?"

I found out later she only hired non-fans. She didn't care if you'd seen her as a mermaid once or twice when you were a kid, but if you regularly quoted the film as an adult, or owned, say, a Sworkas-to-English dictionary, that was an immediate disqualification.

"How would you be able to take me seriously if you'd seen it?" she pointed out a few days later, while wearing a bedazzled eye patch and mismatched fuzzy slippers.

Back at the café, Miles continues to hover.

"Do you mind? I can't concentrate in the vicinity of oglers," I say.

"I have nowhere to sit," he points out. "Have you really come here every single day since you moved to New York?"

My eye twitches. I'd meant for that factoid to boost my credibility as a valuable customer, not add fuel to his mockery. "Yes," I grit out.

"Why? There's this thing called the City all around you, and it happens to be one of the most incredible places on earth—"

For the tiniest moment of lunacy, I think about saying, "Maybe you could tell me where to start? You've survived here fifteen years—you probably know every nook and cranny and I could really, really use a friend here. Anyone who knows what they're doing, because I sure as hell don't," but then reality intrudes, and I remember he's a jerk who's currently insulting me. *Again*.

I turn my back, put on my headphones, and open a chat box to Mary.

Zoey: Greetings from hell.

Contrary, Quite: Are you expanding your horizons?

Zoey: Someone stepped on my foot the first week and broke my little toe.

Contrary, Quite: What are you whining for? It's vestigial.

Zoey: It's probably going to fall off.

Contrary, Quite: I'm sending you a care package.

Zoey: Why? It'll just get stolen. BTW you owe Nick, and I quote, "2k in back weed."

Contrary, Quite: Lies and slander. I only buy front weed. But that explains why he's been so mopey and lovelorn lately.

Zoey: What do you mean?

Contrary, Quite: He had it bad for you.

Zoey: Incorrect.

Contrary, Quite: The other day he asked why I never gave you any time off. Apparently he got tickets for the Bowl and you told him you had to work late all month. ALL MONTH??

Zoey: I didn't like him that much.

Contrary, Quite: All you had to do was tell me you had plans. We could've knocked off early AT ANY TIME.

Zoey: *He* had plans. *I* wanted to work.

Contrary, Quite: Did you taste the fried chicken at Momofuku, yet?

Zoey: Not yet.

Contrary, Quite: Don't contact me again until you do. I mean it. You're partially dead to me, starting . . . now.

Tess Riley was my first client, and her Best Foot Forward had ended in success. It wasn't easy to steer her in the right direction, though; it took several phone sessions to help her realize it was okay to be specific about what she wanted in a partner. New York City isn't exactly running low on single men, but she felt bad eliminating anyone before she'd met them. I told her #FOMO would paralyze her, and then I worked my tail off helping her pursue her eventual match.

All I know about my second client is her name (Bree Garrett), her age (twenty-five), and that she received a Sweet Nothings gift card from her friends on Galentine's Day. Something must have happened between then and now that prompted her into using it, though based on Clifford's memo, it's also possible the gift cards simply weren't working before. I've decided not to read her profile before meeting her. I don't want to be influenced by any labored-over answers; I want spontaneous, combustible stuff so I can help project an authentic, flawed-but-lovable self into the world in the hopes of hooking her an authentic, flawed-but-lovable man.

From the Freelancer's Handbook: Do not present a "perfect" image. No one will trust it. (Nor should they.) Think of that old interview question: "What is your greatest flaw?" And the interviewee says, "I'm just too darn organized." Don't be the organized guy. Add a tiny blemish here and there.

My phone buzzes as I'm headed out of the café bathroom.

A text from Sweet Nothings: **Incoming. Cupid is as Cupid does!**

A split-second later, the call arrives. I let it ring twice, take a deep breath, plaster a smile on my face, and launch my Calm Professional voice.

"Hi, this is Zoey with Sweet Nothings. How may I help you?"

"Basically, my dick picker is broken," Bree Garrett says.

Despite years of Mary's non sequiturs, I'm unprepared for Bree's opening statement.

"I'm sorry to hear that," I manage to reply, while suppressing a coughing fit. "But the good news is, today we start healing what's broken."

"How does this whole thing work?" Bree asks. "Are you my Yentl?"

I'm pretty sure she means "yenta," but even that word is wrong, and I blame *Fiddler on the Roof* for it.

"That's right," I say cheerfully. "Though I'm quite a bit younger than a traditional matchmaker. In fact, that's one of the things we're most proud of at Sweet Nothings—it's more like a peer-to-peer safety net, like a trusted friend is setting you up on a date after helping you vet candidates. We help you express yourself in the most succinct, and, we hope, charming way, in order to get positive responses from the kind of men you'd like to meet. I think you'll be happy to know I have a one hundred percent success rate."

My cheeks get slightly pink. (It's not technically a lie. I'm one for one!)

"Sweet," she replies. "And you're like a spellchecker and grammar bitch?"

"Exactly. Minus the bitch part."

"Good, because I'm not about having my commas policed."

"What's your schedule like? Want to meet in person today or tomorrow to update your profile?" I'm feeling the pressure of the gift card memo to work fast. But I also don't want to push too hard and scare her off. "Of course, next week's fine, too."

Not really, though! It's Cinnamon Toast Crunch Time and the clock started ticking the moment she rang.

"Couldn't I link you to a profile that's already up?" she asks.

"You could, but I've found people will open up in ways they don't expect if we chat in person, and it helps me get a feel for your personality, your likes and dislikes, and what you're look-ing for physically. Because that counts as much as the mental connection."

"Truth."

"We'll sync laptops and find a handful of candidates to reach out to, then see where that leads us. What's your favorite online service?"

"Last week it would've been Flirtville, but there are waaaaay too many STDs in that population," she says.

Ah. Something DID happen to push her to activate the gift card. I have a sudden chilling thought of Clifford listening in on our call. I have no idea how but I don't want her to say any-thing personal over the phone in case it ends up in front of a man who regularly closes out correspondence with, "Smell you later."

"Whatta Catch and Game, Set, Match are good, but those tend to appeal to people who are looking for something more serious. Does that work?"

"YES. I definitely want to go the serious route. Can you meet at Dominik's for lunch on Saturday?" Bree says.

I pull up a map on my laptop and shudder at what I see. Fifty-Fifth Street and Eighth Avenue. *Two* subway rides away.

"Normally that'd be fine, but my cat's sick," I say in a guilty rush. He's so sick he's wasting away, almost as though he doesn't exist. . . . "So unfortunately, I need to stay close to home. I'm in the East Village. Have you heard of Cheese?"

"Is this a 'Bree' joke?"

"No, sorry, I meant—it's a restaurant, called Cheese."

"Do they serve anything besides cheese?"

"I don't think so. If you don't eat cheese we can totally find someplace else." How do you feel about Duane Reade, the only other food-dispensing place on my street?

Miles catches my eye. "Say cheese," he whispers as he passes by.

I roll my eyes. Plus, how did he hear me? I've been speaking very quietly so as not to get on anyone's nerves. At least, I thought I was. Maybe all the talk of cheese got me excited. After all, I can expense the meal.

"Do they serve wine with the cheese?" Bree wants to know.

"I'm not sure."

"I could bring my own bottle."

"Okay, cool. Why not?"

Having a glass of wine is a great idea. Then she'll really open up. Also, I can pretend I have a friend in the city and we're meeting to have wine and cheese, which is a completely normal, well-adjusted, healthy thing to do, rather than, say, going to a cheese-themed restaurant solely because I live, work, and "play" on a single city block.

We settle on a time for Saturday and I give her the location.

"What do you look like?" she says.

"I have two-toned hair. Not because I'm cool, just out of neglect. It's dark on top and turns light halfway down."

"I have one-toned hair, blond, and I'll be in my 1981 *Undersea* T-shirt. I got it at a yard sale last weekend. I almost felt bad paying five bucks! I wanted to be like, 'This is probably worth five thousand, sooooo . . .'"

"Do you like the movie, or is it more about the vintage pop culture?" I'm truly curious. Fandom comes in many forms.

"Oh my God, I loooooooove *Undersea*—you have *no* idea. It's something I never put in my profiles, because I don't want to be labeled a fake geek girl or whatever, but I'm all about wearing costumes at the midnight showing, I can do 'the hair' and all that, and this time for my profile I'd like to be up front about it. Really be ME, you know? Because otherwise, what's the point?"

I bite my tongue. *I'll* be being her, at least at the beginning. But denying that fact is the number-one rule in the *Freelancer's Handbook*:

*Never remind them you're communicating with their poten-
tial dates as a Cyrano. That line of thinking derails the client-
ghostwriter relationship; they might start to wonder whether
they'll be able to bridge the gap between what you typed and what
they do or say on the in-person date. It's best to get in and get out
as swiftly as possible and let the client take over once you've attracted the interest of a good match.*

"You've seen it, right?" Bree says, reeling me back in to the
topic at hand. "If you're going to be talking like me, you have to
be able to at least reference *Undersea*," she adds.

I don't answer right away. I'm too busy shaking my fist at the
universe. Twenty-nine years I avoided that ridiculous film. For
eight of them, it was at the request of the Duchess herself.

"You're right," I agree. "Can I borrow yours for a refresher
course?"

I opt for a minimal bluff by implying it's just been a while
since I watched it. (If Sweet Nothings attracts a fetish contin-
gent we've never heard of and Clifford needs to change the
company name again, I'll suggest Minimal Bluff.)

"Original or director's cut? Special edition or—"

"Totally up to you. Whichever one you can most easily part
with."

We exchange cell numbers so she won't have to call the
switchboard each time she wants to chat. I tell her I'm looking
forward to meeting her and seeing her vintage *Undersea* T-shirt
tomorrow.

Somewhere in California, Mary raises a glass to me and
laughs.

CHAPTER 5

To: All Tell It to My Heart Employees
From: Leanne Tseng
Re: Einsteins

Team,

Here's what I know: You are all creative geniuses who are not necessarily getting the
financial compensation you deserve due to
circumstances beyond all of our control.
Here's what else I know: I think we can har-
ness that creative IQ to try and change that.

Got an idea for a great promotion? An ex-
ceptional tie-in? A snappy (jingle-less) ad?
I'd love to hear it. Off-the-wall and out-of-
the-box are welcome here but, at the same
time, simplicity often wins the day too. An
idea as mundane yet infuriatingly brilliant
as—just off the top of my head—gift cards
could really mean the difference between a

struggling company and the premier one in the field. It's no secret that I want us to be the latter and I hope it's also no secret that I want to take you with me.

Oh, and besides the promises of future glories and promotions, any actionable ideas will also get a $500 bonus.

Yours,
Leanne

MILES

I haven't been running much over the past six weeks. I haven't exactly been feeling motivated to stay in shape, or get fresh air, or treat my body like a temple as much as a mausoleum for dead things, like feelings or a sense of self-worth. Every now and again, I've been doing a loop around Morningside Park, which is just a few blocks over from Dylan and Charles's apartment, but that's mostly been when Charles's passive aggression has gotten the best of me rather than for any sort of health purpose.

I'm not exactly sure why I'm motivated to go to Riverside Park today instead, except that maybe when I start out by playing "The River Is Long, the River Is Strong"—the theme song from *Undersea*—on my phone, it inevitably leads me to listening to the entire soundtrack on repeat. And that soundtrack doesn't deserve a paltry mile-and-a-half run. It deserves a miles-long view of the mighty Hudson River, past marble tombs dedicated to legendary war generals, and beneath majestic branches of cherry blossom trees that have almost, though not quite, lost their last blooms. And I only spend a very, very small portion of it daydreaming about Mary Clarkson in that mermaid suit. And a smaller portion wondering if the Biscotti Bandit really does know her. That girl is a mystery wrapped in an enigma encased inside wonky arm warmers.

By the time I get back to Dylan and Charles's, I'm out of breath and a sweaty mess. My watch tells me I ran seven miles. I used to do a daily five around Prospect Park, but that hasn't happened in months since my former running partner got a monthlong "stomach virus" before dumping me. (In retrospect, I am really, really thick.)

I buzz up when I get to the apartment. Dylan and Charles have both been too busy to make me a key yet, and I've been too mopey to take it upon myself. Besides, I'm pretty sure the situation would have too much of an air of permanence about it for Charles (and maybe even Dylan), if they actually went to the trouble of making me my own key.

"Oh, God," Charles says when he opens the door for me. "Are you crying?"

"It's sweat," I respond.

He peers more closely at me, trying to affirm that the droplets are, in fact, coming from my forehead. "Hmph. I guess," he finally says. "Mind the runner. It's antique Kermanshah." He points to the dark carpet that runs down their hallway, which he carefully pads around in his corduroy slippers.

"I'm pretty sure we bought that at Target. Or maybe Overstock dot com," Dylan comes over and whispers conspiratorially as I'm taking off my sneakers.

I smile at him as a bead of sweat drips down my nose and falls onto their dark parquet floor. Dylan grabs a tissue from the hall table and immediately wipes it up.

Dylan was my roommate in college, and he was a fantastic one. He was friendly, he was neat, and he never made a big deal of whether or not you were the same. He's still all those things, only now he's with Charles, which I think is only possible because he's not overly attached to "nice" as an attribute in a boyfriend.

Maybe that's not fair. Maybe Charles is perfectly nice to someone who hasn't spent the past six weeks invading his personal space, sweating all over his possibly Kermanshah rugs, and filling his fridge up with half-eaten cartons of chow mein. (I always want it fresh, but then I hate wasting food, so the leftovers tend to pile up. It's the ultimate millennial conundrum: determined to be conscientious while simultaneously wanting everything on demand.)

"He hates me," I say as I stack my shoes neatly by the door.

"He doesn't hate you," Dylan replies too quickly, which makes it hard to buy.

Oh, well. To be honest, I'm not sure Charles ever liked me. Maybe I wasn't able to hide the "Wow/How" in my face when Dylan first introduced me to him. The moment Dylan, the epitome of tall, dark, and handsome—the ultimate wingman, since we were never competing in the same pool—walked into the bar, his face flushed and glowing with Charles behind him, I automatically assumed that he had gotten separated from the boyfriend I was supposed to meet by an older, balding, bespectacled gentleman. I craned my head to look behind him for the young, hot dude I was expecting.

Until Dylan put his arm on Charles's and gave me a huge grin. "This is Charles."

It was probably too late to stuff the look on my face back into the box, and Charles noticed. Charles notices everything.

Like last night, when I was trying to figure out what to order for dinner. Charles took one glance at the app I was on and chimed in with, "Let me guess. Chow mein." I switched over to sushi, just to spite him. (Now there is half of a yellowtail/avocado roll in the fridge, too.)

Last week, he must have seen my laptop opened up to three different tabs of Sudoku, a crossword, and KenKen because when I came back from the bathroom, he casually asked me how work was going. "Busy," I lied automatically.

"Really?" he asked. "That second column is wrong by the way."

And today, just as I've peeled off my shirt to hop into the shower, he leans against the wall and comments, "So you finally went for a real run today?"

I bite my tongue to keep from retorting something about how would he know what a real run is, considering the only bit of exercise he gets is running his mouth. *I'm a guest in his home*, I remind myself. *Their one-bedroom home.*

"Yeah," I respond instead. "Riverside Park."

He nods. "A city gem you discovered in *You've Got Mail*?" He grins evilly.

I give him the finger when he turns around. The thing is, how would he know Riverside Park plays a crucial role in *You've Got Mail* if he hasn't also seen the movie? Huh?

He doesn't turn back around but does let me know that, "You know the windows? They're reflective," as he looks me in the eye through one of them. I carefully fold my middle finger to join the rest of my fist.

By the time I've gotten out of the shower, Charles and Dylan have left for a work dinner thrown by Dylan's law firm. "Help yourself to anything in the fridge," Charles has scrawled on the magnetic whiteboard on the front of it. "Seriously. Just. Eat. Them."

I open up the fridge and count the six white cardboard boxes, and the one plastic one of sushi. Aside from a neat row of salad dressing, raspberry jam, and a bottle of ketchup in the door, that's all there is in their fridge. Neither Charles nor Dylan cooks. I used to, if you can call getting all the ingredients and recipes delivered to me in a box once a week real cooking. But since I currently don't have a home to deliver said box to, that's not happening so much anymore.

I hate to admit it, but Charles is right. I should eat the leftovers. I should just heat them up and eat them . . . but doesn't a nice bowl of soba noodles and veggies sound pretty perfect right about now?

Good job on throwing dreamboat my way. I feel like I'm working on a spread for Vanity Fair. It's a text from Aisha. As predicted, it had been pretty easy to sell Jude on her add-on the day after our initial meeting.

He genuinely needs your help, though, I respond. **His pictures were doing him no favors.**

I spoke briefly on the phone with him too, Aisha writes back. **He sounds like Jamie Fraser.**

I wrack my brain, trying to figure out who that is. When I don't respond immediately, Aisha figures out my problem.

Outlander, she writes.

Ah, right, I write back. I cut the cord a while back so I haven't seen the show.

Why does this guy need your help again? Aisha writes.

As soon as I get that message, my phone buzzes with another incoming one. Jude. **Hey. So I've gotten an initial message from a girl I'm interested in. What's my next step?**

I write Aisha back quickly first. **I guess we're about to find out. I gotta go. Cyrano duties call.**

Then I switch over to Jude's window. **Hey. Perfect. You free to get on a video chat? Easier if we talk through the first one together.**

My phone rings almost immediately.

"Hi," Jude says, his face filling up my screen.

"Hey. So which site are we on?"

"Game Set Match," Jude says.

"Great," I respond. Of the many, many dating apps and sites I've worked with, it's actually one of my favorites. The interface is pretty simple and intuitive. And matches are conveniently already sorted into three categories: Game (hookups), Set (a catchall for those who aren't sure what the hell they want), and Match (long-term relationships). "Okay if I access your computer?"

"All yours, chief," he responds.

I click to the remote access program that I already had Jude install on his computer, wait for him to "accept," and then, voilà, his screen is up on mine. He already has the browser open to Game Set Match and I can see the notification that he has one message. I click through.

It's from someone named RayaJack5, whose profile picture is ostensibly of the large cross she apparently wears around her neck, but is, in fact, mostly of her rack.

RayaJack5: Hey. Seems like maybe we'd be a match, so wanted to say: hey.

I see she's in the "Set" category. Well, better than "Game," since Jude and I've already established that he's looking for more than that.

"Okay," I tell Jude. "So, basically, she's leaving the ball in your court. Which is pretty common." Sometimes, people word vomit on the initial contact, trying to get everything that they'd ever want the other person to know about them across in a cramped, convoluted block of text that—more often than not—just reeks of desperation. That's only slightly better than the absolutely infuriating "hey." At least Raya added a bit more flair to hers than that.

"So should I write back . . . 'hey?'" Jude asks.

"Um, no," I respond. "Because think about it. What would 'hey' accomplish exactly?"

Jude shrugs. "Don't know."

"Exactly," I say. "Think of it this way: Every interaction should have a purpose, however small. Whether it's to get to know more about the person, make them laugh, flirt with them, tell them more about yourself, etc. Everyone's busy, right? Why waste your time or someone else's time on something that's obviously not going to work? You ask the right questions, and you won't have to."

Jude laughs. "That might be the most New Yorker thing I've ever heard anyone say."

I shrug. "Maybe. But it works."

I see Jude looking at Raya's message again before turning his attention back to me. "All right then. So what would you say?"

"I'll type it on your screen, and if you like it, you hit send, okay?" I can always get my thoughts together better in writing.

"Sure," he responds.

"Give me a minute to check her profile out," I say.

Jude nods and I click around Raya's profile. She's twenty-three, an assistant pastry chef, and apparently into something called Christian horror. (Is that, like, movies about exorcisms? I'm slightly intrigued.) Ah, she also moved to the city just a couple of months ago.

"Okay, how about . . ." I say before I start typing.

GreatSc0t: Heya. I see you're new to New York. That was me two years ago. Have you figured out whether you love it or hate it yet?

"What do you think?" I ask Jude.

"Great," he says. "That works."

"Okay," I respond. "You've got final approval power with the send button."

"Approved," Jude says as he hits send and the message pings over to Raya. "Okay, so now . . . ah. She's online."

So she is. I see the icon that means she's typing in real time. We wait for her response. It doesn't take long.

RayaJack5: Haven't decided yet.

I wait, in case Raya decides to take it a step further and ask Jude anything about himself. But we get bupkes. Apparently, she's never taken an improv class either.

GreatSc0t: I have a theory that it's almost completely reliant on where you have your first slice of pizza. You have a good one, and you and New York are a Match. You have a subpar one and . . . it might just be Game.

The message lingers as I watch Jude's brows furrow a bit over it. "You don't like it?" I ask Jude.

"No, it's good," he says. "It's just . . . I don't eat pizza. I've been paleo for over two years now."

"Ah, okay," I say, deleting the message, before realizing what he's actually saying. "So you've . . . never had a New York pizza?!"

He shakes his head.

"And you're still here?" I ask incredulously. "How the hell do *you* know if you like it?"

Jude grins. "The hot dogs weren't bad. I had one from one of those carts once."

"I guess but . . . wait. You had it without the bun too, didn't you?"

"Yeah," Jude says sheepishly.

I shake my head. "Impersonating you might be tougher than I expected. Okay, how about this then . . ."

GreatSc0t: I have a theory that it's almost completely reliant on where you have your first run. You pick some-place scenic, on a beautiful fall or spring day, and you and New York are a Match. You end up in the horror show that is midtown in February, you'll be lucky if you can even bring yourself to call it a Game.

"Much better," Jude says, hitting send.

RayaJack5: Running is cool.

Christ. This woman might need our help even more than Jude does.

"Okay, so real talk," I say to Jude. "How much do you like this girl based on her profile and this brief interaction?"

"Er," Jude responds. "I don't know. There isn't much to go on."

"Exactly," I say. "Remember what I said about being effi-cient? Now, if there's something really striking you about her, some chemistry thing that's jumping out at you, then we can keep this going. But, if not . . . I say we give her one more chance to wow us in this chat, or we cut bait. What do you say?"

I see Jude click around on her profile. "The second one," he finally says.

Thank God. I mean, I've dealt with having to steer the conversation with reticent matches on more than one occasion, but this feels like we're parked in neutral.

"Let's give her a real shot though," I say. "Talk about something she's supposed to be interested in, okay?"

"All right," Jude agrees.

"Have you seen *The Exorcism of Emily Rose*?"

"Um . . . yeah. I think I have," Jude says.

Okay. Good enough.

GreatSc0t: Hey, you've seen The Exorcism of Emily Rose, right? Did you know they were originally going to use a dummy to get the character's contortions, but then the actress was so flexible, it's actually just her with very minimal special effects. Isn't that wild?

Jude hits send. We wait.

We wait awhile. This could be a good sign. Maybe Raya finally has something to say.

"Is that true?" Jude asks me.

"Yeah," I respond. "I think it's one of the reasons she got the part."

"That's brilliant," he says.

"We'll follow the little trivia up with a more open-ended question," I assure him. "This is just so that she knows you have some knowledge about something she's into."

We finally hear a ping.

RayaJack5: Never seen it.

Er . . . . okay, I have to ask.

GreatSc0t: Really? When you said you liked Christian horror, I figured that was a perfect example of the genre?

Apparently, Jude is as curious as I am, because he hits send immediately.

RayaJack5: Christian Horror. <u>www.fifty-shades-of-horror.net</u>

I click on the link and my eyes are immediately assaulted by a black website with neon pink writing. I squint trying to read it.

CHAPTER 1

Christian Horror was a lot of things. Bil-
lionaire CEO. BDSM God. Vampire.

And I, Anastasia Silver, was about to be
his cross to bear. Maybe even his . . . Silver cross. Or clove of garlic.

I stop reading. Dear God, is this fanfic of fanfic? And is it turning the whole thing back to being about vampires? Also, what the hell is it with this week and *Fifty Shades of Grey*?!

"So . . . seen enough to make a decision about Raya, you think?" I turn back to the task at hand, trying to keep any judgment out of my voice. After all, I'm not here to comment on our clients' tastes, just to help them find what they're looking for.

"I might have seen too much, mate," Jude says, his face one of confusion. "I don't think this is a match."

Good man. "All right. Let's do this properly, okay? No ghosting."

GreatSc0t: Ah, got it. Must have gotten my signals crossed. Listen, I have to go. But good luck on here. It's been nice chatting with you.

There's no great way to do this. A rejection is a rejection. But better an obvious one than one that says something like, "Maybe chat again sometime?" Because no. They won't.

RayaJack5 doesn't respond, just logs off.

"Sorry that one didn't work out," I tell Jude, "but it sometimes takes a while to find someone worth chatting with."

"Nah, man. I appreciate it," he says. "The 'efficiency'? Is that what you called it?" He laughs. "Well, you were right. It did save me a lot of time."

"I'd suggest taking a gander at your matches yourself," I say. "See if there's anyone who catches your eye. We can initiate the conversation and start it off on the right foot."

"Okay," he says. "I'll take a look."

"Stick with the 'Match' section if you can," I suggest.

"All right. I'll let you know if I find anyone."

"Great," I respond. We say our good-byes and hang up, after which I immediately use my phone to order that cup of soba noodles.

Apparently, the delivery guy reaches the building at the same time as Dylan and Charles, because it's, in fact, Charles who delivers the food to me.

I briefly consider tipping him, but there's no option on Grubhub for tipping the belligerent man whose house you're crashing at. Besides, like any true New Yorker, I don't have cash on me.

CHAPTER 6

To: Da playa-hatas
From: Clifford Jenkins
Re: International Rolllllll-out

It's time! For those of you who've been following along with our press releases (and if
you're not, you should check 'em out), it will
come as no surprise that our global initiative is about to launch. Soon, the lovelorn
in EVERY TIME ZONE (shout out to Russia!)
will no longer be denied our services.

That said, if you receive messages from a
.ru address, send it to Crystal for vetting.
No Svetlanas or Ivans without making sure
they're too legit to quit, awright?

In the meantime, here's your Call to Action:
Download WhatsApp because that's what people
in other countries use to make their love
connections. FaceTime and Skype are circa
2016.

Also: I'm looking for cover models for the
international portal. Just average folk with
international appeal. Brown skin? Black hair?
Beautiful almond eyes? All of the above? Yes,
please! If not, I'll have to use old vacation
photos of She Who Must Not Be Named, ha ha.

But seriously, if you have international flavor about you, do consider it. You'll have
the opportunity to be the face of the company! Stock options and other perks for the
lucky chosen.

Clifford
CEO, Sweet Nothings Worldwide, LLC

ZOEY

I sleep late on Saturday and ration myself to one cup of coffee
while getting ready for my lunch appointment with Bree. At ten
forty-five, Clifford lights up my phone with a video call request
on WhatsApp. I could pretend it's cutting it too close to my
meeting at eleven, but the location's one minute away. With a
sense of impending doom, I answer the video chat.

"Hey champ! I'm calling all the rock stars this morning to
make sure they installed WhatsApp."

Clearly I did, or he couldn't have called me on it. "Ay, ay,
Captain." I salute him, hoping that'll be the end of it.

"Did you, ah, see the memo I sent around earlier?"

"I did, yes. Very cool about the . . ." I quickly scan the memo,
surprised. "Oh wow, global initiative. I didn't realize there was
a demand for it."

"Totes, totes. But, we really are in need of some visuals. Specifically, of people."

"Oh, right. With an 'international flavor.' Like lamb-and-mint chips."

"Good one! You have a mildly exotic face and I was wondering if you're fully American, half, or just mostly. I can ask that because my ex-wife is Chinese."

"Uh . . . I'm pretty sure no employer can ask that."

(Me, two months in, working for Mary, after I messed up some basic accounting: "I hope you didn't hire me because you thought I'd be good at math."

Mary: "No, no, I hired you because I thought you'd be good at meth. Boy do I have egg on my face!")

"Let's backtrack," Clifford says quickly. "Let's approach it from a new angle."

"When you say 'mildly exotic,' are you talking about these 'almond beauties'?" I ask dryly, pointing to my eyes. "They are one-half Filipino, from my dad's side of the family." My father's mom, Nana Dalisay, is the one who raised me in a tidy bungalow by Santa Monica Beach starting when I was ten.

Speaking of the ocean, the more Clifford talks, the more I'd like to walk into one and just keep going. Wave good-bye to Nana and Mary along the shore and slowly submerge myself. My final act on earth will be giving the finger to Clifford as the water rises above my head.

Fat chance of that happening. Now I live in a city truncated by walls, even outside. Is the sky still there? Who can say? It's buildings and windows all the way up for me now; claustrophobia by way of the outdoors.

Clifford proceeds to dig himself deeper. "Could you *pretend* to be fully or three-quarters Asian? Just for the photo's sake? Not like as a representation of your true self or whatever. We are, after all, in the business of pretending, right? It's all part of the same op?"

"Nope. Sorry." I refuse to be the poster child for his cluelessness.

Clifford looks deflated, but his finger guns fly out of their holsters nonetheless. "Gotcha. Okay. All good."

"Gotta run. I'm about to meet a new client."

"Oooh, is she international? Could you snap some shots on the sly and send 'em to Aisha for—"

I'm always happy to refer clients to Aisha, our freelance photo expert, but not without a client's permission, and not so they can secretly be part of an international ad.

I click off, ending the call. If he asks later, I'll say the Wi-Fi in my apartment is spotty. Of course, he has about a million other ways of communicating with me, and right on cue, a new message materializes on-screen.

CliffBar: We got cut off somehow. Good luck with Bree! Go get 'em, Tiger.

I wait, wondering if that'll be the worst of it or if there's more to come. Sure enough . . .

CliffBar: Not like a Tiger Mom, though! LOL. Any kind of tiger. Rawr. See you at the meeting next week.

It's only eleven a.m. but I'm in desperate need of alcohol.

At Cheese, Bree sits at a booth in the back—plenty of space for our laptops—and pours herself a healthy slug of pinot noir. The way the liquid sloshes against the side of the glass makes me nervous. What if she spills some on her special shirt? The shirt is a print of the movie poster for *Undersea*. It's faded, and the material looks whisper-soft. I can see why she likes it. As she mentioned on the phone yesterday, she's got blond hair, which she's pulled into a side braid. That hair combined with her light blue eyes and pale pink lips would normally give off a Barbie vibe, but the fact that she's a bookkeeper at a doctor's office cuts into the stereotype. Still, from the shallow end of the pool, she'll have NO trouble attracting "suitors." I make a private challenge to myself: Secure her a first date within the week.

She stands upon seeing me, and when she moves in for a hug I'm surprised at how emotional the gesture makes me. It's been a month since I've been hugged or touched in any way that didn't feel like the prelude to a knife fight. *My poor vestigial broken pinkie toe.* It doesn't hurt anymore—I don't think it *can*—but if it turned blue and fell off while I slept, I wouldn't exactly be surprised.

Bree's taller than me by a few inches, so my head tucks against her collarbone briefly before she releases me. Her hair smells like coconuts.

"How are you?" I ask. "Does the menu look okay?"

"It looks awesome! But . . ." She lowers her voice as we face each other across the table. "They're not a BYOB. She charged me a fifty-seven-dollar corkage fee. I'm so sorry."

What is *with* New York? At Bottega Louie in LA you can bring as many bottles as you want for free.

Then I remember who's footing the bill and grin. "No worries, really. It's a business expense." Smell you later, Clifford.

Bree smiles back, relieved. "Also, could we, like, pretend I'm not paying you? I liked what you said about 'peer-to-peer' or whatever. I think this'll work better for me if we hang like we're friends and you just happen to be good at online dating, and you're helping me out for fun."

"Sure, no problem. Thanks for meeting me near my place, I really appreciate it." Please don't ask about my cat. I haven't invented his backstory yet.

"Are you farther over in Alphabet City or . . . ?"

"I'm actually right across the street."

"Oh my God! You live there? Those apartments are huge! And they allow pets? Do you mind if I ask what you're paying?"

I'm so gobsmacked by her belief that my apartment is spacious that I'm rendered mute. Besides my broken toe, my shins are littered with bruises from knocking into things because there is nowhere to stand. Also, I can't exactly tell her my old boss owns the building and has knocked 50 percent off my monthly rent, because that might lead to telling her who my old boss IS by pointing to the woman on her T-shirt. Her level of *Undersea* fandom would not recover from that information, and we have tasks to complete today. As much as I love the idea of pretending we're friends on a lunch date, the truth is we're on a mission.

Luckily, the waitress appears and introduces herself before my silence becomes prolonged. Each person on the waitstaff, she explains, goes not by name but by favorite menu item. "I'm Cheesy Nuggets, and I'll be taking care of you today." (And indeed, her name tag reads "Cheesy Nuggets.")

Cheesy Nuggets explains that Cheese is an experimental pop-up specializing in grilled cheese sandwiches and fondue. Since it's on my "company card," I tell Bree to order anything that catches her eye. We both want the extra sharp cheddar toasties with jalapeños, and cheesy tater tots on the side, and she also asks for goat cheese with raspberries and syrup on top.

When Cheesy Nuggets leaves, Bree pours wine in my glass and we clink together.

"I need to stop hitting the sauce," she says, while hitting the sauce. "I think it's the cause of all my problems, honestly." She frowns. "Not *all*-all my problems, just my relationship problems. It's fine if I drink with you, or my girlfriends after work or whatever. But with dudes? Uggggh. Because if I'm feeling relaxed and giddy and uninhibited, it's over way too soon, you know what I mean?

"I don't have regrets, don't get me wrong," she continues. "I partied a lot after college, and it was fun, but I think I'm done with that phase of my life. I'm at the quarter-centch mark, you know? Everyone knows if you don't lock down a husband by the time you're twenty-nine in New York it's, like, *not* happening. Because why would they date an almost-thirty-year-old when there are a kajillion twenty-two-year-olds running around the place who are like, fertile? I really need to find a quality guy. Because my dick picker's—"

"Broken. Right." I'm not likely to forget that phrase anytime soon.

"There's nothing wrong with the dicks *themselves*, just what they're attached to. Here, let me show you—"

Before I can demur, her phone's out and floating about two inches from my face. She scrolls rapidly with her forefinger: dick pic, after dick pic, after dick pic.

"It's okay," I squeak. "I don't need to—"

She scrolls faster. I've never seen such a variety of man parts fly by. "Wow," I say. "That's quite a collection. How long did it take you to amass such a—"

"I didn't take these! I haven't seen even half of them in person. These were just what dudes *sent* me on Flirtville, with no messages or notes attached. I don't get it."

Ahh. Her comment yesterday about STDs reminds me she's had a rough go of it recently. I want to turn the ship around for her.

"Hmm. Let's pull up your Flirtville profile and see if we can figure it out," I suggest.

She sits next to me, making our laptops neighbors. She logs in and tilts her screen so I can see her profile. In response to the question "Something my parents don't know about me" she's written, simply, "DTF."

I think we've cracked the mystery.

"Oh God. I don't even remember typing that," she moans. "I must have been wasted. Anyway, that's another reason I should cool it with the beverages."

We both drink to that.

Bree deletes a letter and types a new one. "There. DTM. Down to marry. That should fix everything."

"That . . . might work," I say. Minimal bluff! "Or, we could cut our losses at Flirtville and start fresh at a different site. What do you think?"

She pushes her hair behind her ears, looking earnest and determined. "Start fresh."

Twenty minutes later, we've synced our laptops to her Game, Set, Match account, and we've filled out her questionnaire with pithy remarks and a humorous but firm declaration that her account is a "dick-pic-free zone."

With her input, I've presented Bree as an outgoing, free-spirited denizen of Hell's Kitchen who enjoyed being single and playing the field but has realized she's looking for something more significant now. She's someone who loves classic action-adventure fantasy films, and walking tours of historical neighborhoods, especially haunted ones. (I love this because it presents a perfect opportunity for snuggling with her dates.) She works as a bookkeeper at a pediatrician's office, where she's also in charge of curating the kids' waiting area with games, toys, DVDs, and a colorful fish tank.

We decide to leave out her affinity for fart jokes. I make note of it and categorize it as a Future Honesty.

Freelancer's Handbook: A Future Honesty is not something to be ashamed of. Instead, think of it as a reward, a prize, even, bestowed upon a match after multiple successful dates. If deployed too early, it risks sabotaging the burgeoning relationship. Protect Future Honesties and save them only for those who prove worthy.

Having devoured our grilled cheese sandwiches and doused the jalapeño flames with more wine, we feast on goat cheese drizzled with maple syrup.

And we're off, filters set for men aged twenty-four to thirty living in Brooklyn or Manhattan who exercise, like animals, and can see themselves settling down within the next few years. Five is our magic number, meaning the number of people whom we plan to "serve" (Game, Set, Match's version of a "poke"). If someone "lobs back," a private chat is activated. If the target of the serve doesn't respond within a predetermined period of time, they land in your "Ace" folder (an Ace being a tennis serve that hasn't been touched by the receiver) and won't appear in your searches any longer. It's a brisk way of dispensing with people who don't respond.

"How long should we give them before we Ace them?" I ask. Bree's halfway through her second glass of wine.

"A week?" she suggests.

"I was thinking forty-eight hours, but let's compromise and say ninety-six."

"Okay, sounds good. Who should we serve first?" Bree asks, looking eager.

"I think we need to narrow it down more. There are thousands of people here."

"Should we tighten up the age range?"

"I was thinking we could tighten up one of the lifestyle categories. You've mentioned drinking gets you into trouble sometimes. What if we filter for nondrinkers, see what comes up?"

"You mean complete teetotal-tarians?"

". . . Yes."

I don't know if "teetotal-tarians" is a malapropism or a new term used by the twenty-five-and-under crowd. The four-year age difference between Bree and me may as well be a generation. I've spent the last two decades hanging out with women in their fifties and sixties, and honestly I think I relate to them more at this point. Although despite what Rude Miles from the café believes, I'm VERY computer savvy.

"Okay," she agrees.

I like that she doesn't fight me on it. It proves she's serious about curbing her drinking for the chance at a longer-term commitment.

I click the appropriate buttons and refresh the page.

The first profile is a rail-thin guy with a wispy mustache and a dreamy look in his eyes. I fear I've led Bree astray. "Nondrinker" might be code for "shoots heroin."

"Sorry, let me adjust this again . . ."

I filter for "straight-edge" instead.

"Ooh, how about this guy?" she says immediately.

MustLoveDogs's profile picture includes (who else?) his dog, whom he's hugging from behind and gazing at with fierce adoration. His description reads, `Seeking someone as wonderful and loyal as my black lab, Henrietta. I don't think I'll ever find anyone as perfect as her, though. LOL.`

"Awww," says Bree. "That's so sweet!"

Before I can stop her, she's reached for her screen and clicked on "Serve."

"Whoops! Okay, um, if that's what you want to do, but I'm not so sure. You know how some people call their pets 'fur babies'?"

"Yeah?"

"I think this is his 'fur wifey.'"

"But he wrote 'LOL.' He's just kidding."

"Yeah . . . I think he's serious. You don't want to enter this fight."

"But I already served him. Can I take it back?"

"No, but that's all right. And who knows, maybe I'm wrong. It's just that Henrietta takes up more of the picture than he does. We can't really see what he looks like, and his only interests have to do with her."

She groans. "See? I told you my dick picker's broken."

"Healing," I correct her. I *need* to get her to stop saying "dick picker." My right eye twitches every time she does.

MustLoveDogs lobs back instantly, which, frankly, is a bad sign.

Bree squints at his message:

MustLoveDogs: Henrietta's birthday is tomorrow! No need to spend a lot—under $100 is great—but if you'd like to come, we'd love to meet you. Woof-woof! (That was Henrietta! :))

"Under a hundred?" Bree sputters.

"Let's reply and move on."

"Don't even! That was gross."

I resist the urge to point out that Bree was the one who contacted *him*. The right thing to do is close it out properly. "He doesn't count," I assure her. "We'll find five more."

Under Bree's account I write:

TheDuchessB: Happy Birthday to a special dog! I'm afraid I'm not available. Hope it's a terrific day. Then I "Ace" him so he won't come up in any more searches. I don't trust "after-hours" Bree not to serve him again by mistake.

We scroll through more profiles.

"This guy might be cool," she remarks. "He's a lawyer."

"He's also into Ren Faire. That's up your alley, right?"

Her face contorts. "Ew! No."

Who knew cosplayers could be so snobby? "But only once a year, upstate. And he's got a nice smile," I point out.

Ignoring me, she points at a muscular dude with a buzz cut. His username is RedPill. "What do you think about him?"

I read his About Me section aloud: "To find out if we're compatible, please complete this sentence. Sully was a hoax—Yes/No."

Bree gasps. "Was it?"

"No!" I shout, before reining myself in. "No, Sully was not a hoax." The Miracle on the Hudson is the one thing I know to be good and pure and true about New York. I refuse to entertain any notion that suggests otherwise.

"I think he wants us to say 'yes.'"

"Probably, but—"

She clicks "serve" and types, "Yes."

I grit my teeth. We need to work on her impulse control.

Two seconds later, a response:

RedPill: You've been auto-subscribed to my newsletter.

"Nondrinkers suck," Bree declares.

I can't disagree.

"How about 'occasional' drinkers, then? 'Everything in moderation' types?"

"Hallelujah. Yes, please."

We order fondue because why not? We've been here two hours already and have barely made any progress. I'm sleepy and headachy, and I'm pretty sure Cheesy Nuggets wants us to tip her out so she can go home. In fact, a different waitress brings us our fondue. Her nametag reads, "Golden Moldies."

"What does *that* mean?" Bree asks, pointing to her tag.

"Your Gorgonzolas, your Camemberts, your Stiltons and Roqueforts. All cheese is basically mold, right? My favorite deliberate moldy cheeses are available on a platter," she replies, somewhat robotically.

"Should we get some?" Bree asks.

"I think we'd better save those for next time," I answer gently. "And I want to apologize, because I think I've been putting you on the spot too much. How about I go through some profiles on my own, play around with the other filters, and I'll send you a list of five later tonight for you to check out. Would that be cool? I won't contact any of them without your approval."

"Do it. Yes. This is exhausting."

We ask for the check and while we're waiting, Bree leans in. "Can I ask about your background?" she asks.

Seriously? What is this obsession with my race today?

"Where do I come from, you mean?" I ask guardedly.

"No, I was wondering if you're married, what your parents are like, anything you want to share. We've talked so much about me—I want to hear your story."

"Oh, okay." My shoulders ease back down. "I've never been married, and my parents are a couple of save-the-world types who met in the Philippines, where my dad grew up. My mom was there with the Peace Corps, volunteering to rebuild houses after Typhoon Herming, and they fell in love. Nine months later, ta-da," I say, pointing to myself.

"Aww, you got to be their new project."

"More like I got folded into the old one. They dragged me from one natural disaster to another until I was ten and my nana put a stop to it."

Her exact words were: *This is no way for a child to live.*

"She got them to settle down?"

I swallow a mouthful of my wine. "Oh, no. They wanted to keep traveling." I shrug. "Which I get. It's part of their DNA. I mean, they coined the term 'voluntourists' for what they do. So Nana and I rented a little one-bedroom place in Santa Monica by the beach."

If I close my eyes and hold my hands over my ears, I swear I can hear the ocean calling me back.

"That must've been an adjustment," Bree remarks. "To go from being free and, like, traveling the world, to being stuck in one place with Grandma?"

"No, oh no, it was a dream come true. No disruptions, no surprises, getting to unpack a suitcase and *mean* it . . . I loved it. Waking up and going to sleep in the same place every night was all I ever wanted."

Nana felt the same way; once we arrived, we never left. We never even took vacations. (Why would we need to? We already lived in paradise.) It was a huge relief. And for college I didn't even have to leave town because Santa Monica City College was right there. My first ten years were spent like a vagabond, and my next twenty were spent with my feet on solid ground, surrounded by comfort and routine, and I know which I prefer.

"What brought you to New York, then?" Bree wonders.

It wasn't by choice, I'll tell you that. . . .

I force a smile. It makes my teeth ache. "I'm supposed to be writing a screenplay. Anyway, I'm boring myself so I can't imagine how it feels for you."

"I'm not bored, I'm fascinated! Where are your parents now?"

I signal for the check.

"That is an excellent question."

Once Bree and I part ways, her *Undersea* DVD safely tucked into my laptop bag, I wonder if I should head to Café Crudité and scour more profiles. That would be the smart, productive thing to do.

But it's Saturday, a small voice inside my head protests, *and you go to the café every day. What if you broke the mold, just once? What if you pretended you were going to the café but instead of going inside, you put one foot past the door, just one extra step, and then another, and kept on walking?*

I adjust my various bags and look inside Crudité as I glide past, trying not to make it obvious I'm scanning for someone in particular, the only person I've said more than two words to outside of work since I arrived.

Why is it I never saw him until the Biscotti Incident, and now I see him there all the time? Is he there right now, clicking away at whatever it is he's trying to clack?

Gazing beyond my own reflection, I see the big table is empty. I could go in and grab it right now, but a victory without an audience is hardly a victory. If he's not there to see me enjoying it at his expense, what's the point? *And by the way, of course he's not there*, I reprimand myself. It's the *weekend*. He has a life.

No reason I can't have one, too.

My bravado lasts precisely five blocks. The entrance to the subway beckons, like a gateway to hell.

I could go down those stairs, but what if I never come back out?

I halt abruptly. My feet refuse to take another step. People knock into me on both sides as they pass, clipping my elbows, giving me dirty looks, but I'm rooted to the spot like a fork in a river. Unless someone steers me to the side or shoves me out of the way, they'll have to go around me. I picture a ladder leading to a pit, and I'm in the middle of it, unmoving. I can't get down the ladder, and I can't go back up, either. I'm paralyzed.

Below me, below ground in the dark, a train arrives, bringing with it a whoosh of sound and a gush of hot, disgusting air that's been living below the city streets for a hundred stagnant years. What madness makes people ride this thing, squashed together with strangers, shaking through the city, jolted every five feet, as though humankind was ever meant to travel that way, underground like rats? Because make no mistake, I'm in rat territory now. Or I would be if I descended. Why can't I stop feeling so scared, so stupid and helpless?

A trickle of sweat drips down the back of my neck. I feel like a lost child. But no one's going to find me because no one's looking for me. They haven't even noticed I'm gone.

I take a deep breath, duck my head, and turn around to go home. My breath comes out in panicked gasps, making me dizzy.

I can't go on like this, I tell myself. And I wish, more than anything, it were true.

Because what if the real problem is that *I can?*

In a city of nine million people who pass me by without a single thought, who would care if I did?

CHAPTER 7

To: All Tell It to My Heart Employees
From: Leanne Tseng
Re: Hypothetically

Team,

I've been speaking to Giles, and we want to offer a bit of general advice. Hypothetically speaking, if you're ever asked to be "the face" of a company you're not actually running—don't. What if the company crashes and burns in a fiery wreck of its own doing and now your image goes along with it? As in your actual image? No so-called bonus is worth that . . . hypothetically speaking, of course.

Now, if said theoretical company uses your likeness without permission, thereby finally giving you legal recourse to light the spark that just happens to culminate in that five-

alarm blaze? I would call that the circle of
life, moving us all, and so on and so forth.
Giles is standing by—just in case this lion-
ess gets her Simba in the form of a sweet,
sweet lawsuit.

Yours,
Leanne

MILES

Charles is a great breakover motivator. If this whole law pro-
fessor at Columbia thing doesn't work out for him, he should
consider a career change. Maybe Leanne could even hire him
as one of her consultants.

I leave the house at around six a.m. now, before he's woken
up, and hit the seven-mile run at Riverside Park. I grab a bagel
and coffee from the cart around the corner, and I'm back at the
apartment by eight a.m., at which point Charles is gone for his
first class of the day, and I get a good twenty minutes of chatting with solo Dylan—my favorite Dylan.

I shower and get dressed—I even bother to put in my
contacts—and am out the door again by nine forty-five, so as
to miss Charles coming home in between his two classes of the
day. This is when I grab the subway and am down to Café Crudité by ten thirty, a perfect lull of time between the morning
rush and the lunch crowd, which lets me stake out the good
table.

I've started looking into the big picture window before I
even enter to see if I can catch the telltale two-toned hair and
wide-eyed stare of Mary Tampa Moore. She's not here today. I
wonder why. Did someone raise an eyebrow at her and send her
scurrying for cover? Moreover, the table appears to be empty

and, when I walk in, there's a *handful* of free biscotti left at the counter. Look at that: Everything's coming up Miles. Who cares why she's a no-show?

I've just grabbed my coffee and biscotti and gone over to the sugar and cream station when I sense something wheeling by in my peripheral vision. I glance over.

It is . . . a stroller. Inside of which is a child of maybe two or three. Is that too old for a stroller? Jordan and I used to joke that children always seem to leap from tiny, burrito-sized wraps to enormous slabs of chunky thighs and grubby hands who some-how look too big to be engaging in whatever activity they're engaged in: drinking a bottle, sucking on a pacifier, whining. "Have you ever seen a kid who's in the in-between phase?" I asked her one day, not long after we'd gotten engaged. "Do you, one night, put down a tiny blob of indeterminate features and then return the next day to hear Seth MacFarlane's voice coming out of someone who looks like a Halloween costume of a gigantic baby?" She laughed, as expected. Less expected was when she said to me, "I don't know. But let's find out soon." I don't think I ever loved her more than at that moment, when I looked at her and knew we were both envisioning the same future.

Anyway. *This* stroller is being pushed by a different mom, a woman in her mid-thirties who is very, very pregnant (definitely plus six weeks). She looks like she might have been awake for about as long as I have, minus the benefit of a long run or a cup of coffee. Her child is screaming, and I can hear her hissing under her breath, over and over again, "Nathan. *Please.*"

This causes no change in Nathan's behavior. But now they are settling down at the large table while she takes out an as-sortment of jangling, screeching, singing, and flashing toys from underneath the stroller and places them on the table in front of the red-faced Nathan, who merely screams louder with every object that emerges. The last thing she takes out is an iPad, which is the sole thing he finally lunges for—immediately quieting down mid-sob.

I look away as I scan the café for another table. There's one in a corner farthest away from the large one, which will make it harder to swoop in and grab the table once Nathan and his mom leave. Oh, well. How long can a two, three-year-old last in a café anyway? I'll just be on high alert for the next half hour.

I squeeze my laptop onto the tiny table, where it takes up the entire surface area, and I log on. There's an e-mail from Leanne asking to check in on me remotely this morning, and one from Jude saying he found someone in the Match pool he thinks he's interested in.

I ping Leanne that I'm ready for her, and she sends me the remote access request, which I accept. I ran this morning; I'm on my second cup of coffee—thanks to Charles, I'm feeling pretty confident that Leanne isn't going to see something she shouldn't.

Then I click through to the profile Jude linked to.

Twenty-five-year-old Bree, aka TheDuchessB. The first thing I notice is the first thing everyone notices on an online dating profile (and the reason Aisha's never going to be out of a job): She's attractive. Blond, tan, and fit, she's definitely playing in the same gene pool as Jude, unless it just so happens that she has a photography consultant too. (Right. What would be the odds?)

Then I start to read. She's looking for something a little more serious. Good listening, Jude. She enjoys ghost tours: nice, quirky little detail. And—what's this—she likes classic, action-adventure fantasy films . . . I put two and two together with the screenname and bingo! Someone I can chat about *Undersea* with? This morning is shaping up to be better than expected.

I start to type a brief but pithy message. In his e-mail, Jude wrote that he has back-to-back clients today and probably won't be able to hop online but has given me his log-in and blessing to send whatever I think is best. He'll get a full report of all messages at the end of the day.

Greetings from the 'Neath, my liege. The Sea Lord sends

his regards, I start out. Then I delete it. Better to include it at the end, a little wink instead of a full-blown geek-out.

From: GreatSc0t
To: TheDuchessB

Hi Bree, [always include their first name. It's the simplest thing in the world, and yet, more than 65 percent of messages are cut-and-paste jobs—and they sound like it too.]

Haunted tours, eh? I ain't afraid of no ghost. But seriously, what a cool idea. I've been in New York for two years now and I haven't even thought to do one of those yet. (Do you think there's one that includes that guy from Twitter whose apartment is haunted? I mean, honestly, some guys have all the luck. Why couldn't a terrifying poltergeist choose my building to plague for all eternity so that someone could snatch the rights to *my* life story. As always, I blame the co-op board . . .)

The café door jangles and I inadvertently look up. It's Miss Flo Rida herself. I see her eye the large table first, her face falling as she registers the full-blown toy shop that seems to live there now. Then she scans the café and stops when she sees me.

I give her a sort of half smile and a shrug. *Guess it's a stalemate today.* But I can't really read her expression back. Within moments, she's looking away, eyeing the only other empty table in the place. She looks at her bag, clearly wondering whether it's worth putting it down and risk getting it stolen or better to possibly lose the table.

Don't do it, I immediately think. Sure, this is expensive AF, $7.99 latte, *Million Dollar Listing* New York . . . but it's still New York. I keep looking at her, sort of trying to will her not to part with her belongings. She walks over to the table anyway though, hesitates, and then takes off one of the arm warmers she's always wearing and places it over the chair.

She doesn't look at me as she walks back to the counter, but I almost smile at her again. That was pretty clever.

With impeccable timing, I hear a *whoosh* informing me of a

new company-wide memo from Leanne, and I'm transported back to the whole reason I'm in this café to begin with: to work, save my career, and prove to everyone—most importantly myself—that I am not just a shell of a man.

I reread what I've written so far to Bree. It's a little out there. It could possibly turn someone off.

The Sea Lord sends his regards, I type in the next paragraph. **And he'd absolutely love to conspire further with you.**

~ Jude

I stare at it for a moment and then, before I can second-guess myself, I hit send. It *is* out there but the truth is . . . my instincts for this stuff are pretty good. At least, when it comes to other people's love lives.

I've just copied the message into an e-mail that I'm about to send Jude, along with a brief intro telling him I think Bree is a good choice, when I get a little ping.

Bree has just jumped online and lobbed back.

TheDuchessB: It's not a poltergeist. It's a phantasm disguised as a child demon. Honestly. Don't you know anything about the Internet famous?

I type back immediately:

GreatSc0t: Must have misplaced my Hashtag Handbook for the Recently Deceased.

A little bit of a shot in the dark. But maybe if she likes classic eighties action/adventure fantasy films, she might also know . . .

TheDuchessB: #Dayo . . .

Bingo.

TheDuchessB: You know, when I was a kid, I always wanted ghosts to move in so that I could dance by the ceiling.

GreatSc0t: Is that why you like haunted tours? You're hoping to become the living embodiment of a Lionel Richie song?

TheDuchessB: Maybe. Wow, my therapist never

cracked that one. And here we are two minutes into a chat . . . excuse me, a "lob."

GreatSc0t: You're welcome. I charge $125 an hour. But I give special discounts to duchesses, especially those of planet Undersea.

There's a slight pause, the first of our conversation.

TheDuchessB: Rule number one of Fight Club: never talk Undersea on a first chat.

GreatSc0t: Oh really?

TheDuchessB: I've been burned. This is strictly an in-person subject. I need to see the whites of your eyes before I can discuss Her Highness with you.

GreatSc0t: Like . . . in the Battle of Bunker Hill?

TheDuchessB: Dating is war, my good man.

GreatSc0t: Touché. I respect that. Soldier to soldier.

I hesitate.

GreatSc0t: Is it too forward of me to say I'd like that conversation to happen soon?

A pause. Damn, did I jump that gun too early?

TheDuchessB: The Duchess acquiesces . . .

Her most famous line, of course, although . . .

GreatSc0t: Uh-oh. Is this a trap?!

She sends through a skull emoji.

TheDuchessB: Whites of your eyes, remember? Don't make me break my own rule on a first chat.

GreatSc0t: Yes, soldier.

TheDuchessB: Captain.

GreatSc0t: Oh, I'm sorry. I thought this was an even playing field.

TheDuchessB: Is it ever?

There's a pause, allowing me to take another glance at Bree's picture. Beautiful and smart. Nice work, Jude.

TheDuchessB: So is it true you're fresh off the boat? Would you happen to have what they call a brogue?

GreatSc0t: Aye. 'Tis true . . . and you should hear how I sound when I say brogue.

TheDuchessB: Woo. Is it hot in here? But, seriously. Keep talking Scot to me.

GreatSc0t: Whiskey. Heather. Kilt.

TheDuchessB: Hmmmm . . . maybe something else we need to save for our in-person meeting.

GreatSc0t: This isn't translating?

Mentioning meeting up in person twice is a good sign.

TheDuchessB: I actually have to run. But this was fun.

Uh-oh. Hope I haven't been reading this wrong. "This was fun" might be the first generic thing Bree has said and it's only a positive about 60 percent of the time. I hope I didn't blow this for Jude. Or myself, as I remember the little remote access icon that's been quietly flashing at the bottom of my screen this whole time.

TheDuchessB: Can we pencil in another one of these? Maybe tomorrow.

Whew.

GreatSc0t: Name the time.

TheDuchessB: Is 9 AM too early?

GreatSc0t: It's perfect. I don't have any personal training sessions until the afternoon.

What Jude does is already in his profile, but might as well work in a nice, organic reminder.

TheDuchessB: Is this your subtle way of reminding me you have muscles?

Oops. Maybe that wasn't as organic as I thought. I should be more careful, especially since this girl seems extra sharp.

GreatSc0t: Yes. It obviously worked, right? You feel very subconsciously attracted to me?

TheDuchessB: Of course. Freud would be having a field day with my id right now.

I grin at my screen.

GreatSc0t: So . . . until the morning sky kisses the stars away, my Liege.

Another pause.

TheDuchessB: You're a little bit of a rule-breaker, aren't you?

GreatSc0t: Only in the best way.

I send through a winking emoji.

She sends one back.

TheDuchessB: I guess we'll see about that. Talk later.

GreatSc0t: Later.

Bree logs off. I copy and paste the conversation to tack onto my unsent e-mail to Jude, feeling pretty pleased about the turn of events. Apparently, I'm not the only one.

Leanne T: Nice work.

Miles I: Thanks!

Leanne T: So . . . can I be relieved of babysitting duties now? Regular Miles is back up and running?

Miles I: Consider yourself relieved.

Leanne T: Thank God.

And then, right before she logs off my computer, one more message:

Leanne T: P.S. I missed you.

I appreciate the sentiment but *is* Regular Miles back? Not really. It's going to take more than eight weeks to accept that the woman I thought I was going to marry has now wholly disappeared from any future scenarios I can imagine for myself. Jordan won't be chatting with me while I cook, she won't be snuggled next to me on the couch while we're watching some Netflix documentary, and she'll never walk toward me down an aisle in a white dress. I inadvertently look toward Nathan and realize that we are never going to stare down at a human we made together, feeling both exhausted and content.

But for Leanne's purposes, sure, I can be back. I can orchestrate other people's romances. I'm good at it. And, luckily, I think Bree and Jude just might make this easy for me.

A projectile something catches the corner of my eye, and I see that Nathan has just lobbed his sock out of his stroller in a fit. I also notice that his mom is stuffing all her items back into a myriad of bags, and stroller hooks, and a large underseat compartment that is stretched below Nathan's purple, contorting body.

I start to gather up my belongings when . . .

What's this?

No. It can't be.

But it is. It's I Am Legend, who has picked up a snack cup that has rolled underneath the large table and is now chatting with Nathan's mom.

"Need any help?" she asks. She then looks at Nathan, opens her mouth wide, crosses her eyes, and makes a bizarre gargling sound.

Immediately, Nathan breaks out into a fit of giggles.

"Oh, God, please," Nathan's mom says. "If you could just keep doing that, I would be forever grateful."

"No problem," Legend responds before kneeling down to Nathan's level. "Did you know I once won a face-making contest? It's because my tongue can touch my nose. See?" She demonstrates.

"Wow," Nathan responds, eyes wide. He sticks out his own short tongue which, of course, just goes straight out.

"The key is to practice," Legend says. "Every day, for at least twenty minutes. And, I'll tell you a secret . . ." She looks around, and whispers, "Cafés are the best place to practice. I learned everything I know while my mom was drinking her coffee."

Nathan nods studiously, while his mom looks at Legend like the Sunshine State is, in fact, beaming out of her ass.

"Thank you," she mouths, tears practically in her eyes, as she strolls a face-making—and therefore silent—Nathan, and his rack of luggage, out of the café.

Legend smiles after them and I can't help noticing what a bright smile she has. It's all dimples. I've never seen her smile before, and the distraction costs me; sometime during that exchange, she has managed to place her bag right on the seat

Nathan's mom just vacated. She glances over at me. Her smile disappears and it's like the sun has gone behind a cloud.

Let it not be said I'm a poor sport, however. I give her a slow clap, and she takes a little bow before sitting down with a flourish. I roll my eyes, but, privately, I have to admit I'm pretty impressed. Maybe MTM is going to make it after all.

Nathan's sock, on the other hand, is doomed to haunt the café floor for the rest of eternity—or at least until the barista sweeps up—reminding us all of his lengthy and memorable residency at Café Crudité. And also reminding me that I should call my mom.

I've been putting it off, listening to a lot of concerned voice mails that have been responded to with brief texts just so she knows I'm alive. But this seems like as good a time as any, if for no other reason than when she scans the screen for clues to my mental well-being, she'll notice that I've showered and am out of the house.

I put on my headphones and start up FaceTime. She answers on the second ring. I see her face for a second before my screen is filled up with the white and purple flowers on her shirt as she hugs the iPad to her.

"Oh, thank God. Ahmad, come here. It's Miles."

She sets up the iPad on the table in front of her and brings her face closer to it, as if that'll help her peer at me better.

"At least you're out of the house. But you look skinny," she says, like all Jewish moms from time immemorial. "Have you been eating?"

My father comes strolling in then, wearing his standard out-fit of a neat, striped button-down with two pens—one red and one black— tucked in the pocket. He is the only person I know who uses an actual pocket protector and is not a stock nerd from an eighties comic book.

"Miles. How are you?" Baba asks. He's been in America for what will be fifty years next year, but he still has never lost his faint Egyptian accent. My mom looking at me with concern is one thing, but my dad doing the same means I should've called them ages ago.

"I'm fine," I say.

"Liar," my mom immediately responds, putting on her cat-eye reading glasses and staring me down.

"Okay," I respond. "Not exactly fine. But I'm doing better." Of course I had to tell them the wedding was off. And of course, this being my parents, I had to tell them why—the real reason. Though I'd let Aisha handle explaining most of the gory details.

"When are you going to come visit?" they say then, practically in unison.

See, everyone thinks that Jews and Muslims are mortal enemies, that my parentage shouldn't even be possible, let alone harmonious. But what they don't know is that there are so many similarities, it's practically laughable. Starting with the parental guilt skills. Separately, they are forces to be reckoned with, but together, they are unbeatable. Like when the Power Rangers all united to make the Megazord.

"Soon," I say.

My mom raises her eyebrows and I just know she's about to call me a liar again.

"I promise," I say. There are very few things that would drag me down to God's Waiting Room, aka Florida, but seeing my parents is one of them. Especially if I'm feeling extra mopey about love, fearing that it doesn't really exist. . . .

Well, they are living proof that it does, that it can be stronger than where you're from, or how you were raised. That it can even be stronger than what your own family is telling you. When my parents got married straight out of Penn State, I don't think anybody thought it would last, not even the one person who supported them the most: Uncle Hassan, my dad's brother and Aisha's father. They were both so young—twenty-one and twenty-two—and everyone thought it was puppy love spurred on by the fact that my dad's student visa was expiring.

But Ahmad and Louisa knew better, their ages and backgrounds be damned. It was very Romeo and Juliet, in that nobody's parents were happy, but with a meet-cute that took place at a frat party rather than a masquerade ball. Louisa's parents wanted grandkids who would be bar/bat mitzvahed (I was, in fact. Maybe the only kid who read a portion of the Quran along with my portion of the Torah, but still. Like the millennial multitasking Jewslim I am, I became a man in the eyes of God/Allah at the same time). Ahmad's parents wanted their son to come home and marry a nice Egyptian woman so that they could see their grandkids.

But there weren't kids, plural. Just me. And I came along fifteen years after their City Hall nuptials. My mom liked to joke that "it took them that long to figure out the schematics for the nursery." Which might be more believable if they hadn't settled for the uber-creative theme of . . . sailboats. In reality, I know they were too busy being in love to think about having children yet. They were young; they had time. As to why there weren't any more after me . . . well, I have heard rumors that I was somewhat of a terror. And by rumors, I mean my mother likes to remind me two to three times a month.

Anyway, back to the Capulet/Montague saga; by the time I was born, Grandpa Frank was gone and Grandma Naima wasn't too far behind. Grandma Ellen came around at the end. I have some memories of being with her, playing near her carpet shoes, drawing on one of her throw pillows, and hearing her cackle in glee and tell my mom not to yell at me—that she thought it was an improvement on the paisley.

But I don't think my dad spoke to his dad ever again. They'd ask after each other, via Hassan. But a hereditary stubborn streak remained in both of them that not even illness or death could tear asunder.

"Maybe for Memorial Day?" Mom asks, trying to pin down an actual date of visitation from me.

"That's a little too soon," I say. "I've got some work stuff going on. But . . . before the summer is over. I promise." I immediately regret this because there are few places on earth more miserable than Florida in the summer. But I see Mom is already jotting something down in the little planner she keeps on the coffee table, so I know I'm doomed to be bound to what I said.

I ask after some of their friends down there and they bring me up to date on who has gout, who has dropped out of the mah-jongg club, and whose kids are getting married/divorced/having babies.

"It's going to be a granddaughter for Julia," Mom says, maybe not even wistfully but in my current state of mind that's what it sounds like to me.

I glance over at the tiny sock on the floor and feel compelled to ask her, "Mom, how do children appear?"

Mom blinks. "Didn't we already have this talk?" She turns to Baba. "I mean, I mostly left it up to you but I thought it was taken care of."

"So did I," Baba responds. "Of course, I taught physics, not biology, so maybe something got a little lost in translation?"

"No," I say. "I don't mean *where do they come from* . . ."

"Thank heavens," Mom says. "I'm not sure I have enough blood pressure medication to explain this to you *now*. Plus my consolation that you were a boy instead of a girl was that I didn't *have* to." She playfully glares at Baba.

"Let me double-check my notes," he says. "I'm positive we had this talk."

"Yes, Baba. We did. I was just thinking how come they morph from tiny babies into overgrown ones so suddenly. Like there's no in-between . . . you know what? Never mind."

"I think this is a lack of food talking," Mom says. "Come here immediately and I'll make you my chili, okay? And mandel bread."

"Yes, Mom," I respond dutifully.

"You never make *me* mandel bread," Baba says.

"You can make it yourself," she responds.

"So can he! He's a thirty-one-year-old man."

"That's true," Mom responds. "But he'll also always be my baby. Aren't you, my little oogle-boogle."

I shake my head, grinning despite myself, as my mom makes kissy faces at me. They're punchy today.

But they've also made me feel better. Because at least there are some parts of my future that are crystal clear.

Like me, a month from now, sweating my balls off at their community pool as I swim laps, much to the delight of my mom's lounging, loungewear-clad girlfriends.

CHAPTER 8

To: You Know Who You Are
From: Clifford Jenkins
Re: A Spy in the House of Nothings

Look, I'm sorry, but this won't be an easy memo to read.

It's come to my attention through RUMINT (rumored intelligence) that we have reason to believe a traitor walks amongst us. An unwitting traitor, perhaps. A useful idiot, for those who know the term. He, she, or they have been doubling for another company that, on the *surface*, appears to serve a similar function to our own.

I get it. Times are tough. Everyone needs to take work where they can find it.

The part that concerns me, on a personal, human level, is that those who serve more than one master risk being taken advantage of (by them, obviously. Not by me). The good news is, there's an easy way out for the person or persons who is double-dipping.

Flip the script.

I'll throw in a title bump and 250 business cards.

You have 48 hours to accept my offer.

Clifford

P.S. See you all at Porchlight at 4 p.m. for the monthly meeting. I may or may not be there physically, but rest assured I'll make my presence known . . .

ZOEY

I thought *Undersea* would be a welcome escape. After my failure to ride the subway over the weekend, and a full evening of procrastination in which I Aced over thirty matches on Bree's behalf, I fired up the DVD and some microwave popcorn. Unfortunately, fully sober at the midnight hour was not a good time to be subjected to wooden dialogue and so-so special effects. I wanted to appreciate the historical significance of the first fantasy-action film directed by a woman, but the outdated, 1980s-style, battle-of-the-sexes banter made me cringe more than cheer, and I abandoned ship halfway through, right at the moment Mary's fins made their debut.

All it did was make me miss Mary, the real Mary.

I went online and Googled *Mary Clarkson Undersea* for the first time.

Playboy, 1996

Long Time No Sea: How Mary "Jane" Clarkson Went from Persona Non Grata to Hollywood's Best-Kept Secret

Ten years ago, at the age of twenty-two, Mary Clarkson landed the role of a lifetime as Duchess Quinnley in the *Undersea* films. Well, film. What was intended to be a trilogy famously went off the rails when the actress, a self-described former adrenaline junkie, insisted on performing her own stunts. She tripped (while in the tight-fitting mermaid costume that launched a thousand wet dreams), hitting her head on a camouflaged rock submerged a foot beneath the water. After a month at the hospital recovering from a broken vertebra in her neck, she punched her physical therapist out cold when he told her swim therapy was the only way to achieve full spinal mobility.

Now, "running at 87 percent capacity," as she puts it, "without ever stepping foot in a goddamn whirlpool, thank you," she lives in a secluded fortress in the Hollywood Hills, as far from the ocean as one can get in Los Angeles without leaving earth. Over several hours, our conversation touched on her short-lived acting career and her new, behind-the-scenes role as Hollywood's most sought-after script doctor whose dialogue and plot tweaks you've seen in two dozen movies without knowing it.

On the assault charge that landed her in prison for four days

"All I ever wanted my whole life was a captive audience, so it was a dream come true, really. The other women, all of whom I've kept in touch with, would say things like, 'I was at Bedford Hills maximum security before this' and I got to say, 'I was in *Undersea*.'"

On her Hollywood blacklisting

"Obviously, it's sexist as all f*ck-out. Male artists get into fights all the time and it just increases their mystique, their virility. It's the Hemingway effect. I give *one* asshole, who I think we can all agree *deserved* it, a concussion, and it's lights-out for *my* career? I'm 'uninsurable on set'? Come on."

On the PEZ dispensers that bear her/Duchess Quinnley's likeness

"I mean, it's cruel. The neck unhinges! How would you like it if your most terrifying moment was captured in candy form?"

On fans who wish she'd Mermaid Up and complete the trilogy

"While I value the opinion of strangers much, much more than my own health and sanity, my scarlet L for liability is not going away anytime soon, even if I wanted to perform again, which I don't. Life is much safer behind a typewriter."

If she could clear up one misconception about her assault charge, what would be it?

"Okay, first off, it was not a punch that knocked him out. No, I threw a copy of Dorothy Parker's collected works at his head. I mean, he should be so lucky. Probably increased his IQ points by double digits."

Is it true you sometimes put on a Duchess Quinnley mask and go to midnight screenings incognito?

"I'll never tell."

You've testified in front of Congress multiple

times advocating for medical marijuana on the federal level. What was that like?

"The C-Span footage is some of my best work. And I think we could've solved the Cold War faster if everyone on Capitol Hill had gotten stoned, I really do."

On becoming a so-called script fixer

"Now I punch up jokes instead of people, hyuk hyuk! Is that what you want me to say?"

I heard you used to rewrite headlines about yourself and mail them back to magazine editors—is that true?

"Jesus Christ, they weren't even trying. How many times did I see some variation of *Undersea* Actress *Under* Investigation. It's not difficult to make a punny headline."

Give me an example . . .

"I don't know, how about 'Mary Clarkson Fin-agles a Role in Jailhouse Rock'? Now *that's* funny. Feel free to use it."

I fell asleep and dreamt I was in the audience of *Cheese: The Musical*, starring young Mary as a golden moldy ("I am bleu / I'm filled with penicillin / Best leave me on the plate / Or you'll be illin' like a villain").

On Sunday, I invited myself to a pity party. According to *Sex and the City*, everyone but me spent sunup to sundown at brunch, guzzling mimosas and howling with laughter over their latest romantic escapades. I was lonely in a way I'd never been in LA, not with weekly visits to Nana, and not with Mary's round-the-clock inspirations.

On Monday, the gods sent me a gift of my own, in the form of GreatSc0t. With Bree's approval ("HELLZ TO THE YEH!"), I have free rein to contact him again.

It's Tuesday now, and I'm eager to instigate a follow-up, but before I do, I need to finish watching *Undersea*, which is why I'm still at home instead of at Café Crudité. (Don't get comfortable, Miles.)

I managed to sidestep a real discussion of the film during my first, admittedly promising, exchange with Jude, but if I'm going to be true to Bree's personality, I can't freeze up during topics that are key to her profile. She's told me more than once she wants to "own her fandom," and the sooner I get Bree situated, the sooner I can collect a paycheck and a new client.

If you get her situated, you'll never chat with GreatSc0t again, a little voice replies. It's the same voice that tried to trick me into taking the subway on Saturday.

Inappropriate, I chastise back. *He's not chatting with "you." He's chatting with Bree. And everything you say to him is on her behalf.* Still, I'm deluding myself if I pretend it wasn't fun flirting with a young, gorgeous Scotsman who's also charming and quick-witted. No one could fault me for that, right?

A spear of doubt lurches through me: What if he's already found someone else to chat up, and he prefers her? Hurry up and watch the movie, woman!

Still in my pajamas, lying on my couch-bed (freelancing has its perks), I click through the chapter menu on Bree's DVD, looking for the spot where sleep claimed me, and trying not to wonder if there's a way to watch the film without, you know, having to watch it. That's when it hits me: Somewhere, someone has already asked and answered that question. Of course they have! I settle in for a YouTube deep dive, hoping to locate a fan-made summary.

What I discover is quite entertaining.

Twenty minutes later, I log on as Bree and type a message to GreatSc0t:

TheDuchessB: Good morning! I have an extremely important question for you: Have you seen the video where some guy sped up Undersea by 123% or something, and now the dialogue sounds like "West Wing on the Moon"? It's a whole different experience!

GreatSc0t: Blasphemous! Someone gave Undersea the Chipmunks treatment?

TheDuchessB: Minus the dubious moral lessons of "doing what's best for the band vs. Alvin's narcissism."

A janky tennis ball animation complete with *swish* noise arrives in a new text bubble. I'm being served by a guy named Andrew. Just "Andrew"? That means he was an early adopter with his pick of usernames, which means he's been on Game, Set, Match since it started, which is a red flag. Against my better judgment, I click "accept."

Andrew: What's up?

TheDuchessB: Not much, you?

Andrew: Do you have pretty feet? And if the answer is yes, I'm about to go to the bar an have a dink, wanna cum?

I clap my hand over my mouth. Is this really happening? When Best Foot Forward got jettisoned as the company name, I figured I was done with this particular population. How naïve I was.

Andrew: Whoops autocorrect LOL. wanna "come" I meant. To the bar for a drink. I see your close by . . .

Before I can stop myself, I've copied the conversation to my clipboard. Then I return to messaging Jude. Handsome, hot, NORMAL Jude.

TheDuchessB: Sorry for the delay. REALLY sorry. I had to Ace someone. You will not believe what he just said to me.

Freelancer's Handbook: Never bring up the other people you may be chatting with. No one wants to hear about the competition. Exceptions include: When the exchange is so batsh*t you need someone to laugh with you about it. Forming a conspiracy of mockery just might bond you together, "us against the world"–style.

GreatSc0t: Sometimes I think they should call it Mace. Can't imagine what you ladies have to deal with out there.

TheDuchessB: Case in point . . .

I paste Andrew's message into Jude's window. Jude (understandably) needs a moment to absorb it.

GreatSc0t: Wow. On behalf of all men, I apologize. Not just for the creepy foot fetish, but the grammar.

TheDuchessB: Thank you! "An" have a "dink"? Should we assume "dinking" has long since begun?

GreatSc0t: YOUR offended me most, personally.

TheDuchessB: It's a toss-up. I think before anyone's allowed on a dating site, they should have to pass a basic grammar test.

GreatSc0t: Co-signed. And a breathalyzer.

TheDuchessB: Anyway, before we were so rudely interrupted, I was going to say I heard somewhere that when Blanca Hinley went over budget in the first half, they couldn't afford the wave machine anymore, so it's literally Mary Clarkson swaying back and forth in the scenes with King Oceano, who's, you know, threatening to replace her legs with fins. Swaying back and forth was a 1000% price reduction from renting the wave machine.

GreatSc0t: Ha ha! I love behind-the-scenes info. Where'd you hear that?

TheDuchessB: Not sure, probably a con.

(Crap. It's not common knowledge. Mary told me that in the midst of a rambling, regretful story while on day five of a bee-pollen-and-charcoal-lemonade fast. I should stop before this gets out of hand and he realizes I've only seen the movie at 123 percent speed. Keep things moving and snag the Hot Scot for an in-person assessment.)

TheDuchessB: Anyway, if you want to see the Chipmunk'd version for yourself, here's the link. Though I hope you'll at least keep my tab open while you watch . . .

GreatSc0t: I've bookmarked the link for later. Your tab has a better view.

TheDuchessB: Oh yeah? *bats eyelashes*

Before he calls BS on my *Undersea* bona fides, I make an impulsive decision.

TheDuchessB: What are you up to later?

A pause, while he checks his calendar. Or wants me to think he's checking his calendar.

GreatSc0t: Working til 5:30.

TheDuchessB: Want to meet for coffee after work?

The first time I spoke to Bree, she said she dressed up in character for midnight movies and could even do "the hair." It's probably something sexy/adorable, i.e., catnip to *Undersea* fans, right?

TheDuchessB: I'll wear a certain hairdo we all know and love.

GreatSc0t: . . . seriously?

Do the ellipses connote lust or horror?

TheDuchessB: Go big or go Flirtville, right?

GreatSc0t: Are you a Flirtville refugee, too?

TheDuchessB: Couldn't get out of there fast enough. There's a DuchessB-sized hole in the wall where I fled.

I'm rewarded with the heart-eyes face emoji. I can't help smiling back at it.

GreatSc0t: Can we make it a brewery? I'm on a mission to test out the local taps.

Shit. Bree and beer don't mix. They're literally an anagram of each other, and anagrams are how the devil communicates with humans. Red rum, etc.

(On the other hand, beer's not *liquor* exactly. It's wheat! It's fine!)

TheDuchessB: Let's do it.

GreatSc0t: Looking forward to it! Here's the address. See you then. :)

* * *

I plunk down $30.06 (two take-out dinners) for a taxi ride to Porchlight, because it's only the second company meeting Clifford has held since I started working for him, and I want to appear to be a model employee. It's galling, per his latest memo, to know he might not even attend, but I can't risk not showing up.

The taxi ride is a sensory nightmare. Besides the endlessly blaring TV that can't be muted or turned off, the a/c is on too high and I don't have my arm warmers to console me. I stare out the window like a dog trapped in a car headed for the pound. To my right is the Hudson River, aka the setting of the Miracle on the Hudson. Sully CANNOT be a hoax. I need Sully. I need the Miracle on the Hudson.

Bicyclists and joggers look loose-limbed and almost free, flying past one another on the surprisingly wide, clean-looking sidewalk along the edge of the water.

Maybe next weekend I'll have the courage to join them.

It's a nice thought, anyway.

"Did he ask you to be the 'international face of the company,' too?" I ask Aisha Ibrahim loudly, trying to be heard over the cacophony of the bar. We've secured ourselves a dim spot in the corner.

She grins and rolls her eyes. "How *ever* did you guess?"

With her smooth brown skin, bootcamp-toned arms, curly black hair, and mischievous smile, Aisha would look great in front of a camera; but her expertise lies on the other side of the lens. She's shorter than me, but fit and mighty from her thrice-weekly kickboxing classes, which I know about because it's the only time her phone's unresponsive. As the photographer and Photoshop expert at Sweet Nothings, she's in high demand, helping our clients slap a Vaseline filter over their online images. That sounds unskilled, when nothing could be further from the truth. Aisha turns profile pics into seamless works of art, covering her tracks so well no one can tell she's cast a spell. Although we've spoken on the phone a few times, this is our first in-person conversation, and meeting her has already made the trip worth it, I decide.

"We could've been famous," I lament.

We clink our four-dollar punch flasks together, purchased with drink tickets Clifford provided. They were given to us by a man in a hockey uniform at the door, whom Clifford has apparently hired as some kind of mascot for the midafternoon soirée. The hockey player's jersey has the Sweet Nothings logo on it, complete with hearts and a cupid arrow. Weirder still: The guy is wearing a mask.

A hockey mask. Inside a bar.

"Sweet Nothings!!" the dude shouts every couple of minutes, for reasons unknown. Is it to amp up the crowd? Is it a team-building exercise? Who can say? Maybe Clifford pays him per shout.

"What is the deal with Clifford's memos?" I groan in my best Seinfeld voice. "Did you see today's paranoid freak-out? My favorite part was the caveat at the beginning."

"The WARNING," Aisha sputters with a laugh.

"That it, quote, 'wouldn't be an easy memo to read.' "

"We've got news for you, Cliffy. None of them are easy to read."

"What was he even talking about? It was more cryptic than usual."

"Oh, oh, oh." She leans toward me to faux-whisper: "I was the subtweet of that memo."

I'm giddy. "No."

"Oh, yes. Clifford wants to train me as a double-agent."

"How . . . what . . ." I stammer.

"Because I also work for his ex-wife's company. The original company."

"You're the 'double-dipper,' " I piece together.

We both make "ew" faces at his word choice.

"He offered to 'read me in' for top-level clearance at Sweet Nothings. He wants me to look through his ideas file, and then he wants my detailed analysis of whether our concepts are better or worse than Leanne's."

"And now he's worried Leanne has asked you to do the same, and you could conceivably be a triple agent?"

"Probably? Your guess is as good as mine."

"How did that whole thing between Clifford and Leanne . . . occur?"

"Their marriage? I know what happened," the masked hockey player says. Aisha and I nearly leap out of our skin at his arrival.

Also, his voice is familiar.

I squint at him, trying to convince myself this isn't what I think it is. Trying to convince myself it's not, in fact, *Clifford* who put on a stupid costume and a hockey mask in order to "infiltrate" his own meeting.

I can hear his thought process for such a stunt: *I thought I'd mingle amongst you, an undercover boss if you will, so as not to intimidate anyone into censoring themselves. I want to hear the word on the street. I want to get a feel for the worker bees, learn what they really think.*

"Yes, yes, the Story of Clifford and Leanne," the hockey player intones, rubbing the chin portion of the mask. "Sometimes two creative souls yearn to collaborate in their pursuits, but the resulting Venn diagram does not overlap in the manner or circumference both had wished for. It's tragic, but those are the thorns of life's roses."

It's him.

Aisha refuses to make eye contact with me. It's for the best; if we acknowledge the situation in any way, we'll lose our shit, and possibly our jobs. Mercifully, Clifford moves to the middle of the room for his great unveiling.

He removes his mask and shouts, "Guys! It's been me all along! Why am I dressed this way? Because, starting this moment, Sweet Nothings is the hockey team of online matchmaking! We brawl for our clients. Defense, offense, we've got your backs! Gather 'round, gather 'round, I've got an announcement to make."

The twenty-odd group of employees encircle Clifford.

He's a boisterous, forty-something white guy whose unadulterated excitement is infectious. I have a sense, momentarily, of what Leanne might have seen in him. Genial and eager, he's the living embodiment of "jump and the net will appear." In his bizarre memos he comes off as Michael Scott from *The Office*, but in person he's more like Jim. Failure, he seems to imply, will only happen to those who aren't lucky enough to throw their lot in with him. I can understand how someone might buy in to his total belief in himself, because what if, just what if, he's right? I can also understand how, after a few years of this, it would wear thin. To put it mildly.

I tune back in to his monologue in time to hear the crux of his new idea: ". . . and I'm thinking, 'There's a tennis-themed dating site. What about a hockey-themed one?' It would be part of the Sweet Nothings family, hosted under the same umbrella of services, and we'd be the in-house counsel, so to speak. We could call our ghostwriting services 'Assists.' Like in hockey, right? And there'd be a discount to anyone *if you use our hockey messaging app.* Instead of serves and lobs and aces and what have you, we'd have Cherry Picking, Clearing the Puck, and Off-Sides. For abusive behavior."

"Do you intend to attract abusive users?" Aisha asks, sounding perplexed.

"Not on purpose," he says happily, then turns his wide, hopeful eyes on me. "What do *you* think?"

"It's interesting," I say. "An interesting thought."

What I don't say: Cherry Picking sounds like a human trafficking site where people bid on virgins.

"Cool. Cool. Thanks for your honesty. I'm going to take the temp of the room, see what's shaking."

"He just admitted he's going to rip off Game, Set, Match by changing nothing but the sports slang," Aisha guffaws once he's out of earshot.

"He really, really did. Should we, like, report this? And to whom?"

"It's exactly what he did to Leanne. One of these days, someone's going to sue his ass and win."

"I believe it," I reply.

We return to our previous table and finish our drinks.

"What's it like working for Leanne?" I ask.

"It's . . . smoother. Less 'kill or be killed' and more 'we're all in this together.' I mean, don't get me wrong. There are times when I can definitely see why she and Clifford were together for so long. But Leanne's more . . . subversive with her business tactics."

We both look over at Clifford, who is now cheering on two freelancers funneling beer through his hockey mask. "I guess it'd be hard to be less subversive," I point out.

Aisha laughs. "I think Leanne's full up on ghostwriters, but if that changes, I could let you know," she offers.

"Would you? Thanks a lot."

"And hey, if Clifford's serious about creating a new dating platform, maybe he'll throw some extra work your way to help write the profile questions."

"If I could design a questionnaire, I'd eliminate all the cliché questions. No more 'Which three albums would you bring to a desert island' crap. I think there should be a section in their profiles about misremembered or misheard lyrics."

"Yesss. I thought 'Living on a Prayer' by Bon Jovi was 'Living on a Prairie' for years," Aisha replies, her eyes sparkling. "And I need to know how someone would react to that before I can entertain the notion of dating them."

I really, really want us to be friends.

"I'd also want to know the weird places people go to zen out. For me it's office supply stores."

She looks at me for a beat. "I should introduce you to my brother. Well, actually, he's my . . ."

I cut her off right away. "Thanks, but I'm not in the market right now."

(Who would want to date a virtual shut-in?)

"You sure? He's a *great* guy. Went through a bad breakup recently, not his fault, but—"

"I've never had a bad breakup. Probably because I've never had a good relationship," I admit. Whoa, where'd that come from? This punch flask must be living up to its name. "Don't the two go hand in hand?" I clarify. "The better it was, the more it hurts when it ends?"

"Maybe. I don't actually think he should have been with her to begin with. But anyway, I could show you a picture. . . ."

"If he's cute, that'll make it tougher to say no," I laugh. "But let's talk later, okay? I've gotta run. My new client has a date straight from work and asked me to help her prep."

"I'm going to take off, too. Secret-agent duties. Are you headed uptown or downtown?"

"I'm headed . . . left, whichever direction that is. Luckily, her office is only a few blocks away, so I can walk."

By a "few" blocks, I mean twelve, and by the time I reach Blue Sky Family Practice, I'm a sweaty, frazzled mess, and my socks have sunk low in my combat boots, chafing one heel. That's what happens when you're convinced the subway's going to collapse while you're inside. Good times.

Clad in a skirt and blouse, Bree ushers me into the large, empty bathroom for patients, where she's putting the finishing touches on her makeup. The wallpaper consists of pictures from vintage children's books. I'm pretty sure it's Bree's handiwork.

I try to ignore the urine samples sitting on a counter by the wall. Most of her colleagues have left, except, apparently, the owner of the hand that reaches through a small wooden window to yank the samples away.

" 'Night!' Bree calls to the hand, which waves, tilting a urine sample this way and that.

Bree focuses on me.

"Did you come from the gym?" she asks kindly. I'm reminded again why I like her; she doesn't mince words but at the same time assumes the best of people.

"Yes, I did." Minimal Bluff. Power walking is exercise, after all. "Did you have a chance to read the messages from this morning? I printed a copy, if that's easier." I dig through my bag and hold the pages out to her.

She'd been brutally honest about skimming our first conversation. (She referred to it as "the blabby blabby.")

"The dates are the important part," she reiterates now. "The rest is noise."

"Absolutely," I assure her. "But reading it is a great way to prepare, see what you've 'already discussed' and take it from there."

I watch intently as she reads our chat from this morning.

She doesn't bat an eye at Andrew's gross interruption.

My reaction to *him* is what sticks in her craw.

"Zoey! You said you weren't going to be a grammar bitch."

What—but—Jude was into it. He agreed with me. He *likes* this grammar bitch!

"Sorry, it's just . . . if someone doesn't care enough to write a good sentence, especially for the first impression—"

"You're supposed to be acting like me, and I wouldn't have cared. No one expects DMs to be Shakespeare."

"Yup. You're right," I say in clipped tones. "If you don't think I represented you well, or it's not something you want to deal with, we can always cancel on Jude—"

"Hell no, have you seen his picture?"

"I have." I nod gravely.

"Sex on a stick. Irish, too, right?"

"Scottish."

"Either way. Me like-y what me see-y."

And what you "read-y" is pure gold, but oh well. She flips to the next page like she's stuck reading a thesis and her torment will never end. She's *bored*.

"Dial down 'the blabby blabby,'" I summarize through gritted teeth. "Got it." But if it had been YOU "blabby-blabbing," you might not have scored a date in the first place, so maybe a little gratitude is in order, eh, DuchessB?

"It's all good. But hopefully he won't have to message you again—hopefully I can take it from here. Nice job getting me this far, though, seriously. He's exactly what I'm looking for."

The operative word being "looking." She certainly hasn't absorbed much from his words.

Bree's eyes widen at what she sees at the end of the last page, and her kindness dissolves, as if it's been thrown in acid. "Why did you tell him I'd do the hair? That'll take at least an hour."

"Oh. Well, I can help, and he's not expecting you until six thirty, so we have time—"

"You know what it looks like, right?"

"Kind of . . ."

Bree tosses the papers to the floor and yanks out her phone. Huffs some more and pulls up an endless array of Google Images of Mary, circa 1985.

"See? It's a big commitment."

Oh God. How could I have forgotten?

It's not a cute side braid or a sexy, ribboned twist. It's a pointed, one-and-a-half-foot triangle, made entirely out of hair, protruding from the back of her head like a traffic cone.

(Mary, regarding an invite from San Diego Comic-Con: "If they think I'm going to tear out what little hair I have left to wear the Pylon Party Hat, they need to triple my fee." I also have a vague memory of a letter in her scrapbook, written to Lorne Michaels at *Saturday Night Live:* "Do I owe the Cone-heads any royalties? Then again, I think I have plausible de-niability. In outer space, no one can hear you scream (about copyrights) . . .")

"What can I do? How can I help?" I ask gently.

"Bobby pins. As many as you can find. Now."

When I return from my errand at, where else, Duane Reade, Bree's in better spirits.

She's changed into a minidress and freshened up her makeup. She reaches for the bobby pins I'm holding and secures the elab-orate 'do while gazing at her reflection in the mirror. "You're sure he loves *Undersea* as much as I do?"

"We've talked of little else." Which you'd know if you'd read the messages!

God, what is wrong with me? Just because she doesn't ap-preciate GreatSc0t's humor on the page doesn't mean she won't appreciate his . . . attributes in person. (But if she doesn't ap-preciate his wordplay, should she really be *allowed* to meet him in person?)

It never bothered me when my first client, Tess, dated her matches. It's moot, anyway; what I told Aisha was true: I'm not dateable in my current state.

"Good luck, Bree. I hope you have a terrific night."

But I cross my fingers behind my back.

CHAPTER 9

To: All Tell It to My Heart Employees
From: Leanne Tseng
Re: Digging Deep

Team,

Love stories . . . we've all got them. Even if, sometimes, we wish we didn't.

This week, I want you to dig deep and get a little personal. It's important for us to work on behalf of our clients, but, also, on behalf of love itself. And the best way to do that is to find the common ground in order to *empathize* with what they're looking for.

Now I can't very well ask you to get personal without doing it myself, right? So here goes: I was in love once. In love enough to get married. On the surface, we didn't seem right for each other. Now, as it turned out,

not too far down from the surface—I'm talking maybe half a centimeter—we weren't right
for each other either. But here's where it's
important to selectively examine what worked
about the relationship. The jokes that made
me laugh, the unbridled enthusiasm and support for my work, and that feeling—however
brief—that I was seen and heard and loved
for who I was. These are the thoughts and
feelings I'd try to conjure up every time I
sat down to work for one of my clients.

At the end of the day, what we do *is* personal . . . as well as being a business.
Success lies in finding the balance between.

Yours,
Leanne

MILES

Huh. That's a memo I wasn't expecting from Leanne. Has she
been feeling nostalgic for *Clifford*? And if that's the case, what
does that say about my chances of getting over Jordan, who is at
least 90 percent less loathsome than Leanne's ex. Though, considering the cheating, maybe I should bump that down to 85.

The brewery with the beer flight specials Jude wants to test
out happens to be located not too far from Dylan and Charles's
apartment.

That's one reason for me to stop by during their date. Another is that I woke up this morning to a stack of *Metro* news-
papers fanned out across the mahogany and glass coffee table
in front of the sofa. They were all open to the classifieds sec-

tion and every single available apartment was circled. Charles doesn't have any classes today, which means he could conceivably be home all day, and having to confront your passive aggressor is just awkward for everyone.

And, finally, I admit it. A part of me wouldn't mind seeing Bree in person, hearing if her humor translates IRL. Hey, I'm supposed to be empathizing with my client's desires, right?

As it turns out, I can't miss her. Holy crap, she actually did do the hair. It stands about a foot above the crowd, a perfect yellow isosceles. And based on Jude's gawking expression as he shakes her hand, I think I forgot to tell him about it, probably because I thought she was joking.

The truth is, she looks . . . hot. Obviously, she's an attractive girl but this adds a ballsy, nerdy element that takes it to a different level. The two of them together look like something out of a catalog (currently, maybe something out of a cosplay catalog, but still). And if Jude doesn't quite appreciate that now, I'm just going to have to huddle with him later and get him up to speed on what a rare find she seems to be.

I slide myself onto a barstool that's catty-corner from their table. I can see them out of the corner of my eye but, more importantly, I can hear them perfectly.

"You look . . ." Jude starts, then hesitates. "Interesting?" Then he catches himself. "Nice?" But he can't seem to stop the question mark from appearing at the end of his adjectives. Maybe I should take my notebook out so that he and I can have a proper postmortem after this.

"Thanks," Bree replies, touching the side of her hair. "Usually, it's a little bit more accurate than this. I didn't have a lot of time."

"Oh," Jude says. And then, nothing. He clears his throat. Then he picks up the menu. "Well, thanks for meeting me. I've heard good things about this place. They have over forty beers on tap and I think at least six of them are low-carb." That might be the most animated anyone has ever uttered the phrase "low-carb" and it was way more enthusiastic than anything he said to or about her. Yeah, the notebook's coming out.

"Right," Bree says, picking up the menu herself. They both seem to be reading it for a while.

"What are you thinking?" Jude asks. "This Monterey Jack IPA looks good. And I think I might give the Wil Belgian Wheaton a go."

"Um . . . ." Bree says, flipping the menu over and then back again. "I'm sorry, but does this place have any food?"

"Oh," Jude says. "Are you hungry? We can ask the waiter for the food menu."

"Yeah, that'd be great."

It takes a while for Jude to flag a waiter down and during that whole time, they don't utter a single word to each other.

It's true what I said: Sometimes people's online humor doesn't translate in person. But with Bree . . . I can't help thinking this is mostly Jude's fault. She put herself out on a limb with the hairdo—if nothing else, an instant conversation piece—and he's not engaging her at all. I've got to talk to him. This girl won't be on the market for long, and I really think he'd be missing out on something pretty special to let her slip away.

A waiter finally comes and informs them there's no food menu except for a forty-dollar cheese plate with a different slice of cheese to pair with each of their beers.

"What do you think?" Jude asks Bree.

"Huh, cheese," she says, and then, "sure. Why not? I'm pretty hungry."

"Cool." He smiles at her. "Do you know what you want to drink or do you need another minute?" Jude asks before the waiter disappears again.

"Oh," Bree says. "Just a Diet Coke."

The waiter blinks at her before jotting her order down. "And you?" he asks Jude.

"Um . . . actually, I'll take a minute," he says.

"Okee dokee. Just holler when you're ready," the waiter says, impressively finding a way to express irritation through the medium of retracting a pen.

"You don't want to try out the beers?" Jude asks Bree.

"Nah. I'm off alcohol right now."

"Oh," Jude says, looking thoroughly confused. I can see him throwing a glance my way. "I didn't know that. I'm sorry. I wouldn't have picked a brewery."

Shit. I'm pretty sure she never mentioned this in our convos, but I am going to have to go back and do a postmortem on myself now.

"It's okay," Bree says. "Maybe I didn't mention it. Who knows?"

"Well . . . do you want to go somewhere else?" Kudos to Jude for offering. But I have to dock a point since he's looking longingly at the menu while he does it.

"Honestly? I'm not sure this hair would survive a trip to another location. So maybe it's best if we stay put."

"Right, okay," Jude says, and then awkwardly picks up his menu again, perusing it with extra concentration.

When the waiter comes back, he ends up ordering a beer flight, along with the cheese plate and Diet Coke.

"So . . ." he says, once the waiter's gone.

"So . . ." Bree replies.

Jesus, this is painful. I'm getting flashbacks to RayaJack5. I wish I could type words straight into Jude's brain for him to speak.

"So . . . you work in medicine? Right?" he finally says.

"I'm a bookkeeper. For a medical practice."

"Ah, right," he says. "How do you like that?"

"I like it. It's more fun than it sounds," she replies.

"You're obviously . . . a fun person." He vaguely gestures toward her head. It takes everything I have not to thunk my head onto the bar.

"I'd like to think so," she says. "And you . . . sorry, I don't remember exactly what you do."

Really? But she made that wry comment when I mentioned the personal trainer thing a couple of days ago. Could it be she's just juggling a lot of matches and doesn't remember the conversations? That's not a great sign, but it also means I might have to amp up my game to make sure Jude rises to the top.

"Personal trainer," Jude says genially.

"Right," Bree says, and then briefly touches his upper arm. "That would explain these."

Jude smiles at her. Okay, this is better.

"So you're from Ireland. Wait, no . . ." Bree pauses. "Scotland."

"Aye." Jude nods.

"Where in Scotland?" Bree asks.

"It's a small hamlet near Glasgow called Auchentiber. It's lovely."

"It *sounds* lovely. Well, when you say it."

Jude smiles. "Thanks."

You'd think the train was finally leaving the station but, uh . . . nope. Another stall, just about a foot away from where they started. Neither of them says anything until the waiter comes back with their drinks and an enormous plate of cheese slivers that takes up almost the entire table.

"Well, cheers," Jude says, lifting his glass to clink it with hers. He brings the beer to his mouth, then stops. "Oh, wait. I'm sorry. I should've asked if it was okay if I drank in front of you. That was rude of me."

Bree blinks at him. "Why wouldn't it be?"

"I just didn't know if you weren't drinking because of some abstinence thing or . . ." He trails off his sentence, thankfully not accusing her of being a raging alcoholic.

"Oh, no. That's not it. I've just given up drinking on dates for now." She leans in and whispers to him. "It's led me to making some bad decisions in the past. So, cheers. Enjoy."

"Ah, got it." Jude smiles at her again and takes a sip.

"Which ones would you like?" Bree says as she takes the cheese knife and hovers it above the plate.

"Actually, I don't eat cheese. I'm paleo," Jude says.

"Oh," Bree says. "So I'm supposed to finish this by myself?"

"I'm sure you can get it wrapped up?" Jude replies.

"Right. Good plan." She then starts cutting the cheese (literally). She cuts and eats the cheese for a long time without a single interruption: no conversation, no gestures, barely even any eye contact. For all his good looks and charm, Jude needs a lot more help than I thought.

"Oh, God!" Bree yells and I glance over. A big piece of her hair seems to have come undone and just landed in what looks like a large pile of feta. "Yuck," she says as she picks up her hair. Jude hands her a napkin. She laughs as she wipes at it. "Guess the Duchess never had this problem in space. Zero gravity and all."

Jude smiles weakly and nods, but even I can tell he has no idea what she's talking about. I guess he's never seen *Undersea*. I've been obsessed with it for so long that I didn't even entertain that possibility. Maybe our first order of business is to remedy that. A very small price to pay to get in this girl's good graces.

"Excuse me a minute. I think I'm just going to go fix this . . ." Bree gestures to her hair.

"Of course," Jude says and he gets up to pull her chair out, but she's out of it and on her way to the bathroom before he can get there.

Once I make sure Bree is out of sight, I walk over to him.

He's running his hands through his own hair. "I've never particularly been up on avant-garde fashion," he says to me.

"Uh, that's not avant-garde fashion," I say. "It's from the movie *Undersea*. Mary Clarkson?"

"Oh," Jude says, and then I see it dawn on him what I'm talking about. "Ohhhh. Right. I remember it. Vaguely. Haven't seen it since I was a kid . . ."

"Well, we might have to do something about that because obviously she is very into it."

"Right," Jude says, though he sounds unsure.

"Don't worry," I assure him. "It's awesome. Easiest homework you've ever had."

"Okay," he replies. "But homework . . . do you really think . . ."

"Shit, I gotta go." I leap onto my barstool as Bree comes walking back to the table. Her hair is down and normal now and she's carrying what can only be described as a cardboard dunce cap in one of her hands.

Jude stands up and this time manages to pull her chair back for her.

"Thanks," she says.

He sits down and smiles at her. "I get it now," he says over-enthusiastically, gesturing toward her head. "*Undersea!*"

"Um . . . yeah," Bree says, but she looks like she's thinking about nothing except placing the dunce cap on his head.

The date does not last much longer than that. Suddenly, Bree isn't so hungry anymore, Jude has finished his flight, and I'm hearing murmurings of "that was fun," with no talk of a further date.

Crap.

Jude comes back to join me at the bar once he's seen Bree out. He orders a water, since he's apparently already filled his beer carb quota for the day. I order a Jameson on the rocks.

"If nothing else, that Wil Belgian Wheaton beer might be a contender for the quest," Jude says. "It was pretty tasty."

"It's not over yet," I reply. "We can still salvage this."

"You think?" Jude asks as he squeezes the lemon into his water. Then he shrugs. "I don't know. Remember what you said about efficiency? Maybe we should just move on."

"I don't think so," I reply almost immediately, even though, normally, if my client wasn't feeling it on the first date, I would

100 percent agree with exactly what Jude is saying. There are plenty of profiles in the sea, especially for a guy like him, and my job is to keep my clients from wasting their time.

But that's the thing. I don't feel like Bree is a waste of time. Sure, this wasn't the most amazing date in the history of romance or anything, and maybe the sort of story they'd have to embellish if it got to the point where they were telling their grandkids about it (on the other hand, maybe it'd be hilarious: the hairdo that almost wiped out their existence). But it could also just be one mediocre date; everything I've seen and read of Bree so far makes me think she's worth another shot. I tell Jude so.

"All right," Jude says. "But I'll be honest: I'm not sure she thinks *I'm* worth another shot."

"Let me think on that," I tell him. "If that's true, I'll come up with something to make her change her mind."

"You're the expert," Jude says, raising his glass to me.

That night, when I get home, it's to the welcome sight of solo Dylan on the couch with a tray of chips and salsa on his lap as he watches *Shark Tank*.

"Where's Charles?" I ask, hoping the answer is something along the lines of "*gone forever.*"

"Having dinner with a former student, one of his mentees," Dylan says.

Okay, fine. I have to admit that's a better answer. Charles and I may not get along, but I'd be totally blind not to realize that he and Dylan are crazy about each other. And if there's one thing I've always been, it's a hopeless romantic.

Here's where I butt up against this problem again: Regular Miles isn't here and I'm genuinely not sure I want him to return. Because being a hopeless romantic meant that I left myself so wide open that I got my heart pummeled, steamrolled, and left for dead.

On the other hand, being totally cynical about love has

thrown me for a loop too. I don't feel like myself; I feel like a version of me that's consistently seeing the world through a smear of Vaseline. Nothing is clear and I can hardly trust any of my own senses. That's no way to live, especially for a New Yorker who needs to be constantly vigilant lest they sit on something unidentifiable and sticky on a suspiciously open subway seat.

I join Dylan on the couch and he offers me a chip, which I take, trying to chew above the tray so that I don't add crumbs to the aggravation of my interminable stay.

"I think Barbara is going to snatch this guy up," Dylan says, gesturing to the TV.

"Maybe. Or Kevin," I reply.

"Ugh. I hope not. He deserves better." Dylan has obviously bought into the villainous portrayal of the investor nicknamed Mr. Wonderful.

Maybe that's the answer. I can be a Shark—an investor in the game of love, but not personally involved. I have the perfect job for it too. I'm not just constantly on the sidelines watching other people's great romances; I'm a real architect of them. I provide the seed money, so to speak. And if I do my job and tend to it properly, I can watch something blossom without being in personal danger if the crop fails.

I don't need to be Regular Miles. I can be Miles 2.0.

And I think that Bree and Jude are the perfect couple to have a stake in.

CHAPTER 10

To: Special Edition Peeps
From: Clifford Jenkins
Re: Results-Oriented Mindset

This is going to sound waaaaay more corporate than you're used to, and I admit it's not how I usually roll, but hear me out, K? The truth is, between the mole, the launch of Puck and Run (working title, gotta laugh!), and what feels like an onslaught of frivolous lawsuits (it's how we know we're top dog, so I'm not worried), I wasn't prepared for the folks over at TIT CENTRAL to place a money-back guarantee on the front of their site. Who does that, right? Love is a many splendored thing, and cannot be rushed, and cannot be forced. They're obviously cynics who think emotions can be quantified by coinage, and that is NOT the Sweet Nothings way.

Still, we'd be foolish not to clap back. So, I've devised a compromise. As of next week,

our clients will have the option of changing ghostwriters if they believe their needs
are not being met. Unfortunately, this means
the original ghostwriter won't be paid, because we can't ask our clients to pay twice
if they're not seeing results. On the plus
side, this new biz model will doubtless attract more clients than we can handle, so
ultimately, it's a HUGE WIN for the Sweet
Nothings family!

Peace always,
Cliff

ZOEY

I think Bree ghosted me.

It's been three days since her date with Jude, and she hasn't responded to a single message I sent asking her about it. I'm freaking out.

If the job interview I had on the phone yesterday for a script coverage position had gone better, I wouldn't care so much, but it ended with the ultimate backhanded compliment: "We're just afraid you're overqualified and wouldn't be happy here."

I'm not sure what I could have done to convince them I don't mind running errands and answering phones. I mean, I did it for eight years just fine; I don't see why I can't keep doing it.

Then this morning I got a reply to a résumé I sent out six weeks ago. No greeting, no reminder of which company it was. Just:

It says here you worked for a script doctor. Do they give out PhDs for that?

When I sent back an explanation of the term, I got this in return:

I'm surprised you didn't get the joke. I thought jokes were your "thing." Anyway, we aren't hiring.

I'm so flustered by the brush-off and lack of money coming in that I can't focus on the script I'm supposed to be writing. I've been stalled on page *two* for weeks, changing the main characters' names and redoing their opening dialogue until I don't even know what the story's about anymore, assuming I ever did.

I know Mary would never kick me out of this apartment, but the idea of telling her I couldn't hack it in the city, considering she gave me every possible advantage, makes me sick to my stomach. After Bree looked so astonished by my address, I researched the building's history. Turns out I should be paying nearly four grand for this tiny room, which is NONSENSE, but it means Mary's more generous than I realized; if I can't cobble together the monthly rent at 70 percent off, I don't deserve to live here. Let someone who knows what the hell they're doing take it over from me.

Because bad news always comes in threes, now Clifford is threatening to renege on my pay for what I thought had been a slam-dunk ghosting job! I need to find out what happened. Voice mails and IMs aren't working, so I decide to log in to Bree's account with Game, Set, Match and search for answers on my own. She hasn't given me permission to do that since I last saw her, but she hasn't NOT given me permission, either.

Maybe it's good news I haven't heard from her. Maybe she and Jude are so loved up they don't have time for anything else. I'll hop in, skim a bunch of gooey missives—I bet Jude gives great gooey—and invoice Clifford for another success story.

Username: TheDuchessB
Password: 1374552x9992080
The login or password you entered is incorrect.

I roll my eyes. That's because it's a bunch of random numbers that correspond to some type of *Undersea* map coordinates. I double-check it and type again, slowly and carefully.

The login or password you entered is incorrect.

I grit my teeth and make a third attempt.

The moment I hit enter, the screen goes black and a single yellow tennis ball smashes into a cartoon player's face. His eye swells up and a few of his teeth fall out. Charming.

Then a message in white text appears:

Please contact an Admin to restore your access. Bye!

Oh shit! How long will she be locked out?

I'm reeling from the implications when my e-mail inbox dings. The message is from Clifford and it's a video. Just what I fucking need! At least I'm at home where no one can witness this lunacy. I click on it and cover my eyes, watching through the sliver of space allowed by my fingers. *When* does he have time to make these?

Oh, he had fun with this one.

The video depicts Ariana Grande singing and dancing, but her face has been sloppily covered with Bree's profile pic. Ariana's brown ponytail shoots out the top of Bree's head, not unlike the party pylon hairdo, come to think of it. She (and the Weeknd, because Clifford's obsession continues) sing that if I want to keep them, I need to love them harder. Then Clifford walks toward me in front of a white screen.

"Here's the sitch-a-roo. Your client filled out a customer survey, and she gave you a"—he cringes—"one out of five for user satisfaction. That's *almost* the worst possible outcome."

What's the worst one? Murder?

"Not everyone's compatible, but this goes beyond that."

No shit! Is my boot compatible with your jugular?

It's really tough for me to fathom how Bree's meeting with Jude could have turned into a bad date. I set her up perfectly; all she had to do was show up and chat about her favorite topic, and she would've been off to the fricking races. Jude and I *connected*. If it went wrong, it's not because of me.

I shut off Clifford's message (right after I hear him say, "Ruh-Roh! Mayday! Mayday!") and pace the length of my $4,000-a-month room. I only take six steps before I'm forced to turn around.

This is bad. This is really bad.

I scroll through my address book, and pause at Aisha's name. I *need* to vent about Clifford, and who better? She'll understand like no one else. But then I hesitate.

A) It's Friday night; she's probably out.

B) If I let on what a big pile of fail I am at my job, she'll never refer me to her other company.

I scroll further and tap call.

"Starry Eyes Retirement, Ruby speaking."

"Hi Ruby," I say, trying to sound cheerful over the lump in my throat. "Is my grandma around? It's Zoey."

"It's Friday, so she's at karaoke bingo tonight. Want me to have her call you back? It won't be until eleven . . ."

"No, that's okay . . . Tell her I hope she wiped the floor with Doris."

I hang up and stare at the walls of my apartment. My eighty-year-old grandmother has more of a social life than I do. I'm happy for her—she deserves it—but I miss her and I miss my old self, the self I used to be, when things made sense and my schedule never deviated.

Wake at six, breakfast in front of the TV, take the 10 to the 405 to the 101, work with Mary all day, take the 101 to the 405 to the 10, home, dinner in front of the TV (unless I stayed late and had dinner with Mary), asleep by eleven, repeat.

If I didn't get out much, it didn't matter; in Los Angeles, there were always people around. I never had to think about it. Nick the weed dealer and I could sneak off alone whenever he dropped by Mary's, so it wasn't like I needed to date. Mary herself threw house parties constantly, and included me as a guest, not an employee. I was always welcome. Part of the group. Never looked down upon.

Maybe that's what my fear of NYC is all about. Here, I feel unwelcome.

Now I have way too much time on my hands and no one to share it with.

Okay. Let's think. What would Mary say about tonight's events?

There's one surefire way to find out. It's only six p.m. in California, not that that's good or bad; arbitrary concepts like "time" don't mean much to Mary.

A voice picks up on the fourth ring.

"Mary, Fuck, Kill, how may I direct your call?" says a smooth male voice.

Stunned, I hang up. My heart beats triple time in my chest. I feel light-headed, and my arms and fingers tingle, the way they always did after a ten-hour day typing. I'm having phantom tendinitis pains from a job I haven't held in months.

Tears fill my eyes. *I'm so stupid.* I should have known.

She's replaced me.

She's replaced me with someone who doesn't choke on the name of the company.

I wipe my eyes and shake my head. She told me I was the best assistant she ever had, and I guess I thought that meant she wouldn't be using an assistant anymore. That after me, she'd just, I don't know, muddle through or something. Focus on adapting her memoir for the stage like she'd always planned to.

Talk about ridiculous. I was her assistant, not her partner, even if she did ask my opinion on the scripts and let me pitch jokes. Just because she gave me an associate title, just because she sent her car service around to pick me up when I had the flu so she could look after me in her guest room and feed me matzo ball soup from Canter's Deli, and just because she took me and

Nana to Catalina Island for Nana's birthday, and just because I thought . . . I thought . . .

Okay, get a grip.

After answering her correspondence for eight years and editing her dictation, you know her almost better than you know herself. So. What would Mary say about Bree? Probably something along the lines of, "When life hands you lemons, make Amaretto Sours."

Preach. I don't have the ingredients for that, but I do have half a bottle of week-old Riesling. I yank the fridge open and take a fortifying chug straight out of the bottle. It shivers sweetly all the way down. Mask of bravery in place, I FaceTime Bree. I feel no shame or guilt. It's after hours, so I'm not bothering her at work, and she owes me an explanation.

Bree appears on my screen, looking chagrined. "I'm sorry," she squeals. "Hiiiiii."

"Hi," I answer, stone-faced. "What happened? Are you okay?"

"Are you in trouble? I'm sorry about the survey, but it kept popping up on my screen and the only way to get rid of it was to fill it out. Besides, it was the truth! That date sucked complete ass."

As opposed to partial ass? "You know, Bree," I say slowly, so I don't explode, "I'm honestly surprised to hear that. Can you walk me through it, please? I want to understand what went wrong."

"He doesn't eat. He only wanted to drink, which you *knew* was a deal-breaker for me. It could not have been more awk. And he didn't even, like, register the frigging unbelievable accuracy of my hair. I DON'T DO IT FOR EVERYONE, YOU KNOW."

"Yet I can't help but notice you seem to have put it up that way again." My teeth are clenched so tightly it's a miracle she can tell what I'm saying.

She sniffs and lightly touches her coif, half of it off-screen.

"There's a Blu-ray party at midnight tonight," she responds huffily. "It's a re-release of the director's cut with eighteen seconds of never-before-seen footage."

"Okay. I'm sorry it went poorly, I really am. Did you . . ." I close my eyes briefly. "Find another ghostwriter?"

"No," she says. "I didn't know that I could."

"You can't," I say quickly. Not until next week, Clifford said. I still have a chance to turn this around. "I get that you're mad, and I apologize profusely for misjudging what would happen. Was there anything you *did* like about him? Anything we can work with?"

"He's ripped," she admitted. "And he's got great eyes, and a killer accent . . ."

I can't help smiling. I bet he does. "Oh, yeah?"

"I think he felt bad that he bombed so hard because he sent me something this morning."

I brighten. "Was it flowers? A note? Can I see?"

"There's nothing to see. You can hear it, though. It's an audio file. I only listened to the beginning, because it looks long."

"Doyouwantmetolistentoitforyou?" I sputter.

If she says yes, I'm still her ghostwriter. If she says yes, I can still make rent. Besides, I'd like to hear his "killer accent" for myself.

She shrugs. "I guess . . ."

"I'll report back in the morning, okay? Send it over and have fun with your . . . um, new eighteen seconds of film—oh, and you might be locked out of Game, Set, Match for a while, but I'm on top of it."

"Should we maybe just start over? Find a new match? This is exhausting."

I pretend I don't hear. "I'll fill you in first thing tomorrow—or, should I give you until noon so you can sleep in?"

"Noon's good."

" 'Kthanksbye!"

The file arrives and I download it to my phone and put my earbuds in.

There are so many ways of communicating online. Facebook, Twitter, IMs, DMs, chatrooms, match services, IG, text, and all they seem to do is increase the distance between us. In that respect, recording one's voice for a private listening session seems almost . . . quaint.

I love it.

"Right. Okay. So, I've always been a fan of those articles in airplane magazines, the ones that do a spread on a city, with an article about 'Three Perfect Days in Toronto' and that. I don't fly often, mostly just to Glasgow and back every other year, but I always take the magazines home with me. I like to think I've amassed a collection so if I ever do find myself in certain cities, I'll have a plan in place, a perfect three days. And I got to thinking, in New York City, every neighborhood, every single one, has its own vibe, something about it that's unlike any other neighborhood. I wish someone would put together a guide to them, a microcosm version—one perfect day. But so far, I don't think anyone has, so I thought I'd take a crack at it. My contribution to this is a walking tour that starts in Hell's Kitchen but takes you to my favorite place in all of New York. If all goes well, I hope it shows you something that you haven't noticed before. And if you end up loving this place as much as I do, maybe we could check it out together sometime."

Oh, mama. His accent IS delicious.

It's my second time listening to the recording. I'm lying in bed, lights out, eyes closed, window open a crack, letting Jude's words pour over me as night envelops the city.

"So, without further ado"—he chuckles endearingly—"welcome to Hell's Kitchen. Let's start our morning with a trip to Holey Cream on Ninth Avenue. What better way to begin the day than building your own doughnut, right? Don't skimp on the toppings—that's the best part. And be sure to order some ice cream on the side . . ."

His voice lulls me into a sense of peace. It's after midnight and I'm drifting on a cloud of contentment.

For the first time since I arrived in New York, the tear that slides down my cheek is one of happiness.

I'm still glowing the next day, Saturday, because Jude's favorite place in all of New York is close to my apartment, only ten blocks away! The High Line apparently runs along the Hudson River, the area I'd made a mental note to explore after my taxi went past it on the way to Porchlight the other week. With a "companion" guiding me, this'll be a snap.

It's seven a.m. and I'm dressed in yoga pants, a sports bra, and a tank top, the unofficial uniform of LA. I'm pumped. I'm elated.

I'm out of shape.

I learned from listening to Jude last night that the High Line park opens right now, and it's invigorating to know I'll be one of the early risers taking advantage of it. After exiting my apartment, I stretch my arms and legs out, and head toward Gansevoort Street in the Meatpacking District. Jude claims that's the best entrance from which to experience the High Line.

Eventually, it dawns on me I've gotten turned around. In fact, I've walked in the complete wrong direction and now I'm on Avenue B. The place I'm supposed to be is now eleven blocks away, not ten, and it's eleven *avenues*, not blocks. Turns out avenues are not the same as blocks. Turns out avenues are about the size of *five* blocks. I'll have to walk an hour just to get to the beginning of the tour!

I curse at myself, then take a deep breath and remember it's my first time actively exploring the neighborhood, and that anything I see today is more than I've seen since I came here, which can only be good. I grit my teeth and march up to Fourteenth

Street. I pass Union Square Park and the New School, and I'm glad I take a moment there to stop and catch my breath because the windows look like rippling liquid. I snap a photo—my first tourist photo!—take a big swig of water, and continue on my way, renewed.

At last I'm at the "proper" entrance to the High Line, and Jude's voice is waiting for me there, like armor protecting me. I pop my earbuds in, fire up the recording, and tune out the noises and chaos. Jude regales me with a brief history of the elevated railway, and the effort to "save" it in 2000 and turn it into a public space in 2009. The history fascinates me. From its beginnings as a train line to an elevated promenade, this place speaks highly of the locals and their desire to preserve a worthy piece of history by renovating the industrial area into a mixed-use park.

The biking and jogging trail widens or shrinks along the water, depending on what else shares the space. It's relaxing and breathtaking all at once. I'm not impressed with the Standard Hotel (LA's is better), but I'm pleasantly surprised by all the artwork along the walk, from sculptures to murals and mosaics. No need to go inside art galleries when so much is free and visible to those of us passing by. There's even a project called *Mutations* scattered on video screens throughout the walk that warms my LA heart.

"I don't know if I'll ever have kids, but if I do, I'm taking them to the Pershing Square Beams," Jude's voice intones, leading me on a detour. "In fact, the Pershing Square Beams might be the only reason to *have* kids. Basically, they scooped out the concrete deck so people can see the original steel beams and frames and walk on them."

It's impossible to resist, and soon I find myself taking part, testing my balance along the beams of the sunken, rectangular gridwork, between which sit little gardens.

It's delightful, and I'm so enthralled by Jude's voice, his calm reassurance and the effort he put into the tour, that I don't even notice I've walked a mile and a half by the end of it. Now I've got to walk back, ugh . . . Yet the smile on my face never drops.

I'm rewarded by a snack he suggests at an Israeli joint called Seed + Mill at the Chelsea Market. They specialize in Nutella halvah, aka my new favorite dish.

When I get home, I shower and check the time—it's only eleven thirty, so I can't call Bree yet. I'm antsy, waiting for the minutes to pass. I'm also unnerved by how much I enjoyed listening to Jude, and pretending his tour was for me, and not her. How on earth could Bree abandon it after just a few minutes? Why wasn't she riveted? Or at the very least, more appreciative?

12:01 p.m. and I'm FaceTiming her again. She looks tired when she answers; want to bet she watched the new eighteen seconds on a loop all night? (Like I'm one to talk, having listened to the walking tour on repeat . . .)

"You've got to give him another chance," I tell her, cutting to the chase.

"Are you sure? Because, like, the part I listened to was a tour of my own block. I mean, it was fine, but I live here. I know the area well, I don't need a—"

"But the effort! The time! You have to admit that someone who goes to all that trouble deserves a second chance."

She purses her lips and wrinkles her nose, and for a split second of insanity, I pray that she'll disregard my advice. She really doesn't deserve him, if she's that uncertain.

But then she smiles and nods. "Okay, you're right. Let's set up another meet."

"Great! Yes."

We chat a little more before I end the call. I flop backward onto my couch bed, knowing I should be happy, I should feel relaxed, rejuvenated, and recharged, but the truth is I'm experiencing my *own* version of the three Rs: relief, regret, and resignation.

CHAPTER 11

To: All Tell It to My Heart Employees
From: Leanne Tseng
Re: Confidence

Team,

A big congratulations is due to Stella Gonzalez. She's only been freelancing with us
for two months, but she's the winner of our
"out-of-the-box/not out-of-the-box idea challenge."

You might have missed it on our site, but
all Tell It to My Heart clients now have a
money-back guarantee. If they're not satisfied we've helped them find a great match
within eight weeks, they get a full refund.
It's great peace of mind for them! It also
speaks highly of *you*! That's right. We can
only do this because we believe in the quality of our work and our employees.

That being said, we did have to carve out a small financial caveat. Please note that if one of your clients activates a money-back guarantee, the company will absorb the loss. If a second one is activated, however, then the money will unfortunately have to be docked from your pay.

But, just keep doing what you're doing . . . i.e., giving 100% to each and every client . . . and all will be gravy.

Congratulations again, Stella!

Yours,
Leanne

MILES

I can pretend that Leanne's memo is the main reason I went so many unpaid hours beyond Jude's TITMH package to write that walking tour. Or that I felt threatened that Stella would take over the only staff writing position Leanne can afford right now. But the truth is I started working on it before the memo even came through.

The day after that disaster of a date, I took myself to Bree's neighborhood and self-assigned a leisurely stroll, making a voice memo of places of interest as I did. I kept my eyes peeled because that was exactly the point: to show her something she might not have noticed before the tour. Not because I was keeping an eye out for the recipient of the tour herself. Of course not.

But I was a little unnerved at how intently I seemed to *not* be looking for her. Or how every flash of blond hair made me do a double take. Which was why once I had a solid idea of what I wanted to include, I took myself to Café Crudité to write out the actual script.

It took me two days to do it, mainly because I was interrupted by another new client—Clark—and had to go through his questionnaire and set up an initial meeting with him. Though at one point, another flash of blond hair at the café distracted me too.

But it wasn't Bree. It was my nemesis au lait, whose hair isn't even fully blond at all, but a confounding mixture of dark and light which—given the very little I know about her—actually seems somewhat appropriate. It was starting to get weird that I didn't know her name, since she had become such a fixture of my time here. But I couldn't very well go up and ask her *now*. "Hi, I'm Miles. Would you mind telling me your name? My inner monologue is running out of clever nicknames for you. By the way, has anyone ever told you your dimples are an exact fifty-fifty ratio of sexy and sweet? Thanks!"

She did, unknowingly, give me a little motivation for the tour though. I thought of how she didn't know the city at all, about how disdainful she seemed of it in our brief interactions, and I got inspired to make it lead to the High Line. It was my absolute favorite place in the city, the place I thought could make even Legend fall in love with New York. Especially once Jude got his hands on it. Or, er, tongue around it. Together, we really were the perfect man. Perfect for Bree, anyway.

Jude was a pretty good sport about the tour. He delivered the file back to me within a few hours and I got the honor of sending it along to Bree.

And then we . . . waited. I figured it would take her a while to listen to it. Maybe she wouldn't have time during working hours. But then five o'clock rolled around. And then six. By midnight, Jude's Game, Set, Match inbox was still empty.

Hmph.

I wasn't super panicked about Leanne's new policy of docking our pay if a second money-back guarantee comes through.

But, by the next day, I'm a little panicked about it.

Especially when I get home in the afternoon to a notice taped up on Dylan and Charles's door. At first, I think it might be a take-out menu (which, I admit, I get a little excited about. I've been in a bit of a rut with my dinners lately). But then I see it's yet another classified section of the *Metro* newspaper, with every available apartment circled in a particularly violent slash of thick red marker.

Honestly, now I'm pissed.

I get it. I've been invading Charles's space. But I feel like I deserve a little credit for trying to be as unobtrusive as possible. And it's not like I *want* to be here. It's not like it was my choice to get kicked out of the apartment I shared with my ex-fiancée. Or to find my job in such a precarious position. Has Charles truly never been down and out? And if he has, hasn't he had some kind person—maybe even what some would call a *friend*—help him get back on his feet?

Probably not, since he's such a miserable person that only sweet, optimistic Dylan would be able to see the good in him at all.

I tear the notice off the door and stomp in, where I hear his unmistakable heavy footsteps in the kitchen. I rage in there.

"What the hell is your problem?" I yell.

"Excuse me?" He looks up at me, stunned, his hands full of two of *my* Chinese take-out boxes, which he's pouring out onto a plate.

Was I going to eat them? Probably not. But are they mine? Hell yes.

"If you want me out of here so fucking badly, maybe you shouldn't also gorge yourself on my food," I add.

He looks down at the food and then up at me. "You've got to be kidding . . ."

I slam the notice down on the counter. "I get it. I may not have a law degree, but I'm not an idiot. You want me out of here. *I'm working on it.*"

"Are you? It sure doesn't seem like it." Charles's face has started to get blotchy and red.

"How would you know?" I bite back. "I'm never here."

"You're here enough," he roars. "Enough to ruin everything."

"What the fuck are you talking about? Because I deigned to put a bead of sweat on your goddamn Ikea rug?"

"No," he says, and now he's actually shaking. A couple of pieces of rice escape the carton in his hand and end up on his precious floor. "Because I bought a goddamn ring for Dylan the day before you moved in here and now I've had no chance to fix up the apartment like I wanted to, or to ask him anything because you will never. Fucking. Leave."

I stare at him, stunned. "You . . . you're going to ask Dylan to marry you?"

"You bet your ass I am," he roars. "Whether you think I'm good enough for him or not."

I have no response to that. And the next words that come are actually from neither one of us.

"Oh . . . oh, Charles."

We both whip our heads to see Dylan standing in the hallway, his hands on his mouth, and the mail he had carried up all over the floor. Apparently, neither one of us even heard him come in.

"Is it true? Are you going to propose?"

Charles's entire face is a frown. "I . . . yes. I was going to. But not like this." He gestures to the half-open cartons on the counter, and the food on the floor and, of course, me standing in the middle of it all. But he doesn't look at me. His eyes are fixed on a point on the ground.

Oh, God. Now I feel like such a shithead.

"Do it," Dylan says, as he rushes over to Charles and takes his hands. "Ask me."

Charles looks up at him. "Really? But I was going to get food from Chez Nous. And there were going to be candles. And that Nick Drake song playing on the stereo."

"I have a good imagination. I can pretend all of that is happening," Dylan responds. "Just ask me."

Charles takes one brief glance my way, but then his eyes slide past me to a side table in their living room. He walks over to it and opens up a small drawer in the back that I've never noticed before. He takes out a ring box.

Then he walks over to Dylan and gets down on one knee in front of him.

"Dylan . . . I've honestly never felt love as crazy as this. Or as perfectly sane either. Everything with you makes sense, in a world where so few things usually do. I don't have to argue a case with you, or make anyone try to see my side. There's only one side here—*our* side. I want you to brighten my Northern Sky forever. Will you marry me?"

Dylan gives a yelp and then he sits himself down on Charles's knee. "Of course I will!" he says, before he takes Charles's face in his hands and kisses him passionately.

Charles starts to laugh. At least, I think that's what that is. It's a sound I've never heard from him before. "Really?" he says. "Are you sure?"

"Of course, you idiot!" Dylan says in between laughs himself. "I love you more than anything."

"And I love you more than anything," Charles says. "Don't you at least want to see the ring?"

Dylan grins as he stands up from Charles's knee and takes the ring box. He smiles even wider. "It's gorgeous." He takes it out of the box and slips on the thick platinum band. I can see a diamond sparkling from within it. "Isn't it beautiful?" He turns to me and shows me his hand.

I smile at him, a genuine one even if Charles will never believe it. "Yes. It is. Congratulations! To both of you." I turn to Charles then, intending to apologize.

But this isn't the time for that. Charles has put his hand on Dylan's back, and he suddenly dips him, and starts to furiously kiss him. Dylan responds.

I spend another second with a sappy smile on my face, watching them, before I realize that, er, I definitely need to let them have this moment alone.

I scoot around them as quietly as I can, pad down their hallway, and leave.

It's only when I've walked half a block that I realize the classifieds section is still clutched in my hand.

Well. Now seems as good a time as any to look for a new apartment.

I think about finding a bar or café to go sit down, but then I come across something better.

Staples.

I walk in and head straight over to the most comforting aisle there is, the aisle of a thousand Post-its. Few things in life make me more zen than knowing that one can take notes on an almost infinite variety of shapes, colors, and sizes of sticky paper. Ever since I was a kid, the sheer possibilities for organization—the thought that no matter how unpredictable life gets, there are tools to neatly catalog it—have been massively appealing.

The whole store is pretty deserted, and there is no one there to ask me what the hell I think I'm doing as I place my back on the metal shelves and slide down to the floor.

I lean my head against a pen display (fine point, 0.7 mm, and comes in five colors. I should give one a whirl before I leave here). So Charles and Dylan are going to get married. I realize that's the first proposal I've ever witnessed that wasn't my own.

But my own proposal to Jordan certainly had a lot of witnesses. It happened at the fancy Mexican restaurant where we'd had our first date. I called ahead to set everything up: the peonies on the table, the ring placed inside a beautiful chocolate rose on top of her flan, and the bottle of Veuve Clicquot afterward. I got down on one knee as soon as they brought the dessert out, so happy to present the ring that had been burning a hole in my pocket for weeks. So happy to watch Jordan's face.

She looked elated. I'd gotten the ring off her Pinterest page, so I knew she liked it. And when she said yes, the whole restaurant burst out into applause. The maître d' even led everyone in a toast to us.

Looking back on it now, I wonder if that's what really made Jordan so happy. The fact that there were people to approve of her big moment, like the real-life version of social media likes. I think it's quite possible that Jordan smiled more at the people applauding us than the person kneeling in front of her. Dylan, on the other hand, hadn't cared how his boyfriend proposed. He just wanted Charles.

I sigh as I pick up the crumpled *Metro* page, not really expecting to find anything there. (I mean, honestly, who lists housing in an actual newspaper anymore?) Sure enough, it's a few room shares with a questionable number of roommates, a $7500/month studio on the Upper West Side, and one ad that I'm not sure should be categorized as a sublet or a missed connection. "Roommate wanted: the brunette in the lemon-print dress that took the A train at 5:16 p.m. on Tuesday. You wear that dress every day; I will make you lemon pancakes every morning. Southern-facing windows, private bathroom (though you're also welcome to share my jacuzzi tub). You pay half for cable and Internet." Either way, I'm considering reporting it for sheer creep factor.

But then one listing catches my eye. It's a building in the East Village, on Avenue A. Actually, I think it's across the street from Café Crudité. I Google the address. Yup. It's a 650-square-foot one-bedroom for . . . this can't be right. $900 a month?

Obviously a scam.

Also. The ad rhymes:

So you want to live in Alphabet City . . .
All you have to do is be witty.
Just have a sit,
And answer me this,
Make the words pretty, not sh*tty.

And then it's followed by an honest-to-God essay question. So maybe it's just some rich, eccentric leprechaun who wants to fill his building up with a certain type of person. That actually makes the price slightly more plausible.

Then I read the question: "If you had to pick one fictional character to be for the rest of your life, who would it be? And why?"

I let out a snort that actually shakes the pen display behind me.

Well, that's easy. Harry from *When Harry Met Sally*. For one, he's not too far off the mark from myself: snarky, slightly embittered, thirty-something New York guy. But with the added bonus that my beautiful, smart best friend eventually realizes she's madly in love with me. Plus I'd get to read as a white dude for once. Win/win.

Look, I don't really know if this ad is legit. But if there's one thing I can do, it's write, especially this essay. So might as well, right?

I stand up, grab one of the pens from behind me, and a notebook from one aisle over. I pay for them, and then head right back to the Post-it aisle where I settle in to wax poetic about eating at Katz's, singing electronic-store karaoke, and delivering zingers about the dance of the white man's overbite.

CHAPTER 12

To: The All-Star Lineup
From: Clifford Jenkins
Re: Out of the office all week

i'm in and out of depositions at the mo,
can't get online much but it's all good, will
update in the a.m., in the meantime send
good vibes to the courthouse (the one in lil
jamaica, NOT throgs neck) i am killin' it
and may even get a copy of the videotape to
inspire you all

C

ZOEY

It's been raining on and off all morning. The air outside Café
Crudité is thick with humidity, as though the streets and buildings have Saran Wrap stretched around them, trapping a layer
of heat and garbage and smoke over our heads. By ducking un-

der canopies on my walk over, I managed to arrive in a relatively dry state, with zero competition for the big table.

It's only nine a.m., but when the downpour starts, and a slash of lightning crackles through the air, it looks and feels like midnight. Unsurprisingly, the place fills up with people who appear mildly traumatized.

Despite Clifford's assurance that he's "killin' it" at depositions, his e-mail has me feeling mildly traumatized myself. If Bree and Jude work out—and I'm torn between wanting that and not wanting that—the Sweet Nothings's check better not bounce. I'm not as panicked about this as I might have been a few days ago, though. For one thing, Clifford's e-mails all tend to blow over, and for another, I'm still buzzing from the hike Jude sent me on and all the wonderful things I saw along the High Line.

Thunder rumbles overhead, the door flies open again, and about eight more people shove their way inside, huddled and shivering.

Miles is among them. He wears an Adidas track jacket (black, with two white stripes down the sleeves and two red stripes at the cuffs) over a soft-looking, gray pocket tee and skinny, dark blue jeans that cling to his fit body. His face is clean-shaven, and his hair is damp and dripping from the rain.

In short, he's cute AF.

An observation I'll be taking to the grave.

He runs a hand through his thick brown locks, pulling them away from his eyes and inadvertently giving himself a side part.

Stop looking at him, I order myself.

The floor's slippery and the last one in, an older woman whose glasses are fogged up, almost takes a spill. Miles holds his arm in front of her like a bar so she can steady herself. She nods gratefully to him and he nods back, guiding her ahead of him in line.

Hmm. Downright chivalrous. Quite the opposite of his behavior with me. Which one is the true Miles? Angry shouter, or courteous caregiver?

The café is so crowded now that every table may as well be the Big Table—they're all coveted, and tension fills the room as it dawns on the customers in line that soon, there will be nowhere to sit. They can't go back outside, though. Orders and names are shouted, hot drinks are dispensed, and the air vibrates with the hum of people shifting into and around one another, arguing about where to sit. Any second now a fight may break out.

". . . But I'm waiting for a friend," a middle-aged woman protests when a soaking, uninvited guest plops down in one of the few unoccupied seats remaining.

"When they get here, I'll leave," the interloper snaps. "But there's nowhere else to . . ."

"Double up, folks. Make it work," Evelynn booms, hoisting a gallon of oat milk onto the counter.

Instinctively my gaze swings back to Miles. I stare, hard, and wait for him to meet my gaze. When he does, I jerk my chin toward the chair opposite me. He's not nearly as wet as the latecomers, and since I'm being forced to double up I'd rather it be with a mostly dry person.

Miles peers behind him and from side to side, unable to fathom a universe in which I would invite him over. He points to himself, a questioning look on his face.

"Yes, you," I shout.

He wastes no time bringing his drink over and depositing his annoying messenger bag made of tarp. Today it probably saved his computer.

"Thanks."

"Better 'the devil you know,' right?" I ask. "Besides, I'm in a good mood today."

He glances at my plate of biscotti and I yank it closer to me. "Not THAT good a mood," I clarify.

He rolls his eyes. "I wasn't going to—"

"My generosity extends as far as my paycheck."

"Starving artist?"

"Sort of. You too?"

It would explain why he spends all day on his laptop. He's probably a novelist. One of those guys who writes a book from a woman's POV and then swims through an ocean of praise about how sensitive he is.

He nods. "Okay if I clear this?" He motions to my collection of notebooks and papers. "Set it on the bench next to you or something?"

"Sure."

We reach for my leather-bound notebook, a gift from Nana, at the same time. Our fingers brush and the contact makes my stomach flutter, which is flat-out wrong. I inhale sharply and pretend it didn't happen. He doesn't seem to notice, just lifts my notebook and pens and hands them to me to make room for his laptop. I can't help but notice how artistic his fingers look—and then I notice something catastrophic: a loose sheet of paper has fallen out of my notebook and flutters to the floor. He bends over to get it.

"Don't!"

He sighs. "What is wrong with you? I'm just picking it up."

"Give it to me—" I waggle my fingers impatiently. My strange reaction has piqued his curiosity.

"What is it?" he asks.

"Nothing."

He holds up the paper and squints at it.

"It's private," I insist.

"Is this a . . ." He turns it sideways and my cheeks get so hot I may burst into flames. People could gather around me to keep warm.

"It's a tally," I say, hoping to hasten him along. "Just a tally, nothing important—"

He won't be deterred or hurried. " 'Table Champion,' " he reads aloud, "with dates and initials—who's MHH?"

"No one," I stutter. "What? I don't know."

He tries and fails to muffle his laughter. "Did you . . . make a *chart* for which of us gets the table each day?"

"MHH," I grit out. "Miles. High. Hair."

His hand flies up to his hair, and it's my turn to smirk.

"Miles-High Hair?" he repeats, looking hurt. "Me, Miles? How do you know my name?"

" 'It knows my name!' " I shriek sarcastically.

He sets the tally between us and sits down. His legs are so long he has to tuck his knees flush under the table or they'll invade my space. "How *do* you know my name?"

"They only say it every day when your order's up."

"Only someone who'd been listening for it would notice, though."

"You're right; you caught me. I just had to find out the name of the stranger who YELLED AT ME for no reason."

He cringes. "In my defense, that was one of the worst days of my life."

"Me being a tiny bit greedy was one of the worst days of your life?" I retort. "Can we switch lives, please?"

"No, the bad stuff went down before I came to the café. You being *a lot* greedy was the last straw."

"You can sit here," I mutter. "But that doesn't mean we need to talk."

"You know my name, but I don't know yours," he says simultaneously.

I clear my throat. "Zoey Abot."

Silence. We look at each other for a second, as though waiting to see if the other will hold out their hand for a shake. Neither of us does. I think about the way our hands touched earlier and decide it's for the best. It's been a freakish enough encounter already.

"My miles-high hair doesn't just happen, you know," he says amiably. "I have to have had a particularly atrocious night of sleep."

"What happened last night, then?"

"Ouch. Guess I walked right into that one. Why do you keep a tally of who wins the table?"

"I wanted to see if there was a pattern. Days you didn't show up, so I wouldn't have to race here. I'm winning, by the way. Sixty-five percent of the time."

"You must be proud."

"Which begs the question, why do you keep coming here, when I'm so clearly dominating the competition?"

"A) I couldn't care less who gets the table. The fact that you do says way more about you than it does about me."

The other tables are comically bad. What a liar! He cares. He cares so hard. I can feel my blood pressure rise, just looking at his smug face while he talks.

"And B) Free Wi-Fi, usually no big crowds, and I don't have to worry about gorging on junk food because they don't sell any. Speaking of, I think we should order something."

Strangely enough, I agree. It'll fend off the vultures and keep us safe from Evelynn, who might otherwise kick us out into the storm to make way for customers who actually eat.

"I think you're right. No kale muffins, though."

"Pool our resources?" he suggests.

Two starving artists empty every pocket, purse, and wallet, placing our wrinkled dollar bills and a handful of coins onto the table. Miles systematically organizes them and announces that between us, we've got $14.87.

"There's only one item on the menu we can afford," I point out.

"Black bean and quinoa bowl it is," he says, snapping the menu shut.

"I've never tried it."

"Me neither. It looks pretty good, though."

He orders it and returns the menu to the holder on the counter.

More silence. I should ignore him and get back to work. But what he said a moment ago gnaws at me. My writer-brain is curious, eager to collect a story that might be useful for a character one day. The odds that he'll tell me something juicy are slim, but it's worth a shot.

"You said it was one of the worst days of your life. Personally, or professionally?" I ask.

"Both. Times ten."

Now I'm *dying* to know. I tilt my head in a manner that's intended to convey openness and warmth. He takes the bait:

"I'd just found out my fiancée was pregnant and I wasn't the dad."

My mouth falls open.

"Want to guess who the dad is?" he says, loudly.

"I . . . I'm so sorry—"

"Yoga Doug. YOGA DOUG. And who can afford therapy, right? I mean, I was actually considering starting an anonymous Twitter account so I could air out my grievances into the void. You know, for free."

I almost smile despite myself. "That sucks. Yoga Doug sounds like a Yoga Douche. Still doesn't excuse your behavior toward a stranger, but I understand it better . . ."

"What about *your* behavior?" he protests. "Demanding way more than your allotment of snacks? Ordering me around like you owned the place? What was that all about?"

I was hangry and I hate it here would sound pathetic, especially in contrast to what he'd been dealing with that day, so I shrug, which is very mature of me.

"Like I said, I'm in a better mood today," I say. "As it turns out, some New Yorkers are extremely thoughtful. None of the ones at *this* table, mind you, but—a new friend, he, um, showed me around and gave me some advice on great restaurants. Really took the time to think about what I might like."

Minimal Bluff. But who cares, it's not like I'll ever be talking to Miles again. Barring another flash flood, perhaps, but even then, I'll think twice.

"A friend?" he repeats. "Or a 'friend' trying to take advantage of your naïve transplant status from Swamptown, USA?"

What on earth is he babbling about? "Swamptown? Where is it you think I'm from?"

And why has he formed an opinion about it either way?

He leans back in his chair. "If I had to guess, I'd say Florida."

I gasp. "Get out." I point to the door. "I rescind your invitation."

He stands, stunned. "What did I . . . ?"

"Sit down."

He does, looking perplexed. "To be fair, your outfit's a little—eccentric . . . to put it mildly . . ."

"Who cares about my outfit! Do I look like someone who would tolerate hanging chads?"

"That's a little before our time."

"It's still a topic of conversation among my friends."

"How old are your friends?"

"Ancient. For the record, I'm from California," I sniff proudly. "The Best Coast."

"That's debatable. Aren't you about two seconds from falling into the sea or getting blown up by nuclear weapons? In between throwing yourselves bloated award shows every weekend, that is." He does an obnoxious little song-and-dance from his seat. " 'Hooray for Hollywood' . . ."

"You seem nice, Miles," I snap. "This has been oodles of fun."

"What can I say? I'm in a good mood, too. Found myself a new apartment, in a sick location, for an even sicker price."

"That *is* good news," I pipe up. "The other side of town, is it, near an entirely different café?"

"You'd like that, wouldn't you?"

"Oh, *I* wouldn't mind either way—considering my sixty-five-percent success rate"—I tap the tabletop lovingly—"but *you'd* be better off. I was only thinking of you."

Evelynn brings the black bean and quinoa bowl over. She stares at us for a moment, then says drily, "You guys finally figured out you could share the table, huh? What did it take, three weeks?"

"Ask Zoey here. She keeps a *record*."

"We're only sharing it for today," I correct her. "Inclement weather and all."

Her expression doesn't change. "Uh-huh."

She leaves, and Miles and I peer down at the bowl of food we're apparently sharing.

"Can we have a separate bowl?" I call to Evelynn's back, which stiffens.

We await her return in silence, but when she swings by our table again, she's empty-handed. Wordless, she lifts the bowl up to reveal a plate underneath and pivots away again.

"It's smaller than I expected," Miles remarks.

"$14.87 doesn't buy what it used to."

I scoop approximately half the quinoa onto the plate.

"I know we discussed your greed earlier, but could you at least *try* to make it equal?" Miles asks.

"What are you talking about, your portion is clearly larger," I respond.

There's a gleam of humor in his eye. "Does Evelynn need to come back and intervene?"

"That sounds like the title song in a musical. 'Intervene, Evelynn!' " I sing, to the tune of "Hello, Dolly." What is happening?! He just sang "Hooray for Hollywood" and now I'm channeling Broadway? Whatever, who cares.

He shifts the bowl and the plate so they're side by side and peers skeptically at them. I can't stop an annoyed snort from escaping.

"For fuck's sake, pick one," I gripe.

He slides the plate closer to him and pushes the bowl at me. "Ladies first."

"What am I, your food taster? Seeing if it's poisoned?"

"You do seem violently determined to keep this table. I don't know what lengths you'll go to."

I place a forkful of black bean quinoa on my tongue. My eyes widen and I contort my face as I force the food down.

He looks nervous. "Well?"

"It's . . . fine," I choke out unconvincingly, reaching for my glass of water and taking a hearty swig.

His nose wrinkles. "That bad, huh?"

"No, nooo," I hedge. "You'll probably like it. Why don't you take a nice, big, enormous bite and find out?"

He looks mournfully down at his food. "Great."

He digs his fork in and scoops out the smallest possible portion, gingerly raising it to his mouth.

A moment later, sounding surprised, he says, "It's delicious. It's really, really good."

I giggle, unable to pretend any longer. "I know."

"Why'd you try to trick me?" he sputters.

"I thought if I made you think it was gross, you might set it aside and I could take it home later."

"You're like . . . a con artist. Are you sure you're not from Florida?"

"Seriously, if you say that one more time . . ."

He devours another couple of bites. "Just answer me this. What's with your arm warmers? And your boots? Nothing about your ensemble makes sense. It's like you're dressed for two different countries, like your top half is at war with your bottom half."

I'm not sure I like the idea of him contemplating my top and bottom halves. Though God knows I've contemplated all of him from the moment he arrived in his clingy wet clothes. A blush threatens to overtake my face again.

"On cool days, it's nice to have the arm warmers on outside, and on hot days, when they crank the a/c all the way up, it's freezing inside and I can't type if my wrists and fingers are cold. Either way, I need them."

"Also to hide your commuter tan?"

I stare at him. "How do you know about my commuter tan?"

Now I'm pretty sure he's the one who's blushing. He tries to play it off with a shrug. "You had the arm warmers off once. Your right arm looked pale compared to your left. I assume from wasting away your life inside a car all day."

He's right, of course. Not about wasting away my life but about how the lopsided tan came about. My left arm out the driver's-side window naturally got more sun while driving to work each day.

"At least the sun shines where *I* come from," I shoot back, nodding to the dire weather outside.

Miles is clearly determined to get back to why he finds my sense of fashion perplexing as opposed to, say, why he's been staring at me so keenly that he knows my tan lines. "And the boots?"

I let him squirm a little before I answer. "My first week here, someone stepped on my foot and broke my toe. I can't risk it happening again."

"Pro tip: Some women wear sneakers to commute and then put on high heels at the office."

"Are you honestly suggesting I change into high heels while I sit at a café?"

"It's basically your office, though, isn't it?"

"I haven't gotten any work done since you sat down," I point out.

He mimes zipping his lip and throwing away the key.

Twenty minutes later, as I sit staring at my blank screen, I have to admit it wasn't his words that were preventing me from working; it was his presence.

It's hard to concentrate with him sitting here. He's probably judging my every breath and movement, finding them lacking in some way.

Florida, I scoff. *How humiliating.*

The next time there's a flash flood, I'll splash home in my apparently ridiculous boots. There will be no repeat offer to share this table, I guarantee you.

Right. Back to work. I've somehow made it to page three of my screenplay, but now I don't like the setting. Or the characters. Or their dialogue.

Why can't the finished script magically appear on my screen so I can *fix* it instead of having to *write* it? Why can't I skip ahead to that part?

Reflexively shifting my laptop so Miles can't see the screen, I check Bree's account for any new messages.

There is one unread one.

GreatSc0t: It was my pleasure. If I may be so bold as to ask, what toppings did you get on your doughnut?

I had thanked Jude for the walking tour, wanting him to know that I—I mean, Bree—was still interested. But I hadn't mentioned meeting up again yet, knowing that a little suspense couldn't hurt at this point since *he* was clearly so interested.

Now seems as good a time as any.

TheDuchessB: I could tell you, but maybe I'd rather just show you sometime. ;-)

I'm thinking about what to follow that up with when I get a ping. He's online.

GreatSc0t: You name the time. I'm there.

I have to double-check Bree's schedule. Before I can write back, I get another message.

GreatSc0t: Choose wisely re: the time. You may not have lived until you've had a butter pecan/rainbow sprinkle/Boston creme doughnut at 2 a.m. on a school night.

TheDuchessB: Rebel.

I'm grinning at my screen and I don't even care that Miles might notice and make fun of me for it. But a quick glance his way reveals that he's far too absorbed in his own work.

TheDuchessB: I'll get back to you with my sched soon.

CHAPTER 13

To: All Tell It to My Heart Employees
From: Leanne Tseng
Re: Last Night

Giles,

I've made an executive decision that you
need to get back over here and do that thing
you did approximately 37—no let's make it an
even 40—more times. My retainer demands it.
I'm in bed now. Naked. Waiting for you to
come. (So that I can come . . .)

L

MILES

65 percent of the time? Zoey has beaten me to the table 65
percent of the time? That's ludicrous. I clearly need to up my
game. Though it's nice to know her name, finally. I mean, for
psychological warfare purposes.

The bad news is, I now live across the street from Café Crudité. Bad news for Zoey, obviously, because her stats are about to take a major nosedive. Miles-High Hair, is it? I'd like to see Zoey Scaredy-Toes beat my commute now.

There's only one word for my new apartment, by the way: spectacular.

I got a response within an hour of submitting my essay with instructions to take my security deposit and first month's rent to an old-fashioned smoke shop on Avenue B, where it took me a minute to find the small, old Polish man camouflaged amongst the large selection of bongs (beautiful glasswork, I noted) that were stacked on the front counter. He didn't respond to my hello, just stuck his hand out for my envelope with the checks, looked them over briefly, and then handed me two keys in return.

I admit I was slightly nervous about what I'd walk into when I put the key in the door. After all, I had done this whole thing sight unseen and the rent was ridiculously cheap. I was expecting some catch: maybe vermin, maybe dead body chalk lines—neither of which was a deal breaker, by the way.

What I walked into was a revelation. A bright, airy, true one-bedroom. The kitchen and bathrooms both had some once-neon pink tiling that were somewhat eighties chic, but everything was functional. The living space was definitely big enough for a couch and a dining (or, let's be real, pinball) table. Wall to wall, the bedroom could fit a full-size bed *and* a dresser. I was on the fourth floor and the building even had an actual elevator! It wasn't working when I got in, but that was hardly the point.

If there was a catch, I didn't want to know what it was and, quite frankly, I'd probably be fine with it. As I'd established with Bree earlier, haunted apartments were all the rage anyway.

What the what?! It's a text from Aisha, but I don't know what she's freaking out about. I send her back a question mark.

I take it you haven't read Leanne's e-mail yet . . .

I saw it come in but since I'm about to run out of my apartment to grab *my* table, I haven't opened it yet.

But Aisha's text piques my curiosity. I take out my phone as I walk to the front door. I'm just about to click on Leanne's subject line when I hear a deep voice ring out in the hallway, "I'm coming out!" Ah, my mysterious neighbor. Not sure if they're a big fan of Diana Ross, auditioning to be an off-brand *Price Is Right* announcer, or possibly making sure the building knows their sexual orientation at all times, but despite the fact that we've never met, I've heard that greeting every single day that I've lived here. You gotta love New York.

I read Leanne's message once.

By the second time, I probably no longer need that cup of coffee. I'm up.

I text Aisha back exclamation points.

Leanne . . . and GILES . . . are . . . , I write.

Boinking. Yes, it would appear so. Now everything makes SO MUCH SENSE.

She's right. Not just all of the little favors Giles has been doing for the company, but also how much more relaxed Leanne has seemed in the past month. I mean, writing an e-mail about her love story with Clifford?!

I half expect to get an "unsend" e-mail—one of the most pointless functionalities in Outlook—or maybe even a follow-up message from her once she realizes her mistake. Then again, I also half expect her, in a typical baller Leanne move, to just let it stand, daring any of us to make mention of it.

Either way, I don't have too much time to ponder, because it's five fifteen a.m., and I need to get over to the café.

I hurry across the street, putting my hand out to warn a speeding taxi to let me by, and am just about to open the door when I sense movement by the picture window.

Un. Fucking. Believable.

The café has been open for all of fifteen minutes. How the hell did she beat me here? Is she sleeping in the back alley? Is she secretly Evelynn's roommate?

She smiles sweetly at me—dimples set to "maximum destruction"—when she sees me walk in, then makes a big show of opening her bag, uncapping her pen, and marking something on her crazy chart.

What a waste of a perfect smile. For a second, I wonder what I'd do if she were my client. She's beautiful, obviously. She's intelligent. But she's also clearly unhinged. Could I copywrite that away?

Probably, I think to myself with a smirk. *I'm really good at my job.*

Scaredy-Toes Zoey rolls her eyes at me, almost as if she can hear my thoughts. I clear my throat, feeling uncomfortable at the idea, and vow to ignore her for the rest of my time here. I get my drink, find the table farthest away from the Table of Champions (damn it! . . . now she's got me calling it something idiotic), and open up my laptop to get to work.

TheDuchessB: Will you take "Random Questions" for 100?

I smile at my screen. This will make it easier to swallow my defeat today.

GreatSc0t: Always.

TheDuchessB: What's your most embarrassing misheard lyric?

I think about it for a second, but the answer comes pretty quickly.

GreatSc0t: You know that Blues Traveler song "Run-Around"? It was on the radio a lot when I was a kid . . .

Though, on second thought, was it? Jude is a few years younger than me . . .

TheDuchessB: I know it.

Oh, well. Luckily, she doesn't seem to be doing the math.

GreatSc0t: I always thought it said, "Use your violin to speed things up." And I figured it was about a magical violin that could make things go in fast-forward.

TheDuchessB: Wow . . . that might make it a better song, actually.

GreatSc0t: I used to dream about owning said violin. Especially during naptime.

TheDuchessB: Not a fan of taking a leisurely sojourn in the middle of your day?

GreatSc0t: As a three-year-old boy? Er . . . no.

TheDuchessB: And now?

GreatSc0t: If I'm taking a midday sojourn . . . I prefer to have company. ;-)

There's a lag in her response. Maybe that came across as too sleazy. I quickly start typing up a damage control message, but I don't get to send it.

TheDuchessB: Sooooo . . . are you still down for meeting up?

YES! I almost pump my fist into the air. I've been waiting days for this. Or, I guess I should say, *we* have. Jude and I.

GreatSc0t: Of course. Holey Cream, right?

Though now that I think about it, Jude probably doesn't eat doughnuts.

TheDuchessB: Actually, there's this other place I've been meaning to check out. It's a pop-up cheese shop called, very cleverly, Cheese. It's in the East Village.

It's actually down the block. I've seen it. But then I remember, Jude doesn't eat cheese, either—a memorable point from their first date. Then again, maybe so many other things went wrong that she doesn't remember. Either way, the fact that she's giving Jude another chance is a big deal and we shouldn't give her any cause to change her mind. I can probably get Jude on board; luckily, he's one of my more affable clients.

GreatSc0t: I'm in. When would work for you?

TheDuchessB: Thursday night?

That's two nights from now. I have to double-check Jude's schedule but . . .

GreatSc0t: Let's pencil it in!

Jude is fine with Thursday night. He's even fine with Cheese. Sort of.

"I guess I'll eat beforehand?" he says to me.

"Maybe," I respond. "Or . . . I don't know. Could you save your calories for the day or something and just eat a small amount? It would be less awkward. . . ."

Jude blinks at me through FaceTime as if he's thinking of saying something. Maybe another deserved question about why we are trying so hard for this one girl. But then he lets it go.

"Sure," he finally says. "I can have Sunday dessert on Thursday this week."

"Great," I say. And now to tell him the other idea I had, which was, in large part, inspired by Leanne's accidental e-mail.

Jude needs this date to go well. I need this date to go well. It's not that I don't trust Jude to not have another stilted conversation disaster . . . okay, it *is* that I don't trust him.

"So, do you remember how I mentioned we have a gold package? That comes with a conversational coach who can sit nearby and feed you lines on a date?" Who would ostensibly be Giles, of course.

"Er . . . yes, I do," Jude says. "But I have to be honest . . . I'm not sure it's in my budget to get another add-on. The photo package . . ."

"Totally, totally," I respond right away. "And it normally is an add-on, but we're actually testing out new equipment . . ." New equipment that Aisha and I have to go to Best Buy to figure out . . . "So we're offering a steep discount right now. Only fifteen dollars for a onetime date."

"Oh," Jude says. "That's not so bad . . ."

"Yup," I say confidently. "It's a very good deal."

"All right. I'll think about it . . ." Jude says.

"Great!" I say. "Do you think you could have an answer by say . . . eight p.m.?"

Because Best Buy closes at nine. And Aisha is not free tomorrow. Out of the two of us, she's the tech whiz, and I'd be more comfortable if I had her with me.

"Tonight?" Jude asks.

"If you wouldn't mind. I just have to make sure everything is in order and our coach is available." I'll let him know later that our regular coach will magically not be available and he is going to end up with me.

"Um . . . all right, sure. Why the hell not? Let's just do it."

I grin at him. "Great. You won't regret it."

I do get a weird kick out of going to Best Buy with Aisha. Because, inevitably, some employee takes one look at my tiny, female cousin and assumes she needs help when it comes to electronics. And then she gets to run circles around their technical knowledge. One time, when she was helping me pick out a router for the new Brooklyn apartment, some smug dude in his thirties actually asked her if she knew what a modem was. Her silence was only her trying to figure out if she should answer or just fall back on her kickboxing.

"We basically want the most unobtrusive Bluetooth headset we can find," she says as she scans the aisle we're in, while I keep an eye out to see if any employees will dare to approach us. I could use the entertainment. "Simplest way is to just have him sync it to his phone, then you call him, feed him lines or what have you and, bada boom."

"Sounds good," I respond.

"I actually found this spy set online." She looks up at me, her voice going up in pitch along with her obvious enthusiasm. "The ear receiver is invisible, goes deep in your ear and needs a magnet to remove. Then you put this necklace around your neck as a receiver, and there's even a Morse code tap thing in your shoes so you can tap out an SOS to whoever's listening."

"Wow," I say. "Who would need that?"

"Um . . . actual spies?" she responds.

"Right," I say. "Or, like, a really hopeless TITMH client."

She laughs. "Yup. You should talk to Leanne. See if she can spare a grand to get one for the company."

"Good idea." I smirk. "I'll also point out that she can spend a lot of time going over the minutia of it with our conversation coach."

"Yeah, right. Like you would dare bring Giles up to her ever again."

"You're right," I respond solemnly. "As far as we're all concerned, Giles is dead. No, he never even existed."

"I aspire to be as badass as Leanne," Aisha says, and sighs as she takes one of the packages off the shelf. "This one should work. But it's a hundred fifty bucks."

"Ugh," I say as I look at it. "I guess it's an investment."

She stands up. "Are you really that worried about the money-back guarantee? I mean, it's a two-strikes-and-you're-out sort of deal, so even if for some reason Jude activates it, you'd still have another shot."

"It's not that," I say, and then hesitate. "Well, it sort of is. I also just, you know, want to make a good impression. On Leanne. I fucked up so much last month." Even though it's not really that either. Would I be doing this for any other client? Or, better question . . . would I be doing this for any other *match* except Bree?

I don't even want to go there because I don't want to give myself the chance to confirm the answer.

"Oh, excellent," I say, as I see an extra-confident-looking dude in a blue polo strolling over to us, opening up his mouth to ask Aisha if she needs help. I take a step back, ready to enjoy the show.

*   *   *

Jude comes to my apartment to test out the headset and then we walk over to Cheese together. But I go in first, telling him to take a stroll around the block before he enters. I don't want to risk Bree seeing us together.

I go into the restaurant and assess the situation. There aren't too many people there. A trio of young women sit at one table, and, behind them, another woman in sunglasses and a fedora-type hat slouches into the corner of her booth. Probably a celebrity of some sort, but I won't risk tarnishing my "I'm obviously a real New Yorker" demeanor by deigning to look closer to find out who it is.

When the waitress comes over, I ask to sit at the booth closest to the door. I slide into the bench facing the rest of the tables, giving me a perfect view of wherever Jude and Bree choose to sit.

I call Jude and he answers on the first ring.

"I'm outside the restaurant," he says quickly and quietly. "And I see her. She's about five feet away."

"Great," I say. "No need to respond to me anymore. I'll just listen in and will be talking to you when necessary."

Jude doesn't say anything, but I hear him greet Bree and then, a minute later, see the two of them walk through the door.

I order food as they are getting seated, so that the waitress will have no reason to have a prolonged interaction with me. And then I settle in to concentrate on the conversation happening twenty feet away.

CHAPTER 14

To: All the Single Ladies
From: Clifford Jenkins
Re: Side Gig

Hello, my fine friends of the female
persuasion,

Rebound relationships are tough. A balancing
act. Some people indulge in a dirty, nau-
seating affair as swiftly as possible, with
whoever happens to be nearby, without regard
to professionalism, hygiene, office harass-
ment policies, or standard human decency.

After stomping on love's carcass,
/ they need an unsatisfying fling
/ to help numb the sting
/ of losing "the real thing."

(Anyone have connections to Eminem or Ken-
drick Lamar? I don't spit rhymes on the reg,

but this one's screaming out for a song; I'll even give it to him for free.) Anyway, we all know people like that, amirite? Not me, though. I'd rather enter into something meaningful. I was reflecting about it tonight, after knocking back a few, and I realized I have access to some of the best creative and romantically inclined minds in the country when it comes to finding and keeping someone special. To that end, I invite you all to submit a poem (no stealing the one above, haha!) for me to put up on my profile (link below), which I plan to go live with on Thursday. It's my first time on a dating site since . . . the obvious . . . and I need to make a good impression.

Let's keep this between us for now. I don't think the dudes need to know at the mo'. (There I go again . . .)

Winner gets a cool $150 and my gratitude.

Yours,
Clifford

ZOEY

One-fifty for a poem? Are we talking sonnet or couplet? (And did you notice the time stamp?? 3:37 a.m.??) I text Aisha as I wait for the elevator. I haven't seen the Sleeper inside all week, which I think is a record.

LOL! Srsly. I could be down for a limerick. Between this

and my other boss's digital get-down (don't ask), I'm setting up a filter. Unless the subject line says "urgent" or "paycheck" all their e-mails are going straight to archive from now on, she writes back.

And then whenever you want to feel profoundly uncomfortable, you can binge them instead of this torturous slow-drip, I reply.

Yes!

I'm about to respond with something along the lines of, "We could make a party of it" when the elevator arrives and I chicken out. We'll see each other at the work meetup next week and I'll test the waters in person, see if she'd like to grab brunch sometime. I don't want to come on too strong; I'm sure she doesn't lack for friends, so I need to make my move organically, pretend it just came to me in the moment. Maybe a café near the High Line.

I tap my foot a few times. The elevator's here but the doors aren't opening. It sits for a moment, and then it's called back down to the ground floor and leaves me behind. *Sad trombone.* Twenty seconds pass before I take a deep breath and head for the stairwell.

Outside, en route to Cheese, I earn squinting double takes from strangers as I walk by. My brown trilby hat, ponytail, artfully shredded jeans, and Holly Golightly sunglasses convince people I'm Someone, if only for a second. If I ever need to disguise myself again, though, I'm stuffing a BabyBjörn with salami. #MillennialMom for the win.

It was easy to get myself invited on Bree's second date with Jude. Over FaceTime, looking contrite and concerned, I offered to drop by in case she needed a bailout. After all, in her view, it was my fault the last date bombed; I owed her one. I told her if it's as much of a dud as the beer flight, she can Ace him for good.

At which point maybe I'll set up a Game, Set, Match profile of my own and . . . nope. Nope nope nope. Keep it professional,

Zoey. Enjoy the opportunity to check him out IRL and leave it at that. Your rent depends on it.

Luckily, she enjoyed Cheese the first time (minus their outside bottle policy) and was happy to go back. She told me to hide in a booth at the back. I don't *need* a disguise, but it made us feel better about me tagging along. If I'm incognito, she can more easily pretend I'm not there and/or that we don't know each other.

Her signal for an intervention will be if she loudly asks their server for a Monster Mozzarella to go. But if she orders the Ricotta Mousse with Balsamic Pepper Cherries to split for dessert, that means she's having a good time and I should skedaddle.

The back of Jude's head is sexy. It's the only part of him I can see from my vantage point, but it's excellent. It has a high fade, with adorably messy textures and flow on top. Sort of like if Miles-High put a little effort in, instead of his patented "I slept wrong, oh well, guess I'll go out in public!" look. (I still can't believe we shared a table last week. I've been checking my weather app each morning and it's clear skies ahead, thank God.)

You can tell Jude works out a lot, but not because he's huge; he's *streamlined*. He probably has abs like a washboard. And yet, he's not a meathead or gym rat, not even remotely. His texts are funny and clever and his profession is, dare I say, altruistic—using his superior knowledge of the human body to help others attain their goals. There's something noble about a job like that.

I wonder if he has any female clients. . . .

Bree looks great. Her hair falls softly down her back, and her crop top and linen pants are casual yet flirty. Was it my imagination, or did Jude look relieved at her choice of outfit and hairstyle?

Right now she's telling him about her last visit: "They made me pay sixty bucks to *open* my bottle of wine. Can you believe it?"

Actually, they made *me* pay sixty bucks, but she's allowed to embellish for a better story.

"Once we get to know each other better, assuming I don't make a guddle of this date, I hope you'll pick out some wine pairings with me sometime, because I'm hopeless at that. My area of knowledge is strictly beer."

Guhhhhh. *Guddle.* He's so hot and humble. Bree better acknowledge how hard he's trying. If she doesn't thank him for the walking tour, I might have to stand up on the table and wave my arms to get her attention. Also, it's both intoxicating and strange to hear him talking, live and in the flesh. I've been listening to his recording on nights when I can't sleep and his smooth, elegant voice always lulls me into a sense of peace.

"It's brilliant really, this place focusing on cheese. When I was in Switzerland, you could order a plate of cheese—"

"Swiss cheese?" Bree interrupts.

"Exactly!" he says (points for enthusiasm). "And with a side of fruit it makes for a perfect meal, so I'm glad you suggested this."

"Thanks for giving it a try."

My daydream about Jude hiking the Swiss Alps shirtless is interrupted by the arrival of their appetizer: cheese curds. Jude picks up four small pieces and . . . juggles them. It's charming and unexpected, and Bree laughs. Score another one for Jude!

He flounders and drops two on the floor. Bree bends down.

"Five second rule," she declares.

"One, two, three, four, five," Jude says.

Crouched on the floor, Bree looks up at him.

"Six," he adds, ominously.

She pops one in her mouth, eats it, and swallows.

"I live on the edge, baby," she says with a wink, and returns to her seat.

He laughs and raises his hand for a high-five and I no lon-ger know what I'm witnessing. If my date essentially licked the floor of a public restaurant, that would be a problem for me. Either the five (or six) second rule also exists in Scottish child-hoods, or he has no intention of kissing her later? (Or ever, one can hope?)

"Do you have any female clients?" Bree asks, eerily echoing my own thoughts from earlier. "Are most of them ramping up for some big event, or summer bikinis, or is that a myth?"

"I mostly work with blokes to be honest, but there certainly is a lot of eye candy at the job in general."

That's a bit . . . odd to mention. How he likes to ogle women at the gym. I mean, it's not offensive exactly, because of course we all like to check out attractive people, especially if they're a bit sweaty and working their bodies into a frenzy in spandex, but—

"Wouldn't it be the *worst* if you were, like, watching a super foxy girl, just a perfect specimen, running on the treadmill next to you and she suddenly let loose with a big ol' fart?" Bree says with a giggle. Then she does a sound effect. A SOUND EF-FECT.

I almost spit out my food. Jesus Christ. She's just thrown her Future Honesty at him. The future is now, apparently.

Far from disgusted, Jude responds instantly: "That's hap-pened! That's really happened to me before!"

"Noo."

"Right hand to God, when they're running it's like they can't hold it in! And then it makes a 'rat-a-tat-tat' like a car engine burst."

He slaps his hand on the table, and they're both laughing so hard the other customers look over.

So far, this date can be summed up thusly: floor cheese and farts.

Huh. Well, okay. Maybe they needed a silly icebreaker after

the awkwardness of their first date, and now they can move on to, shall we say, less flatulence-based conversation. Props to Jude for being so willing to go with the flow. His laughter sounds genuine, too, and since Bree's facing me, I can see how pleased she is that they're connecting.

Jude truly is a saint. A handsome, kind, witty saint. Maybe the "rat-a-tat-tat" sound effect wasn't witty per se, but I like to think he's overlooking all of Bree's behavior because of our—I mean, her—messages the last few weeks. He's willing to put in the extra mile to make her happy, because he thinks I'm—I mean *she's*—worth it for the banter burning up our keyboards.

They move on to discussing Bree's job, and when their main courses arrive, their body language is easily decipherable. She's touched his arm twice, and he's helped the waitress clear away Bree's old dish to make way for Bree's new one. Thoughtful, considerate Jude.

I dig in to my *kanafeh*. It's divine, but I can't help feeling glum over their obvious enjoyment of each other.

It's good, I remind myself. *This is what you're aiming for.*

Then I hear the chilling words: "We'll have the Ricotta Mousse with Balsamic Pepper Cherries to split, for dessert."

No.

Jude leans across the table toward her. "Why wait for cherries when I've got these perfect lips right here?"

Did he just . . . refer to his own lips as perfect cherries? Or did he mean hers? If he meant his own, that'd be a bit egotistical. Unless he's flirt-joking. Yes. That must be it. He's being ironic. And you know, he's not wrong. His lips are pouty-plump and would probably feel *amazing* gliding up and down someone's—Oh. God.

They are kissing. *They are kissing.* I jump up from the table and walk swiftly past them, only to see Bree's hand sliding up Jude's thigh under the table!

Outside, I pace. My mind fills with images. They're going to leave and they're going to go back to his place or her place and they're going to keep kissing, deeper and wetter, and then he'll lift her up effortlessly because he's a freaking *gym trainer* and she'll lock her legs around his lower back and he'll carry her to the bedroom, and . . . I can't let this happen. I just can't.

I dial her number. I get voice mail. I dial again; same result. I text her madly: **I'm outside. MAJOR emergency. I need your help. PLEASE!**

A minute passes and Bree exits the restaurant. Her lipstick is smeared halfway around her face.

"What happened? Are you okay? Are you hurt?" she asks, patting my shoulder.

"I'm fine, I just had to get you out of there."

"What are you talking about? I did the good signal." She looks longingly back inside the restaurant. "Did you mix it up with the bad signal?"

"No, I vetoed it."

"Why? We're having a great time!"

"You can't sleep with him. It's too fast."

"You asked me to give him a second chance, and now that I have, and it's working, you think it's a mistake? This is exhausting."

What *doesn't* exhaust her? "This has nothing to do with me. It's what you wanted. Here's what you said to me the day we first talked. Look, I wrote it down."

I thrust my smartphone in her face, cued up to the notes I took upon meeting her.

DOES NOT WANT TO HAVE SEX TOO EARLY.

(I may have caps-locked, italicized, and underlined it just now to hit the point home.)

Her nose wrinkles and she paces alongside me. "But . . . I'm fully sober. And I want this. Him."

"WELL, YOU CAN'T," I blurt out.

"You're kind of freaking me out right now."

I back off and take some calming breaths. "Here's what I think. It's awesome you guys are feeling each other, it really is, but the worst thing you could do right now is get physical." *Why am I quoting Olivia Newton-John? Why* are *my friends so old?* "You decided to use Sweet Nothings so you could have a different outcome, right? I wouldn't be very good at my job if I didn't at least *try* to help you stick to your plan. If you're having fun tonight, you'll have fun again another night, and another one, and each date after that, until it's a meaningful situation, and, also, you know, it'll be *so* much hotter and more satisfying after all that waiting and waiting, all that buildup rocketing through your bodies, it'll be like . . ." I make an "explosion" noise, complete with hand movements, and I think I'm turning myself on, which is disturbing. I might even be panting. "And then if you want to"—I pause—"take it to the next level, I'll be cheering for you every step of the way." God, I sound creepy.

She blows a puff of air and slowly nods. "I guess you're right."

"Make an excuse, say good night, and leave him hungry for more. If he messages you later, I'll handle it, okay? I'll take it from here. You just go home and chill."

She continues to nod. "Okay. Yeah. Thanks for looking out for me, Zoey."

Bree smooths her hands down her thighs, straightening her pants, and reenters the restaurant.

I head home, my heart pounding a mile a minute.

CHAPTER 15

To: All Tell It to My Heart Employees
From: Leanne Tseng
Re: Speed Ghosting

Team,

Stella does it again! Our feisty freelancer
has come up with yet another brilliant idea.

Over the next week, we're running a promo.
Anyone can sign up for a free "speed ghosting" session with us. What does that mean?
It means they get one free ghostwritten chat
session with a match of their choosing. Our
goal? To retain between 30-50 new clients.

Now while we cannot pay you for the speed
ghosting sessions themselves, there will be
a $250 bonus for anyone who can turn our
prosaic penny-pinchers into full-fledged clients. So let's do this.

And brava, Stella!

Yours,
Leanne

MILES

Will the record please show that I never told Jude to say any-thing about farting? In fact, very little of that conversation ac-tually turned out to be mine. Definitely not worth the price of admission—namely the 150 bucks I paid out of my own pocket for that headset.

It started out fine. I did feed him the line about the wine pair-ings, though he cleverly Scotified it by using the word "guddle."

And then, before I knew it, he was talking about eye candy at the gym. "No, Jude," I said. "We don't want to talk about other attractive women . . ." but before I could tell him why, the two of them were off and talking about gas. As in passing it. Well, I guess that was one way to divert the conversation.

Apparently, the correct way because suddenly they are heav-ily making out in the middle of the restaurant and straight into my inner ear. I have to take my headphones off at one point because it's like listening to a porn podcast.

That might have been a mistake because before I know it, Bree is flying past me and out of the restaurant.

Shit. How did things go downhill so fast?

I look over at Jude, who is looking longingly past me at the door. I'm about to go over to him when the door flies open and Bree comes rushing back in. I don't have my headset in so I don't hear what she says, but she bends over the table for a mo-ment, throws what looks like a piece of paper at him, and then leaves for good.

Jude smiles at her retreating form and then saunters over

to me, lipstick smeared all over the lower half of his face and a sexed-up haze in his eyes. His hair was already too artfully mussed up for Bree's pawing to make a difference.

"You were right. She's amazing," he says to me, still drunk on pheromones.

"What happened?" I ask. "Why did she leave?"

"Her friend had an emergency," he replies.

Huh. "A friend with an emergency" is usually code for someone who was on standby to interrupt the date at a preset signal. But from everything I saw—and heard—it sure didn't look like Bree wanted to be interrupted.

"That's odd," I say.

Jude shrugs. "I thought maybe she might've been bailing on me, but then she kept saying how sorry she was. And slipped me this before she left."

He hands over a cheddar-colored napkin with a kiss stain on it. If I squint, I can make out what looks like an "IOU more of this" in something that looks like chalky grease marks.

"What did she use to write this?" I ask.

"Ricotta mousse," he says, grinning. "She's insanely sexy, no?"

"Yes," I admit. Because she is. In every way. She's got looks, personality, and—apparently—a healthy disregard for inhibition. Good for Jude.

Bastard.

"I'm going to text her," Jude says, taking out his phone.

"What? No!" I say, knocking it down from in front of his face. "It's too soon."

"Really?" Jude asks, puzzled. "I mean, she was just sitting on my lap and, uh, I'm not sure Little Jude was in on the plan to play hard to get. Just, you know, hard." His eyes twinkle, as if he's delighted with his clever pun.

"Right. I get it," I respond curtly. "Even so. Let's give her a little time to think about you. Keep some of the mystery going."

"O-kay," Jude says slowly. "You sure? Seems a bit like playing games just for the sake of playing games."

"Trust me," I say firmly. "There has to be just a smidge of game-playing, at least in the beginning. We'll keep it short. You can text her tomorrow." His face lights up. "Night," I amend.

"If you say so," he says, but he looks disappointed as he puts his phone away.

After he's left and I'm settling my bill, I give myself a post-mortem. If I were in Jude's position, would I have texted Bree right away?

Abso-fucking-lutely. Probably before the door closed on her way out.

So why did I stop him?

It's because you have perspective, I tell myself. *Little Jude—or Little Miles, I guess, though I haven't actually named my dick— isn't steering the ship for me, so I can look at the situation from a more logical standpoint.*

Right?

Right. That has to be it.

I focus on that instead of the strange other feeling that's cropping up in the back of my mind.

Relief that the kiss didn't turn into something more.

And then, disappointment that it didn't.

Which is the proper emotion. I want this to go right for my client. I want what he wants.

I ignore the little voice telling me now: *You're not disappointed because Jude didn't get laid. You're disappointed because now the sexual tension will be drawn out. And what could have been a one-night stand? Could turn into a slow-burn romance.*

I put my headphones back on and drown out that little voice completely with an Iron Maiden Spotify playlist.

By 4:55 the next morning, I've taken a half-hour jog around Tompkins Square Park, showered, gotten dressed, and am casually reading a book as I lean against the side of Café Crudité. I even wait a respectable minute after Evelynn has opened up the café before I saunter in, giving her a big smile and a hearty "good morning."

She narrows her eyes at me before grunting a greeting back.

The table is all mine, of course, and I triumphantly place my bag on its bench before I walk over to the counter.

"How are you doing?" I ask Evelynn before I order, trying to think of something else specific I can ask about and realizing that—despite the fact that I've known her name for over a decade—I don't know a single other thing about her.

"Fabulous," she responds drily. "You?"

"Great!"

"Mmm-hmm," she says shrewdly. "Beat your girlfriend today, huh?" She nods in the vicinity of the table.

"What do you mean?" I ask.

"Anyway. What'll it be? The usual?" This sad excuse for a conversation has clearly been all that Evelynn can handle at 5:04 a.m. on a Tuesday.

"Yup," I respond. "Oh, and how about a muffin. Carrot raisin."

"Living dangerously," she mutters, not even remotely under her breath.

I smile at her as I slip a five in the tip jar, but she barely even glances at it.

Okay, so maybe I need to try harder to get into Evelynn's good graces.

I sit at the table and for the next few hours I am ostensibly working on a couple of new clients. Clark has made initial contact with a guy who looks promising and I'm crafting his response message. Diego has signed up for this new speed ghosting initiative (I'm beginning to think I may have to put out a hit on Stella), and, though I thought his free chat session went well, I am currently fielding a multitude of questions from him about the packages and trying to work through his reluctance to sign up.

I say ostensibly because in reality, I am waiting for one of two alerts. The bell of the front door signaling that Zoey has come in and seen me basking in the spoils of my victory; or the Game Set Match ping from Jude's open profile, signaling that TheDuchessB has started a chat.

Three times I go to start a chat myself.

I'm trying to woo a jaded barista into deeming me worthy of morning chitchat. I write the first time, then delete.

Do you think Mary Clarkson kept the costumes and, if so, do you think any of her boyfriends ever had her role-play with them? I try the second time and delete it again.

The thing is, I don't need to be writing her at all. I told *Jude* not to text her until tonight and he needs to make the first contact for real at this point.

So moving on from misheard lyrics, what's one song everyone loves that you can't stand? At the risk of having you never speak to me again, I'll take the plunge and go first: "The Rainbow Connection."

I hit send. Apparently, I'm unable to talk sense into myself at this point. But why?

Christ, isn't it obvious? the little voice says.

TheDuchessB: SACRILEGE.

If it wasn't obvious before, the huge smile on my face and the way my fingers fly across the keys should make it so.

GreatSc0t: But just think about it . . . there *aren't* so many songs about rainbows. Just like . . . "Over the Rainbow." The whole song is built on a lie!

TheDuchessB: Do you hate the Muppets too? And sunshine? I'm starting to get worried this isn't going to work out . . .

GreatSc0t: Of course I don't hate the Muppets. Well,

at least not all of them . . . can we maybe discuss Miss Piggy's narcissistic personality disorder though?

TheDuchessB: MISS PIGGY IS AN ICON AND A TREASURE. Though I agree she and chipmunk Alvin would make an epic crossover. As of this moment, I'm a Pigvin shipper.

I laugh out loud. At my laptop screen. While in public.

And, of course, that's when I can no longer deny what's actually happening.

I like Bree. As in me, Miles.

And if there's one thing that breaks all the rules, not only of my job, but also of my own self-prescribed romantic exile, it's that.

The #1 rule of your job: It's a job. Always make sure you're keeping yourself from getting too personally invested in a client or a match. When dealing with love, emotions can run high. Keep yours in check.

So, no. This cannot happen.

This *cannot* happen.

GreatSc0t: Whoops. Running late for a client. Let's discuss at a later time . . . hopefully in person. ;-)

And then I log off. I need to remember to tell Jude this convo happened.

More importantly, I need to remember to back the fuck off.

The best way to do that? Make sure Bree and Jude get together. No more weird, sabotaging pseudo-advice. No more off-the-cuff chat sessions.

From now on, I'm following my own *Freelancer's Handbook* to a T and making sure this goes to its natural conclusion of happily ever after. For them.

CHAPTER 16

To: Zoey Abot
From: Aisha Ibrahim
Re: Fw: Hamptons Emergency

HE NAVIGATED AROUND MY FILTER THE FIRST TIME
OUT! WILY BASTARD!

p.s. THERE IS NO SUCH THING AS A "HAMPTONS
EMERGENCY"

p.p.s. SORRY FOR SHOUTING BUT HOW IS CLIFFORD
IN THE HAMPTONS WHILE I'M WORKING A THIRD
JOB

p.p.p.s. CONGRATS ON WINNING THE POETRY CON-
TEST

Begin Forwarded Message:

To: Party People
From: Clifford Jenkins
Re: Hamptons Emergency

Ugggggggh, the house I'm renting this weekend has a leaky sink, broken locks, and the
blinds are torn. What's a guy gotta do for a
little privacy?

Anyone know a reliable crash pad for a dude
in need? I'll owe you a crisp high five.

Also, keep up the good work, my soldiers
of love. Not a single person has asked to
switch ghosties since the plan was imple-
mented. That speaks super highly of each and
every one of you. I always knew I'd hired the
best in the business, and here's the proof!

Fist bump to Zoey A., aka the Zo-ster, for
knocking my socks off her with her wicked-
ass prose for my profe.

Namaste,
Clifford

ZOEY

The reason Clifford liked my poem was because I copied his
e-mails into a word cloud app to uncover his most-used phrases,
then fiddled around for a few hours until the sentiments
rhymed. (He was definitely the kind of person who believed
poems must rhyme.)

I'd fed his own words back to him. You—Only Better was the original name of his company, after all. Of course, instead of writing ethically gray-area poetry, regardless of the paycheck, what I *should* have been doing was opening Final Draft and starting page four of my screenplay. And what I should be doing now, instead of reliving my win, is hauling ass to Café Crudité.

The problem is, it's already twenty-five past six. Miles will have snagged the good table by now, and rage suppression doesn't leave much room for creativity. He commandeers it more often than not on Wednesdays; not sure what the outlying factors are. I need a new chart that analyzes his frame of mind and not just the nuts and bolts of arrivals and departures.

I need a life.

I decide to stay home today and deny him any caffeinated schadenfreude. Caffeinfreude. It gives me a kick imagining the moment he realizes he could've slept in. In that sense, *I've* won the day.

An alert arrives on my phone: $150 (the poem payoff) has arrived in my PayPal account. *Godspeed, Clifford, may it bring you a match. And may she have some type of language barrier situation going on so she can tolerate you.*

Final Draft dares me to open it. Simultaneously, my apartment requires dusting. Funny how that happens.

Armed with dampened paper towels, I dust while listening to music. Then I close my eyes and just listen to music, hoping to coax my muse out. The problem is, I don't like any of my screenplay ideas. When I was a teenager, I wrote fanfic (aka "fixing what TV shows did wrong, or expounding upon what they did right") and I always assumed it was practice for writing my own stories. That was supposed to be the goal, after all. And when I got the gig with Mary, I told her I wanted to be a screenwriter. I'd barely heard of script doctoring, didn't know there were people whose jobs it was to help shape *other* people's screenplays. But Mary sent me here to write original material—she's subsidizing me, essentially. It's what she thinks I should do, so I have to keep at it. I have to at least *try*.

When I needed a creative jump start in LA, I'd stroll the La Brea Tar Pits. The thick, primal, bone-trapping smell reaching out from the earth's sordid past comforted me for reasons I couldn't begin to explain. Random fact: La Brea in Spanish means "tar pits," so we're all actually going around saying The Tar Pits Tar Pits.

When that didn't work, well, I'd get stoned. That's not an option in New York, unless I go through the trouble of procuring a medical marijuana card. (What would I say my health issue is, "dependent on weed"?) There is wine in the fridge, however. I just need half a glass, something to mellow me out, get rid of the low-key panic running through me all the time.

Half a glass turns into three or four. I've never been a day drinker, so chalk that up as another reason this city is ruining me. Six hours of buzzed YouTubing later, I guiltily open Final Draft. I have wasted this whole day. Nothing's working! Everything I write I end up deleting.

My hand darts of its own volition to a different folder: my secret treasure trove of Jude messages, copied and pasted from our conversations the past few weeks.

The only person who makes me feel even *slightly* like I'm not drowning is Jude. I click on a document, and relief settles on me like a soft, cool, satin sheet.

Right before dinner, Bree tells me to message Jude later to confirm their upcoming plans tomorrow. She can't do it herself because she's going out with her girls and they apparently confiscate each other's phones. (*But how will the rest of us spend our evenings if we don't get to see what they eat?* I wonder sarcastically.) I'm just sore because three days ago, Bree and Jude snuck off on a smoothie date without me knowing.

Worse, it was her favorite date so far! The one I had nothing to do with!

Pride and (what else) prejudice war inside me. Pride that my so-called dick-picker is superior to hers and landed her a great match. Prejudice because I don't think she's on Jude's level, and never will be. I'm not ready to give up texting privileges with him, despite her instructions not to linger while messaging him tonight.

Was it inevitable that I'd fall for him? If you toss a twenty-something (I can claim that age for one more week) into a new city with no friends or support, force her to cyber flirt with eligible, attractive men who self-describe as "seeking meaningful relationships," what do you think is going to happen?

You can see why, then, I'm not in the mood for a brief conversation. And why I might wait until eleven p.m. to do it.

TheDuchessB: You up?

GreatSc0t: Is this where I make the requisite double-entendre?

TheDuchessB: If you must . . .

GreatSc0t: I'll find a way to resist.

GreatSc0t: Hard time sleeping?

TheDuchessB: Little bit. You?

GreatSc0t: Hard *something*. (ba-dum-dum) Sorry. I repressed the first joke, but suppressing two in a row is a bridge too far.

TheDuchessB: Like farts. Suppressing them. LOL

Ugggggh. I loathed typing that. But it's "in character."

The pause after my fart joke seems endless; did I do it wrong? Maybe they've passed that phase of their interactions and it's no longer amusing? Not that it's a recognized phase anywhere else on God's green earth. But no, soon enough a new message pops up.

GreatSc0t: LOL yes

TheDuchessB: Just confirming tomorrow's shindig.:) Almost today's . . .

GreatSc0t: Cool, really looking forward to it.

TheDuchessB: If I woke you, I can go, we'll be seeing each other soon, so

GreatSc0t: No that's okay. I'm definitely awake.

TheDuchessB: Want to guess my favorite sleep game? You get three tries.

GreatSc0t: Okay. Based on my own experience, is the game 1) Let's All Panic About Not Being Able to Sleep 2) The Sheets Are Bunched at the Foot of the Bed, So Now I Must Curl My Foot Into a Crude Hook to Grasp and Pull Them Back Up 3) The Mystery of the Pillow That No Longer Has a Cool Side

TheDuchessB: All excellent guesses. *buzzer noise* But all wrong. Here's how you play the Sleeping Game. You close your eyes and try to convince yourself you're in a different bedroom. Could be the same house, could be someone else's house, as long as it's a place you know well and can recreate in your mind.

Tonight I'd been imagining my guest room at Mary's in as much detail as I could: the bedside drawer with the loose handle, the alarm clock, reading lamp, tissue box, desk, wall mirror, basket of yarn and crochet hooks, ten-inch TV on the dresser, and the bookshelf composed entirely of lurid murder mysteries from the 1970s.

GreatSc0t: How do you win?

TheDuchessB: To win, you have to experience doubt about your surroundings, convince yourself you really ARE in that other room, on the king- or queen-size or whatever-size mattress, AND that you're on the opposite side of the bed. If you roll over, you'll fall out of bed.

GreatSc0t: That's how you win? By falling out of bed?

TheDuchessB: I've never won before, but yes—that's the objective.

GreatSc0t: Your goal is to concoct a fantasy world that feels so rich and real you'll injure yourself.

TheDuchessB: PRECISELY

GreatSc0t: I think I'd rather picture the occupant of a different room. Her face, for example. Her hair. The person I'm thinking about is pure tidy when it comes to styling her hair.

I've never heard that expression before, but for some reason it causes a pleased blush of warmth to spread through my limbs, which is ridiculous; it's not MY hair he's talking about. If he knew Bree was a construct, that she was two of us and we could be separated out, which one would he pick? Is there any universe in which he'd pick me?

I think of Mary, pushing me out the door, all the way to the opposite coast, then hiring a new assistant like it was nothing, like the last eight years meant nothing.

I think of my parents, so pleased with themselves for going where the wind takes them that they've never tried to steer themselves in my direction.

TheDuchessB: Why thank you. I try ;) I think you might have been onto something, when you asked if I couldn't sleep.

GreatSc0t: Have you tried counting goats? Much better than sheep, for obvious reasons.

TheDuchessB: Sheep go to heaven, goats go to hell.

GreatSc0t: Yup. Cake!

I doubt Bree listens to Cake. Whoops. Oh well. And if I'm digging my own grave here, might as well make it worth the trouble.

TheDuchessB: I haven't heard from my parents in a while. Which isn't unusual, but . . . sometimes it bothers me.

GreatSc0t: Not super close?

TheDuchessB: Let's put it this way: I don't know where they are. I couldn't even begin to guess. They're "free spirits."

GreatSc0t: Were they always like that? Or is it an empty nest / retirement thing?

TheDuchessB: Always like that. One time when I was 8, we went to see the circus in Morocco, and they encouraged me to join it. They would've been overjoyed if I'd run away from home and joined the circus. Because that's their definition of living. But living with them already WAS a circus.

I know I'm playing with fire talking about my own life, but I've kept details vague enough, I think, that I can get away with it. Also, before we sign off, I can always pretend I was joking or something.

Because who would have parents like that?

CHAPTER 17

MILES

GreatSc0t: I get it. My parents' love story is so epic. And mostly that's a really nice thing except . . . sometimes it's a lot to live up to. How could my own romances ever compete?

No way in hell should I have written that. Because of course it doesn't describe Jude's life, but my own. I don't even know the deal with Jude's parents. Maybe they divorced in some sort of epic Highlands land grab and one of them ended up getting a Scottish castle in the settlement. This is something that would be easy for Bree to fact-check the moment she and Jude get a little closer.

But I can't help it. I guess I know my time with Bree is winding down and there's a part of me that needs to let her know how much I understand exactly what she's saying. And maybe there's a part of me that wants her to understand me—Miles me—even if just for the briefest of moments.

TheDuchessB: Maybe we could find a way . . . ;-)

There's a small pang, knowing it can't possibly be true, not for me and Bree anyway. But I can help orchestrate something like that for Jude and Bree. That's enough, right? Of course it is. That's what I've been telling myself all along.

TheDuchessB: So are we still on for tomorrow?

GreatSc0t: Definitely. Can't wait.

TheDuchessB: See you then.

It's a relief that she ends the conversation, because the startling truth is I'm not sure I would have been able to.

It's also ironic that we spent most of the conversation talking about beds because the foam mattress I ordered last week finally arrived today. Filling my new apartment up with furniture has been more problematic than I anticipated. I had my couch and pinball table delivered from my storage unit, but Jordan kept the bed and everything else that we'd bought after I had—stupidly, as it now turned out—sold all the rest of my own stuff when we'd moved in together. Not that I wanted the bed we'd shared, but three months of sleeping on a couch was reminding me that I—and my joints—weren't exactly eighteen anymore.

Now I spend the rest of the night with the lonesome duty of putting together a bed frame that I bought on Craigslist (from a promised "bedbug-free" home, though I 100 percent You-Tubed how to inspect it for myself) on my own. I hammer it together and watch the miraculous science of a tightly packed wad inflating into a full-size mattress in mere minutes, trying not to think about how this is the most excitement my bed has seen in months. And when I put on my new sheets and lie on it that night, I try to focus on the fact that my couchhead days are over, instead of focusing on the empty stretches of time ahead mirrored by the empty space beside me.

I've been at the café for almost four hours the next day before Zoey deigns to walk in. Thank God. It'd be an utter waste to have gotten here early—again—without the satisfaction of watching her mark up her Table Champion sheet. Besides, I've been feeling mopey this morning and I could use a little boost, even if it comes in the form of winning a truly inane game that nobody except the two of us even knows exists (though that's not entirely true: Evelynn has obviously begrudgingly been keeping track too).

I settle into my chair a little more, purposely making it scrape across the tile floor. She glances my way, but only for the briefest of moments, and with no reaction. That's when I notice that she's on the phone.

"Saturday? I'm . . . I'm free. I mean it's my b . . ." Zoey gets in line behind the counter. There is one person in front of her, a portly, middle-aged man, and he is giving his order loudly to Evelynn. Zoey scoots a little to the side and cups her phone. "No. Of course it'd be great to see you," Zoey mumbles, only she doesn't sound like she means a word of what she's saying.

Mr. Outdoor Voice has just finished booming out his order and steps aside, clearing the way for Zoey. "Could you just hold on one second, Dad?" She blinks up at Evelynn, looking as if she doesn't remember why she even went up there in the first place.

Evelynn waits a moment before she asks, "Usual? Medium drip?"

"Yes," Zoey says and then, after scanning the glass counter, "actually, no. I'll also get that quiche Lorraine. And, um, a slice of zucchini bread. And a mini red velvet cupcake. And . . . what's a vookie?"

"Vegan cookies," Evelynn responds.

"Yeah, sure. Three of those."

Evelynn grabs her tongs and starts putting the baked goods on a plate while her coworker begins to heat up the quiche.

"I'm back," Zoey says miserably into the phone as she pays for her food, grabs the plate, and moves over to wait for her quiche. She listens for a while before responding. "At a café." Pause again. "In the East Village."

"Quiche Lorraine," Evelynn calls out.

"Oh, that's me," Zoey says and she goes to grab the plate that

Evelynn just put out. Only she seems to forget that she's already holding another plate, along with her phone. The cookie plate goes clattering to the floor, shattering into pieces and throwing all of its baked goods to the four corners of the café. As she futilely tries to grab for it, her phone goes flying out of her other hand, but not before she must've accidentally hit the speaker button because suddenly a scolding female voice is booming out from the floor.

"I really hope you're not contributing to the blatant gentrification and homogenization of the East Village, Zoey. Of course you know we met a family in Ethiopia who had a restaurant on Second Avenue for years before they were priced out, and then do you know what moved into their space? A molecular Ethiopian-slash-Japanese fusion bistro. Run by a Vegas conglomerate. This is exactly the sort of thing that keeps us from ever coming back to the States."

"Why don't you get your coffee from a nice bodega? Or a food truck?" a male voice calls out.

"A *real* food truck," the woman clarifies. "Not one of those artisan grilled cheese affairs run by the trust fund offspring of the one percent."

"Obviously," the man says.

Zoey is on her knees now, frantically pressing the speaker button on her phone. Only it doesn't seem to be working. I think because her hand is smeared with cream cheese frosting from her unsuccessful attempt to grab at the red velvet cupcake.

I walk over, kneel down to take the phone from her, and press the button for her.

"Thanks," she mumbles, her voice shaky. She looks at the phone in my hand like it's a ticking time bomb.

I don't know what possesses me but I hold it up to my ear and speak into it. "Is it okay if Zoey calls you back?"

"Who is this?" the startled voice that I assume belongs to Zoey's mom says in my ear.

"This is her comrade, Vlad," I respond smoothly. "We're just about to start our march in Washington Square Park. Workers of the world, unite!" And then I hang up the phone.

Zoey gives out a loud honk, a laugh that is dangerously close to becoming a sob.

"Good thing this is made from renewable sugarcane instead of ceramic." Evelynn has walked over with a broom and is pointing to the plate, which has broken into three large pieces instead of shattering into a million.

"Sorry," Zoey says as she reaches over to clean up.

"I got it. Don't worry," Evelynn says, her voice softened just a tad, as she begins to sweep.

Zoey nods, biting her lip and, in another sign of an impending breakdown, giving a loud sniffle.

I suddenly remember that I have a clean HankyBook in my messenger bag. Jordan and I bought a three-pack last year (I realize now she kept the extra one for herself). It's a handsewn Kleenex substitute, made of 100 percent organic cotton and shaped like a book with eight small pages. You use it like a handkerchief and turn the page each time you have a new use for it. And when it's "full" so to speak, you toss it in the laundry. It's supposed to last for years. I'm not quite at the level of composting, but I try to do my part here and there.

I walk back over to our table, and grab it out of my messenger bag. By the time I've made it back over to Zoey, the tears are falling fast and free.

"Shit," she says, wiping at her face.

"Here," I say, crouching beside her and handing her the HankyBook. She stares at it in confusion.

"What is this?" she says, holding the floral-covered fabric book between her thumb and forefinger.

I explain the basic gist. "Just turn to a new page—it's perfectly clean."

She starts to open it, but she's turning in the wrong direction, to the previously sneezed-in section, which is terrible on many levels. "No!" I shout. "Never go backward. Always forward, always moving forward."

She flails and flings the HankyBook at my chest. "I don't want your analogy rags!"

Her cheeks are still wet. I give up on saving trees and hand her a fistful of napkins.

"I guess it *is* a good metaphor for life," she sniffles. "Never go back. Always move forward. Easier said than done, though."

She peers at me with her mostly dry eyes. Her eyelashes are damp and I don't know why, but it's pretty. "Why are you being so nice to me? Comrade," she adds, a small smile on her face.

"I . . . I just wanted to make sure you marked down who won today in your little chart," I respond as I hold out my hand to help her up. "The last *two* days, actually. Go ahead, open your notebook. I'll wait."

She laughs. "I thought you *couldn't care less* who gets the table."

"I don't," I say. "But since you're the one who wants to keep score, I just want to make sure you're doing it fairly." We've both unintentionally walked over to the big table so that we're now standing on either side of it.

"Uh-huh." She noisily slides out the chair she's standing by and sits down in it. "You really think you won two days in a row?"

"Unless you've somehow managed to get your hands on an invisibility cloak, I'd say so."

"And to think, I was sleeping that whole time. Having a long, luxurious, good old-fashioned lie-in." She stretches out her arms in demonstration. "Still think you won?"

I rap the tabletop with my knuckles. "This isn't fun unless you're angry about it."

She sighs. "I think I'm already too emotional to add anger to the mix today. Sorry about them, by the way." She gestures with the hand that is still clutching her phone.

"Honestly, I've always wanted to try out my stringent leftist persona," I say. "I'd say it suits me."

She laughs. "Maybe. Except for not really being a Vlad."

"I could be a Vlad!" I say, sitting down in the chair across from her. "I think you're being closed-minded."

"You're right." She nods solemnly. "I shouldn't be so prejudicial about my idea of a Vlad. I apologize."

"Accepted," I say.

"Anyway, I wish Vlad could come with me on Saturday when apparently, I'm going to have to have dinner with them."

"Your parents?" I ask.

She nods.

"Well, if you really mean it . . . he could. In a way." I'm not sure exactly why I'm offering her this, except that I've felt very off the past couple of days and I would love to restore some order to my life, even if it's in the form of turning my forlorn café nemesis back to my sarcastic café nemesis. Besides, it still stings that I spent $150 on that headset for nothing.

"What are you talking about?"

"I have a way to feed you lines during your dinner. If you want."

Zoey is staring at me incredulously. "I would think you're joking," she says slowly, "but from what little I know of you, that seems like the exact sort of thing you would have."

I shrug. "I use it for work."

"Why? Are you a dialogue coach or something?" she asks.

"Something like that."

"Huh," she says. "Not what I would've pegged you for."

"And what would you have pegged me for?" This ought to be rich.

"I don't know. Social media manager for one of those hipster mail order glasses companies?"

"Wow. That's . . . oddly specific." Has she actually spent time pondering what I do?

"Anyway," she says. "I actually write lines for a living too." I cock my head at her until she clarifies. "Screenwriter."

"Ah. LA. That makes sense. So, got it. You don't need help with your dialogue then." I shrug.

"Yeah, well . . ." She looks down at her closed laptop. "I do a pretty good job for fictional characters and . . . other people. For my own life—not so much." She looks up at me, eyes glinting in a disarming way. "You know what? I'll take you up on that offer."

I stare at her and blink. "You will?"

"Sure," she says. "If you meant it, that is, and weren't just trying to find a way to prolong a conversation with me." She smiles sweetly, batting her eyelashes an extra time or two.

"I meant it," I say. "This is about a headset. And a service I can offer. That's all."

"Cool. Works for me. Can I get your number and text you the time and place of the dinner?"

I take out my phone briskly, determined to show her this is strictly business even though . . . it isn't, unless I'm in the business of offering conversational coaching to random enemies I make at cafés.

We exchange numbers and then I decide I've worked enough for the day. I gather up my bag. "Enjoy the table," I say. "But don't forget. The tally."

She shakes her head at me. "Here. You can watch me do it." She slowly takes out the notebook, opens up to the right page, and makes two exaggerated marks underneath the MHH column. "Satisfied?"

"For now," I say. "See you."

When my alarm rings at four fifteen the next morning, I consider sleeping in. I remember Zoey's taunt that that's exactly what she had done the past two days. I hit snooze.

At four thirty, it goes off again. Does her little table tally really matter? Besides, maybe we've reached a new level in our relationship, one where we act more mature than a five-year-old. I hit snooze again.

At four forty-five, I bolt out of bed. I don't have time for a run, but I take the world's quickest shower, throw on a T-shirt and jeans, and slip out the door with my hair still wet. I've just put my key in to lock the door behind me when I hear my enigmatic neighbor yell, "I'm coming out!" Finally, this mystery will be solved! The doorknob turns. I face the other door, waiting with bated breath.

She's not looking up when she emerges, and her blond-brown hair is covering most of her face, so my mouth is gaping before hers is.

"Aaaaaaaaaaah!" she screams when she finally realizes there's a human body standing right in front of her. And then, when she realizes exactly whose human body it is: "How did you get into my building?" She's literally clutching at her heart, and looking at me as if I'm some sort of stalker who might've followed her in here.

"It's *my* building," I say.

"You have got to be fucking kidding me," she hisses and I don't know why it bothers me so much that she seems totally offput by seeing me there.

But it triggers an unpleasant feeling in my gut, powering the force of words that come out of my mouth. "I can't believe *you're* the one yelling into the void every time you leave your apartment!"

"It's not into the void," she snaps. "It's because this hallway is so damn small, my neighbor told me to do it as a *courtesy* so that we don't bowl each other over. Courtesy . . . maybe you've heard of it."

I snort. "I should've known. Who the hell else would actually be scared of coming out into a HALLWAY? Probably the same person who seems to cower at the thought of her own parents coming into town."

The way Zoey glares at me, I think I may have finally stepped over the line. I'm about to open my mouth to apologize when she suddenly surges ahead, ramming into my shoulder, and zooming past me to go thundering down the stairs.

I know exactly where she's going. And despite her head start, *no way* is she getting there first.

CHAPTER 18

ZOEY

My head swells with the theme song for *The Amazing Race*.

I knew a woman who worked in postproduction for that show. She said the camera guys had to run, too, to keep up with the contestants and get the shots they needed. It cracked me up envisioning entire entourages booking ass in crowded cities, frantically dodging all manner of obstacles at airports and train stations, burdened with heavy, expensive equipment.

Today I'm not laughing.

I've learned something about Miles today: He's the type of person who turns things around on you, takes what you've told him and twists it to hurt and belittle you. In other words, the exact stereotype of a New Yorker. Why had I allowed myself to think he was better than that? Was it the HankyBook that tricked me? And if so, why? In retrospect, he probably wanted to infect me with whatever plague it's carrying. I should've known better; the first time we interacted he showed me his true colors. Imagine if I'd really opened up to him! The very idea of it makes me shudder.

Footsteps thunder above me and I take the stairs two steps at a time, almost tripping and falling when my foot lands wrong. Just what my broken toe needs: a sprained ankle to go with it.

He sounds fast. Fuck. I haven't smoked pot in weeks—shouldn't that count for something? I don't expect to sprint like a cheetah, but in comparison to the beginning of the year I've been a paragon of health. And wait a second, toking is supposed to expand your lung capacity—I swear I read that somewhere—so what's the deal with the stitch in my side and my gasping, labored breaths right now? Should I remove my laptop and toss the bag at him to slow him down?

"Did you move here so you could win?" I shout upward. "That is full-on, Shake 'n Bake CRAZY."

No response. I resist the urge to stop and look behind me. I take the corner at full speed, using my palms to ricochet off the wall. I make it to the ground floor, gasping, my chest heaving, only to see the elevator doors open and Miles dart out ahead of me.

Today of all days it decides to work? For him?

"Can we stop for a second?" I call after him, panting.

He's already out of the building, and a vision of him soaking wet, wearing an Adidas tracksuit jacket the day we shared the big table, enters my brain. He's a *runner*. Of course. This is probably a warm-up for him; he won't even break a sweat.

Even if he weren't so athletic, my inability to cross the intersection in anything resembling a timely manner will prevent me from winning, but I'm not about to make it easy for him. Winded and sore, I zigzag through pedestrians on the sidewalk, muttering angrily to myself. Acting—whaddaya know—like a New Yorker.

I don't think I've moved this fast since I was nine years old, fleeing "the fuzz" in Manila with my parents after they released a bunch of weasels in a government building connected to President Estrada. It was widely known he'd benefited from a stock manipulation scheme. This act of rebellion was their "audition" to join an underground group, and they passed with flying colors. (Shortly after, Nana issued her ultimatum: *This is no way for a child to live. Come with us to California, or let me have her.*)

Speaking of California, if Miles and I were there now, I'd have creamed him in a drag race. He probably doesn't even have a driver's license.

As predicted, Miles beats me to the café, but to my confusion, he hasn't yet gone inside. He lingers on the sidewalk, peering in.

"Is it closed?" I gasp as I near him.

"Worse." He points.

I look through the window. The pregnant mom and toddler from a week ago are back. Correction: The no-longer-pregnant mom, toddler, *and* newborn, are back, settled in at our table. Er, my table. *The* table.

Suddenly the race seems winnable.

"I got this," I say with a smirk. "We're practically sorority sisters."

"Yeah, no, she just arrived," Miles says. "She's not going anywhere."

I frown. "Really? Won't she have to breastfeed soon?" The newborn is wailing its wee head off. The window partially shields us from the sound, but by the looks of the other customers, it's pretty bad.

"Sure, but she can do it right there," he reminds me.

My phone shakes with a rapid-fire flurry of texts. Bree.

Tomorrow's the big night! Pink or green?

Attached are two images of the different lingerie she's choosing between. Shit!

I shouldn't respond. It goes beyond my purview as a ghostwriter, and I don't have time for this. But the idea of her and Jude bumping pretties jolts my nerves.

NOT YET, I text-scream. **YOU'LL REGRET IT, TOO SOOOOON**

"Are you having a seizure?" Miles asks, leaning over to see what's got me texting so madly.

I shove my phone away and glare at him. "Did you seriously move to my apartment building so you could set up shop here every morning?"

He looks disgusted. "How was I supposed to know it was yours? The real question is, why have you only gotten the table sixty percent of the time when you live across the street? How did I get it *any of the times*?"

"Better question: Why can't you just let me have it?" I shout.

"Why should I?"

"Because I can't go anywhere else!" I grit out, shame and anger clenching my teeth together.

"Where were you going to meet up with your parents? Cheese?" he replies sarcastically.

"No, they already booked a place," I reply testily. "In Midtown."

Thinking of Cheese makes me think of Jude, who would NOT be shitty to me about my fears, which, by the way, do not include my parents. They're a whole different subcategory of misery. (Jude, who's about to get laid, unless I can convince Bree it's not yet the right time.)

"Now if you'll excuse me . . ." I nudge his shoulder with mine and enter the café.

Baby Mama clutches her grande latte with tense fingers. She looks like she's entered a fugue state; the baby's shrieks haven't abated but the mom's vacant gaze seems to imply she's on a different plane of existence.

"Tough day, huh?" I ask gently.

"I know nobody wants me here," she says. "But where am I supposed to go?"

"I hear you. I get it," I say emphatically, hoping she'll infer that I have kids stashed somewhere, that I've been on the front

202 / TASH SKILTON

lines too, and maybe mine are grown or at school or—has camp started yet?

"Do you want some help getting them packed up, or . . . ?" I prompt.

"My coffee's gone cold," she mutters, to no one in particular.

"Let me get them to reheat it for the road," I suggest with a sympathetic nod, and reach my hand out for it.

Her response is to pull the mug closer to her chest as though I'm a threat.

I fold a napkin into a passable bunny and turn my back to them, letting the bunny peek out from over my shoulder. I loved origami as a kid and some of the shapes are imprinted in my brain. The baby goes silent with curiosity. The toddler, Nathan, squeals.

"That's cute," the mom says tonelessly. "How did you do that?"

I hand the bunny to Nathan—who promptly lets it unfold, perplexing the baby—and provide her with a tutorial.

After a few minutes of companionable conversation, I nod toward the kids. "They might prefer a jungle-gym type scenario. . . ."

The mom's eyes flash. "What about what *I'd* prefer? Besides a time machine or a Swedish massage."

"Not suggesting you leave now," I backtrack quickly. "No, no, take your time, just *eventually*, after you've had a rest . . ."

"There is no rest," she says. "There is no peace."

"It's just that some people are trying to work," I murmur before I can stop myself.

Miles, standing by the sugar and cream area, drops the sugar. Eyes wide, his gaze darts between us. Even without his reaction, I know I've screwed up.

"I'm not a pariah. I'm allowed to be out in society!" she says. "And this is not an office!"

"Can I get an amen?" (Evelynn, loudly, by the iced tea dispenser.) "Can I get a hallelujah?"

The baby suddenly burps up whatever it most recently ingested, dousing its onesie.

I'm guilt-ridden, and head to the bathroom to find paper towels so I can help the mom for real, without ulterior motive.

When I return, though, she's vanished, and Miles sits at the table. I want to scream. I seriously want to scream.

"Practically sorority sisters, huh?" he mimics me, deadpan. "So when are you guys going to be braiding each other's hair?" He makes a big show of spreading out all his items, making it crystal clear I'm not invited.

Our truce, or whatever the hell was going on the day of the storm, is officially over.

Worse, I have no support for dinner tomorrow with my parents.

Unless . . .

I place the paper towels on the sugar and cream stand and slump over to the smallest table, where I promptly reopen the texts from Bree.

She's responded to my crazed cock-blocking with the words, **Why wait? Tomorrow's the perfect night!**

Because you're coming to dinner with me and my parents. Their treat, I type back.

Her response is slow to arrive: **Huh? That's nice of you, but rain check. My plans are going forward.**

My face feels warm. While I'm suffering through appetizers, she'll be enjoying Jude's company, and more. Inviting her to a family dinner was an immature, desperate move, but I wish it had worked. Barring that, I wish I could rewind the last twenty-four hours and get a do-over. A time machine, like the mom mentioned. At least before, Miles was going to accompany me via earpiece to the meal.

Now I don't even have that.

CHAPTER 19

To: All Tell It to My Heart Employees
From: Leanne Tseng
Re: Wedding Season

Honorable Bridesmaids, Groomsmen, and Guests,

Wedding season is in full swing which means that, in addition to the loved-up couples you are all about to celebrate via cutesy hashtags, you'll be coming across plenty of bystanders reexamining their own love lives.

To that end, please find attached our newly redesigned business cards (thanks, Georgie!). You should all be getting a box of them in the mail by the end of the week. Break the ice with your wedding tablemates, find out who's in need of our services, and slip them a card.

Piece of (fondanted within an inch of its life) cake.

Yours,
Leanne

MILES

I get Leanne's uncharacteristically Cliffordesque e-mail as I'm unlocking my mailbox and there, as if she summoned it, is a heavy cream envelope with calligraphy boasting my new address, the first piece of non-forwarded mail I've gotten here.

I tear it open while I'm waiting for the elevator.

It's a thick piece of cardstock with a small, classy watercolor flower painted in the corner.

Save the Date for Dylan and Charles's Wedding
Brooklyn Botanic Garden

Well, it looks like I might get a chance to become the world's least classy wedding guest—per my boss's directive—sooner than I expected. The date I'm saving is apparently three months from now.

I stare at it incredulously. When Jordan and I were planning our wedding, it was absolutely impossible to find any venue in New York less than eighteen months out. Otherwise—and it pains me to think this now—we might have been married already.

Not to mention, I had actually priced out the Garden and, I mean, insert a cartoonish whistle here. Granted, Dylan and Charles are paying for it on two lawyers' salaries and not those of a matchmaking copywriter and a holistic lifestyle coach. (And no, the irony of two people whose jobs were to make other people's lives feel fulfilled, while their own were falling apart, doesn't escape me.)

I'm too curious not to take out my phone and text Dylan right away.

Got your Save the Date. How did you manage to get a date so close?

He texts back almost right away. **There was a cancellation!**

I can practically hear his glee at whatever poor couple's mis-

206 / TASH SKILTON

fortune has led to a canceled wedding. Which is very unlike
Dylan, but weddings do strange things to good people.

Can't wait.

It's a lie and it isn't. I want to see my best friend marry the
man of his dreams. But the thought of attending a wedding
right now is still exhausting and I can't see how that could
really change in three months. I can't even imagine having a
plus-one to bring, unless . . .

My mind flashes to Bree for a moment. I picture her on my
arm, beautiful and funny, making snarky references to the *Undersea* wedding scene while the string quartet starts up *Pachel-
bel's Canon*.

But Bree most likely won't even be in my life at that point.
While, on the other hand, *some* people seem destined to haunt
it for all eternity.

I'm at my own door now and glance over at the closed door
down the hallway.

Maybe I should just ask Zoey to be my plus-one. The way
things are going, she'll probably already be there anyway as
Charles's maid of honor.

At five p.m. the next day, with the Bluetooth headset stowed
away in my messenger bag, I knock on Zoey's door. It takes her
a minute to answer and, when she does, she looks surprised to
see me.

"Yes?" she asks testily. She's dressed up in a magenta dress
with blue polka dots and navy heels. She has dark pink lipstick
on to match and a pair of silver earrings shaped like wishbones
in her ear. If I'd seen her passing me by on the street, I might
not have recognized her except as another pretty girl in New
York.

"Hi," I say, momentarily forgetting why I came here and instead picturing Charles and Dylan's Save the Date.

"Hi," she responds flatly, her hand on one hip. I now realize the polka dots on her dress aren't polka dots at all, but tiny little typewriters. Cute.

"Your dinner is still on tonight, right?" I say, indicating my bag. "I have my headset."

"Oh," she says looking taken aback. "I didn't think you'd still do that after . . . everything."

I frown. "Why not?"

"I just figured, after what happened yesterday, our truce was over. So why would you do anything nice for me?" She shrugs.

"Isn't that all just a game?" I ask.

She looks hard at me for a moment. "Not for me. Not when you choose to throw the one tiny insecurity you know about me back in my face."

I never did apologize for calling her out on being scared of her parents. "You're right. I'm sorry about that comment. It was out of line."

She shrugs. "Whatever." And then she goes to close the door.

I put my hand out to stop it from clicking shut. "But I can still help you."

"No, thanks," she says. "I don't need to give you any more ammo. And my parents . . ." She shudders.

"Come on, Zoey. I wouldn't do that."

"Wouldn't you?"

I shake my head. "No. Promise. It caught me really off-guard that you've been my neighbor this whole time. But that was a really crappy thing to say. I'm sorry."

She looks at me. "*And I'm a shithead, Zoey,*" she prompts.

"And I'm a shithead," I concede.

"*Whose wardrobe looks like it came straight out of the Smarmy Hipster catalog.*"

I look down at my black T-shirt, eggplant blazer, seersucker shorts, and boat shoes before looking back up at her. "I am rocking this."

I catch the hint of a smile on her lips. "If you say so. Vlad."

She takes her purse from the hook by her door. "I'm only doing this because I need some help navigating the subway. And you owe me for being such a jerk."

"Fair enough. Where are we going?"

She checks her phone. "A Spanish place on Fifty-Fourth and Ninth."

"An authentic one, I assume? Not one bought by someone who subscribes to the Smarmy Hipster catalog?"

She flashes me a real smile this time. "One would assume. Oh, and I have one request. No subway transfers."

"Hmmmm, okay," I say. "But it might be a bit of a trek crosstown to get to the right subway." I eye her shoes.

"Fine by me." And to prove her point she expertly walks away from me. I've watched her walk to the end of the hallway before I remember that I'm supposed to be going with her.

Zoey is quiet all the way to the subway and down the stairs. Her posture is stiff as we wait on the platform, her gaze focused on a distant point. I almost get the sense that she's repeating a mantra in her head. I wonder if she has some form of agoraphobia.

"So. Is there anything I should know about your parents before we go in?" It serves the dual purpose of getting information and maybe even distracting her from her anxiety.

She sighs. "Where to even begin," she mutters.

"How about their names?" I say.

"Liz and Melvin."

"And how did Liz and Melvin meet?"

"Peace Corps," she says flatly.

"Ah, do-gooder types."

"Well, actually, here's where it gets interesting." She shifts her bag from one shoulder to the other. "*They* think they're do-gooder types. But, honestly, I think their two main interests are traveling and soapboxing about whatever issue du jour they've decided to foster at the moment. So now the Peace Corps is a corrupt organization and the real way to heal the world or what have you is to be on the ground . . . at whatever location has the best background for their travel blog and—now—Instagram account. I guarantee you my mother will bring up their follower count within two minutes of us sitting down."

"I see," I say, remembering the brief tidbit of conversation I overheard on the phone. "And so where are they based out of now?"

"Last I heard, Central America. Grenada."

"Perfect for selfless acts and selfies, eh?"

She gives a small laugh, as if surprised that I've understood her parents so quickly. "Exactly."

The train pulls into the station. I notice a group of people getting up to leave it one door down, so I indicate that we can grab their vacated seats.

As soon as the train starts moving, she's back to staring off into the distance again and taking deep breaths in and out. I decide to keep talking. "So when's the last time you saw your parents?"

"Oh . . . I don't know," she says. "Maybe three years ago now? Actually, I think exactly three years ago. Because it was my twenty-seventh birthday."

"It's your birthday?" I look at her again, suddenly understanding the dressing up.

She looks over at me. "Dirty Thirty," she says with a small smile. "According to some, my dating expiration date."

"Who told you that?"

She waves it off. "No one. Forget it."

"Well, happy birthday," I say, feeling bad that I had no idea and therefore didn't even bring her one of Café Crudité's cupcakes or something (especially now that I know she likes red velvet). "I'm sorry . . . I bet you'd rather not be spending it with me."

She shrugs. "Honestly, if it wasn't for this, I'd probably be holed up in my apartment." She looks briefly at the wall of midriffs that is now placed squarely in front of us on the crowded train. "Which would probably be an improvement. God, I miss LA."

She wraps her arms tightly around her knees.

Keeping her mind off things is tougher than I realized. It might work better to get a rise out of her. "What could LA possibly have that New York doesn't?" I ask.

"Legal weed," she grits out.

I laugh, surprised. "Well, you have me there."

"What, I'm supposed to leave my emotions up to fate?"

"You know, there is booze. Prohibition ended here in 1933 just like it did everywhere else."

"It's not the same. I just want to be mellow," she says, so quietly I almost don't catch it.

"It's not a mellow city, I'll give you that. But I think that can be a good thing." When she doesn't respond, I add, "Don't worry. We're almost there." Looking up at our fellow commuters, I notice a pregnant woman standing a few people down from us. I glance quickly at her face just to make sure it's not Jordan in case fate has decided it loathes me today. Relief washes over me at the same time that the woman senses me looking at her and meets my eyes. I gesture to her, asking if she wants my seat. (I'd like to think I'd do the same thing even if it *was* Jordan but, look, I'll be honest and say I'm not sure, okay?) She shakes her head.

"I'm getting off at the next stop," I mouth.

She considers and then flashes me a smile of yes. "Thank you," she says as she comes over and takes my place.

"No problem," I say as I stand up and squeeze myself in by the pole in front of Zoey. She's looking at me, but turns her gaze away after a second.

"This is us," I say as we pull into Fifty-Seventh Street. A herd of commuters are now crowding around the door, clearly about to stream out of the train. I don't even think about it, but I take Zoey's hand to lead her out of the car and navigate through the swarms of people who are heading toward the exit stairs. I only let go to let her walk in front of me as we make our way up.

We don't talk as we walk the crowded streets, her trailing slightly behind me as I traverse the three avenues to the restaurant.

When we get to the corner of Fifty-Fourth and Ninth, I pull her aside and take out my Bluetooth headset, turning it on.

"So just put this in your ear," I say as I take out my phone and dial her number. "Can you hear me?"

"In stereo," she says. She's smoothing out her dress, her fingers moving up and down the fabric nervously. It's both strangely endearing and kinda hot.

Jesus, I need to get laid soon if the sight of a girl's fingers on her dress is making me think dirty thoughts.

"Um, you walk in first," I say, pointing to the restaurant. "And I'll come a few minutes behind and try to get a table where I can see you. Just remember not to react to what I'm saying to you."

She nods.

"See you in there," I say with what I hope is an encouraging smile.

She just nods again as she turns around and walks to the restaurant.

"Oh, and by the way, Zoey."

"Yes?" she says, though she heeds my advice and doesn't turn around, continuing to open the door of the restaurant.

"You look really nice today."

CHAPTER 20

ZOEY

I don't spot them right away; I'm too busy trying to figure out if agreeing to be Miles's ventriloquist dummy to get through dinner with my parents represents the precise moment I lost my mind, or whether that occurred when I held his hand as we were getting off the subway. Either way, it's too late—RIP Zoey's sanity, wish you were here!—and I'm no longer capable of assessing anything with a clear head.

As my eyes adjust to the dim lighting of Lo Busco, Lo Busco, I find them in the largest, swankiest booth. They sit on the banquette against the wall, cushioned against the red velvet, which will place me solo across from them. Mom's hand is frozen in a wave, her expression curious and wide-eyed as she tilts her head to the side. Instinctively I wonder who's caught her eye, because I know it's not me. Did Miles not give me enough of a head start? Has our cover been blown and she's wondering if I brought a "date"? The very idea would've been hilarious to me yesterday: me and Miles existing anywhere other than Café Crudité. Surely, we'd pop like bubbles if we ever encountered each other in the real world. Yet here we are, more than acquaintances, not quite friends.

Of course, would anyone other than a friend have offered to do something like this? I swallow hard and look behind me. Sure enough, there's someone there; two someones. They look to be mid-sixties, Cruella de Vil black-and-white hair for him and a feathery pixie cut for her, probably a power couple of some sort, but I don't recognize them. The maître d' does, though, and steps out from the podium to greet them and escort them to a table a few down from Mom and Dad's.

My parents' heads swivel as one unit to watch them and for the second time tonight I consider bailing on the whole thing. I mean, honestly, what is the point? They perked up more at spotting two strangers than seeing their only kid, and I hate that I refer to myself as a kid around them, that I revert to a six-year-old jumping up and down to get their attention.

I duck my head and barrel toward their table.

"Hi guys, great to see you, I'll be right back, just gotta . . ." I make some type of swirly motion with my finger that's supposed to mean "freshen up" but *could* mean dunk my head in the toilet. Which might be preferable.

In the cramped hallway outside the ladies' room, I test out my tech connection with Miles.

"Abort, abort," I whisper.

He chimes in right away, soft in my ear. "Already? What's going on?"

"Imagine your parents looking past you to see if someone more interesting has entered the womb."

"Room?"

"I know what I said."

"Huh."

That's one of the reasons I loved working for Mary so much: She never looked at me that way, and she knew actual stars. She *was* an actual star. Academy Award winners or MacArthur Geniuses could show up at her house and they'd have to wait until our conversation was finished before she'd acknowledge them.

Which is why it hurts so damn much that she's replaced me.

"So, I'm thinking, we came all this way, right," Miles continues reasonably. "And I've had a look at the menu, and I think it's worth staying, if only for the free meal. Tonight's special is *cochinita pibil*, which is slow-roasted pork wrapped in a banana leaf . . ."

"I *know* you didn't just tell me what to order," I remark.

"Ha. Sorry."

"It sounds delicious. That's why I'm pissed."

He chuckles. It's nice to argue with him again. This is what passes for normal in my life these days: arguing with Miles. It gives me the strength to go back out there.

"Are we doing this?" he asks.

I nod, before remembering that he can't see me. "Yes. Okay."

Back at their alcove booth, my parents stand to greet me. Mom's bright-eyed in a polyester-velvet jumpsuit, a pleather fanny pack covered in teeny tiny rhinestones serving as a belt. Dad wears a cashmere hoodie and hemp drawstring pants. I assume both ensembles were organically sourced or at the very least Jaden Smith–approved. He commented once on their Instagram, years ago, and they still bring it up as though they're old friends.

"Did you see who was behind you?" Mom asks, pecking each of my cheeks with a kiss. She smells like incense and sage.

I roll my eyes, vindicated.

"Only the owner of Food for Thought Media," Dad pipes up, and squeezes my arm. "We need a self-self with him before we go."

(Yes, that's what my parents call selfies of more than one person.)

"A top-shelf self-self," Miles replies.

My lips quirk and I try to keep my expression neutral, but it's not exactly easy.

"You look lovely," Mom says, pressing my hand to her cheek.

"We're a bit crunched for time, so we ordered for you," Dad says. "Oooh, and here it comes now."

"One vegetarian medley, two *cochinita pibils*," the waiter declares, placing the vegetarian dish in front of me.

I have never been vegetarian.

"Seriously?" Miles groans.

"It's our cheat day," Mom explains. "But I'm betting you don't get nearly enough vegetables in your diet."

"Ah," is all I can say.

"Seriously?" Miles repeats. His commentary is a salve against their hypocrisy, but it's not exactly helping. I can say "Ah," all day long without his assistance.

Perhaps sensing this, he changes tack. "I'd hate to see you guys go without veggies! And wouldn't you know I spend most of my time at a vegan café, so no need to worry. Let me just scoop a bit of yours on my plate. Since you have *two*."

I repeat his words verbatim and slightly robotically. Mom and Dad tilt their heads but don't stop me from snatching a portion of their meat.

"He's getting up," Mom hisses, bumping Dad with her elbow.

"Zoey, stop him," Dad urges, nodding at me.

"Stop who?"

"Food for Thought," he whispers urgently behind his hand.

I'm not quick enough doing whatever it was my dad envisioned me doing (tripping the guy? Flashing my tits?) to stop Mr. Mogul from passing by.

"There goes that plan," Mom sighs.

"What was the plan?" Miles asks. "Kidnap him?"

I repeat his words before I can stop myself.

They glance at each other, apparently trying to assess whether or not I'm being sarcastic.

"Well, no, I just thought we could engage him for a moment and perhaps slip him our new business cards," Dad replies slowly.

"Take a look. Tell us what you think," Mom adds, unzipping her pleather fanny pack and procuring a fistful.

"Maybe Zoey can set one on his table," Dad suggests.

"Or crawl underneath it and pop out during dessert," Miles deadpans.

I snort but don't have the guts to repeat it.

Mom slides the new business card over to me, a sly gleam in her eye. The card reads "Eco-Friendly Tourism. *We* curate a Zero-footprint trip, *you* get Peace of mind. And spirit!"

The copy editor in me begs to fix their sentence fragments and random capitalizations.

"You changed your business model again?" I ask. They are now travel agents, it appears.

"With the exception of the plane ride, it's carbon-footprint–free," Dad crows.

"Sounds great," I say.

"Does it?" Miles asks.

"So," Mom prompts, leaning in slightly. "Tell us about New York."

"It's the greatest city on earth, obviously," Miles jumps in.

My eyes narrow and I wish I could mute him for a moment. I'd rather he not hear this part of the conversation, because if they're genuinely asking, now's my chance to get a little parental advice. I take a deep breath, ready to spill my guts about how lost and lonely I've been feeling. It's not like Miles and I are going to hang out after this. It's a one-shot deal, a spontaneous good deed on his part that won't be repeated. Of course, anything he hears tonight could be used against me in the apartment hallway. But it might be worth it—after all, Mom and Dad have lived in six out of seven continents. They must have experience feeling disoriented or unsure of themselves.

"It's a lot tougher than I expected."

Dad nods, and says, "We were surprised to find out you're not working for Marly anymore. From what Nana said, she really pulled the rug out from under you."

I don't bother to correct Mary's name.

Mom makes a clucking sound and shakes her head. "Sending you across the country like that."

"You know when we came here tonight, we had half a mind to ask if you'd like to join us on the next leg."

I'm stunned. They want me to travel with them?

"But we forgot how much you hate change, how much trouble you have adjusting to new things," Dad continues. "Any little difference used to set you off."

"Some people aren't cut out for travel. We learned that with you right away, didn't we?" She pats my hand. I pull it protectively toward my body.

"It wasn't the travel I minded," I say quietly.

"Of course it was. You and your nana are cut from the same cloth. That was always our burden," Mom chuckles. "Your generation and Nana's generation had more in common than either of you had with us."

"You never know which traits will be passed on, and which ones will languish," Dad agrees.

"And no one ever tells you how difficult it is to balance parenting and sense of purpose. How jarring it is when you have to give things up."

"You *didn't* give anything up," I interject. "You *didn't* find balance. You sent me off with Nana."

"Well," Mom huffs, "you can't say we weren't all happier that way. You most of all. You thrived living in a single location."

She's right, of course, but that wasn't the point I was trying to make.

"What do you remember about Indonesia?" I ask.

They glance at each other, perplexed. "Indonesia?" Dad says. "Indonesia when? We've been there three or four times. . . ."

"The time with *me*. After Manila, but before Nana took me to California," I clarify.

"The weasels," Mom reminisces, delighted. "You helped us with the weasels."

"I'll never forget it," Dad adds, slapping his hands together. "What a rush."

"Not Manila. Indonesia," I repeat, my voice sharp and gaining volume. "What do you remember about Indonesia?"

"Why don't you come right out and tell us what you're referring to?" Mom says, leaning forward.

They don't remember. They really don't remember what caused Nana to put her foot down. There's no point in having this conversation if they don't remember.

A light bulb practically materializes above Dad's head. I take a deep breath. *Finally.*

He turns to Mom. "Hon, hon, where's the treat?"

"What treat?" Mom asks.

"The one Nana sent."

All the fight leaves me. I'm not going to get any answers from them, let alone the answers I want or need. Maybe it's for the best. I'd almost forgotten Miles is listening in, he's been quiet for so long.

"For what it's worth"—and just like that, his voice fills my ear—"I don't think it's true, that some people aren't cut out for things, or that they can't change. People can always adjust, people can learn to enjoy new things, even if they didn't before."

For a moment the rest of the room falls away, and it's just Miles's voice, murmuring thoughtful words in a careful tone. Kind words. Encouraging words.

And then reality interrupts.

"Hand her the cornbread *bibingka*, Liz," Dad urges.

I refocus. It's been way too long since I've had Nana's and my favorite dessert. The combination of creamed corn, rice cake, and coconut milk crisped to a light brown fresh from the oven always made my mouth water, especially since Nana adds extra sugar on top. Even a stale, room-temperature one would be amazing right now; the best birthday present ever. I perk up, imagining biting into the sweet, chewy texture.

Mom swallows, eyes wide. "That was for Zoey?"

"Yes!"

She slowly unzips her bedazzled fanny pack again and pokes her finger around.

"I ate it on the airplane," she confesses. And indeed a few sad crumbs fall out of the pack.

"Did they . . . just try to . . . bribe you with cornbread that doesn't exist?" Miles says.

"Pretty much," I answer without thinking.

"What's that?" Mom asks.

"I can't believe you ate it," Miles prompts.

"I can't believe you ate it," I mimic dutifully, but the words have no bite.

Time to face facts: I'm not a tough New Yorker.

The name of the restaurant is Lo Busco, Lo Busco, which can mean "I search," "I look" or "I want." Pretty sure my search has come to an end. Had I really thought using someone else's words would change the way my parents treated me? That if I stood up for myself, they'd behave like entirely different people toward me?

"It was a long flight," Mom mutters defensively, re: the stolen cornbread.

We dig in to our meals—my mushy vegetables are indistinguishable from each other save for the colors. But five minutes later, the waiter brings over a cupcake with a candle poking out.

"Did you order this?"

"No—"

"Is it going to cost more?" Dad harangues the waiter.

"Bought and paid for," the waiter responds, and leaves us to it. Dad gestures to Mom. "You know I don't like surprises on my bill. Especially if the icing is made from anything other than fair-trade sugarcane."

"None of that high-fructose corn syrup for us," Mom explains.

"You know it's *devastated* the farming industry. Between the four billion russet potatoes for McDonald's and the high-fructose corn syrup on everything else, it's a wonder any other crops are cultivated," Dad continues, but I tune him out because I've noticed a note beside the cupcake.

"Happy Birthday, from Vlad."

Maybe I can't be the person they want me to be. And they can't be the people I wish they were.

But damn if it doesn't feel good to laugh.

CHAPTER 21

To: All Tell It to My Heart Employees
From: Leanne Tseng
Re: Brilliant New Idea

Team,

I wanted to draw your attention to a new add-on service we're offering to our alumni: wedding hashtags! A newsletter will go out today to all our current or previous TITMH clients. So sharpen up those punny skills in case we get a few requests our way.

And I'd be remiss if I didn't highlight—once again—Stella, who was inspired by my previous e-mail to suggest the new add-on. If she were a hashtag, she would be #stellaR. We could all learn a thing or two from her about consistent brainstorming.

Yours,

Leanne

MILES

Zoey is different on the train ride back. It's possible it has something to do with the two tequila shots I treated us to after her gagluencer parents finally left the girl to enjoy what was left of her birthday in peace.

"Oooh. That one. Right there," she tries to whisper, but I'm pretty sure the tequila has nulled all sense of her actual volume. "It says 'Let's toast to me' in gothic-style writing. Next to an image of a toaster. No contest." She points halfway down the car, where I can see the ink in question on a hairy calf.

I've introduced her to my favorite summertime New York game: Can you find the worst tattoo in this place? She's taken to it like a fish to water.

"Damn it. You're right. That may be hard to beat," I concede. "But want to know the real best place to play this game?"

"Do tell."

"A water park. Preferably on Long Island or New Jersey. I once saw an entire chest devoted to a jacked-up Britney Spears circa red catsuit. I only knew it was her because it had her name in bubble letters below it."

"No," Zoey gasped, cracking up.

"And it would've absolutely won the game if I didn't see, five minutes later, 'No Regrets, No Apologies' scrawled across someone's upper back. In Comic Sans. With 'apologies' spelled wrong."

Zoey gives a huge, hearty bleat, the kind of laugh that causes at least six people to look over. The matching grin on my face comes of its own accord.

"Back home, Venice Beach would probably be a good place to play. Or Magic Mountain."

"You still think of California as home?" I ask.

"Yeah. Well, no. I don't know." She sighs. "There was a person there who felt like home but then she's also the one who kicked me out, so . . ."

A person who felt like home—a girlfriend? I look over at her and realize that I really don't know that much about her. And maybe I'd like to.

"Isn't this our stop?"

"Shit!" I say, grabbing her hand and getting us out of the doors right before they almost slam shut on us.

We're no longer holding hands once we're underneath the streetlamps and neon bodega signs that light the way back to our apartment building. But we are walking close enough to each other that our skin brushes more than a couple of times.

When we get to our building, Zoey uses her key to open the front door and heads straight for the stairs.

"No elevator?" I ask.

"What's the point? It only works twenty-seven percent of the time," she says. "It's a waste of energy."

"The energy . . . pushing a button?" I arch my eyebrow.

"And the anxiety of will it or won't it actually come. Besides, why spend $125 a month on a gym membership when everyone in New York basically has their own Stairmaster right at their disposal?" She looks down at me, coming up behind her on the stairwell.

"Ah, but the $125 a month is not for the equipment, it's for the privilege of comparing every inch of your body to the professional gym rat working out next to you, keeping your sense of self-worth at a standard low- to mid-range level."

Zoey thinks for a second. "I have Instagram for that," she says before she pushes open the door that leads to our floor.

She stops right before we get to my apartment and turns around. "Everything about today should've sucked but, honestly, it was nice just to get out. I really haven't been doing that as much as I should since I've been here."

"I've noticed. Maybe we should remedy that." The "we" feels like it echoes in the tight hallway.

"Thank you. For today." Zoey smooths down her dress again and I get an inexplicable urge to touch the fabric too.

Instead I clear my throat. "You're welcome. Though I don't think I was much help."

"You were," she replies. "Just having someone there was helpful."

Someone? Meaning it could have been anyone? I try not to let my voice betray the weird sting I feel. "Anytime. I'm here for all your dressing-down needs. Your sarcastic quips, your passive-aggressive rejoinders, your what have you."

She smiles. "You should put that on a business card."

"Not a bad idea. I could use some extra cash flow." I wonder if I should pull a Stella and suggest a title rebrand to Leanne.

"Well, if I can ever return the favor, you just let me know."

I laugh, and I'm not even sure why. The words are out of my mouth before I can think better of them. "I don't think I'll need help talking to my parents anytime soon. . . ."

Something flashes across her eyes and I think it might be the same flicker of hurt that just inadvertently passed through my own. But it's gone before I can open my mouth to apologize.

"Good night," she says, and turns around to enter her apartment before I can answer. I know it's impossible, but the space she just occupied suddenly feels cold.

I'm sitting at our table—well, actually, I guess *my* table since I've claimed it and Zoey hasn't come in yet to see my victory—when a pregnant belly comes straight into my view for the second time in two days.

I quickly glance around to see if there are any other tables available and when I realize there aren't, begrudgingly look up to ask the owner of said belly if she would like my seat even though I haven't been able to gloat to Zoey today.

Then I freeze.

Yesterday, I only had a mild, unfounded panic attack that I might see Jordan. Today, faced with the actuality of her in front of me in the flesh—rounded belly and all—I'm too flustered to even panic. Then I notice the smug face and corded arms of the person standing behind her. Doug, our once joint yoga instructor, now my ex-fiancée's baby daddy. I feel like all the air has been sucked out of me, along with any thoughts, vocabulary, basic brain functionality (oh God. Am I going to pee my pants?).

"Hi, Miles. I didn't think you were still coming here." Jordan smiles at me in the way that sometimes has those celebrity twinning apps telling her she looks like Julia Roberts.

"Hi," is all I can muster. And then a very stilted, "Jordan."

"Hey there, buddy. Long time no see," Doug says. He looks like he's smirking but, honestly, he could just be one of those people who is totally oblivious to anything that doesn't directly relate to his chakras or whatever. I never could tell before and I'm certainly in no frame of mind to make astute character observations now.

Jordan places her hand on her back as she eases into the chair across from me. Doug plops down next to her. "So, how have you been?" she asks.

Fuck me six ways to Staten Island. Is this really happening? Are they really expecting me to make small talk?

"Fine." A pause. "You?" Because despite the alarm bells, my brain seems to have reverted back to the vocabulary level of Jordan's fetus. I can't think of *anything* to say: anything original, anything biting, anything with any meaning.

"Oh, you know. They say the second trimester is the best one. But it's like, what's the best day of a prison sentence, you know? I'm still so freakin' nauseous." She looks over at Doug and gives that tinkly laugh that I used to think sounded like bells and I now think sounds like the tinny music that comes out of singing Christmas lights.

See, Miles, the kind of brainpower that comes up with that sort of analogy would be great right now. What was going to be on my business card again? Sarcastic quips? Passive-aggressive rejoinders?

"Though, thankfully, the actual heaving is over," Doug says

with a cadence that sounds like it would be right at home in a *Beavis and Butt-Head* revival.

"Thankfully for *you*," Jordan responds, with a little bit of bite. "I still feel like shit. You just don't have to hear it." She gives another laugh, one I recognize as not being entirely filled with humor.

Doug's returned chuckle makes me think he has no such realization.

But "Sure," is all I can think of to say. God, *I* want to vomit.

Jordan turns her attention back to me. "By the way, there are still some things left at my apartment if you want to come get them. I think a couple of T-shirts. The ring too." The ring gets lumped in with T-shirts. Of course. I glance quickly over at Doug, who seems to have no undue reaction to the fact that we are now blatantly talking about how, you know, I used to be engaged to the girl he was fucking behind my back. The stupid smile has never even left his stupid face.

The thing is, I should get that ring back and I should sell it. Lord knows I could use the money. But the thought of going back to that apartment is making me even queasier. "You can . . . keep that," I manage to spit out.

"Hey there, hi there, ho there!" a chipper voice rings out.

It's Zoey. And the faux chipperness makes her sound deranged, even though the big smile on her face looks relaxed. I blink at her, my sudden-onset muteness apparently not solely reserved for my ex.

Jordan looks up at her. "Who's this?"

"I'm Zoey," she says, and holds out her hand. "And you are?"

Jordan grazes the tips of Zoey's fingers and looks over at me and then back at her, clearly trying to assess our relationship. I almost wish I could tell her that Zoey was my girlfriend and rub her face in it. But of course, Zoey would reel at that lie the moment she heard it and then I'd be more pathetic than I already am.

"I'm Jordan," she finally says. "The ex-fiancée, as you might have already heard." Another laugh. Seriously, what kind of fucking bells did I ever hear before? "And this is Doug." She touches her belly and then squeezes Doug's arm.

"YOGA DOUG!" Zoey says, with a laugh of her own. "Yes, I've definitely heard. And maybe you've heard about me too?"

Before I know what's happening, Zoey slips herself into my lap and grabs my face with both hands. She gives me a huge grin that only I can tell is laced with a smirk, and then brings her lips to cover mine.

Maybe it's a prerequisite in LA that everyone there knows how to kiss someone like they're starring in the climactic airport scene of their very own rom-com. I even get a hint of her tongue grazing my lower teeth. She doesn't hesitate for a moment. There's nothing about this kiss to suggest it's just a ploy. Nothing, maybe, except for the fact that I'm sitting there like a limp rag doll.

Finally, my brain and body seem to spring into action, as I wrap my hand around the back of her neck and kiss her right back.

After all, we New Yorkers know a thing or two about putting on a good show too.

CHAPTER 22

ZOEY

Did I *have* to kiss him? Probably not. But given the way he responds—shock yielding to an embrace, his hands spanning the length of my back and sending warmth through my body—I regret nothing.

I was going to count five Mississippis but after the first Mississippi I've lost track. His lips are soft and welcoming as we slide right into a real kiss. At least, it feels like a real one to me. My heart flutters rapidly and the pulse of it fuels our movements as we take turns brushing our lips against each other's. If I'd actually been greeting the person I was dating, it would not have gone on for this long, and I definitely wouldn't have straddled him.

But I'm not greeting him, I'm *claiming* him.

He'd looked so lost. So outnumbered.

It reminded me of dinner with my parents last night. He'd gotten me through it, and I wanted to do the same for him, repercussions be damned.

The good news: Miles can kiss.

The bonus: He chose today of all days to order a cinnamon

sugar vegan doughnut. I've been wanting to sample one, and now, in a sense, I have.

Delicious.

For the briefest moment, I imagine we've been transported someplace private. Some place where we don't have to stop. His dark hair is soft and thick in my fingers, and I fight the urge to make a glorious mess of it, make it look the way it did the day we met. Remembering that day, the way we went for each other's throats before even knowing each other's names, makes me kiss him harder, and it's the sweetest vengeance I've ever experienced.

When we pull apart, I'm hyperaware of my breathing. It's second nature to reach out and touch his lip, to steal the last of the powdered sugar at the corner of his mouth. I smile at him in a manner that can only be construed as, "Yum." He stares back, his rich brown eyes bright with pleasure and surprise, taking me in. It's hard to pull my gaze away. I like the way he's looking at me. So much so, I have to remind myself it was a ruse; a onetime act of compassion.

"Hi," I say.

"Hi yourself," Miles replies, sounding dazed.

A cough cuts through my self-induced fog. Jordan.

"How come you never say hi to *me* that way, babe?" Jordan's baby daddy—excuse me, Yoga Doug—says, and elbows her in the ribs.

She ignores him, her eyes on me. "How'd you two . . . meet?"

I slither into the seat next to Miles and lean forward, propping my hands under my chin. "Oh my gosh, it's the cutest story. Where to start?"

I can feel Miles's eyes on me and decide to needle him a little.

"I was new in town," I begin. "Completely freaking out— West Coast born and bred—and he was a breath of fresh air, took me under his wing like a helpless baby bird. Pure luck that I should meet the kindest, most patient, most generous guy right off the bat like that. And we've been inseparable ever since."

From the corner of my eye, I see Miles's expression go from shocked to a knowing grin.

"That's . . . nice," Jordan demurs.

"So very nice," I agree. "You haven't heard the wildest part, though."

Miles shifts nervously. Not to worry, Miles, I got you.

"What's the wildest part?" Yoga Doug asks.

"Well"—I lower my voice and glance around the café like I'm sharing a scandalous secret—"*I* was single, and *he* was single. No one was dating anyone, or in a relationship, or living with someone, or, like, planning a wedding. Can you imagine?" I giggle uproariously. "*Both* people free like that?"

Jordan and Yoga Doug blanch slightly and look away from each other. The floor must be fascinating. Maybe they're studying the tile pattern for nursery inspo. The great thing is, they can't quite tell if I *know*-know or if I'm Looney Tunes.

Miles bites his lip and a moment later his hand settles on my thigh in a light squeeze. Hint received; I'll switch topics.

"Anyway! When's your due date?" Before she can answer, I cut her off. "Of course, those are meaningless because nobody *really* knows. It could be any moment! I used to know an ultrasound tech—he says they just guess. They literally guess! Boy or girl? Or are you keeping it a surprise?"

Jordan pats her stomach. "One of each, actually."

My gaze instantly shoots to Miles, who looks as surprised as I feel. Poor guy. I wish I'd kissed him double now.

"Nooooo," I gasp. "Twins? That's so much work! But hey, you must be excited for Halloween."

Jordan looks perplexed. "What do you mean?"

"Oh, like doing themed costumes?" Yoga Doug chimes in. "We could be the Incredibles or something."

"What? Oh, no, I meant you won't need a costume! Super jealous over here. So jelly."

"I'm—sorry?" Jordan says.

"You get to be Tired Mom. It's a thing! Look."

I pull up a Google Images search and shove it in their faces. Sure enough, image after image of Tired Mom costumes flood the screen. The outfits consist of messy bun-hair with Cheerios stuck in it, dark under-eye bags, a stained T-shirt and burp cloth over yoga pants, a reusable Starbucks cup, a BabyBjörn with a plastic doll baby inside, a second plastic baby doll taped around a leg like it's clinging there, a Target bag overflowing with diapers and wipes, and a comically large bottle of wine.

Jordan's eyes widen and she hoists herself up. "I'm ready to go, hon. How about you?" she asks Yoga Doug.

"Uh, sure . . ." He seems unnerved. His gaze flutters over mine and I smile like a madwoman.

After they leave, Miles lets out a whistle.

"Too much?" I ask.

"You told her her life is a Halloween costume."

"It is! You dodged a bullet."

He rubs the bridge of his nose and I fear I've gone too far. After all, there's a good chance he *wanted* the bullet. Er, bullets. And even if he didn't or doesn't, it still must have stung like hell to see his ex-fiancée and her cheating partner saunter in.

"You didn't have to . . ." He trails off.

I look away, hoping he doesn't see the blush that's crept across my cheeks. "It's nothing. You helped me, I helped you."

Neither of us speaks, and then both of us do.

"Look—what you said about—"

"Anyway," I interrupt brightly, "my work here is done, so I'll leave you to it." I offer him a gentle smile and stand.

"Stay."

We look at each other.

"I think Evelynn would be pissed," he clarifies. "I mean, now that she's seen the table seat four people, if I pare it down to one, that'd be a serious waste of space."

For the next two hours we work side by side. Every once in a while, I look up, only to see him glance away.

Every time he shifts in his seat, adjusts his notebook or laptop, or gets up for something, my breath halts and my heart pounds. I don't order any food because I can still taste the powdered sugar from our kiss and I want it to stay that way.

That evening, as I'm unlocking the door to my apartment, a noise within halts me in my tracks. Paralyzed, I can only watch as the knob turns from the other side.

Fear turns to relief as Mary flings the door open, her smile wide. She wears a Black Keys T-shirt, tartan capelet, and stirrup pants, her fingers clutching the stem of a martini glass. Which is a bit alarming, considering I don't own any, nor do I own the ingredients for any kind of cocktail; did she . . . walk out of a bar with it?

Without missing a beat, she asks, "What's a better title for my one-woman show: *Fin and Tonics*, or *Legless and Loving It*?"

"How about *A Good Merman Is Hard to Find*?"

"I've missed you, kid."

She pulls me into a hug and I sink into her embrace, my throat tightening with the effort to hold in a sob.

I pull away before I succumb to tears. "What are you doing here?"

I walk inside, close and lock the door behind me, and set my laptop bag down.

"Got the greenlight for my one-woman show. But more importantly, Nana asked me to bring you something," she replies.

We sit on the couch and Mary riffles through her bag. There's no luggage anywhere, so clearly she's not planning to spend the night. From her bag she retrieves an aluminum-foil–wrapped object and offers it to me.

"*Bibingka!*" I peel it open and gaze adoringly at it. "Thank you for not eating it. Your restraint is appreciated." I display no such restraint and shove half the treat in my mouth.

"Why would I have eaten it?" Mary asks. "She made it for you."

"Tell that to my parents," I say around the mouthful I'm chewing.

"Huh. That explains why Nana referred to it as 'the backup.' " She drains her glass—I still don't know where it, or its contents, came from—and regards me over the rim of her spectacles. "Were you alone on the big three-oh?"

"No, actually, I . . ."

Her eyes widen and I quickly change the subject. "When did you start wearing glasses?" I ask.

She used to say she'd rather get hit by a bus than give up her contact lenses.

"I don't need them to see," she assures me, a twinkle in her eye. "It's a shorthand, alerts people to my intelligence."

I grin. "A warning beacon, good idea."

"Who'd you spend your birthday with?" she asks. I should've known I couldn't deflect her that easily.

"No one. Just Miles, from next door." I flap my hand toward the shared wall.

She taps her chin. "Miles, right, the new tenant. Decent writer. I approve."

"There's nothing to approve!"

"Your lips say *no* but your eyes say *oh, yes.*"

"My eyes say nothing of the sort." *My lips were too busy kissing him.*

"I've got all night," Mary threatens, settling into the couch cushions and placing her stolen (?) martini glass on the side table. "You can't kick me out of my own property so you may as well spill the juicy details."

"We go to the same café, that's all," I reluctantly acknowledge. "It's across the street. And he came to dinner with my parents."

"Why?"

"Like I said, he lives next door."

"Lives next door, goes to the same café . . . Sounds convenient. Reminds me of Nick, Mr. Fresh Hot Dick delivered straight to your door—"

"Oh my God!" I'm blushing furiously now. "Nick was not—delivered straight to my door. It was your door."

"You didn't have to go anywhere, get dolled up, or exert any effort whatsoever. You think I didn't notice you two getting handsy? God forbid you meet someone who doesn't come to you on command, who's not willing to fit into your schedule—"

"I can't even follow this conversation, so . . ."

"How's your broken foot?" she asks, concern etched on her face.

"My toe? It's been better, I'll say that."

"What are you taking for it?"

Without waiting for a response, she moves to the bathroom, her plaid capelet flapping behind her. Next thing I hear is the sound of a medicine cabinet being opened and pillaged.

"Groan. Is this all you have? Dammital?" she calls out.

Dammital is her nickname for tramadol, a synthetic painkiller that's not up to her standards, apparently. "I'll send you something better once I get back to LA." She makes a toking motion.

"Please don't," I beg. "I'll get thrown in jail."

She gasps and I follow her gaze to Bree's *Undersea* DVD on the bookshelf.

She picks up the DVD and shakes it at me. "I let you out of my sight for two seconds and this is what you do? You're tainted now."

"I had to watch it for a job," I answer defensively.

"Any job that requires *this* is not a good job."

"It's the only job I could get! Because you fired me!" I burst out.

"No, I relocated you. For your own good—"

"I don't even know what that means! I was happy in LA!"

She studies me. "Were you?"

"Yes."

"What were you happy about, specifically?"

"The beach," I blurt out.

"The beach, right. Which one? Venice? Santa Monica? Ventura?"

"Santa Monica," I answer, unaware I've walked into a trap.

"Santa Monica, of course! The one closest to you. When's the last time you went?"

"Fine," I grouse. "I miss the Getty."

"Oh really? You must have seen the exhibit on medieval beasts. How was it? Tell me everything."

"Fine, the Hollywood Bowl!"

"I know for a fact you haven't gone there in years. Nick asked you to go, and you could have gone, but you said no, like you said no to everything that wasn't work. I won't be your excuse anymore," she says. "I won't be the reason you don't make plans, or put yourself out there, or risk anything with anybody."

"I'm *so sorry* I was a good assistant," I snap. "I'm *so sorry* I took my position seriously and worked hard to help you."

"You want to talk about work?" she responds calmly. "Okay, let's talk about the script you're writing."

Shit.

"I'm still settling in," I protest.

She looks around. "I don't see any new pictures on the wall. No new shower curtain, no kitchenware, it's almost like nobody lives here."

"Look, I—"

"You've been here over two months. You must have *something* to show for it?" she prompts.

"The script's . . . not really flowing," I say. "I keep starting and stopping and then changing my mind. Nothing's coming together."

"Get out of the house," she suggests. "Find a new place to write, it'll reset your brain."

"Yeah, like I said, there's a café—"

"Not the place across the street. Not the place Miles goes, not the place you've been going every day. A new place."

"I can't," I whisper.

Her expression shifts from frustrated to gentle. "Why the fuck not?" she asks kindly. She's always wielded curses differently from other people, using them to soften her words instead of underline them.

"I'm not scared of traveling," I insist, my parents' condemnation still rattling around in my brain. "I'm not scared of change."

"What, then?"

"The subway. It's the goddamn subway. It reminds me of Indonesia."

The look she gives me is so pitying that I want to turn away, take the words back. Because unlike my parents, she remembers what that means and how it affects me. "I know how stupid it is," I go on. "I know it doesn't make sense that I never had this problem in LA, I know it shouldn't bother me here, but knowing it and feeling it are two different things—I can't explain. I'm sorry." I trail off and force back my tears.

"Different city, same problem," Mary says to herself. "Aw, kid. Come here."

She leans forward and gives me a long hug. The sob I've been suppressing since I walked in unleashes itself and tumbles out. I press my head into her shoulder and she pats my back and smooths my hair.

"I can't believe your one-woman show is happening and you didn't tell me," I tell her soggily, pulling away.

"I'm telling you now. I'll be here on and off for the next two months, scouting theaters and rehearsing. Hope that doesn't cramp your style?"

I wipe the last of my tears away. "Do you have the play with you? Need a pair of fresh eyes for it?"

She frowns. "Ones that haven't been crying, for example? You don't need to concern yourself with that."

"Can I see it?" I crane my neck to look inside her bag.

She retrieves the script but holds it close to her chest. "I don't think it's a good use of your time. I don't want notes, I don't want feedback. You're not on the clock."

"I'll read it for fun. It'll be my birthday present."

"My visit's not enough of a gift for you?" she teases.

I hold out my hand.

She reluctantly hands over the loosely bound pages.

"Help me decide," she says, at the door. "Should I spend the night with my first husband or my second one?"

"They're the same person," I remind her, an old bit of ours.

"Are you sure? They felt like different people. Or maybe *I* felt like a different person."

She married Geoffrey the first time in 1986 and the second time in 2008, specifically November fifth. They were optimistic about Obama. By the time I started working for her, they'd separated—again—but I guess whenever they're in the same city they forget why.

We say our good-byes, after making plans to meet up when she has free time later in the week.

I curl up on the couch to read.

The first line is begging for a punch-up. I know I told her I wouldn't make notes, but . . .

I cross out "A stew of regrets" in her opening monologue and change it to, "Regrets, I've had a stew" so she can sing it as a satire of Sinatra's "My Way," which I've retitled "My Waves." Mary's got a killer singing voice few people know about, so why not highlight it? Before I can stop myself, I've altered the lyrics of the song so they correspond to Mary's experiences.

Regrets, I've had a stew,
And most of them were underwater.
I did what I had to do, even if two films were slaughtered.
And though, I enraged some nerds, and studio heads along the byway.
But so what? I punched the doc
And did it myyyyy waves

Before I look up, it's one a.m., I'm on my third pass-through, and I have no intention of stopping.

CHAPTER 23

To: All Tell It to My Heart Employees
From: Leanne Tseng
Re: Retreat, retreat

Team,

I just wanted to let you know that I'll be spending the next four days at the Online Romance International Federation's International Conference of Executives (or . . . ORIFICE for short. Don't worry, I plan to lead a workshop about their branding and, not any less grievously, why anyone would include the word "international" twice in one title.).

The retreat is in the wilds of Pennsylvania and I've been told Internet service can be sparse. If something is urgent and you don't hear back from me right away, shoot an e-mail to our senior copywriter

```
Miles (miles.ibrahim@titmh.com), who should
be able to answer your question.

Yours,
Leanne


To: Miles Ibrahim
From: Leanne Tseng
Re: Out of office

Miles,

I'm putting you as my out-of-office emergency
contact. Just remember, you wrote the hand-
book for the company. And also, don't fuck
this up.

XO
Leanne
```

MILES

Zoey and I are still kissing. We've never stopped kissing. My hand keeps brushing against her dimple until I can't take it anymore and I move my lips there to kiss the perfect little well it makes in her cheek. My fingers move into her not-quite-brown, not-quite-blond hair.

Wait. It's not Zoey at all. Her hair is now fully blond. Actually, it's up in an elaborate triangular-shaped hairdo that throws my entire frame into permanent shadow.

Now I'm not kissing Bree either, but a faceless bridesmaid in a poufy pink dress at Charles and Dylan's wedding. Except that Charles and Dylan don't have any bridesmaids. Only groomsmen.

"Flight attendants. Please prepare for landing."

I finally wake up before my brain has tricked me into thinking I'm making out with an air hostess too. My neck feels like it's been glued around someone else's for at least two days. Moving it is going to hurt like a bitch, but I have to do it. I let out a groan as I roll it around. The elderly woman sitting on my right purses her lips at me in disapproval. Hopefully, I wasn't doing anything that made it obvious I was having hot, but also mildly disturbing, kissing dreams. The thirteen-year-old kid to my left has his headphones in and has been playing video games this whole time, so at least I won't be accused of corrupting any young minds. (Though judging by what little I can see of his game, it looks like it might be dirtier than anything my thirty-one-year-old brain can dream up anyway.)

I look past the older woman out the window and see the flat landscape, brown faux Tuscan-style architecture, and bright blue backyard pool rectangles of Fort Lauderdale drawing ever closer.

I purchased my ticket at one a.m. last night, which is how I ended up in the middle seat. I hadn't been able to sleep. Suddenly, the thought of Zoey and her surprising lips being just a thin wall away from me was too much to bear. It didn't help that I could hear what sounded like a lot of laughter coming from her apartment—and I didn't think it was her television. If I let myself think too hard about it, I was sure I'd convince myself that it was tinged with flirtiness too. She was with someone.

Why should I care?

It was a disturbing cycle of thought that was never going to end until I went online, purchased the ticket, and decided to remove myself from the situation as quickly as possible.

I texted my mom at seven thirty this morning with a **Surprise! I'm due to land in three hours.** She was ecstatic. It made me smile too. After all, I had promised to visit them before the summer was up. I was just fulfilling my prodigal son duties, *not* running away from . . . whatever.

I was already at my departure gate when Leanne's e-mails came through. I had no idea I'd be her emergency contact so I just hoped nothing came up for the two hours I was in the air, especially since I'd neglected to tell my boss that I'd be out of town for a few days. But, then again, isn't the beauty of working remotely that there is no out-of-town/out-of-office to worry about? I check my inbox as soon as I land and am relieved to see it devoid of anything urgent.

Mom's grinning face and four layered paisley scarves are waiting for me when I exit the terminal. She runs over and sweeps me into a hug. My dad grasps me next, his three pens digging into my chest as he proves that smothering is yet another thing they have in common. "You are *finally* home." Just like the guilt trips.

I grin back at them though. I can't help it. Even though I've never personally lived in Florida, I *am* finally home. Because despite all the culture and grit and coolness factor New York has going for it . . . it doesn't hold a candle to the feeling of my mom's fringed scarf brushing against my shoulder as she keeps her arm around me while they lead me out of the airport.

As always, my parents' house is set to a frigid forty-seven degrees. I dig through the drawers of the guest room for the Mickey Mouse sweatshirt I dropped off here a few years ago on my stopover from Disney World to see my parents with Gemma (she was a bit of a Disney freak). It's a little tight in the shoulders. Huh. Guess I wasn't as into working out when I was with Gemma; that might have been a part of Jordan's world that I'd gotten sucked into. Though, unlike the fanaticism about the Mouse House, maybe this routine would stick.

I wonder what habit Zoey is into that I could pick up?

Wait, what?

I groan. One damn kiss and rom-com Miles is back and ready to fall in love at the drop of a hat.

"Love is stupid," I mutter sulkily as I slip onto the stool at my parents' breakfast counter.

My mom visibly perks up. "Are we ready to talk about Jordan now?" she asks as she slides a heaping plate of veggie omelet in front of me.

"I never liked her," my dad says as he brings over a tall glass of orange juice and sets it by my plate.

"Yes, you did," I respond. "You both did." I point to one, then the other with my fork accusingly before digging into my late breakfast.

They look at each other before Mom takes the reins. "Well, maybe. But only because we thought she made you happy. And because she was about to be our daughter-in-law. Retroactively, we can hate her, right?"

I think it over. "I guess it would be the appropriate parental response."

My parents nod triumphantly. "Now, drink up," Baba says as he points at my glass. "It's fresh-squeezed."

"Of course it is." I take a sip. "Why else would you live in Florida?"

I focus on my plate but from my peripheral vision, I can see my parents eyeing each other with the shorthand they've honed over forty-six years. I bet it'll be my mom who speaks . . .

"So . . ." Mom says. Nailed it. "Are you seeing anyone?"

I guffaw, nearly spitting out my eggs. "Are you kidding? You know I just got my heart and life and really nice apartment situation massively shattered, right?"

"I mean," Mom starts, "I wouldn't really say *just*."

I stare at her incredulously. "It's only been three months."

My parents shrug in unison. Baba speaks up next. "We just thought, knowing you . . . you'd be ready to get out there again."

"Well, I'm not. I'm probably never going to be ready." But even to me, the words sound more like a bratty teenage declaration than anything with real meaning behind it.

I ignore that thought.

"How about we go out to dinner tonight? My treat," I say.

"Oh, we'd love to," Mom says.

"But we have tickets to see Tom Jones at the community center," Baba finishes.

"We might be able to call in a favor and snag an extra ticket. Want to come?" Mom asks.

They are looking at me expectantly. What's my alternative? Curl up under a blanket and scroll through four hundred cable channels like an anthropologist discovering the life habits of a bygone species?

On second thought, that does sound tempting. . . .

But then I catch the expectant look in my mom's eyes, smile, and say, "Sure. I'd love that."

The favor they call in is from their friend Meredith and, judging by the way Meredith keeps shoving her phone in front of me, set to her daughter's Facebook profile, I get the feeling that the favor might actually involve me more than I thought.

This feeling is fully corroborated during intermission.

Meredith has left me to "look after her phone" while she goes to the bathroom. Which leaves my mom with the perfect opening.

"Angie lives in New York too," she says in a way that I'm sure she thinks is casual.

I have to stifle a laugh. "You don't say."

There's a pregnant pause while she studies the smiling redhead that is Meredith's full-size screensaver and then says, as if she just came up with this conclusion, "She's pretty, isn't she?"

I hand the phone over without looking at it. "Here. I think you should be in charge of Meredith's phone."

"Maybe you could just friend request her," Mom says. She's never been long on subtlety. "I know she wants kids, soon, too—just like you."

"Mom. I already told you. I'm not ready to date anyone."

"How do you know if you don't try?" she asks.

I look over at Baba in a futile bid for some backup but, as per usual, he's just there to bolster Mom's argument like an overeager assistant DA. "We've met her. She's very nice."

"I'm glad," I say. "For Meredith. And Angie. And you guys if you had to spend time with her. But the answer is no. I need a break from romance, okay?"

They glance at each other. "That must be pretty hard considering your job," Mom says. "Helping people to write their love stories."

"I write lies," I respond bluntly, thinking about Jude, who barely even knew what *Undersea* was. Even if he and Bree make it to a few dates, I screwed that up for them by becoming too invested in the conversations as myself. It's like I can't win lately: I was failing at my work by being too cynical, and then I failed by becoming inadvertently smitten. I sigh and glance over at my parents who—as ever, when they are sitting within two inches of each other—have their hands lightly clasped together. "How do you two even do it? Stay in love?"

"Love is easy . . ." Baba says infuriatingly. "If you just remember one thing: It looks like it might be those beautiful wedding photos on Instagram. And it feels like it might be those butterflies when you've just met and you're flirting. But it's actually when you're cleaning up your kid's vomit at four a.m., and you manage to crack a joke that makes your spouse smile."

Mom breaks out into a wide grin. "Oh, the *Exorcist* one!" She giggles. "I remember that!"

I'm shaking my head—but smiling too despite myself. They're ridiculous and ridiculously hard to live up to. Maybe that's been my problem this whole time. But then I glom on to something else my dad just said. "You know what Instagram is?" I ask.

"Actually . . . Meredith's daughter gave us a tutorial." He winks at me. "She's just racking up points, right?"

I laugh. "You guys are relentless." Meredith comes back and my mom gives her phone back with what I'm sure she thinks is a secret code smile: *Mission going well. Let's recon at mah-jongg tomorrow.*

That night, as I take my usual back-seat spot in the car like the child I'll always be to my parents, I think about all my plans, how for so many years I believed it would be me and Jordan cracking jokes about our kid at four a.m. I guess that'll be Doug's job now. Though, let's be real, his talents might lie more in cracking open a coconut water (or even an actual coconut) than a joke.

I snort. It felt good to stick it to Jordan—even just a little—the day before. But that wasn't even me; it was Zoey. And if I'm being completely honest, maybe that's the part that felt the best. Laughing with her. Sharing the private joke with her. Feeling her lips on mine . . .

Shit.

Shit, shit, shit.

CHAPTER 24

To: All Sweet Nothings Employees
From: Clifford Jenkins
Re: Last Will & Testament

Guys,

Wow. Okay. Here we are. What I'm about to say is shocking. There will be no preparing you for what follows, but I know you're strong, and I know you'll endure, so I'm just going to come right out and say it.

This may be my final e-mail on this earth, and if any of you are called upon to bear witness to my state of mind, you may need to produce a copy of this e-mail, as well as the attached postcard from 24 hours ago, when a rich, full life was still ahead of me, in order to prove that the person I was and the person I'm becoming are not one and the same. You see, it has come to my attention that the location of this "retreat" (and I use sarcastic quote marks here!!!!!) is highly suspect. Not only is the Wi-Fi incredibly unreliable and spotty (I PRAY THIS E-MAIL GOES THROUGH) but our surroundings—the woods, the rural, rural woods—contain something that's worse than ticks, worse than lice, worse than a rabid racoon. During our trust-walk exercise today in said woods this morning I was blindfolded, and during my time without sight, I brushed up against a tree that contained, I can't believe this is happening!!!!!, a neuro-caterpillar. For those who are unaware—which was also me prior to the orientation meeting last night—neuro-caterpillars are specific to this region and they will fuck your whole life up forever! I'm talking one bite will fry your circuits and take control of your neuro-linguistic programming. (For the layperson, this means they will start to take command of your thoughts, and ultimately, if not treated IMMEDIATELY, your behavior ITSELF.) I am currently awaiting an emergency doctor from the mainland—shit, the city—see, it's already happening, I'm unable to regulate my sense of direction, it feels as though I'm on an island and no man is an island but here I am, an island in my own mind, trying to help you to understand.

I can HEAR you asking: "What can we do to help?" As I already mentioned, SAVE THIS E-MAIL. Save the proof. SAVE THE POSTCARD.

It will become necessary in the upcoming legal storm I'm about to rain down on these motherfuckers.

The work continues.
Send light and love, I'm begging you!
Clifford (BUT FOR HOW LONG?)

ZOEY

The e-postcard in question, the one we're supposed to save as proof that Clifford used to be normal (?) prior to the caterpillar bite, is from a "wacky photo booth" at the Online Romance International Federation's International Conference of Executives, apparently taking place in Pennsylvania. Clifford wears a Groucho Marx glasses-and-nose mask as well as a feather boa in front of a whimsical backdrop, while standing under a sign that reads ORIFICE and pointing up at it, laughing.

Two days after I sent Mary my ideas for her one-woman play, she arrives at my/her/the apartment with takeout from Remedy Diner, a heavenly mixture of roast turkey and brie sandwiches with truffle mac and cheese on the side. Between this meal and my far-too-regular visits to Cheese, it may be time to admit I've developed a dairy dependency.

Also, it pains me to admit it but NYC's takeout beats LA's. I should poll Miles about his favorite places since we're next-door neighbors and could conceivably go halves on something sometime. Then again, that would involve me conceding that something about his city is superior to mine and I'm not eager to hear his smug response.

Mary doesn't bring up my e-mail so I'm not sure she's seen it. E-mail's never been her strong suit; when I worked for her, she once hit reply all to a group message with a picture of a rash that she thought looked like Al Capone, only to discover the entire production office of *The Ellen Show* had opinions. The thread went on for days and we got very little else done that week.

After we've settled in with our decadently gooey food, I hand her the bound copy of her play, my notes written neatly in the margins.

"What's this?" she asks.

"Your play."

She continues eating. "Did you think I might be running low on copies?"

"No, this is . . . these are my suggestions for it."

"Right, I got your e-mail."

"Oh." I'm surprised she never responded, but then again, she's been really busy. "You probably haven't had a chance to read it. . . ."

"I read it."

I look up, nervous and confused.

"But as I said before, it's not for you to worry about," she says, and it finally dawns on me: She hated my notes. *Hated them.*

Oh my God.

What if she always did?

Was that the reason for the apartment, the new life, the push out the door? It's so obvious! She sent me to New York to get rid of me with a clear conscience because she couldn't justify keeping me as an employee when my ideas were this bad. And because she's softhearted, she wanted to make sure I'd be okay.

"You just worry about yourself, and your own writing, okay? Keep plugging away. I know you'll get there," Mary says, but her words are drowned out by a buzzing in my head that's quickly replaced by a buzzing IRL: a FaceTime call coming in on my laptop. Normally I would ignore it, considering I have company, but it's from Bree.

"I'm sorry, I have to take this. For work," I say, dazed by the upsetting questions whirling around in my brain. There's no time to analyze what I've discovered and how it changes my perspective on everything.

Mary's up already, wiping her mouth on a napkin and gathering her items. "No problem, I'll clear out." In her haste to give me privacy, she knocks her play to the floor and that's where it's still sitting, pages bent back, after she leaves. I don't bother picking it up and smoothing it out. What's the point?

I return Bree's call. She answers on the first ring, looking . . . flushed. Endorphin-filled.

Like some kind of morning after.

Er, afternoon after.

"Hey lady," she singsongs. "Guess who got lucky last night? And with whoooom?" She sounds like a self-satisfied owl.

Unless she reversed course and decided to return to her one-night stand ways, I'm pretty sure I don't want to answer the second part of that question.

I congratulate her, my throat tight. She offers to provide all the "deets" and I politely decline. And whoosh, just like that, it's over. I'm out of Bree's life. Out of Jude's. They've knocked cosplay boots or whatever and my services are no longer needed.

Which means any second now—yep, there it is: Clifford's video and bonus cash appear in my inbox. The song blasting out of my speakers barely registers.

The bonus cash is nice, but the flaming hoops I jumped through to get it were not worth the angst. Clifford's latest ripped-off song plays on a loop: Apparently, I'm a maniac, maniac on the floor. I can't scrape by on Clifford's nonsense alone, and let's face it, he's only going to get worse, with or without neuro-caterpillars eating his brain.

He could've just as easily pulled the plug on my work with Bree, and I'd have ended up with nothing. I can't live like that. It's time to get serious about finding other freelance work.

I don't know how long I sit there, staring vacantly out the

window and trying to muster up the energy to take stock of my situation. A knock at my door cuts through the mental fog.

Has Mary come back? I warily get up to open the door, but no one's on the other side. There is, however, a bottle of champagne on the floor with a note from Sweet Nothings attached. Wow, that was fast.

I pick it up and someone calls my name. It's Aisha. Uh, why is it Aisha?

"Oh my God, he doesn't . . . make you . . . deliver the champagne?" I squawk.

"It's a gig economy—what can I say?" She grins. "Just kidding, I'm strictly photography. This happened to arrive at the same time as me."

"What are you doing here?"

We meet each other halfway, between Miles's place and mine.

"This is where my brother lives! I'm watering his plants while he's out of town. He's taking one for the team; whenever one of us visits a set of parents, it buys the other one at least a month of no guilt."

"Your brother is Miles?" Mind. Blown. To hell. Though now that I look more closely at her, I can see the family resemblance.

"Cousin, actually—I'm so used to thinking of him as a brother that I always slip up. But yeah—he asked me to keep his orchids alive while he's away."

"He's capable of keeping something alive? Huh . . ." My cheeks warm because against my own free will I'm thinking about that kiss. He'd certainly made *me* feel alive. And Aisha should probably never know that.

This is too weird. I'm going to ignore it until it goes away. Drinking should help . . .

I hoist the champagne bottle and tilt it toward her. "When you're done, want to join me?"

She grins. "I probably shouldn't, but . . . yeah, let's do it!"

Fifteen minutes later we sit on the couch and clink our coffee mugs together: "To the gig economy," I offer.

"To family members always willing to send you job listings," Aisha adds, raising her mug in the direction of my shared wall with Miles.

"Did he help you get Sweet Nothings?" I ask, surprised.

"The job beforehand, actually, which led to Sweet Nothings. Thank goodness, or I'd have been asking him for a loan," she admits with a rueful smile. "Of course, *he* would never work there. Anyway, I take it this means your latest client fell in love?" Aisha asks. "Congratulations."

"Yes, unfortunately."

"Unfortunately?"

"I sort of . . . developed feelings for the guy. The match. So unprofessional, right?"

"You know, I think it's understandable that you'd start to feel things for the people you're meeting or helping. When you're flirting that hard, I'm sure it's not always easy to turn it off."

"Thanks for saying that. It's just—he was so clever and just really nice and—" *Easy on the eyes.*

"If you're looking for clever and nice, honestly, I'm not just saying this, but M—"

While she speaks, I take my first sip of the champagne and dear LORD it's foul.

"Oof, I'm sorry, I—" I race to the sink and spit it out. "Undrinkable."

Aisha cringes and slides her coffee mug away before its skunk scent can infiltrate her innocent nose.

We look at each other and laugh. "What is wrong with him?" she ponders.

"Why send champagne at all if you're not going to buy a tasty one?" I cry.

"You didn't hear this from me, but I have it on pretty good authority that Sweet Nothings won't last the year," Aisha says. "It's heading toward an Old Yeller solution at this point."

"What makes you say that?" I joke. "Was it the last ten e-mails?"

"What will you do if it goes under?"

"I have no idea. I was supposed to be in New York to find my own voice and work on original material, but every time I open my script file, my whole body tenses up. I've been *miserable* trying to force it. My old boss doesn't think I'm good enough to revise her work and that's the real reason she fired me. You want to know the saddest part? I only just figured it out. Like, an hour ago." I laugh ruefully. "Talk about clueless."

"Wait, did she actually say that to you?"

"She didn't have to. And it sucks because editing and giving notes and bringing out the best in people's writing is my favorite thing in the world. It's exhilarating to shape someone's work like that. As crazy as Sweet Nothings is, *that* part of the job I loved. Now I just have to find a way of making a living at it."

"That's the big question, isn't it? How to make it viable."

"Are you able to make a living from photography?"

"I'm getting there," she says. "It doesn't always go smoothly but I'm learning as I stumble. But the way I think about it, I can take a job I hate and try to learn to like it, or I can do something I *love* and try to become great at it. I mean, what better way is there to spend our lives, really?" She shrugs. "Doesn't mean it's easy, of course." She checks the time on her phone. "Shoot, I gotta run, but next time we'll drink something that isn't from the ninety-nine-cent store, okay?"

"Good plan." We hug good-bye, and a couple of hours later, I'm still sorting through what she said.

Underneath my jealousy over Bree and Jude's intimacy, I feel proud. I got them together, I shaped that romance. My *words* did that.

What else can my words do?

On a whim, I sign up for a free website platform and begin typing.

Hmm, what to call it . . . A to Z Edits? No, Z to A. For Zoey Abot.

My fingers fly across the keyboard. "Need fresh eyes for your manuscript, screenplay, theatrical play, college essay, or corporate presentation? Lend me your voice and I'll polish your pages until they shine. From proofreading to copyediting, rewrites, and more, I'll go through your project backward and forward . . ."

There was a time when I'd have asked Mary to vouch for me so I could slap a big ol' referral quote at the front of the site. That time is over. I don't have her approval or her support for this, yet I'm doing it anyway. Maybe it's a big mistake, but at least it'll be *my* mistake to make.

I have a weird urge to walk down the hall and tell Miles, which is ridiculous (what was *in* that champagne?). Still, I can't help being curious about when he'll return from his trip and what he might think about my new venture.

CHAPTER 25

To: All Tell It to My Heart Employees
From: Leanne Tseng
Re: I'm back

Team,

I wanted to let you know that the retreat has been cut short. I'm attaching a photo so you can see why.

Why, yes, that is my ex-husband—and soon to be ex-CEO of Sweet Nothings—screaming like a banshee at an innocent caterpillar who had the misfortune to crawl up his arm. Said caterpillar was immediately snuffed out and bagged for testing. Despite the rest of the attendees assuring the conference organizers that Clifford was unlikely to ever go through with the lawsuit he was shrieking about, they were spooked enough to cancel the rest of the conference.

In other news, the dearly departed caterpillar was tested and found to be your standard, run-of-the-mill creature who never got
the chance to become a butterfly. (I mean, if
that's not a metaphor for everything Clifford touches, I don't know what is.)

Yours,
Leanne

MILES

The plane ride back home offers *The Shop Around the Corner*
as one of its two dozen movie options and I can't help myself. I
mean, it's a *classic.* And Jimmy Stewart and Margaret Sullavan
are criminally charming as two rival store clerks who have no
idea they've been romantically corresponding with each other
as they banter and argue. I know I have a dopey grin on my
face by the time the film ends and I don't even care that anyone
sees. Maybe it's not such a bad thing that Old Miles is creeping
back in.

I get back home in the early afternoon and take a post-flight
shower. Since I'm already clean, I think I'll forego my daily jog.
But maybe I could do with a cup of coffee.

I open the door and nearly bowl over someone in the hallway.
In my haste to retreat, I trip over the doorstop and end up flat
on my back, looking up the nose of a person who I quickly realize has starred in both my childhood comforter and childhood/
teenaged/let's-face-it-adult dreams alike.

"We have to stop meeting like this," she says with an amused
smile.

I scramble up. It's Mary Clarkson. THE Mary Clarkson.

"You're . . ." I stop and stare at Zoey's door, which she apparently just came out of. "She's . . ." I stop again. Then I try to gather my self-possession and figure out what a normal person would say to another normal person in a situation like this. "So sorry," I mumble.

"Didn't anyone explain the building rules to you? You gotta announce your presence every time you step out into the hallway."

"Er . . ." I'm getting flashbacks to hearing Zoey-before-I-knew-she-was-Zoey yelling "I'm coming out!" on a daily basis. "Right," I say. "Sorry again."

"Don't sweat it, kid," she says. "You're *When Harry Met Sally*, right?"

"Um. Miles," I say. I know Mary Clarkson has famously been an advocate for legalization. Maybe she's stoned.

"No, I mean your essay."

It takes me a second to remember the weird essay I had to write to get this apartment. My eyes widen. "Wait . . . that went to you?"

"Always invest in real estate. That's my best piece of advice." She thinks for a second. "Also, third act problems are almost always first act symptoms. But that may not pertain to you." She gives me a firm tap on the shoulder. "Hmmmm. Muscly. Good writer. Handsome. You might do very nicely for her."

I have no idea what she's talking about, but I think I really ought to Google her and make sure she hasn't recently been accused of erratic behavior. Mary Clarkson is a national treasure and we are all responsible for making sure nothing terrible happens to her.

"Her, uh, who . . . ?"

She nods her head in the direction of Zoey's door. "Don't be a star-bellied sneetch. Invite her to a frankfurter roast."

"A star-bellied—?"

"Seuss, PhD, the early years, originally printed in *Redbook* magazine, though I assume you're more familiar with the collection it appears in, the aptly named *Sneetches and Other Stories*?"

I have a vague memory of some cautionary tale about snobbery on a beach or something, but I don't have the guts to ask whether a "frankfurter roast" is metaphorical. Before I can form any other words, she saunters away, tossing a "See you around, kid," behind her back.

"Bye," I say in a daze.

Mary. Freaking. Clarkson.

I take a second to collect myself before I practically skip out the door and across the street to Café Crudité, visions of mermaid costumes dancing in my head. As soon as I'm close enough to see past the glare, I spot the telltale arm warmers through the big picture window and grin. Even the bell that goes off when I open the café door seems to sound extra jaunty as I walk over and plant myself in front of Zoey. She seems to be absorbed in her work so it takes her a second to notice me.

When she finally looks up, I say, "You actually *know* her."

"Um, hi," she says. "And what? Who?"

"Mary Clarkson!" I say. "I saw her come out of your apartment. You weren't kidding about knowing her."

Her eyes narrow. "Why would you think that I was?"

"I don't know," I say. "She's just . . . Mary Clarkson." I flail my arms as an ineffective way to give those words their due significance. "And I thought maybe it was just part of our banter or something."

"Banter. Right," she says humorlessly. "Well, despite how lame you think I am or whatever, yes, I actually do know her. Because I actually did have a life and a meaningful job and connections before I came to this godforsaken town." She looks back at her laptop and stabs a couple of keys.

"Come on, Zoey. New York isn't all bad, is it?"

"I've yet to be convinced otherwise," she mutters.

"I mean, look, it can be tough. But it can also be wonderful.

In New York City, every neighborhood, every single one, has its own vibe, something about it that's unlike any other neighborhood."

She gives me a strange look. "Is that line from a brochure or something?"

"It's from *life*, Zoey. I mean . . . have you ever even been to the High Line?"

"Believe it or not, I have," she says.

"On a spring day? Near sunset? With New York City itself glittering beneath your feet? And autumn in New York! You haven't even ever experienced it. Sure, it only lasts like eight days, and is also the title of a subpar Winona Ryder/Richard Gere flick, but it's going to be the most glorious eight days EVER. The leaves in Central Park turn actual colors! The air is genuinely crisp! The light is golden!"

Zoey gives a slight laugh. "You really, really love it here, don't you?"

"What's not to love?" I grin at her. Maybe it's my celebrity sighting euphoria, but for just this one moment, I'd do anything for her to feel a little of the wonder I feel for this magical city that can break you, and jostle you, and ice you out—both literally and figuratively—and yet, keep you deeply and eternally under its spell. And that's when I realize that maybe I've never completely been brokenhearted, cynic Miles, because this city is the one thing that I'll be in love with forever.

"There's plenty not to love," she says, and rolls her eyes, though she seems to mean it a tiny bit less. "And I think you're just being nice to me because you found out I know a celebrity. And not just any celebrity, but your teenage crush."

"No way."

"Really?" she says. "You and your hand never spent some time getting to know each other beneath a poster of Duchess Quinnley?"

"I . . . didn't say that."

She laughs.

"My point is . . . that's not why I'm being nice to you," I try to recover.

She gets another gleam in her eye. "Oh? Was it the kiss? Have I replaced your Mary fantasy? I'm hot stuff, right?" She waggles her eyebrows.

I want to have a witty comeback. Instead, I think I might actually be blushing, though—luckily—my darker complexion tends to hide it pretty well.

And then, thankfully, I'm saved by a buzz. I look at my phone. It's Jude.

"I have to take this," I say.

"By all means," she responds, and then goes back to her laptop, as if this whole exchange has been nothing but . . . banter. My own word comes back to haunt me as I fling the door open and take Jude's call outside, away from prying ears.

"Hi, Jude," I say, trying to sound like a professional and not a thirty-one-year-old man who has just been flustered by a little innuendo from a girl.

"Hey, man. How are you?"

"Good. How's it going?"

"Great." He laughs on the other end. "Actually, that's why I'm calling. It's about Bree."

"Oh?" Through the café's picture window, I can see Zoey slam her laptop shut. She starts to gather up her belongings.

"Yeah, I think we're going to take this thing completely offline."

Bree. I feel the slightest pang at her name but then again, it could be the warm exhaust that a passing city bus just blew my way. "You're saying you want to close your account?"

"Let's do it."

"Okay then, it'll be down by end of business today. And hey, I'm happy for you, Jude. That's great."

"It is. *She* is. I'm really happy. And I want to thank you."

"No problem. It's my job," I say, as the bell jangles next to me and Zoey walks out. She nods briefly when she looks my way, but then crosses the street without a glance back.

I feel compelled to follow her. Unfortunately for me, Jude feels compelled to wax poetic about how much he thinks I may have changed his life.

"I really think she might be the one," he says. "I mean, the other night we took it to another level, if you know what I mean. And, by God, that girl has got everything. Absolutely everything."

"Right," I say, as I watch Zoey hail a cab, get in it, and leave.

"Turns out she's into costumes in the bedroom too," Jude says and it sounds like he's actually physically settling in somewhere to give me the full details.

I walk myself back into the café and take my own seat at the now empty big table. I guess I may as well make myself comfortable too.

CHAPTER 26

To: My true norths
From: Clifford Jenkins
Re: Everything's NOT okay. But it will be,
soon, with your help.

First things first: I know everyone's been
very concerned so I want you all to know
that after multiple tests with a neurologist,
an entomologist, and a spiritualist (gotsta
cover all my bases, what-what), everything
has come back clear. Your boy has not been
stung by a neuro-caterpillar and his brain
functionality remains at 110%. HOLLA!

But said brain has also been doing some
soul-searching and—well—maybe it's taken a
near-death experience to realize that life
is short. And the truth is, your formerly
fearless, previously unperturable leader is
shook. Being forced to confront one's own
mortality along the razor's edge like that

changes a man. A man and a CEO. Knowing what I know now, I've got some hard choices to make. One moment you're rafting through the raging waters of life and the next you're crashing ashore on an island of cannibals (no exaggeration, there was some serious "snake eating its own tail" every-man-for-himself *bullshit* occurring on that retreat that will haunt me the rest of my days. You never truly know an ex-wife until your life is in her hands).

For now, I'm putting out the word—and I hope you'll do me a solid by reaching out to your friends and fam who might be able to help—that I'm in the market for a gently used hyperbaric chamber to help with the night terrors. May your dreams be sweet, calm, and caterpillar-free. That is what I fervently wish for each and every one of you. More soon, once I've caught up on my oxygen therapy sleep.

Humbled,
Cliff

ZOEY

I'm weirded out that Miles ran into Mary. It was only a matter of time, I guess, what with her letting herself in and out of the apartment, but I can't help feeling that two worlds have collided and I've lost something in the process. Worse, he's being suspiciously nice to me now.

Our discussion of the High Line and its mutually agreed-upon splendor had me itching to experience it again, so I bailed from Crudité pretty quickly to do just that. I need some air, and it's become my go-to place for gathering my thoughts.

I stroll at a brisk pace (am I going native?), lumbering in my combat boots and muttering to myself (definitely native) until I make a conscious effort to slow down and take in my surroundings. Instantly, Jude's voice fills my head—I have his tour memorized at this point—calming me down and helping me analyze recent events more clearly. And there's that line about each neighborhood in New York having its own vibe. It must be from a tourism campaign or something. Why else would Miles have said it the exact same way?

An hour later I return to my apartment, shower, and change clothes, my thoughts still circling back to Jude. Besides the chats that I never should have saved, his walking tour is all I've got left of him. I scroll through my phone, wondering if there's any way to justify one last contact with him.

Guiltily, I flick through Instagram. I never outright followed Bree on IG, but I know her handle ("Breeast94" for "Bree Beast," but of course it looks like a misspelling of "Breast" because that's my ex-client for you!) so it's easy to locate her feed. As if I needed any more reminders that she's in lurve, her most recent post is of her and Jude, time-stamped last night, snuggling on her couch. She's holding up the latest re-release of *Undersea*, the one she waited in line for all night, with the apparently riveting, never-before-seen, extra footage.

Her caption is strange to say the least: "can u fathom he hasn't seen undersea since childhood?! wuuut! someone needs a spanking! #rightingsomewrongs #datenight"

Great, now I'm picturing her spanking him with the Blu-ray case.

But hold up. He hasn't seen the film since childhood? What in the name of Quinnley's hairdo is she talking about? Jude was *extremely* adept at discussing the movie. I was the one who flailed for dear life whenever the topic came up. Thinking back, though, the way Bree described her IRL interactions with Jude, he almost seemed like a different person from the one I "knew."

Though I guess if you met me and then met Bree, you'd realize pretty damn quick that we're not exactly twins, so . . .

Wait. A. Mother-Loving. Minute.

My fingers shake as I close out Instagram and tap my phone contacts.

Because how exactly does a semi-recent transplant wax so very poetically and authoritatively about his adopted city?

Aisha picks up on the fifth ring. The words fall out of my mouth like a toxic oil spill. "Sorry-to-bug-you-I'll-make-it-quick-it's-just-I-need-to-ask-you-something."

"Hey, Zoey, you okay? You didn't drink the rest of that rotgut from Clifford, did you?"

"What does Miles do? What's his job?"

"He's the top ghostwriter for Tell It to My Heart. I thought you knew that? He and I both worked there before Clifford took off and stole the rules of engagement. The handbook *Miles* wrote." She chuckles.

The words I need to say are lodged in my throat. "Do you have any idea if he, by any chance, put together a walking tour for a client recently, or anything"—I cough frantically—"of that nature?"

"Yeah, he put a lot of thought into it. I've never seen him so invested in a client before. He scripted out a whole intricate thing and had his client record it, which was kind of amazing because the client has a Scottish accent."

My phone slips out of my hands.

Her voice calls out, "Zoey?"

Instead of squatting and picking up the phone like a functioning human would, I opt to join it where it fell. Boneless, my body drops down and I ooze like a slug toward it, my cheek mushed against the hardwood floor.

"Okay thanks, talk soon, bye," I mumble in the general direction of the phone.

This can't be happening.

Miles is Jude. JUDE IS MILES.

Our late-night chats come rushing over me, swirling around my brain as I remember how they made me feel: like a teenager with a crush. How the *ding* of new messages from him made my heart beat faster. How cared about the walking tour made me feel; STILL makes me feel. Even though it was never meant for me.

This whole time it was Miles's words in Jude's voice. Or was it Miles's voice with Jude's face? I'm so confused.

Miles *can't* be Jude. Because that would mean . . .

Okay, calm down. Let's go about this rationally. I need to prove it beyond a reasonable doubt. (Prove it *where*, Zoey, in the Court of Love?) Before I can think through the consequences of what I'm doing, or what kind of domino effect it might create, I log in to the chat service I last used with Jude. Or rather, "Jude."

"Thinking of you," I type, fingers tripping over each other. I attach a sound file, and press send.

My first choice was "California Dreamin'" by the Mamas & the Papas, followed by Katy Perry's "California Gurls," but both of them feel too on the nose. Eventually I settle on the Beatles' "Drive My Car." Fuck you, Miles! LA eats NY!

I stand on shaky legs, move to our shared wall, and push my ear against it. A moment later, I hear the telltale burst of music. *Beep beep, beep beep yeah.*

It's all too much. In a sense, I kissed Jude! Jude's brain, anyway. But I also kissed Miles and now they're one and the same! What does this mean for our friendship, er, enemyship?

Nothing. It means nothing. I may have been desperately

crushing on Jude, but that *doesn't mean* Miles was crushing on Bree/me. He was just doing his job.

My phone lights up with Mary's picture. Dazed and out of it, I pick up. "Hello?"

"Did you get my belated birthday present? I dropped it off this morning."

That must have been when Miles ran into her.

I guess I don't respond quickly enough because she adds, "Check the coffee table."

An envelope sits there, inside of which is a gift certificate for two massages at a chic hotel spa in Brooklyn. Her play with my margin notes has vanished. Maybe she chucked it in the trash. Maybe she shredded it. Clearly, it was too embarrassing to continue existing in the world.

"It includes a one-night stay," she explains.

"Thank you," I stammer. As usual, Mary is outrageously generous. Perhaps it's her way of softening the blow that she thinks I'm a hack?

A massage sounds glorious, but there's no way I'm traveling to another borough. The only reason I made it to dinner with my parents was because Miles literally held my hand.

"Don't thank me yet. There's an addendum to the gift, and it's time sensitive," Mary says ominously.

"What do you mean?"

"As promised, medicine for your anxiety is on its way, arriving any minute now."

For the second time in twenty minutes my hand goes slippery and the phone nearly tumbles to the floor. I clutch it and whisper, "You didn't."

"Oh, but I did. It'll be delivered to Hotel The with your name on it within the hour. It's en route from Geoffrey's as we speak."

"No, no, no," I moan. "What if a sniffer dog finds it?"

"Do you know a lot of five-star hotels that employ sniffer dogs? You're going to want to be there before the staff gets their hands on it, I'd imagine."

"You know it's illegal here, don't you?" I groan.

"For now. They're inching their way toward legality. Maybe by the time you arrive, the law will have changed!"

"Not helping. Why would you do this?"

"I figured you might need an incentive to get across town. Looks like I was right," she adds brightly.

"You couldn't have sent me fresh avocados? Because I miss those, too!"

"Fresh avocados don't reduce stress or lower your inhibitions."

"This is adding to my stress. Exponentially! How am I supposed to get to Brooklyn?" I pace in a loop around the couch, my breath speeding up. "I don't even know which subway lines to take."

"You could always ask that winsome neighbor of yours to escort you."

"Miles-High Hair?"

"Oooh, you're at nickname status? Nice." She makes some type of satisfied clucking sound.

"Asking him for help would be haphazard as fuck."

She laughs. "I don't think I've heard you swear before."

"What are you talking about? I had to swear every time I answered the phones for Mary, Fuck, Kill."

"But you wouldn't. You'd strategically swallow the middle. And now look at you, raining down f-bombs like a real-life New Yorker."

"You don't understand," I say, quietly. "I can't ask him."

"Why not?"

"The thing is—it turns out—uggh! He's different than I thought, and I can't decide if I hate him or—the . . . opposite of . . . that. So even if I agreed with you, which I don't, it's way more complicated than that," I say.

"Uncomplicate it. Go next door and ask him. And Zoey? Tick-tock. Unless you want to be called down to the precinct to answer for your crimes."

She hangs up.

Panicked—I now have less than an hour to get to Brooklyn and intercept the package—I take a deep breath and shout, "COMING OUT!"

Pulse skyrocketing, I step into the hall. It seems longer than ever, as though I've already smoked the pot and everything's slower and stretched out. Yet somehow my feet propel me forward until I'm outside Miles's door. I grit my teeth and knock.

The music within cuts off. My shoulders tense, and my breath hitches.

He opens the door, his expression blank.

"What's up?" he says, leaning against the doorframe.

"Code Green," I gasp. "I wouldn't bother you if it weren't an emergency. . . ."

CHAPTER 27

MILES

"What's the matter?" I ask, concerned. I've seen that look of panic in Zoey's eyes a few times now and I have to admit I like it less and less every time.

She swallows. "I have to get to Brooklyn."

"Your emergency is . . . Brooklyn?"

She thrusts an envelope at me. "I have to get here. ASAP."

I read the return address. It just says:

Hotel the
Gowanus
Brooklyn

"I don't know where that is and it's unGoogleable!" She taps at the name of the hotel and . . . I can see where she might have a problem. "Why would anyone do that with a business name?!"

Based on the non-address address and the minimalist but also graphic-designed-within-an-inch-of-its-life aesthetic of the gift certificates inside, I have an idea why. "Ah. A hotel so hip, even the Internet can't find it," I explain. There, of course, isn't a phone number or e-mail address either, just a social media handle. "Have you tried the social channels?"

"No address there either. And, um . . . it's actually time sensitive I get there. Like, right now?"

"Emergency massage?" I ask her, peeking at the gift certificates inside the envelope.

"More like emergency Mary Clarkson sent a bag of weed to my name there and I really don't need an arrest record right now on top of everything else," she says.

I feel a little lightheaded at the mention of Mary's name again but I know that's not why I say what I say next. A friend needs my help; it's that simple. "Okay, let's go then."

Except it's not that simple because as soon as we exit the apartment building, we are greeted by a mob scene. It feels like at least half of New York City has descended upon Avenue A, a lot of them dressed in either yellow or orange. My first thoughts are some sort of flash mob stunt or maybe they're filming an episode of *Black Mirror*. But then I see one of the girls in a yellow shirt up close. She's holding a tray and her T-shirt reads "Feeling Gouda?" above a logo for the restaurant Cheese.

"Excuse me." I grab her attention. "But what's going on here?"

"It's National Cheese Day!" she yells at me over the noise of the crowd and the DJ who's spinning what I'm pretty sure is a song by the String Cheese Incident.

"Er, okay," I say. Next to me, I can feel Zoey tense up and I remember her aversion to crowds.

"Brie?" the girl in the T-shirt says to me as she holds out her tray.

"No, thanks," I respond immediately and then reach out to take Zoey's hand. I look for a way around the million people who seem to have descended onto our street to score free cheese (I mean, I can't exactly blame them), until I think I've found a way to tunnel us out of here.

We duck under platters of Camembert and Havarti, limbo in between plastic cups of prosecco, and practically have to army crawl our way out from under a group of college guys who have apparently invented a new game that looks a lot like cheese rind Frisbee.

By the time we make it to the subway station, the DJ has switched over to playing the Beatles' "Getting Better," only he's getting on the mic and screaming "cheddar" instead of "better" at every juncture. We're blocks away from the fair at this point, but can still hear every word.

Zoey is looking over at me accusingly and I can almost hear the anti–New York tirade forming in her head.

"It's . . . not our best look. I'll give you that," I say.

She gives a small laugh, before she turns forlornly to look down the subway stairs.

"Do you want to take a Lyft or something?" I ask, looking back at the throngs behind us, and the farmer's market ahead. We'd have to walk at least a few blocks to get to someplace a car could actually drive through.

She looks down at our joined hands. "No," she finally says. "I think I want to try to do this."

She takes her hand back to walk down the stairs in front of me. We're on the platform before she speaks again. "I wasn't always like this, you know. Scared of all the noise, and crowds, and being underground." She's staring across the tracks at an advertisement but her voice seems more intimate than I've ever heard it.

"What happened?" I ask softly.

"I was ten. In Indonesia with my parents. It was post Peace Corps, but before the travel blog. I think somewhere in their foodie period. This particular afternoon, they were trying to find the best oxtail soup in Sumatra, and I was tired and sun-burned and just wanted to stay behind and finish reading one of the Baby-Sitters Club books I'd brought with me. I had just settled in under a cozy blanket fort when there was an earthquake." She takes in a shaky breath.

"No," I whisper.

"I just remember my book almost jumping out of my hand and I couldn't figure out what was happening. I went to grab it and then . . . part of the ceiling collapsed, and I was trapped between some fallen plaster and the bed. It felt like I was there for hours, screaming for nobody because I knew my mom and dad were too far away to hear me. It was probably twenty minutes, half an hour at most before the hotel staff found me and got me out. But it just . . . stayed with me. The dark, the rumbling, the feeling of everything closing in on me, pressing in on my skin, and, worst of all, that dread that no one was ever, ever going to find me. . . ." She goes quiet as we hear the rumble of the F train in the distance. And for the first time, I hear it a little differently. The screech, the vibrations, an unseen something hurtling through space toward us. It *is* terrifying.

The train stops in front of us and the doors open. I don't move. I let her decide whether she wants to get on. She hesitates only a second before she steps in and gratefully sighs at the smattering of empty orange and yellow seats surrounding us. Compared to the madness we just left outside, it's practically meditative down here. Except now I know that's not true for her.

She sits down and I sit down next to her. She catches our reflection in the window across from us and then gives a little laugh. "Don't look so worried," she says at my expression, turning to face me, and reaching over to physically smooth my eyebrows up. "I was okay. And then my nana came to the rescue for real and took me back to sunny, wide-open Los Angeles and I honestly never thought much of it again until I moved here. I really wasn't expecting New York to trigger all of that, especially since the threat of actual earthquakes in LA never did. But I guess something about the combination of sensations here just . . . has."

I nod. "I mean, looking at it from that perspective, it makes sense. And I'm sorry if I was ever a jerk about it."

"What are you talking about? You fit in perfectly with my instantaneous decision to hate New York. I couldn't have asked for a better archetype." She smirks at me. "Anyway, I have to admit that my chill attitude in Cali *might* have also had something to do with the readily accessible weed that blessed my life."

"Ah," I say. "So now it's Mary to the rescue?"

"She may be well-intentioned but it's more like interference than rescue. That's sort of her MO." She looks down at the envelope in her hand. "By the way, do you have *any* idea how to get here?"

"I have a general idea of where to go," I say. "And I know someone in the neighborhood who should be able to help us figure it out. Good news is, no transfers. We just have to take this train for a while."

"Great," she says as she leans back and closes her eyes. "Just wake me up when it's all over, but only if we've managed to elude jail. Otherwise, I'd rather be unconscious."

She keeps her eyes closed for the rest of the ride and I can't help but sneak glances over at her from time to time. If I was living in my own handbook, I'd consider her confession to me a Future Honesty. How many people does she ever tell about that earthquake? I'd bet it isn't many.

I nudge her gently when we get to Smith and Ninth, and we exit the subway into the bustling street filled with shoppers and brunchers. I walk a few storefronts down before entering Gus's Leather Emporium and Pub. Half the store is manned by an ancient cobbler who looks like he was transplanted straight from 1900s Italy to grumpily sit in front of his rack of high-end and extremely shiny shoes, wallets, and purses. The other is manned by a guy with a pointed, chest-length goatee and a beanie. They are both named Gus (Sr. and the III), but it's the younger one who's my friend.

"Miles! Long time no see, bud. How's it going? Who's this?" He turns eagerly to Zoey.

"Hey, Gus. This is Zoey." I like Gus, but his proclivity for shooting the shit is not going to work to my advantage at this moment. "I wish we could stay for a drink, but we have a sort of emergency. Do you have any idea where this place is?" I show him the envelope.

"Oh, yeah," he says, nodding. "It's on Third Av and Third Street. Where that artisanal mayo shop used to be."

"Artisanal . . . mayo?" Zoey asks.

"Yeah, real shame they had to close that down," Gus says with a shake of his head. "It was practically an institution."

"Right . . ." Zoey says.

"Thanks, Gus," I say.

"You sure you can't stay for a drink?" Gus asks. "We have six new IPAs on tap this week."

"Some other time," I say, and I immediately make a mental note that I should tell Jude about this bar.

"How far away is that?" Zoey asks as we leave and start making our way down Smith.

"About six blocks this way and three avenues that way." I point.

"Well, aren't you a runner?" she asks. "Let's go!" And she takes off sprinting down the street, surprising me as she expertly avoids shoppers, scooters, and strollers. It takes me a moment before I take off after her.

She's faster than I expected. "Are you secretly a runner or are you just extra motivated by weed?"

She laughs. "The latter. Also, I seem to be extra, extra motivated by beating you, so . . ." She puts on a burst of speed just as the light changes, leaving me in the dust.

I laugh. It wouldn't be too hard to catch up to her, if I really wanted, but it's somehow more fun this way. Chasing her.

She's followed my directions until she's ended up on Third and Third. I see her jogging in place in front of a large, slate gray building that appears to have no door, and no signs, but does have seven different hot pink spotlights that illuminate seemingly random parts of the slate.

I'd bet my last pair of boat shoes that this is Hotel The. And judging by the way Zoey is staring incredulously at it, I think she's figured it out too.

"The unGoogleable hotel also has no door. This *must* be it," she says when I reach her.

"Yup," I say as I look up at the pink spotlights. Are they some kind of Morse code that points to an entrance? I try to see if I can decipher it, and then try to remember if I ever actually knew Morse code.

"Ah! A lead!" Zoey, on the other hand, has spotted a black-clad gentleman who has just put out a cigarette and seems to be disappearing around the eastern corner of the building. We follow him quietly, like we're spies tailing our mark, but by the time we get to the corner ourselves, he seems to have disappeared into the ether.

"Now what?" I say.

"There!" Zoey points, and I see that a cellar door is closing, blending into the alleyway again as soon as it's shut. She walks over to it and stares down at it. "But this has to be a service door . . . right?"

I look down, and see one more neon pink dot of light shining right at the center of the almost invisible door. "Er . . . no. I bet this is the entrance." I reach down and pull the metal handle open and we are greeted by a set of slate-gray stairs that go down into a pink-lit hallway. "Normally, I would say 'after you,' but I'm actually not sure whether it's chivalrous to send you down to your hipster death first."

Zoey laughs. "You know what? I'm feeling extra brave today. I've got this." She goes down the stairs and I follow her. We come to another black door and open it, relieved that we are, undoubtedly, in a hotel lobby. As long as we accept the fact that the interior designer of said hotel must have created it after an acid trip and an Escheresque fever dream.

Almost all of the furniture and décor is in shades of black, white, or gray, including the enormous chess set that apparently also serves as seating for the lobby bar. (I don't know how comfortable it can possibly be to perch oneself atop a rook, but the girl wearing a Mister Rogers cardigan as a dress is making it look shockingly easy.) The neon pink lighting theme continues inside, where it is joined by bursts of blue and green that sporadically appear on the tiled gray wall behind the concierge desk. I'm sure it's meant to look mysterious and cool, but it honestly reminds me of nothing so much as a sweaty rock climbing wall.

"Welcome," murmurs a tall twenty-something dude in all black, including his tiny round sunglasses. "How may I serve you today?"

"Hotel The, right?" Zoey says, and I can tell she's considering telling him about how ridiculously hard it was to find the place.

"It's actually Hotel *the*, not *The*. Lowercase t." He smiles politely.

She stares at him. "I'm speaking it. How can you tell what case I'm speaking?"

"I can tell," he says, the smile still in place.

"Right, okay," I take over, thinking maybe Zoey has forgotten the urgency of our mission now that she's faced with the overwhelming, totally understandable urge to punch out the concierge of Hotel the, lowercase t. Although, come to think of it, I feel like no one in this place would bat an eye if Mary had sent over a Trojan horse packed with weed. "So, this is Zoey Abot. I believe she has a reservation here. And a package waiting for her."

"Let me check," the concierge says and he starts tapping at his desk, which has a built-in black laminated keyboard. There are no letters on the keys.

"Ah, yes. Wonderful. One of our canal-view rooms."

I nearly choke on the air I was breathing. "As in . . . the Gowanus Canal?" Aka Brooklyn's wretched hive of scum and body bags? Do people pay extra to *overlook* that?

"Of course. I see you have two massages booked for tomorrow morning. Wonderful. And here . . ." He presses a button and a slot opens somewhere near his feet. He extracts a small white box tied with red bakery thread. "This must be the package."

"Yes! Thank you!" Zoey snatches the box so fast, I half expect it to burst open and comically spill dime bags everywhere. But it stays intact.

"May I have your ID and your phone?" the concierge asks. Zoey hands them both over. He taps her phone on a device and hands it back. "You're in room 922. Just tap your phone to the door to unlock it." He says this smugly, as if he's expecting us to ooh and aah at the hotel's fancy tech.

"Like when I pay in Walgreen's?" I ask innocently, and am gratified when I see the flash of irritation in his eyes.

"The elevator is that way," he says brusquely. "Enjoy your stay."

Zoey hugs the box to her and we step away from the concierge and go around a corner to where a shockingly normal elevator is. I was half expecting to be sent up in a wicker dumbwaiter.

"Wow, this place is . . . something." I'm actually feeling sorry I won't get to go up to Zoey's room and experience the rest of this bizarro world with her.

"That's one word for it," Zoey says, as she takes out one of the massage gift certificates from the envelope. "Here. This is for you. For all your help."

"It was nothing. You don't have to do that," I say.

She laughs. "Am I supposed to get two massages at once? I think it was always meant for you, actually. She wanted you to have it."

"She . . . Mary she?" I can hear my own voice squeak at her name.

"Yes, Mary." Zoey rolls her eyes. "Maybe when you're getting your massage you can pretend it's *from* her, from her."

"No, it's not that . . . just, why would she want me to have it?"

I can see Zoey blush a little, but she waves it away. "Who can ever really know why Mary does what she does? But anyway . . . thanks. For bringing me all the way here." She holds the box up. "Looks like I'll live to be on the outside for another day."

I point to the box. "Does it reek?"

She sniffs it. "Hmmm . . . not really. Actually it smells like . . ." She peeks inside. "Sugar. Damn it, Mary! It's brownies."

"Brownies?"

"Well, I'm pretty sure they're pot brownies." She sniffs inside the box. "They definitely are. But I wouldn't have thought it was that urgent if I didn't think there was an enormous lump of marijuana just sitting here!"

I laugh. "You know what, I'm glad you did. This was fun."

She smiles at me. "Yeah. It was." She opens the box up and holds it out to me. "And one of these for your troubles?"

I look at the tempting little squares. "Why not?" I take one and bite into it. "Wow, these are good," I say in surprise. "A little herbal but almost . . . I don't know. Like it could be a fancy mint flavor or something. Nothing like the atrocities my roommate used to make for parties back in college."

"Well, we are refined potheads, Mary and I." Zoey takes one too.

I can't help but realize that she hasn't called down the elevator yet so we're both just standing there, chewing, the scent of chocolate hanging between us.

I'm hit with this overwhelming urge to kiss her, to see if she tastes different from me even though we're eating the same thing. Something tells me she does. And the way she's looking at me, I wonder if she would want me to.

Then she reaches out and touches my bare arm and keeps her hand there as she says to me, softly, "Thanks for making this fun for me today."

I look down at her arm. It doesn't move. And then I look up

at her face, at the tiny bit of chocolate stuck in the corner of her lips. Our kiss at the café was sugar-tinged, too, as though our kisses make up for the way we scrape and fume at each other. If I kiss her right now, it could be a continuation of that sweetness, of being good to each other. I want to show her we can be good to each other—that I can be good to her.

I bring my hand to her face and my lips down to hers.

CHAPTER 28

ZOEY

The elevator dings and we tumble inside, still kissing. I manage to slap at the button for floor three, and we kiss while gliding past the first and second floors—thankfully, no one gets on—and we don't break apart until we reach our destination. The doors open behind me and I pull him backward into the hallway. Before I fall from our shared momentum, Miles wraps an arm around my waist to steady me, and before I can blink, my back's flush against the wall as we make out like it's prom night. Anyone could walk by and we wouldn't notice.

Miles's lips are the best combination of soft and firm, his hands are warm as they skim up and down my arms, and his tongue is a cool, subtle peppermint mixed with chocolate. The taste of him spreads awareness throughout my body, a cascade of sensation.

I'm not sure how we get through the door and into the room; one of us must have slammed the *special key card of the fuuuuuture* against its panel, but once we're inside we're back at it, kissing with renewed vigor.

Breathless, my hands splayed on his chest, I hold him at bay for a moment.

"I feel like I'm taking advantage of you," I whisper.

He looks amused. "You're not."

"I drugged you, and now I'm having my way with you . . ."

"We drugged *ourselves*," he reminds me. He slides his fingertips against mine, the barest movement, yet it sends tiny shockwaves through my hand. I close my eyes, in thrall to his touch. A ball of heat unfurls in my belly.

"Besides," Miles says, "doesn't the weed take a while to, like, overcome us?"

My eyes pop open. " 'Overcome us'?" I quote back, laughing. "You mean, 'kick in'?"

He grins. "Right."

"It'll take at least an hour before we'll feel the effects," I admit, "but West Coast weed is way stronger than you're used to."

He raises a skeptical eyebrow. "I can handle it."

"Famous last words."

He's the one who steps back this time, putting distance between us. "But obviously we can stop if—"

"I don't want to stop," I say quickly. "Unless *you* want to stop—"

In response, he moves back in and sweeps his mouth lightly across mine. He feels so damn good, so strong yet gentle, that I have to fight down a moan. It's been way too long since I've been kissed like this: reverently.

"What if we set a timer, thirty minutes to be on the safe side, so we'll know when to cool things off?" I ask. "After that we go back to the way we were before. Except stoned."

"Sure, if you like." He looks adorably disheveled. "But how will we pass the time?"

"I'm game for whatever feels good," I clarify softly. "Do you have a condom?"

Miles nods, a wicked smile curling his lips.

With my phone timer up and running, we're kissing again, and I cannot, *cannot* get enough of his mouth.

One of his hands cups my chin, gently, like I'm something

precious to be kept safe. His other hand spans my hip, hauling me closer, and there's nothing gentle about the way his thigh presses flush between my legs. The moan that escapes my lips belongs entirely to him.

He turns me in his arms so my back is pressed against his front.

"Just so you know," he murmurs in my ear from behind, his words languid and full of promise, "I'm going to make every second count."

My pulse jumps and my knees threaten to buckle. I swivel again in his arms so we're facing each other, and I run my hands roughly through his hair. It's just as thick, and soft, and perfect as I imagined it would be. It's time to admit I've been thinking about this for a while.

So many emotions flicker through my mind. All the anger, all the hours I've spent *glaring* at him from across the café (*wanting* him, I realize now), *needing* him, or at least needing to grip his hair in my hands and tug, hard, the way I am now. But it's tempered by the realization that what's happening between us isn't spontaneous lust, or at least not *just* spontaneous lust; it's grounded in something real—for me, at least. We've had more than two dozen "coffee dates," we had that dinner with my parents, we've had hours and hours of flirtatious banter online, at night, in my head, as I walked around the High Line . . . He's unaware of the last half, but the way he's kissing me, like nothing could ever separate us, tells me he's happy to be here in this moment.

I glance at my phone.

"How's the countdown going?" Miles asks into my neck, nuzzling it. His warm, strong hands coast over my body, and I lean into his touch, craving it, wondering why I've spent my life thus far without it.

"Twenty-seven minutes left."

He yanks his shirt off and I help him.

"Hurry, hurry," I urge him. Holy hell, his abs are firm. I can't take my eyes off him. His runner's body, lean and smooth, is a gorgeous canvas. I drop to my knees so I can paint his chest with my lips.

"You're—you're—" I stammer.

"Less talking, more stripping," he teases me.

I rise, kiss the smirk off his face, and proceed to remove my shirt and jeans.

Now it's his turn to gaze, and the heat of his eyes—centered on my black bra and lacy panties—makes me flush all over.

"You're stunning," he says quietly.

"Less talking, more stripping."

He tugs his jeans off, and his boxer briefs are black too, as though we planned it that way. I grab his sculpted butt and grind against him in a rhythm he matches stroke for stroke.

"I wonder how many times I can make you come in twenty-seven minutes," he muses. His finger traces my bra strap and he lowers his face to run the tip of his tongue along my collarbone. "I'm going to bet three."

"Someone's got a healthy ego," I remark, but I'm breathless when I say it.

"Are you really going to argue with me about this?" He lifts off my bra and his mouth encircles the tip of my breast, pulling at my nipple agonizingly slowly.

"You're right," I gasp. "Go Miles. Go team." I've decided he can lord it over me as much as he wants as long as he keeps doing what he's doing. I clutch the back of his head and only then does he kiss his way down my stomach the way I've been silently pleading for him to do. His mouth is soft and feather-light as it grazes my skin, but when his face moves between my thighs, his tongue is strong and firm, his movements assured. Dammit, he's right, I'm so close to coming . . .

He circles his thumb leisurely, then persistently, faster and faster until I shatter around him.

"Oh, God," I cry out, going boneless.

Pleased, he rises up off his knees and holds one finger up for me to see. I can barely focus on his triumphant expression.

I kiss his fingertip and glide his finger into my mouth. I'm still coming down from the heights he sent me to, and not even his gloating will ruin it. "There's no way you'll get two more out of me, though, not with the time left . . ."

Five minutes later, condom in place and me poured over the side of the couch, Miles proceeds to prove me wrong. His hands grip my hips while he thrusts, and I'm rounding the corner on orgasm number two when suddenly, a blue light pops on from under the couch's armrest.

"Um," says Miles, his voice strained. At our stillness, the light blinks off again.

"Are those—motion lights?" I ask.

He thrusts again. The light goes on.

"I . . . think so?"

We stay still, testing it out, and I give him a squeeze with my inner muscles.

"Oh, damn," he moans, his hand sliding along the small of my back as he steadies himself.

I squeeze again.

He thrusts again. The light comes on.

It's strangely beautiful.

We continue our dance, our movements—and corresponding light show—gaining speed. I reach between our bodies to rub myself, and Miles covers my hand with his so I can guide him, show him what I like. The extra warmth and pressure of his hand sends me over the edge again.

My heart trips over itself, and when I recover enough to speak, it's to say, "My turn." We change positions on the couch so I'm in his lap, riding him, and it's beginning to feel plausible that I might actually have orgasm number three—so annoying! so good!—when I notice the time—

"Miles—" My voice is a purr I didn't know I could make. "We have a minute left, so . . ." We change positions again. The time limit inspired us to get creative with a wide variety of them, but now it feels right to take things to the bed.

"You want me to time it just right?" he says, above me, pumping deep.

Can he *do* that? Because that would be unbelievably hot. The sound I make is a muffled affirmation into his neck.

The seconds pulse down around us as we mentally make our count, together.

I breathe the final seconds into his ear, encouraging him. "Five, four, three, two, one . . ."

"Zoey," he gasps. His mouth falls open and I arch up to kiss him as he comes, joining me at last. His arms tighten around me, cushioning me from his reckless movements. The sound he makes flatters my ego.

The alarm's buzzing but we both ignore it. The weight of his body feels good, but soon enough he's shifting off me to fall on his back beside me. Our bodies cool while twin smiles linger on our faces. Eventually I get up to shut off the alarm.

"Remind me, I'm just curious, how many did you have?" he asks once we've tidied up and regrouped on the bed. He ticks off one, two, three on his hand and shoots me a questioning look. I want to flick him on his smug nose. But I feel too relaxed to muster the effort.

"I lost track," I admit, ducking my face, my cheeks warm.

"I'd be happy to make you a chart. I know how much you love charts," he says, smiling.

I laugh. What would we call it? Sex Champion?

"Still sober, by the way," he adds.

"I'm sober, too," I reply. "Just . . . high on life." Giddy, if we're being accurate.

"Same."

We're still basking in the afterglow when a weird thought

hits me. "What if Mary only *told* me she was sending pot, but these are just regular brownies?"

He looks appalled. "Would she do that?"

"She would do just about anything, but, probably a good idea to hang out for a while either way. I don't want to send you anywhere before we know."

"Yeah? You sure?" he double-checks.

"Make yourself at home. Or should I say, make yourself at 'Home the'?"

"Out of curiosity, is this"—he vaguely motions with his hands—"a normal day with Mary?"

"She had her 'meds' delivered weekly, if that's what you're asking."

His eyes bug out. "Wait . . . did Mary *pay* you in weed? Does she use weed as currency?"

"No, but it was a job perk. Like health insurance."

"Is that really what you miss most about LA?"

At the moment? I think, shocking myself, *I miss nothing.*

"Don't say the beach or the weather or the people," he adds.

"Did you just tell me how to *answer*?"

"I'm narrowing the scope. Those are too obvious. Surprise me."

"Okay . . . I miss beer-can chicken from A-Frame in Culver City. Pork fried rice, and pickles, and street corn."

"Can I tell you a secret? A little-known fact about New York?" Miles motions for me to come closer, and when I lean in, he continues, "We have restaurants here too. Crazy, I know."

"Do you ever," I concede. "I got takeout from this amazing place, Remedy Diner, the other day. Next time I order, we could split something."

He blinks and I realize I've assumed way too many things about our situation. I quickly backtrack. "I mean, you wouldn't have to come over—it would just be convenient to share if I'm already calling them. You know, split the delivery cost." I don't give him time to respond before I continue. "As for LA, what I miss is awards season."

"Awards season?" he teases me. "Since you don't have weather seasons?"

"Do so. But I like the Golden Globes the best, the most free-wheeling one—"

"The drunk one," Miles clarifies.

". . . and the most likely to purchase Mary's jokes." She rarely attended in person, preferring to stay home with me, create themed menus, and break out the champagne cocktails at eight a.m. We'd make a day of it, beginning with red-carpet coverage and taking note of which of her submissions made the cut. A couple of her fans on Twitter always tried to guess which zinger had Mary's name on it.

The room is dark now that the furniture's motion detector light isn't being, er, activated.

"Where are the lamps in this place?" Miles wonders, getting up.

"I thought I saw a switch by the mirror. . . ."

He moves toward it and flicks the switch. Oddly, the mirror remains dark but a chair on the other side of the room lights up.

"Are you fucking kidding me?" Miles says under his breath.

It becomes a game; who can find the most pointless light source.

I locate a switch under a desk. Does it correspond to the desk lamp? Of course not; it's connected to the headboard. We spend the next few minutes turning on the furniture. The room remains mostly shadowed.

"Let me guess, the coffee machine connects to the TV," Miles says.

I spin in a circle, taking in the small, frightfully hipsterish room. "There is no TV."

He falls dramatically to his knees and raises a mock fist. "Nooooooo."

I flop back onto the couch, triggering the armrest light, and laugh.

"I have a very serious question for you," I say. "Are your legs floating? I think mine are."

"Not at the present time. No, let me check." He giggles.

It's so endearing I have to actively stop myself from kissing him. That part of the evening's over now. We had our thirty minutes and now we're done.

I flash on Bree's selfie with her and Jude, and a wave of guilt crashes over me. Miles doesn't know I'm Bree, or that I know he's Jude. I should tell him, but why complicate things when this is a singular event? It's never going to happen again.

The day with him has been lovely, and I don't want to risk ruining it for no reason.

"What is it you do, again?" Miles says. "For money."

"What do I 'do for money'?" I throw a pillow at him. "You make it sound sordid."

He rubs at his eyes. "The words, they are difficult."

"Well, for Mary, I was her personal assistant, which entailed anything from picking up food at Koo Koo Roo to taking her emotional support ferret out for fresh air—"

"None of those words make a real sentence or job description—"

"But that ended a while ago, and this past week I quit my most recent job, a weird freelance thing, because I decided to start my own business." Now would be a good time to tell him I worked for his company's rival, but how do I even start? *Funny story about my last gig . . . and all those late-night messages you sent to "Bree" . . .*

He's appraising me. "Wow, congratulations on starting your own business. That's a big step."

"Thanks. I think it was time."

"I need to stay longer," Miles says, "if that's cool, because, uhhhh, the thing is . . . I can't move. I'm feeling—the opposite of floaty. What's it called when—"

"Couch-locked. Me too. This is actually my favorite part about weed," I tell him. "That feeling when you can't move or get up or go anywhere, and you don't mind!"

"That sounds *terrifying.*"

"No, it's not," I protest. "The point is you're happy about it, because you're exactly where you want to be. Settled. Content. Like falling in love."

Oh my God. Did I say that last part out loud, or just think it?

"You think falling in love is like being high?" Miles asks.

I guess I *did* voice it. Ugggggh. "Doesn't everyone? At first, I mean? The newness of it all?"

"Okay, Valley Girl." He giggles. "This stuff *is* strong."

"I warned you! You said, and I quote, 'I can handle it.' "

His expression contorts. "Is that how I sound to you? All pomp and poss?"

"Do you mean 'pompous'?"

He looks confused. "Isn't that what I said?" He remains on the floor, a goofy smile plastered across his face.

"Can you crawl to the couch so we can be couch-locked together?" I ask.

He slowly makes his way over to me and oozes up the side of the couch.

Luckily, I keep my next thought to myself. It takes effort, to think it instead of say it. That there really is nowhere I'd rather be than couch-locked here with Miles.

CHAPTER 29

MILES

I startle awake from the kind of sleep that feels decadent, deep, and delicious, like a Sunday lie-in that goes on until noon. I'm surprised to find myself still on the couch, even more surprised by the arm that's draped over my bare chest. I peek down my nose to watch Zoey's face, relaxed in a way I've hardly ever seen, her breath gently tickling some of my chest hair.

I close my eyes again, settling deeper into the expensive upholstery. I remember what happened last night, but I'm feeling too peaceful to analyze the whys and hows of it. Maybe Zoey is onto something with her West Coast weed. If this is the way she felt all the time, no wonder loud, cranky, sober New York isn't cutting it for her.

Five minutes later, I feel her stirring and when I open my eyes this time, she's looking back at me.

"Morning," she says with a shy grin. "How are you?"

"I'm pretty great, although it sounds like we're in the middle of a countdown in *The Hurt Locker*. Should we look for a wire cutter, do you think?"

She giggles and glances at the far wall, which has dials and hands screwed into it so that it is not so much a wall as a giant, loudly ticking clock.

"I didn't even hear that until now. How is that possible?"

"To be fair, we were kind of preoccupied." Before I can stop myself, I'm running my fingers through her tousled hair.

She leans into my touch and closes her eyes, and then makes a move to roll off me.

I tug her gently back. "Last night was . . . surprising. In the best way."

Zoey bites her lip, looking nervous, though I don't know why she would be.

"Speaking of surprises . . ." she trails off. "Actually, let me get dressed, and then we'll, um, talk." We need to "talk" already? Does she regret what happened between us?

She's rolling off me again, still naked, and I can't help but stare at the way her curves are silhouetted in the morning light.

She catches me and sticks out her tongue, lightening the mood again. "Times like these I wish I lived in the movies. Where an artfully draped sheet is never more than an arm's length away."

"Times like these, I'm glad you don't," I say, grinning wickedly at her as she hops into her panties. She rolls her eyes but I see a smile too.

She has just finished putting on her shirt when she stops dead in her tracks. "What the hell . . ."

I look over to where she's staring. In front of the door are three different room service carts, each one filled with an assortment of half-eaten food.

I finally get up and fumble around for my own clothes before I walk over to look at them. "Did we get the munchies last night?" I don't remember anything about ordering food.

Zoey is laughing. "I guess so. But just . . . what is all this?"

I peer more closely at the trays. "Um . . . I think it's mostly an assortment of avocado toast." And it is. At least a dozen kinds, topped with everything from quail eggs, to cayenne pepper, to what looks like it might actually be a melted blue raspberry Blow Pop (I mean, I have no idea, but I have never seen anything else edible that was that shade of blue). There's also a half-drunk bottle of champagne along with three carafes of juices, a large bowl of what appears to be mushroom-shaped gummy bears, and a plate of what I'm almost positive is Hot Pockets, but is probably marketed as artisan roast prosciutto tartines.

Zoey grabs one of the gummy mushrooms, sniffs it, and then places it in her mouth before immediately spitting it back out into a napkin. "Oh my God. I think those are truffle-flavored." She nearly gags.

I laugh before realizing an inconvenient truth. "Oh, crap. We are probably going to have to pay a small fortune for all of this."

Zoey shakes her head. "Knowing Mary, she probably gave them her credit card and told them I could charge anything I want to it."

"Wow, that's really generous."

"She's a generous person," she says softly and in that instant I get a small inkling of just what Mary Clarkson means to her, and it has nothing to do with what she means to me or millions of other celebrity fiends.

Zoey sits on the edge of the bed, hands folded in her lap. "I need to tell you something," she says, her fingers twisting together. Shit, maybe she really is having second thoughts about our evening.

"Okay." I join her on the edge of the bed, but not too close. I want to give her space for whatever she's gearing up to say. My stomach clenches and I tell myself it's just hunger.

"Remember that weird freelance job I mentioned? The one I'm planning to quit?"

"Yeah, sure—"

"It's Sweet Nothings," she blurts out in a rush. "I work as a matchmaking ghostwriter just like you and what's more—I . . .

I . . . Look, I wouldn't even tell you this except I think we might have the potential for something good. Maybe even something great. You and me, that is. The *real* you and me."

My head's spinning. "I don't follow."

"I'm DuchessB. And you're GreatSc0t, and we've been—well, flirting our nuts off online and it's been amazing. At least, for me it has." She covers her face for a moment and then shakes out her hair. "Oh, God. I'm so sorry. I should've told you last night, before we—but I didn't, and now . . ."

"You're TheDuchessB? You're *Bree*?"

She nods, tears sparkling in her eyes. "I'm sorry. Do you hate me now? Actually hate me, not Table Champion hate me?"

Before I can answer—it's a *lot* to process—she jumps up, clearly ready to bolt. "I can leave. You can still have a nice lie-in and get a massage and spend it imagining me getting hit by a city bus because, let's face it, that's probably going to happen to me at some point."

"When did you find out?" I ask, trying to keep my voice neutral.

"Yesterday," she says quickly. "Right before I knocked on your door."

"You're the one who sent me 'Drive My Car'?"

"Yes. And chatted with you, and laughed at all the things you wrote, and loved the walking tour. For what it's worth. Probably not much."

She looks down, and gathers her items off the floor.

I stop her with a hand on her wrist. Slowly, her eyelashes, her beautiful eyelashes, lift and her gaze meets mine.

"You're the Pigvin shipper?" I ask, my voice almost reverent with the ridiculous words.

She lets out a small, nervous laugh. "Yes. And, just so we're clear, I will defend the sanctity of 'The Rainbow Connection' until the day I die."

Bree and Zoey are the same. One perfect package. One witty,

insightful, hilarious, sexy, gorgeous package. The girl I've been thinking about almost nonstop since we started interacting on-line. The girl I was literally angry at Jude for "stealing" is here in a hotel with *me*, and she flat-out said she thinks we could have something good together.

My face hurts from smiling. "This is the best news I've heard all year. This is unbelievable."

She smiles too, tentatively. "You're not—filled with rage?"

I tug her toward the bed as I simultaneously stand up so we meet at the halfway point and I kiss her like our lives depend on it.

When we come up for air, she's beaming at me, all traces of her earlier tears gone.

"Do you know how many ghostwriting jobs I've had?" I ask.

"Aisha said you're the top ghostwriter . . ."

"But I've never thought about the client after hours before. *Really* thought about her. Wondered what she was up to, what she was thinking, how she was doing—wait, you know Aisha?"

Before she can answer, there comes a loud, extremely lifelike "Moooooo" from somewhere in the room. We jump apart, as if we've been caught getting handsy at a junior high dance—that inexplicably takes place in the middle of a farm.

"Is that your ringtone?" I ask her.

She looks at me in mock disgust. "First you think I'm from Florida, and now you think my phone moos? Have you no shame?"

Moooooooooo.

We stagger around the room trying to discern the source.

Finally, I locate a plastic udder (because of course) hanging off the bottom of the bed frame. I pick it up and, disturbed, put it to my ear with a tentative "Hello?"

A rude voice drawls, "You're late for your dual massage appointment."

"We're going to need to reschedule the massage for another day. When's checkout? At noon? Thanks."

Zoey grabs the udder from me and tosses it behind her, then crawls into my lap. "We have three more hours to run amok on Mary's dime."

She kisses me and I roll us so she's on her back and I can lavish her neck and collarbone with attention.

"We know we're good at going fast," I murmur between love bites. "So let's try it slow this time."

"How do you think they're going to check us out? Beam us up?" she asks.

"I was thinking they'd make us play chess with the lobby chairs. Only the winner gets out," I retort, swinging our clasped hands.

"My chess skills are a little rusty, but my will is strong," she replies. "I feel confident."

But there is no one manning the lobby when we get there, except a sign in almost illegible calligraphy saying that our phones will automatically be deactivated when we leave so there's no need to check out.

"That's anticlimactic," Zoey says.

"Seriously. I'm docking a star from my Yelp review."

We leave the hotel through the cellar door and emerge on the sidewalk to a beautiful day: slightly overcast, and a little breezy, which is a welcome change from the unseasonal heat of the past week. I look around and realize for the first time that I haven't set foot in Brooklyn since I got our stuff out of my old apartment with Jordan. Until now.

"Hey," I say, struck with an idea. "Do you have anything planned for the next couple of hours? There's someplace I'd like to show you if you're free."

"Sure. I'm free."

"Would you be okay taking the subway? We can also take a Lyft."

She smiles. "I think I'm feeling relaxed enough. Let's do it."

I take her hand, but we don't talk much for the next half hour as I guide her through Gowanus, to the R train, and finally out at Court Street. It's almost like we don't need to, that despite having a million zingers at the ready for each other, we're just as content in companionable silence. Which I hope is the miracle it seems and not just an after-effect of Mary's potent weed.

When we're close to the end of Montague Street, I tell her to close her eyes and lead her the last couple of steps. "Oh, wow," she says when I tell her to open them. "Wow." It's worth the repeat. "What is this place?"

"It's called the Promenade," I explain. It's a wide pedestrian-only pathway built right next to the water, with the whole of Manhattan's famed skyline spread out before us. The Brooklyn Bridge looks close enough to touch. The Empire State Building, puncturing the slight mist of the overcast day, appears somehow even more magical, like a spire that could take you up into the clouds.

"It's incredible," Zoey says. "Is that the Statue of Liberty?"

"Sure is," I say.

She shakes her head in awe. "You know, in all the time I've been here, I don't think I've ever actually seen her."

I'm not terribly surprised, given that I don't think Zoey has ventured very far from the ten-block radius surrounding our apartments. But I don't mention that. Instead I ask, "Shall we?"

She nods and we start the stroll. Charming old brick buildings with vibrant burgundy gardens frame us on one side, while the blues and grays of Manhattan's established skyscrapers— and the oranges and yellows of those yet to come—frame the other. It's a strange clash of history and progress but somehow, here, it just works.

"You should see it at night," I say. "Or even better, sunset. All lit up. Everything reflecting in the water. It's like stepping into a postcard except, when you're here for real, you realize no photo can truly capture it at all."

Zoey nods. "I get that. Believe it or not, LA has places like this too. The Hollywood sign, for example. As cheesy as it sounds, I don't think I ever failed to stop and stare at it, even if just for a few seconds, whenever it came into view. I'd remind myself that this thing I had seen a million times in pictures, and TV, and movies, here it was in front of me, in the flesh. Or steel, as it were." She takes a deep breath. "Can I tell you something?"

Curious, I nod. "Go for it."

"I'm glad we got high together," she says. "But I'm even more glad it wore off, so I could experience this for real, like you said. Things like this—the surprise of it, the beauty of it—don't need enhancements and I think sometimes I need to be reminded of that. Of what's out there."

"Leaving your emotions up to fate, was that how you put it?"

"Yeah. Exactly." She pauses. "And I'm also glad we sobered up so that I could tell you the truth. So it's *really* for real. Being here with you."

I smile at her. In front of us, a couple starts to kiss, which reminds me of something I read recently. "You know, the Promenade was listed in an article: 'The Top Ten Places to Kiss in Brooklyn.'"

Zoey cuts her head to me. "Is that an invitation?"

"Absofuckinglutely," I reply as I place my hands around her waist, dip her back, and bring my lips to hers. We could be in our own postcard right now, especially when it starts to drizzle. Sure, in real life, it's kind of annoying to be pelted with cold rain, but in the picture postcard version, it would only enshroud us in a light mist and add a sheen to the concrete to make it that much more romantic.

I guess I'm not the only one to think so. The other kissing couple in front of us breaks apart. The guy laughs and says, "I guess I better make this quick." And then he's down on one knee.

Rain or not, everyone surrounding them pauses for a moment to stop and stare and smile, maybe something like Zoey's

Hollywood sign. There's applause when the girl squeals and says yes. Someone even hands them an umbrella as it's clear they came unprepared. Someone else offers to take their photo.

Zoey looks up at me. "Don't worry. I'm not expecting you to copy everything they do," she says wryly.

I smile. What I don't tell her is that I considered proposing to Jordan here too before I ultimately chose the Mexican restaurant. For a split second, I get a flash of the sliding door version of my life, the one where Jordan and I are still together, reminiscing about our own romantic moment here. The version of my life in which I'm about to be a dad.

A rumble of thunder saves me from my own treacherous brain, and then the rain starts pouring down in earnest. "Should we go home?" Zoey asks.

I nod and we start running toward the subway.

Is it a little strange that we're going to the same "home," despite having only gotten together the night before? A little. It's also convenient.

Best. Walk of Shame. Ever.

We're going down our shared hallway and I can see she's heading toward her own door, but I tug her back to mine and kiss her rain-soaked lips. "I'd be remiss if I let you go home in these soaked clothes," I say in between kisses. "You could catch a cold."

She laughs. "That's very chivalrous of you. I mean, this hallway *is* on the drafty side."

"I'm a very thoughtful person," I murmur, as I try to put my key in my door without breaking our embrace. It takes a minute, but I manage to do it. She gives me a little sarcastic round of applause before I grab her hands to pull her inside. I can think of other things I want to be doing with her smart hands and smart mouth right now.

CHAPTER 30

ZOEY

Waking up in Miles's apartment is like waking up in the fun-house mirror of my own place. Everything's the same but facing the opposite direction. He's still asleep, which gives me time to reflect on the bonkers-but-wonderful twenty-four hours we've shared.

Between bouts of lovemaking, we stayed up late, talking and sifting through our interactions from our respective dating platforms.

Beep. Beep. Beep.

Miles immediately shuts off his alarm, then rolls over to wrap his arm around my waist.

"No one needs to be up at four a.m. to try and snag the big table today," he croaks out.

My eyes are already drifting shut because for the first time since we met, I get to sleep in without a second thought. I let out a contented sigh and fall back into dreamland.

Four hours later, showered and dressed, we're at the intersection across from Café Crudité when Miles turns to me and says, "Do you have any pressing work to do today?"

I wanted to add a portfolio section to my site, but is it really *pressing*? As pressing as, say, how much I'm enjoying getting the real GreatSc0t in the flesh and all to myself? "Not really, why?"

"We *could* go to the café and share the big table and put up with Evelynn's knowing looks—"

"She *so* had us figured out—"

"And play footsie under the table and interrupt each other every five seconds to share something funny we see online—"

"And be completely insufferable and feed each other little pieces of stale, day-old biscotti—"

"Or, we could assume this day's a wash and play hooky. What do you say?"

I link my arm through his. "Where to?"

I recognize our destination as the Pershing Square Beams, one of the coolest spots on Jude's—er, Miles's—walking tour.

While the rest of the city hustles through their workday, the two of us take a time-out to balance along the beams, jokingly trying to push each other off-balance. Because that's what we do best.

For lunch, we grab hot dogs and pretzels from a cart and sit on a bench facing the Hudson.

"You want to know something? The walking tour kind of saved me," I admit, keeping my eyes on the water so I don't have to see his reaction. "I was in a bad place, completely holed up, and it came along and got me out of the apartment right when I most needed it."

"I actually got the idea of it from seeing how you were struggling," he says.

"Seriously?"

"Yeah."

"I loved that line about not being sure if you want kids, but that the Pershing Square Beams would be a reason to have them. It cracked me up."

Miles smiles. "Yeah, well, that might have been one of the

few times I tried to remember I was writing for a *client* and not myself. Jude and I had never discussed whether he wanted kids, so I tried to keep it vague. Of course, *I* want kids. The Pershing Square Beams is only one of a million reasons to have them."

"Really?" I ask.

"Of course. Don't you want kids?"

"Ehhh, I don't know yet, but I'm leaning toward no."

He stops mid-chew. "Oh, really?"

"Have you seen the look in that mom's eyes? The one who's always in Café Crudité? I mean, her baby is effing adorable but no, thanks." I shrug. "Who knows though? I still have a lot of time to decide."

"People always *say* they have a lot of time, but then all of a sudden they're in their thirties or whatever and it gets complicated, you know?" He looks intense all of a sudden, the way he looked the day we met.

"Hey, lighten up," I say, patting down his messy hair.

"I'm just thinking about Leanne. My boss at TITMH. Sorry, Tell It to My Heart. She was going to have kids with Clifford, and now they're divorced, and it's like"—he mimics me—" 'who knows' now. Which sucks." He clears his throat. "I'm guessing."

I've clearly hit upon a touchy subject. And I don't know if I want to ruin an otherwise perfect day. Besides, that portfolio isn't going to write itself. "Playing hooky has been awesome, but I think I should get some work done."

He stands. "Yeah, me too."

"Want to meet up the day after tomorrow? I could call to rebook those massages at Hotel the . . ."

He perks up. "Yes! I've got some errands to run that morning. Will you be okay getting there on your own, or—"

"Shoot me a point-by-point instruction manual and I'll make it my personal treasure hunt."

"You got it."

We seal the deal with a kiss.

CHAPTER 31

To: All You Beautiful People
From: Clifford Jenkins
Re: All Good Things

UPDATE: the hyperbaric chamber is up and running and rentable by the hour if anyone's in need. My time spent dreaming, reflecting, and inhaling oxygen like never before has brought about an epiphany, son! As much as I've enjoyed the hell out of working with all of you at Sweet Nothings, it was never genuinely *my* baby.

So it's time for this fly butterfly to spread his wings and fly with his next new MONEY-making idea. I don't want to give too much away, but let's just say that hockey uniform ain't going to be gathering dust in my closet anymore. But wait, there's more! I wanted to personally extend an invitation to any one of you who wants to dive into this swimming

pool of cold, hard cash. Anyone who joins
me will automatically get stock options and
P.O.I.N.T.S. (the caps are intentional . . .
you'll see) as a signing bonus. Your shot's
wide open!

And keep an eye on your e-mails in regards
to suiting up for "batting practice." (wink,
wink . . . can't spill too many details but
this will all make sense SO SOON.)

Until then,
Namaste,
Clifford

MILES

"This might be a new masterpiece. Even for Clifford." Aisha
looks up from her phone. "I think I may have just gotten fired.
But also offered a new job."

She passes her phone across the table to me. We're having
dinner at one of our favorite ramen places, but she's been waiting for an e-mail from a gallery interested in exhibiting some of
her pieces so she's been apologizing while obsessively checking
her phone.

I skim the e-mail. "I . . . can't even count how many different
sports metaphors are bungled in here. Oh, wait . . . he's going
to open up a sports bar, isn't he?"

"Probably," Aisha says as she takes her phone back. "I'm sure
all the bartenders will be dressed in jerseys."

"Um, sexy jerseys, Aisha. Come on."

"Million-dollar idea," she says. "And what do you think the
acronym P.O.I.N.T.S. is for?"

I think for a moment. "Pants Off, I Need to Shit."

Aisha snorts.

"That sucks about your job though," I say. "Are you going to be okay, money-wise?"

"What are you talking about?" Aisha says as she twirls some noodles around her chopsticks. "We are about to make some serious bank with Clifford's sexy jersey sports bar. SON."

"You're right." I nod solemnly. "So you're picking up the bill tonight, right?"

"No way. Elders always pay," Aisha says before sighing. "It's not great timing, I'll admit. Not that working for Clifford has ever been even remotely pleasant or predictable, so maybe it's for the best that I figure out a different gig. I hope Zoey's going to be okay too. Speaking of which . . ." She waggles her eyebrows.

"I knew I shouldn't have told you. . . ." I groan.

"Oh, but I'm so glad you did. Did you know I came *this close* to setting you guys up?"

"You did?" I ask.

"Yup, because you're perfect for each other." She expertly pierces a mushroom with the end of her chopstick and plops it in her mouth. "Though I can't believe you lived next door to each other and didn't know she worked at Sweet Nothings."

"Well, we were kinda busy hating each other," I explain.

"Foreplay. Nice."

I almost can't resist the urge to throw a piece of soggy bok choy at her. "*Anyway.* I think she's going to be just fine despite the demise of Sweet Nothings. She's decided to start her own freelance business. But I'll check in with her when we have our date tomorrow morning."

"A *morning* date? Oh my God, you guys are soooo in your thirties," Aisha teases.

"Yeah, enjoy all four months left of your wild twenties," I reply. "Once midnight strikes on your birthday, you get an immediate shipment of Ensure and drugstore reading glasses."

Aisha pauses. " 'Cause that's what you're going to send me, isn't it?"

I smirk as I lean back in my chair. "You bet your boxing gloves."

I'm up early the next morning so that I can run my errands and still have time to shower and dress. After all, when I finally saunter over to Hotel the, I want to look good.

I've just exited my building, shutting the heavy front door behind me, when I hear a shaky voice call out, "Miles."

I turn around and it happens so quickly that I don't recognize her by her voice or her face. She's run into my arms, sobbing, and it's honestly the sense memory of her body pressed into mine that finally makes my brain identify who she is and just what is happening.

"Jordan?" I say incredulously as she sobs into my arms. "What is it? What's happened?" I move her a little away from me to make sure she's still pregnant, even though I could feel her belly between us.

She looks a mess though. Liquid leaks from her eyes and nose, her dark, curly hair is wild in the way that I always liked but that she never did so she'd carefully tame it every morning. "I . . . I . . ." She takes in a deep breath and I know she's counting to seven in her head, the way she always tells her clients to do when they're having an anxiety attack. She finishes the breathing exercise and looks up at me, her hand going to her stomach. "I don't think I can do this."

"The babies?" I ask, stunned. The fact that she wants kids has never been a question. Or, at least, it wasn't for the Jordan I knew—which, admittedly, might never have been the real Jordan.

But she shakes her head. "I want the babies. Just . . . I don't think . . . with *him*."

"Yoga Doug?" I say and Jordan starts a little at the shared nickname we once had for him. I'm guessing that's not what she calls him anymore. Maybe she doesn't even remember until now that we used to make fun of having such a meathead for a yoga instructor, all our jokes about how he probably thought namaste was Sanskrit for "Nah, man."

"He . . ." she starts again, but then is racked by a fresh wave of sobs.

"Hey, it's okay," I say as I gently move her out of the way of a swinging satchel carried by a harried businesswoman. "Do you want to come up?"

She nods and I reopen my front door. The ride up the elevator and walk to my apartment is silent, except for the occasional sniffle from Jordan. She doesn't look at me the whole way. When we get inside I invite her to sit on the couch and offer her a glass of water, which she accepts with a nod.

When we've both settled in, I wait for her to begin speaking. When she doesn't, I take the lead. "Did Doug leave you?" I ask as gently as I can. I mean, I won't win the fight, but, if that's the case, I will still gladly go over and attempt to punch him out.

"No," Jordan says, putting her glass of water on the table. "I mean, I don't know. He's freaking out. *I'm* freaking out. The thing is . . ." She wrings her hands, takes another deep breath to compose herself, and finally looks at me. "He was never supposed to be the father of my children, Miles. That was always supposed to be you."

I could say something right now about how she was the one who ruined that the minute she let someone else's sperm inside her. But I look at her tearstained face and her rounded belly between us and I just can't.

Memories tug at me everywhere. For two years, my brain's synapses fired away with visions of the two of us, visions of our future. And there were always (at least) two children in the picture. There are two children here with us now.

Jordan's next shaky breath is a small "oh" and her hand goes to her belly. "They're kicking. Do you want to feel?"

I hesitate for a split second. Then nod.

She takes my hand and guides it to the right underhand side of her belly. I immediately sense it, the little spasm. It feels like electricity coursing through from her body to my hand; it feels intensely real.

"This one's the kicker. Baby B, as she's creatively called," she says with a small laugh, the little bells laugh. "Baby A is chill. He seems to flip over every once in a while, but this one . . . Another kick. "She's a firecracker."

"Like her mom," I say.

Jordan smiles and then her face cracks open. "I don't want her to be a screwup like her mom," she says, her voice thick with tears. "I screwed up the best thing I had going, Miles. And I don't want my kids to suffer for it. *Our* kids, if you can find it in your heart to let that happen."

Baby B knows her cues. She reaches out to me again, a tiny wave—or a fist bump if she's anything like her dad, her real dad.

But it's her mom who is openly sobbing now. And the only thing my heart knows to do in that moment is to hold her and let her.

CHAPTER 32

ZOEY

I've learned nothing if I thought yesterday's e-mail from Clifford would be the last time I'd hear from him. He can't resist continuing his copyright infringement streak by sending me a clip of 'N Sync's "Bye Bye Bye" with his own lyrics dubbed over. "I know that we'll make more dough, it ain't no lie. Just wait until you hear the SCORE, you won't say bye, bye bye."

I forward it to Miles and chuckle to myself, imagining his reaction.

Then I pull up the hand-drawn instructions (complete with color-coded illustrations and landmarks) that Miles taped to my door last night so that I can re-create the path from our place to Hotel the.

During my trek, I fluctuate between terror and laughter. To keep my mind occupied during the subway ride, Miles included a blank page where I'm supposed to take note of the best and worst tattoos I find, and he'll grade my pictures upon arrival.

Feeling like a smug regular by the time I reach the ridiculous underground hotel, I even help a new guest locate the way in.

"It looks like a service entrance, doesn't it?" I smile knowingly. "Here, I'll show you."

Good deed done, check-in complete, and fluffy robe (it has cat ears, natch) on, I'm relaxing in the spa lounge waiting for Miles and taking in the décor.

In the fireplace is a Lite-Brite creation of a Yule log, the magazine selection consists entirely of back issues of an obscure trade publication called *Fashion Mannequins Quarterly*, and the seats are shaped like large hands and made out of memory foam; I can't wait to hear what Miles has to say about this.

Our names are called so I send a quick text to my errant partner-in-crime: **You okay? Where are you?**

"I just need five minutes," I explain to the masseuse.

"It will be deducted from your massage time," she replies before turning on her (thigh-high!) boot heel and exiting the waiting area.

More than ten minutes pass—and I'm pacing with agitation at this point—before my phone buzzes with his response: **can't talk rn sorry**

Over the next day, I tell myself a dozen times that there's a simple explanation—a work or family issue has come up—and that any second now he'll tell me what's going on, and I'll be able to offer a sympathetic ear.

One day turns into two days.

Two days turns into three days.

On day four, I realize that not only isn't there a simple explanation—there's no explanation. There is never going to be one.

By this point, I've sent five texts and left two voice mails. The voice mails started out concerned: "Could you call me back, just let me know if you're all right?" and slowly evolved to "So I guess this is just . . . over?"

When I hang up that final time, tears spill out of my eyes. I wipe them away as fast as I can, but they keep coming. I splash cold water on my face from the kitchen sink, and wipe myself dry with a dish towel. It's rough against my skin, harsh and unforgiving.

My thoughts race, back and forth, back and forth. I'm an oil painting from Picasso's Blue Period; the original image is one of sadness, but I keep slapping angry new coats of paint on the canvas, trying to hide it, hoping no one will go digging and scraping at it and find out how many layers there are.

What did I do wrong?

Was I just too much? Did I come on too strong?

Was I too "me"?

Did he get tired of me that quickly?

A knock on the door has me drying my face again. It can't possibly be Miles. Right? But what if it's Miles? Shit. I don't want him to see me so broken. I hold my breath and look through the peephole. Mary stands there, ferret Frank on her shoulder, a lit cigarette dangling from her lips and one in her hand—she sometimes forgets she's already smoking and lights a second.

I unlock and open the door and usher her inside.

"Finished rehearsals early, thought I'd stop by and see what's new," Mary says, putting out both cancer sticks in an ashtray on my coffee table that says "Ash me no questions and I'll tell you no lies." She keeps it here for whenever she makes an impromptu visit. "I have a pair of tickets for previews if you're interested. No pressure. You kind of lived the play, after all."

"You know you don't have to do that. I get that we're not . . . part of each other's lives anymore," I mumble.

She looks affronted. "Says who?"

"I'm not on your payroll, but you keep giving me things— why do you keep giving me things?" I ask, hating the painful, pleading quality of my voice.

"What things?"

"This hugely discounted apartment, the spa day, the massages." I lower my voice, jerk my head toward the shared wall. "*Miles.*"

Her hazel eyes sparkle with mischief. "Didn't realize I'd gifted him to you. Something happen?"

"You definitely engineered it. And don't change the subject, please."

"Just tell me the good stuff and then we'll get back to your thing," she says.

Despite my confusion and misgivings about her serial drop-bys, I settle beside her on the couch and find myself giving in. After all, who else can I tell?

"It was wonderful. We had the best time at the most preten-tious place ever."

"Then why do you look so miserable?"

"Because it's already over and done."

"How do you know?"

I shrug. "He ghosted me. I don't know why I'm surprised. I mean, why would he choose me?" I look away and bark out a laugh to cover up the truth of the next statement. "No one else has."

"I say this with all the love and respect in the world, but what a fucking absurd theory to have."

Startled by Mary's raised voice, Frank jumps to the floor and slips under the couch.

I swallow tightly. "Is it? My parents never wanted me around—stop, it's true—they confirmed it completely at dinner when I saw them—and *you* didn't want me around, and, and, two seconds after you shove me out the door . . ."

"I didn't shove you out the door—"

"You literally did, and slammed it on me."

"Not in a bad way!" she protests.

"And two seconds after you shove me out the door, you hire a dude-bro to manhandle the phones," I snap back. "How do you think that made me feel?"

Her brow wrinkles in confusion. "Darren? He waters my

plants and I asked him to pick up the phone ONCE. Did you call me? When? What happened?"

"It doesn't matter. The point is—"

"Your gran wanted you," she interrupts forcefully.

"That wasn't a choice. She was the only family member left— she *had* to take me in."

"But she adores you."

"I know. And I adore her, too. But it's not the same thing as having a parent who wants you around. When people have a *choice*, I'm never the one they choose," I add shakily.

"All of this is nonsense," she roars. "Why do you think I pushed you out of the nest?"

"Because you think I suck, obviously; you couldn't even look at me when I gave you notes on your play—"

"Because I want more for you! You shouldn't be stuck emulating me—look at me!" She stands up so I can see her full outfit: sailor shirt, leather culottes, striped tights, and high-heeled penny loafers. A feather boa not owned by me also hangs on the coatrack. (It's not owned by Mary, either; it's Frank's.)

We stare at each other for a moment.

"You were dealt a shit hand in the parenting department," she says. "It's true. But you're wrong about something. Parents *shouldn't* want you around. Not forever. The good ones don't. It's selfish to keep a son or daughter home when what they need most is to find their way in the world." Mary never does anything quietly, but right now she is, so I lean in, in time to hear her say, "You're the best kid I could've hoped for. And if I'd kept you as my personal assistant, you'd never have had the chance to spread your wings, write your *own* scripts, and fly. I sent you away because I want the world for you."

Tears fill my eyes for the second time today.

"Don't you remember what you told me the day you interviewed for the job? You wanted to be a screenwriter. As for thinking you 'suck,' that is ludicrous with a side of bullshit. I value your input, and your ideas were clever, but for a memoir adaptation to *be* a memoir adaptation, I think it all needs to come from the filly's mouth, don't you?"

"Yes, I get it—"

"Good. Now go write your own stuff, willya?"

"I don't want to," I grit out. "You think I do, and maybe eight years ago I did, but I've changed—it isn't what I want anymore. I can't do what you want me to do!"

She waits.

"There are seven basic plotlines in the world," I tell her. Nothing she doesn't already know, of course. "*Could* I write a Boy Meets Girl, or a Man Versus Nature? Yeah, probably. But so could anyone else. It's not the plot that matters, it's the *way you tell it*.

"I always figured revising other people's work was meant to be practice for creating original stories. But what I realized is I'd rather take someone else's idea, their one-out-of-seven story-line, and flip, twist, rearrange, and improve upon it so the audience will *think* they've never seen it before. George Orwell said, 'Good prose is like a windowpane.' I want to be so good, no one will know I was there; they'll be so engrossed in the story, they won't even see the words. I like editing and shaping, not starting from scratch. Actually, I don't just like editing, I love it. So that's what I'm going to do."

"I didn't know you felt that way," she replies. "I thought I was holding you back, forcing you to adopt a voice that wasn't yours."

"I want to adopt *lots* of voices—not just yours, though I like your voice—it taught me so much . . ."

Her eyes sparkle. "This is amazing. Do you know what this means?"

". . . no?"

"You're rebelling. You're following your own path. That's all I ever wanted for you. I'm ecstatic!"

"You are? Then what the heck are we yelling for?" I want to know.

"You were pissed that I assumed I knew what was best for you. That's a pretty bad look for me, huh?"

"It's okay," I say, meaning it.

"As for Miles . . ." She waits until my gaze meets hers. "You didn't come here to meet a guy."

"But I *did* meet a guy—"

"There's a whole city out there—a whole life—that has nothing to do with that café and nothing to do with this building, and if it's too tough to live here anymore, we'll find you a new place. It won't be as *good* as this place, but . . ."

"He isn't going to make me move. I was here first," I snap.

"True. I'll raise his rent sky-high, just his, and—"

"No, we're not kicking him out either. If it's a ghost he wants, I can be a ghost. Check *this* out." I make a big show of opening Miles's contact info on my phone and hitting "block" with a flourish. And then I even go over to Aisha's and do the same thing—from now on, my life is Ibrahim-free.

"That's the spirit! Take what you've been given and rewrite it. Change the plot, switch the dialogue, make it work. Be your own script doctor; you're in charge of what happens next, not him."

With Frank on her shoulder, feather boa wrapped around both of them, she gets up and makes her way to the exit. "Let me know about those tickets."

"When did you find out your show was going to happen?" I ask, as something clicks into place in my mind.

"Hmm?" she says absentmindedly, securing a new cigarette in her mouth. "March, I think. Why?"

March. The month she abruptly fired me and sent me to New York.

"Mary . . . did you send me here so we'd still be in the same city?"

"That would be crazy," she says, her lip curving up, and a second later, she's gone. I laugh out loud, and between that and the release of tears earlier, I'm feeling slightly better.

Just because Miles won't be with me doesn't mean I can't explore the city on my own.

I'll start by expanding my café horizons.

CHAPTER 33

MILES

"To the groom and groom!"

Everyone is still holding up his or her champagne glass but I have already downed mine.

I forgot that it was Dylan and Charles's joint groom shower until about forty-five minutes ago when Dylan texted me. I threw on some clothes and arrived half an hour late. I gave an impromptu speech that was mostly cribbed from the TITMH *Freelancer's Handbook*. But judging by the smiles, it was either coherent enough or everyone was already too buzzed to care.

I feel like I'm off the hook and can spend the rest of the party quietly finding a corner to blend into, willing the intricate, hand-cut paper decorations hanging from Dylan and Charles's ceiling—all sorts of animals, from cranes to tigers to peacocks—to make a staggeringly vital life decision for me.

It works for about two minutes before both Dylan and Aisha come to corner me. "Thanks for the speech," Dylan says.

"Yeah. Nice one," Aisha says, eyebrows raised, because of course she knows exactly where most of it came from.

"No problem," I reply. "Great party."

"Anyway," Dylan says. "Can we talk about you now? Are you okay?"

I'd texted both Aisha and Dylan within minutes of Jordan leaving my apartment and begging me to please think everything over. But then, after a few of their exclamations and threats that they'd disown me if I even thought about taking Jordan back (Aisha, of course), I told them I needed some time to sort things out before I could really discuss it. And I hadn't answered anyone's calls or texts since. Not theirs. Not Zoey's, I think with a pang. Not until Dylan's reminder that it was their shower today.

The problem is I haven't sorted anything out at all. My mind is just as jumbled as it was six days ago.

"I guess . . . I'm not really okay," I admit to Dylan and Aisha. "I honestly don't know what to do." I run my hands through my hair. "I know it's easy for you guys to tell me to leave Jordan. But we have history. And maybe . . . a future."

"But they're not your kids," Aisha says gently.

"But she said she wants them to be . . ." I sigh. "Maybe I want them to be. Maybe this is my last chance to have a family."

"What about Zoey? I think you're in love with her," Aisha says.

I look around at all the decorations, at the manifestation of love that is this party, even at Charles so giddily laughing at something with one of his friends. And how can I deny it? "Of course I am. With everything about her. Everything except . . . she told me she probably doesn't ever want to have kids."

"She told you that?" Dylan asks.

"When?" Aisha chimes in. "In what context?"

"In the context that I said I could think of a million reasons to have kids, couldn't she? And she said, not really."

"But did she *know* that it was a deal breaker for you?" Aisha asks.

"Of course not!" I say. "We were on what would probably be

considered our second real date. I mean, come on, Aisha. Have you read my handbook? Who brings up having kids as a real topic of conversation on a second date."

"Except it wasn't a second date. Not really and you know it," Aisha says. "Look, I don't know what you should do about Jordan. Only you know that. I know if you decide they're going to be your kids, they will be. And they'd never know the difference. But I just really want you to think about this, Miles. Because is it more important to you that you have kids, or that you find the right person to have kids with?"

"You can't make someone who doesn't want kids have kids," I say.

"No, you absolutely cannot," Aisha says. "But you owe it to yourself—and Zoey—to give her a real chance to understand the stakes. Let her know it's not a jokey question for you, not a reason for a quick comeback. It's time you were Heart on Your Sleeve Miles again. For Zoey. She deserves that."

After the party, I run. I'm in a button-down, slacks, and loafers. But I don't care. It's the only thing I can think of doing to clear my head.

I get flashes of my life with Jordan, of all the times we jogged together through Prospect Park, of pushing each other through sprints around the lake, of sometimes picnicking by the baseball fields so we could watch the Little League games. The ones with the youngest kids were our favorites, the kids who didn't always know which way to run, or who could barely even hold up their lightweight bats. It was such a sweet moment to witness, a first.

And then I get flashes of my time with Zoey. We don't have years' worth of memories. What we do have is all sparks and excitement, wit and passion. Would it fizzle out after a few months? Would it ever turn into anything more than that first blush of romance? I think we're in love . . . but can we stay there? Could we ever have what my parents do?

I don't know.

At Union Square, I hop on the subway and I let the air-conditioning dry my sweat. I get off at the familiar stop, I walk the steps to the familiar stoop. But I no longer have a key so I have to ring the bell. The buzzer still doesn't work and it takes a minute for Jordan to slowly make her way down the stairs. She smiles tentatively through the glass doors when she sees that it's me.

So many things are the same, but everything's different.

She opens the door and I say the one thing I know to be true. "If I said yes to you right now, it would be coming from a place of fear." I take a deep breath. "I know I'd get to be a dad and that's something I've always wanted. But it's not the *only* thing. Because that dream has someone else in it, too. Someone I love deeply for her own sake. Someone who loves me back just as fiercely. I can't give up on that, Jordan."

Jordan blinks at me. "*I* love you, Miles."

"Do you?" I ask gently. "Or do you love the idea of me? Are you envisioning the four of us"—I gesture to her belly—"as a profile picture? The 'likes' pouring in?"

She scoffs. "That's not fair."

"You weren't fair to me," I say. "And if I came back now, I wouldn't be fair to either of us. Or to Doug. Those are his kids, this is his family photo. Give him a chance to step up to the plate. Give him a chance to surprise you."

She hesitates. "Like that time we caught him scarfing down a whole bag of Funyuns in the bathroom before class?" she asks softly.

"See? He's not without his charms."

She gives a small smile and pauses before she speaks again. "Is this because of that café girl?"

I can't keep myself from flashing back to that first kiss with Zoey, when she was pretending to be my girlfriend just to help me save face with Jordan. "Yes. Even though I may have screwed that up. But it's also because . . . we don't belong together, Jordan."

She stares down at her belly, cradling it. "*My* dream of a family had you in it, Miles. Because you were the first person I was with who made me want that." She looks up at me. "I knew it was a long shot. But I had to try."

"Try with Doug."

CHAPTER 34

ZOEY

As the sole proprietor of Z to A, I've edited two college entrance essays and one corporate presentation. Not much money's coming in—I offered discounts if they spread the word to other possible clients—but it feels good to be in charge of my life. I also tried out not one but two non-Crudité cafés, with mixed results. The first didn't have free Wi-Fi (booo) but the second one had day-old chocolate croissants on offer, which IMO, beats the snot out of biscotti anytime.

The next day I drown my sorrows in a liquid lunch at the Half King. I'm two pints in, editing a corporate presentation for a far-flung trade show, feeling buzzed and disoriented in a city that, let's face it, I've never belonged in, when a new e-mail comes in.

```
To: Z to A Editing Service
From: VP@Night-Light Films
Re: Sample Pages

Hello Zoey,

Mary Clarkson sent us some sample pages of
your work. We especially liked the way you
```

riffed on that old *Playboy* interview where Mary says she never punched a guy, she clobbered him with the collected works of Dorothy Parker (you changed it to "the *portable* works of Dorothy Parker, known for their velocity"). Cute stuff.

We'd love to get on the phone and discuss the possibility of getting your thoughts on a script that's in production. It needs tinkering, and we're eager to see what you could bring to the process. We know we're not the only production company interested in you . . .

(They're not? I wonder, dumbfounded.)

. . . but if you're willing to hear us out, we'll make it worth your time. Assuming the phone interview goes well, we'd need you back in LA by the end of the month to get started. Send us your availability for a phone call, and thanks,

Jon Klein, VP, Night-Light Films

My heart rate speeds up. This could be the escape hatch I'm looking for. I could hightail it back to LA and put an entire country between me and Miles. First I instant message Mary.

Zoey: Should I take a call with Night-Light Films?

I'm not expecting her to get back to me for a while, but they must have broken for lunch at the Roundabout Theatre because two minutes later, my phone dings.

Contrary, Quite: Your choice, just don't submit notes

without a contract. They might be getting ideas from a bunch of writers, keeping the notes, and not hiring anyone. Wouldn't be the first time. Fuckers.

Zoey: Is it nepotism? Should I feel gross/unqualified?

Contrary, Quite: You should always feel gross and un-qualified, all the time. NO, of course not! Nepotism is the lubricant Hollywood runs on. But for the record, I never told them I had a daughter.

As if the tears I've shed over Miles the past week weren't enough, a fresh group gathers in my eyes. It takes some effort to tap out the next letters.

Zoey: Thank you.

Contrary, Quite: I helped get your foot in the door, the rest is up to you. My last piece of advice: Don't do it the way you think I'd want you to, or the way you imagine I might go about it. They don't want me. They want the person that edited me. (Don't worry about my feelings—my ego's a bounce house.)

Zoey: ♥ Guess what, I'm going to Momofuku today.

Contrary, Quite: Enjoy!

Next thing I know, I'm on the subway—breathing hard, sometimes bending my head down between my legs, but on the subway, nonetheless. In the Financial District I get sidetracked. I visit the Charging Bull statue and Battery Park. I try to do an adult thing and take a wildflower tour in the perennial garden, but the aquatic carousel inside a giant, metallic-and-lavender-hued fish looks more my style (blame the booze or adrenaline, your pick). The colors and light patterns almost trick me into believing I'm underwater. I also feel weightless, which makes me giggle.

Later, at Fuku's at last, I eat a spicy fried chicken sandwich with *vada pav*, slaw, and rice pudding, washed down with a strawberry lemon slushie. I relish the meal—so long in coming, but so worth it—taking the time to savor each bite, let the flavors and textures mingle on my tongue. There's probably a word for it created by mindfulness experts ("slow bites" or something), but today, I'll just call it "living." I don't look at my phone a single time. I don't take images of the food and post them across social media. I live in the moment, until I'm comfortably stuffed and fully sated.

It's not that New York has better food than LA, I realize. They're both wonderful in different ways. I keep thinking, "I can't wait to tell Miles that I . . ." and then stopping myself, midsentence.

I think back to why I went along with Mary's crazy suggestion that I fly out to New York. Why I accepted the tickets, and packed a bag, and got on that plane, and headed to the East Coast. I'd spent so long being afraid of change, of trying anything new, and suddenly, as we went wheels up at LAX, I'd felt so electrified my body could barely contain it. Then the fast pace, noise levels, chaotic crowds, and subway fears took over. Without Miles, I don't think I ever would have gotten out of that headspace.

If it turns out my time in New York was only an extended dream sequence, and I'm heading back to LA at the end of the month, I'd better make the most of this city while I still can.

My phone call with Night-Light Films is set for tomorrow at noon.

I can admire Mary without trying to *be* her. I can acknowledge that her work inspires me, without emulating it. I'm not her cookie cutter or anyone else's, and what's more, I don't need to be. Can I trust my own talent? Trust my own instincts?

I guess we're about to find out.

CHAPTER 35

MILES

I think Zoey's ghosted me. I text; I call. I get no response. I get Aisha to text her and she gets nothing in return either. I can't exactly blame Zoey. After all, I did it to her first. But I *need* to talk to her.

I keep hoping I'll run into her. But I don't. Not at the café, not in our hallway. I don't even hear her. One day, I knock on her door and then find myself with my ear pressed up to it, checking for signs of life. There's not even the sound of a whirring air conditioner. I don't think she's there.

Feeling dejected, but not wanting to fully entertain the possibility that she really might be gone for good, I head to Tompkins Square Park for a run. That's when I spot an altogether different set of familiar faces.

Bree and Jude, together, stepping out of Cheese. They are both chuckling, leading me to guess that Jude has made some sort of Little Jude joke.

Jude spots me before I can decide whether to walk by without acknowledging them and gives me a huge grin. "Miles!" He comes over and slaps my shoulder.

I smile back. "Hey, Jude. How are you doing?"

"I'm great!" he says, sounding like he really means it. He pulls Bree over. "Babe, come here. You have to meet someone. This is Miles. My profile ghostwriter."

My jaw drops. In all the years I've been doing this, I have *never* had a client introduce me that way to anyone, let alone the match I helped them snag.

But Bree is laughing. "Sounds like we owe you one," she says as she adoringly looks over at Jude.

"I'm sorry but . . . you know about me?" I stammer out.

"Yes!" Bree says. "Because you want to hear something hilarious? Turns out we were both using ghostwriting services for our profiles."

I screw my face into something I'm hoping represents surprise at this shocking revelation. "Wow. Really?"

Jude laughs. "Turns out we hardly chatted online as ourselves. Isn't that wild?"

"Wild," I repeat.

"When we figured that out, it made sense that you'd only seen *Undersea* once," Bree says to Jude.

"And that you'd take me to a cheese restaurant, even though I was paleo," Jude responds.

"Not anymore!" Bree says with a smirk.

I look quizzically at Jude.

"Er. Well, when you start playing strip fondue, I mean . . . bread is kind of essential to dip into . . ." Jude starts looking Bree's body up and down and I hold my hands up.

"Got it," I say.

"Anyway, it's a good thing we ignored most of whatever it was you and . . . what was your writer's name, babe?" Jude turns to Bree.

"Zoey." My heart stutters at hearing her name said out loud.

"Right. Zoey. We ignored most of what you guys talked about." He looks over at me good-naturedly. "You almost ruined it for us, mate!"

I slap on a smile. "Well, I'm glad we didn't."

"Us too," Bree says. "We have to run. We actually have tickets to the preview for Mary Clarkson's one-woman show. And I've convinced Jude to take me even though he knows *nothing* about her, obviously." She giggles.

"See you around?" Jude says.

"Actually . . ." I say, an idea spontaneously forming in my head. "I have a massive favor to ask. . . ."

Now I just have to figure out how to find her.

I didn't think it was possible, in this day and age, for someone to be truly unreachable. Especially someone who literally lives next door to me. My brain hums with all the ways I might get hold of Zoey. Do I sit in the hallway all day and night with my laptop? Would that make me a fire hazard? I even consider contacting Clifford (ugh) and calling her through him. Though I wonder if she'd really be likely to answer his call over mine. I mean, it's Clifford.

But who does she even know in New York besides us?

And then I finally answer my own question. I slowly pull up my phone and search through my e-mails, looking for an address I wrote to once. Now that I know who that mailbox belongs to, it is way more nerve-racking to be writing her without resorting to any of my fanboy thoughts.

She also, apparently, is getting ready to put on a one-woman show, so what are the chances she'll even respond?

But I have to try.

CHAPTER 36

ZOEY

Today's coffee shop, Hole in One, is seventeen blocks from the apartment, half of which I walked and half of which I rode the subway to get to. I haven't been to any café more than once since Miles ghosted me. I'm expanding my horizons block by block, widening the circumference of my explorations, and I've been keeping vampire's hours to minimize our chances of coming across each other in the building or on the street. I even slept at Mary's a couple of times to dodge him.

Two days ago, I saw him on the High Line, zipping toward me in his Adidas tracksuit, and without thinking, I lifted my hand in a wave. Turned out it wasn't Miles after all, and I don't know why seeing a stranger run past felt like losing him all over again, but it did.

I still feel dizzy each time I descend into the darkened tunnels of the subway, and my heart still speeds up at the roar of an approaching train, but the difference is that now I don't let it stop me.

Hole in One is not, as I'd assumed, a golf-themed restaurant begging to be ripped off by Clifford, but a doughnut joint.

A message from Mary chimes in.

Contrary, Quite: Congrats on "Radioactive Wolves of San Francisco."

(That's the script I'll be doctoring for Night-Light Films.)

Zoey: Thank you! 🦊 Aw-ooooooh

Contrary, Quite: Aw-oooooh! Where u at, as the kids say (or did once)

I do a pin drop on Google Maps at Hole in One.

Zoey: You nearby?

Contrary, Quite: No, but I have a special delivery headed your way.

Zoey: Noooooo. Leaving now!

Contrary, Quite: Nothing illegal, I swear. Promise me you'll sit tight till it arrives.

I'm at a small table in the back, enjoying a cinnamon twist and e-signing a contract with Night-Light, when I see him walk in.

Oh no.

A breath dies in my throat and I turn my back but it's too late. He's walking toward me, his expression impossible to read. I'd done so well avoiding him, too! My heart pounds and I wipe my mouth with a napkin, hoping I don't have any cinnamon crumbs on my face. I'm so focused on my own dread that I don't see he's holding a large take-out container in his hand until he sets it on the table in front of me.

He opens it with a flourish before he speaks, "Cronuts. Scones. Canelés. Tartlets. And . . . *jumbo* biscotti. Take your pick."

I look down at the treats and then up at him. "Hi . . . What is all this?"

"Quality day-old products. I hit every café I could find below Thirty-Fourth Street."

Unsure of what to say, I settle for something resembling our normal bickering. "You mean we fought over stale biscotti when we could've been fighting over cronuts this whole time?"

"Not just any cronut," he clarifies. "Maple bacon."

He nudges the container toward me.

"I'm not all that hungry," I say.

"Oh. Work going well enough that you can buy lunch now?" His eyes are soft, questioning, as if he genuinely cares how my work is going.

"It's getting there," I say. We look at each other for a moment. "What are you doing here, Miles?" I can't stand the way my voice hitches. I wish I could be nonchalant.

"Is it okay if I sit for a second?" he asks and I nod. I don't trust myself to speak; I'll either rage at him or sob, and the way my pulse speeds up as he settles across from me, I have no idea which emotion will win. I wasn't sure I'd ever talk to him again, but suddenly here we are, as though nothing's changed, as though he didn't shatter my heart.

He swallows tightly. "I'm here to apologize. I went off the grid for a few days and I need to tell you why. I don't expect you to understand, given how you feel about having kids—"

Now I'm *really* thrown. "What do kids have to do with anything?"

"You don't want them and I do, and . . ."

"Wait, hold up. There are days I do, and days I don't. I don't think I should be pinned down about it at this stage in the game."

"You're right, but Jordan came to me, the day I was supposed to meet up with you. She said she wanted me to be the twins' dad. I freaked out and I didn't know how to handle it and by the time I came back to myself, I couldn't get ahold of you."

"I blocked you," I explain, my mind spinning. "After four days of nothing, I'd had enough."

"I'm *so* sorry. I brought you something to let you know just how much I mean that." He stands up and in his haste he knocks over his bag—that ridiculous, stupid, obnoxious, holier-than-thou, upcycled bag that makes my heart clench to look at because it's so very Miles and even when I hated him, I *missed* him.

He gets on the floor to clean up his stuff and retrieves a thumb drive which he holds out to me, still on one knee. "I hate that I might have ruined the city for you, so I put together some new walking tours for you to have. I got Jude to record them because, let's face it, that accent. And in case you never wanted to hear my voice again," he finishes in a rush.

From far away, it probably looks like the world's most ridiculous high-tech proposal. I look at the thumb drive but I don't take it. If I take it, does that mean he'll walk out the door, and we'll be done for good? I'm paralyzed, uncertain what to say or do. He stands up awkwardly, sets the drive on the table, and glances over at my laptop, the screen open to my airline ticket purchase.

"You can't leave New York," he blurts.

I glance between him and the screen. "Why?"

"For the same reason I turned down Jordan. I'm in love with the girl I've been speaking to for these past couple of months. I think about her all the time. What she says. The way she thinks. She makes me laugh. And someone once told me that a relationship is all about finding that person who makes you laugh on the worst, most god-awful days."

My pulse jumps and I find it hard to speak. *In love with . . .* "Who told you that?"

"It . . . it was my dad, okay?"

I can't help it; a smile pulls at my lips. "A life without lows makes the highs meaningless." In love with *me*. He chooses me. "Was this a recent heart-to-heart with your dad or was this a Brady Bunch moment of yore?"

"Listen, I promise you can tease me about my parents all you want," Miles says heatedly. "Only keep teasing me. Don't stop teasing me. Don't leave."

"I took a new job in LA. . . ."

He slumps forward, rests his head in palms. "You did?"

"But I'm not moving back. I told them I'd only accept if I could telecommute."

"So what's the flight for?"

"They agreed to an in-person meetup every six weeks." I shut my laptop and suddenly there's no barrier between us.

He looks chagrined. "I just confessed all that for nothing?"

"No, not for nothing. You once asked me what I miss most about LA and here's the real answer. I love when you're in your car and the music on the radio overtakes you, so you pump it up so loud it vibrates through the steering wheel. The bass hits, you're gliding along the 405—which never happens unless you hit it just right, on a Sunday morning maybe—you're soaring along, you own the whole city, and when that perfect song hits, it creates this dome around you in your car. You're moving around amongst all these other people but they can't touch you."

"Sounds lonely," he points out.

"It was safe," I tell him. "Because it was separate. I had my own bubble, and I never had to hear other people's noises, never had to bump up against the rest of the world. I would go to work, and I would come home, and sometimes I would smoke pot and numb myself to every kind of emotion. I don't want to do that anymore. These past few weeks with you, I've felt so many things, good *and* bad, but even getting hurt . . . it's not as bad as not living." I scramble to locate and open my notebook—flipping past the Table of Champions chart—and show him my new list. "There's so much I want to see in New York, so many things I've never done. I haven't ridden the Circle Line yet or eaten at a Russian supper club or browsed the shelves at the Strand bookstore. I haven't taken a horse-drawn carriage around Central Park or wandered the marble cemetery in the East Village or toured the row houses and jazz museum of Harlem or pitted the best pizza places against each other or tasted enough exotic dishes at Chelsea Market or explored Museum Mile or watched my breath swirl in the air while ice-skating at Rockefeller Center. I haven't even seen a Broadway show!"

Miles looks at my list, touching each item like it's a precious thing and I know it is, to him. "The new walking tours have a lot of those things covered."

I take his hands in mine, and look him straight in the eyes. "I want to hear them in your voice. Because I want you walking beside me while you speak. I've fallen in love with New York and I've fallen in love with you, too."

He opens his mouth but I reach over and press a light fingertip against his lips.

"Will you show me your New York? Can we start fresh?"

His response is to cup my face in his hands and pull me in for a passionate kiss. It feels like coming home.

"Yes, yes," he murmurs, when we break apart. His thumb gently brushes a tear from my cheek. He leans in and kisses the spot where it slid.

A waiter comes over and asks Miles if he wants anything. "You'll need to spend ten dollars if you want to plug into the Wi-Fi," he adds.

"That's okay. We don't need Wi-Fi today," Miles tells him. "We have a lot to talk about."

"Yes."

We grin at each other across our table.

"Clifford's e-mails alone—" I sputter.

"His e-mail signature from the old days still haunts me." Miles shudders. "He used to sign off as 'Da Big Red Dawg.'"

I laugh, and it feels so good. Being on the same side, laughing together.

Miles is right. We have so much to talk about—in the real world, offline, as Zoey and Miles and nobody else.

"I think it's time for a new chart," I announce. "We should taste-test and rank all the snacks you brought us."

I flip over to a fresh page in my notebook, blank with possibility, just waiting for the story of Zoey and Miles to be written.

Four Months Later

To: All Tell It to My Heart Employees
From: Leanne Tseng
Re: On the up and up

Team,

Happy news today: After a meeting with our accountants, I can confirm that our revenue is on the rise. Now that we're the only major player in the game, I feel confident in adding two more people to our full-time staff.

Everyone, please offer your congratulations to Aisha Ibrahim, our staff photographer, and our newest staff copywriter, Stella Gonzalez. You deserve it, ladies.

Yours,
Leanne

To: Aisha Ibrahim
From: Miles Ibrahim
CC: Zoey Abot
Re: Promotion Celebration / We Came In Like a Wrecking Ball Party

Bravo!! We're back from LA. (Zoey's standing over my shoulder, so I've been instructed to confess—under threat of setting fire to my boat shoes—that their sushi annihilates New York's. Dammit!)

Anyway, can't wait to celebrate your promotion tonight at Zoey's. Or should I say Zoey-and-Miles's? We'll provide the sledge-hammers, cake, snacks, non-Clifford-style bubbly; you provide the arm strength. Mary gave her blessing to let us tear down our shared wall. We're allowed to smash to our heart's content before the professional crew comes in.

See you soon!

MILES

In case those scenes in *Ghost* haven't convinced you, let me assure you that renovating a New York City apartment is very, very sexy. Zoey even wore Demi Moore-esque overalls while we destroyed a wall, got sheetrock inside all of our champagne glasses, and drank it to our heart's content anyway. I may have lead poisoning, but it was all worth it.

I roll over now to pull Zoey closer to me, my muscles feeling well used and achy, but my hands are met with crumpled sheets instead. I force one eye open.

Not only is Zoey fully dressed but she's almost out the front door already.

"Hey," I call out to her, my voice still filled with sleep. "Where do you think you're going?"

She looks back at me. "Where else?" she asks. "There's a very large, empty table waiting just for me."

"You've got to be kidding me."

"Listen," she says, as she pulls her wet hair into a ponytail. She even took a shower already? "If you think a few rounds of mind-blowing sex are enough to keep me from my destiny of Table Champion, you don't know me very well."

I smirk. "Mind-blowing sex, eh?" I say, folding my arms behind my head and leaning back into the headboard. "Go on."

"My mind is blown and my strategy is sound," she says, as she pulls open our door. "Flattery just bought me another thirty seconds. See ya!" She slams the door behind her.

"You're ruthless," I yell, but I also don't attempt to move out of bed. If this is the consolation prize for losing Table Champion, I don't think I mind one bit.

Besides, I know she's saving me a seat.

Acknowledgments

SarvenazTash: Hey

SarahSkilton: Hey

SarvenazTash: Hmmmm . . . well, that accomplished nothing. Maybe Miles is onto something in his handbook.

SarahSkilton: So we have to do the acknowledgments. How do you want to handle it?

SarvenazTash: Well, we have to thank Alicia Condon, of course, our amazing editor at Kensington. And let her know how much we appreciate her enthusiasm and love for Miles and Zoey's story. Working with her has been a pleasure and a joy.

SarahSkilton: Victoria Marini at Irene Goodman is our rock-star agent: smart, empathetic, and all-around awesome. We're indebted to Lee OBrien and Maggie Kane as well. Thank you so much!

SarvenazTash: Also, from Kensington, we are very grateful for our publicist Jane Nutter, as well as the fabulous efforts of Lynn Cully, Jackie Dinas, Alexandra Nicolajsen, Kris Noble, Laura Jernigan, Susanna Gruninger, and Carly Sommerstein. Also a very special thank-you to Elizabeth Trout, who was the very first Kensingtonian to read and love this book and who started the chain of events that led to its home. We'd also like to thank superheroine agent Lia Chan at ICM, and the incomparable Ronald Bass for his enthusiasm, ideas, and one of the most unforgettably delightful meetings of our careers.

SarahSkilton: To my sister, Rachel "HankyBook" Murphy: I love you so much and your support means the world to me. Thanks for being an early reader of all my stuff, from the published to the unpublished and everything in between.

SarvenazTash: And to my sister, Golnaz Taghavian, one

of the most discerning readers/watchers of rom-coms that I know. Thank you for being a beta reader for this; I knew if I could get you on board, I'd done us proud. (#TeamMusic-FromAnotherRoom4eva.)

SarahSkilton: I need to thank the wonderful Amy Spalding for always making me laugh (and making me meals!) when I most need it; Leslie Sullivant and Lisa Green for our nights at Rose & Crown pub talking writing; the RWA Santa Clarita branch; Lynne "Early Reader" Kadish for the kind e-mails; and Stephanie "Dammital" Sagheb for fabbo movie nights. Elliot "Cheesy Nuggets" Skilton is my favorite little guy, and Joe "Love of My Life" Skilton is the reason any of my books exist at all. My parents Earl & Ros Hoover and Lydia & Richard Skilton have endlessly supported and encouraged me, and I'm extremely grateful. Carrie Fisher and Nora Ephron helped inspire this story; we miss you.

Lastly, thank you to Sarvenaz Tash, the only person I can imagine collaborating with on a novel. After we met on Twitter in 2011, you literally opened your home to me a few months later when I was in NYC (and many times since). Your generosity, talent, work ethic, and creative spirit are unmatched. I have loved writing this book with you and it still makes me laugh *every time* I look at it. Thank you, thank you for your friendship. I treasure it more than I can say.

SarvenazTash: I'd like to thank the rest of my wonderful family, especially my mom, Haleh, and aunt, Homa, for too many things to list here; my aunts Hengameh and Haideh—I miss you both so much; my in-laws, Arlene and Michael, for their constant support and enthusiasm; my husband, Graig (whom I met-cute on—true story—the Staten Island Ferry), for making me laugh every single day; and Bennett and Jonah, who were generally no help when it came to the writing of this book but enrich my life in every other way. I can't wait to dress up as Tired Mom for Halloween with you two.

And, most of all, I'd like to thank my writing partner, Sarah Skilton. Writing this book with you will always be one of the greatest joys of my life. It's been my beacon of light and hope and SO much laughter over the past two years. It was the place I retreated during the darkest times (and without fear of neuro-caterpillars). I'm so honored that you've shared your talents with me in this way. And even more grateful that I can call you one of my best friends.